Angels' Blood
Murder in the Chorus

Angels' Blood
Murder in the Chorus

Roberta Mantell

INDIES UNITED PUBLISHING HOUSE, LLC

Copyright © 2025 by Roberta Hershenson
robertamantell.com

Published by Indies United Publishing House, LLC
This is a work of fiction. Any references to historical events, real people, or real places are used fictitiously. Other names, characters, places, and events are products of the author's imagination, and any resemblances to actual events or persons, living or dead, is entirely coincidental.

All rights reserved worldwide. No part of this publication may be replicated, redistributed, or given away in any form without the prior written consent of the author/publisher or the terms relayed to you herein, except in the case of brief quotations embodied in critical reviews and certain other noncommercial uses permitted by copyright law.

Paperback ISBN: 978-1-64456-799-9
Kindle ISBN: 978-1-64456-800-2
ePub ISBN: 978-1-64456-801-9
AudioBook ISBN: 978-1-64456-802-6

Library of Congress Control Number: 2025902943

Design by Rita Skingle

INDIES UNITED PUBLISHING HOUSE, LLC
P.O. BOX 3071
QUINCY, IL 62305-3071

indiesunited.net

Dedicated to my mother,
Florence Mantell,
who passed her love of music to me.

"It does not seem that woman will ever originate music in its fullest and grandest harmonic forms. She will always be the recipient and interpreter, but there is little hope she will be the creator."

—*Woman in Music*, George P. Upton, 1880

1

PIPER MORGAN kicked off her stilettos and ran down the backstage ramp toward the staircase. A soprano died on those stairs tonight, but who? The alto who found the body could not give a name.

Please not someone I met today. Piper's thoughts were like a prayer as *Messiah*'s "amens" rang in her head and the sounds of panicked chorus members grew fainter.

She moved on shaky legs past the maze of vacant dressing rooms. It was eerily quiet here, the air deathly still. Her heart pounded—not from fear but from the thrill of doing her job. After the scream she had dashed from the risers and slipped past the stagehand to cover this breaking story. Now she was alone, an arts reporter at a death scene. She imagined the headline of the story she would write.

**CHORUS DEVASTATED AS
SINGER FALLS TO HER DEATH**

At the staircase, she stifled a scream. A still figure lay at the bottom in a pool of blood, concert clothes in a heap and a slim arm jutting upward. The face was turned away, while a dark bun unraveled in bloody strands.

Piper's knees went weak. Several women in the New York Luminoso Chorus wore that hairdo tonight. Like the talented Daphne Paige, who sang an angelic solo at the dress rehearsal. And Nicole Jennings-Barlow, the conductor's wife, who told her about a "secret" chorus mystery before they went onstage. She had not met the others, but their updos looked stunning atop their scooped black blouses, long black skirts, and pearls.

Now one of them was dead. Piper hitched up her silk tuxedo pants and was taking a step down, to identify the body, when a deep voice rang out.

"Move away from the staircase, ma'am."

2

Fourteen Hours Earlier

Maestro Todd Barlow lifted his baton from its velvet case and polished the pearly shaft until it gleamed. He would not admit to honoring his baton in this way, as if it were Siegfried's sword. But he dearly loved his stick, a gift from his parents when he graduated from the conservatory. *To our beloved Todd, for a life in music,* was inscribed on its curved handle.

The baton inspired him to "preserve the music of the past and empower the music of the future"—the motto of the New York Luminoso Chorus and its 120 singers.

"We must always seek new music," Barlow liked to say, though he was partial to the old. The works of the masters were in his bloodstream, the *Stabat Mater*s, *Requiem*s, and *Gloria*s that choral conductors like him had kept alive for centuries. Few women in that musical canon, as his dear wife never tired of pointing out. Despite centuries of toil over candlelight, just a handful of Claras, Fannys, and Ceciles had broken through the symphonic ceiling. In May, he would do his part to remedy that injustice, when New York Luminoso premiered a work by the forgotten 19th-century English composer Lisha Lovington.

But this was December, *Messiah* time, and tonight he would travel a well-worn path back to the 18th century to conduct Handel's beloved oratorio—the standard money-making version, not one of those jazzy modern *Messiah*s set on Mars or in a soup kitchen. New York Luminoso had brought Barlow prominence, respect, and, six months ago, a whack on the head in the form of Daphne Paige, a radiant singer in the soprano section who had taken up residence in his brain. He'd never imagined straying from Nicole, his wife of eight years, who also inconveniently sang in the soprano section, but he was in love.

He was reviewing the score when his cell phone rang with a Schubert tune, jolting him from the Baroque period into the

Romantic. Daphne, he thought, grabbing the phone like a lovestruck adolescent.

"Hello!" he burst out. "What are you doing this morning? I miss you!"

"How nice; I miss you, too," his wife said dryly. "I'm calling to remind you to pick up your tails from the cleaner, as you requested. And while you're at it, we need some milk."

Barlow grimaced. The eminent Nicole Jennings-Barlow, philosophy professor at Anderson University and the best-selling author of *Philosophy for a Happy Life,* had him cornered.

"Sure, I'll get the tux," he said through gritted teeth. "And the milk."

"And don't forget, that arts reporter will be singing with us at the concert tonight." Nicole went on as though nothing had happened. "She'll be at the dress rehearsal, too, name of Piper something from *New York News*. She's going to write a feature about the chorus, Todd, so let her sing no matter what her voice sounds like."

He made a face. "What if she's tone-deaf?"

"We've got to put business first. You know we need good publicity to attract a paying audience to Carnegie Hall in May. Lisha Lovington is not exactly a household name."

"Yeah, I know." His mood plummeted.

"So, a positive feature on the chorus is what we need," Nicole spoke with her usual confidence. "I hope you're focusing on *Messiah* today, by the way. We need it to be great tonight."

"Yeah, with a tone-deaf journalist singing off-key."

"Try to remember that an audience brings money. Publicity brings an audience, not to mention a better shot at grants. Therefore...."

"Therefore, let the reporter sing," he said glumly.

"Correct."

"Fine. But she'd better write a glowing article about me in return."

"I hope so; bye."

Barlow liked to say Nicole was the brains of the chorus while he was its heart. She was always right, always strong, and always on top of her game. A rock, in other words, while he was the water flowing over it. He was too afraid of her not to love her, and he did love her, when he thought about it. But when he thought of Daphne, he only asked himself how to stop loving her, so he could repair his fractured life.

It was Nicole who had found the Lovington *Requiem,* an 1899 masterpiece that would surely bring its unknown composer lasting recognition. And heap recognition on himself, too. The manuscript had languished unseen until last spring, when a friend gave Nicole a box of old music materials from her grandmother's attic.

"And it's never been performed, Todd." Excitement had made her cheeks glow. "I looked it up, and there's no record of a requiem attributed to Lisha Lovington. No other major works, either, only art songs."

The *Requiem* was a gift, allowing him to champion a neglected woman while addressing the sexism in music that lingered to this day. Audiences cared, and they flocked to the conductors who took a stand.

His focus gone, he set out for an invigorating walk to do his errands. Passing the mailbox, he removed a hand-addressed letter and slit it open with a fingernail. At once a horrible smell filled his nostrils, like a mix of rotten flowers and old dog poop. It came from a single sheet of triple-folded music-composition paper he smoothed out while holding his nose.

The page was arranged like a song, with his beloved's name stretched like a title across the top.

DAPHNE PAIGE

The words below rose and fell on the staff like notes.

**WE KNOW WHAT YOU ARE DOING MAESTRO
STOP THE FILTH OR ELSE**

Barlow broke into a sweat. He and Daphne had been so discreet, avoiding eye contact at chorus practice, limiting their public interactions to a nod, and meeting at an upstate motel whose dreariness was surpassed only by its remoteness. Skilled amateur singers who paid to sing onstage with a professional symphony orchestra would never frequent such a place.

Unless it was a chorus singer doing what he was doing—cheating on their spouse.

Barlow tore up the letter, stuffed the pieces in his pocket, and continued downhill. His darling Daphne did not deserve a scandal. She was so trusting and accepting, never demanding more of his time, or calling him at odd hours, or—heaven forbid—expecting him to leave his wife. He supposed her life was too full to want more from him, although he sometimes wondered if there were other reasons—other men, for example. He didn't have the courage to ask.

A scandal would be even worse for Nicole. A cheating husband, a prominent figure acting like an ass. He must confess his affair to her. But if he confessed and did not promise to stop it, she would demand a divorce. He would have to end his affair—unthinkable—or lose the spacious house his rich in-laws had given them as a wedding present. A poor kid growing up, he enjoyed the fruits of success, even if his wife's trust fund paid for most of them.

Moving out would be like knifing himself in the heart.

3

Piper watched as the chorus went through its warm-ups: tongue trilling, lip buzzing, neck rolling, limb shaking, and accelerating runs of scales and arpeggios. New York Luminoso was not just a grayer-haired version of her college chorus, where she had sung as an alto; it was on a whole different level.

She soaked up the vibe as the chorus prepared for the "dress"—the rehearsal with the orchestra. Barlow—the singers called him Maestro—stood before them in jeans and a sweatshirt, a shimmering baton in his right hand. He was as pale as a poet and mid-30ish, with an older man's gravitas. He was picky, too. Don't stress that syllable, stress this one. No American R's. "And keep your eyes on me!"

Piper's old chorus habits kicked in as she watched him for the downbeat. She felt a shiver as the strings played the opening measures and her dream assignment became real. She was here to produce a feature worthy of her job as an arts reporter for the *New York News,* known as *NYN.* She would write an article with grit, nothing delicate or flattering, no puff piece. Something to open readers' eyes to the passions and furies in a group of folks singing their guts out for the simple joy of doing it. Yeah, like a bunch of gladiators dodging one another's chariot blades. That kind of joy.

She was honing her craft toward a single goal: becoming one of *NYN*'s crime reporters by age 30. Now she was almost 29.

Barlow had placed her with the tenors, though she knew *Messiah*'s alto part by heart. "I need to bulk up the section; there are never enough men," he'd said.

Not that she was bulky, he added, getting flustered as he looked her up and down. He was a nervous guy who seemed as worried about her sight-singing skills as she was, but she figured he craved press attention as much as any artist she had met in her five years on this beat. Egomania came with the territory when you had to tell people to look at you all the time.

A grandmotherly woman tenor had greeted her warmly. "Hi, I'm Zandy Stewart; welcome to the family. Singing tenor is a blast." Piper thanked her and reached into her bag for the notepad that was as essential as a body part. *Interview Zandy*, she wrote.

During pauses in the rehearsal, she made longer notes.

Anderson Performing Arts Center is a splendid jewel located on the campus of the State University of New York in suburban Anderson, 30 miles north of Manhattan. It has five theaters ranging in size from intimate to orchestral, and we're singing in the orchestral one, known as Theater One until some benefactor steps up and gets his or her name engraved on the wall. There are 1,500 red velvet seats, a perpetually open gold curtain, and gold-toned balconies curving toward the stage.

But I know the dark underbelly of the place—the maze of cinder-block corridors one level below the stage where the dressing rooms are located, reached by a ramp, and the chorus's women's room another level down. Women call the bottom level the Dungeon, with good reason. While soloists have private toilets in their dressing rooms, and men have a bathroom in their dressing room, the women must brave a steep and narrow metal staircase if they need to go. Since the Dungeon elevator is usually out of service, disabled choristers have to ask—or beg—the soloists to let them use theirs. It's an illegal outrage, and I plan to expose it—after I finish the chorus piece.

She made notes while singing, too, because thoughts must be captured before they drifted away.

Barlow waves his arms as if only music matters. Artists inhabit invisible worlds...

"Eyes here, and that means everyone!"

Looking up, she saw the maestro glaring at her. Later she would tell him she meant no disrespect, but notes were as important to her job as they were to his—just in a different way.

Slipping her notepad under her music book, Piper noticed how professional the sopranos sounded. Really impressive, no flat notes or off-key warbling. She and her chorus buddies had dubbed the sopranos "angels" because of their heavenly voices.

But now an alto screeched loudly off-key. Barlow dropped his arms, and the chorus and orchestra dribbled into silence. One hundred and twenty pairs of eyes stared straight ahead, not giving up the offender. Finally, a bass could stand it no longer and laughed. Barlow smiled, too. He looked attractive when his face relaxed like that.

"I agree, an accidental solo can be funny, folks," he said, wiping his brow. "But ladies, please, if you don't feel comfortable on the high notes, don't sing them, okay? Don't ruin things for the rest of us, thank you very much."

"Everyone knows who did it," the tenor next to Piper whispered. "Diva Daley, calling attention to herself as usual. But Todd doesn't embarrass people by calling out names."

He was a cute, fresh-faced guy of about 20 who gave his name as Riley Webb. Piper hoped Riley would gossip some more.

"There she is." Riley tipped his head toward the riser below them, where a red-haired alto was giggling into her hand. Diva, the off-key culprit, was plainly embarrassed. You couldn't get away with much in a chorus, which was where the gladiator blades came in. Most singers in Piper's former chorus had been kind and empathetic, but a few were ready to cut you to shreds. They would badmouth you until no one would sit near you. It had never happened to her, but it was grist for her article.

The story idea took off one morning as she and her now ex-friend Vicki Jewel sipped their lattes at Captions, the *NYN* café. Vicki was a freelance publicist with a knack for good pitches, and the two became friendly over the years. Vicki's description of her favorite client, the New York Luminoso Chorus, was intriguing, especially the "sexy backstage tales" she promised to tell. Piper recalled some sort of trouble in Luminoso, widely considered one of the best avocational choruses in the Hudson Valley. A nasty love triangle had led several members to drop out. But that was ancient history.

Piper couldn't wait to peer behind the scenes at a first-rate adult chorus. Never mind that Luminoso rehearsed 30 miles north in Westchester County, while she lived in midtown Manhattan. She had a car, courtesy of *NYN*, and commuter trains ran every hour. She had pitched her editor, Moss McCarthy, right away.

> *Hey, Moss, how about a first-person view of a top chorus, telling who joins these unpaid groups and why? Showing the blotches beneath the stage makeup, the strains when so-called angelic singers work to make heavenly music together. Do those angels ever want to strangle each other for singing flat or botching a rhythm? I'll bet they do. Want me to join the excellent New York Luminoso Chorus and find out? I'm a pretty good alto, and I know my way around a music score.*

Hallelujah, yes! Moss texted back. *You can't go wrong with angels' blood.*

Vicki connected her with the maestro, then grew distant. The morning coffees ended, along with the friendly calls. Piper asked why but got no answers. Did Vicki feel Piper had intruded on her turf? Did she resent being unattached while Piper had a boyfriend, as she once hinted? Vicki would not say, and Piper stopped asking.

She approached the feature with two assumptions: First, an adult chorus was packed with sexual tension and drama due to the passions whipped up by singing your brains out. Second, singing expanded your lungs but left you emotionally and physically vulnerable. She was ready to be wrong on both counts, having learned the old-fashioned way to base her writing on evidence.

A jab in the ribs stopped her daydreaming. "Sing!" Riley whispered, but she had lost her place in a fast-moving fugue. Trying to sing the tenor part was like speeding down an unknown mountain road on a moonless night in the fog. She was lost, lost, lost, flailing for a foothold on the crest of the music. She suppressed a wild impulse to laugh, floating along until Barlow stopped to consult with the concertmaster, and the bad, beautiful dream was over.

The chorus stayed seated while the orchestra began a cacophonous round of retuning. All except the concertmaster, who huddled with Barlow. Piper tried to lip-read their conversation but was sitting too high on the risers to see.

Riley nudged her. "See that tall guy watching the rehearsal from the back of the hall? That's Hunter Bell, musicologist and consultant to the chorus, rumored to be overly fond of the conductor's wife. And over there, to the right in the second row of sopranos"—Riley seemed to relish this—"is the conductor's wife herself, Nicole Jennings-Barlow, the one with dark hair in a bun."

Piper followed Riley's eyes. "Who's the good-looking soprano sitting two rows behind Nicole, the one wrapping her hair on top of her head? They look like sisters."

"Oh, that's Daphne Paige. The maestro gives her private lessons."

He stressed the word *private,* and Piper made a note to interview Daphne. "Is she any good?"

"She rocks." Riley grinned.

"I suppose Barlow teaches a lot of these people." Piper imagined sibling rivalries, the singers competing to please Daddy Maestro.

"Some of them. I think he gives Daphne the most time—because she's so talented." He kept a straight face. *Good material; follow up,* she noted.

Riley was squinting at the soprano section. "Now I see the resemblance. Daphne is like a taller and younger Nicole. But they aren't really alike." He shook his head. "Daphne is fun, but Nicole—well, you'll see."

"See what?"

"She's whip-smart and uses that whip. Look out."

"Ooh, I'm scared." Piper winked at him. *Talk to Daphne,* she jotted on a sliver of notepad not covered by the music book. *Also interview Riley, Diva, Nicole, and Hunter.*

The music resumed without warning—a rushing stream of sixteenth notes that looked scary on the page. Rather than dive in and make a Diva Daley kind of mistake, Piper moved her lips and pretended to sing. Her eyes drifted to the empty balcony, where her live-in boyfriend of one year, Dr. Theodore Shay, would be sitting tonight. Theo ran a busy orthodontic practice a few blocks away from their one-bedroom Murray Hill co-op. He had a short attention span in concert halls, being too tall for most seats at six foot three. After twisting and turning to get comfortable, he usually gave up and left early.

Piper loved Theo despite his ever-present scent of orthodontic bonding glue. But he was pressuring her to get married, and she was not yet ready to be a wife.

Now a solo soprano voice rang out in the hall. Piper was far from an opera buff, but she had never heard a voice so pure and angelic. It soared on the highest notes and mellowed as it moved down the scale.

The chorus exploded with applause when the solo ended, and Barlow paused the orchestra.

"Who was that great singer?" Piper whispered to Riley.

"Daphne Paige. She nailed it, don't you think?"

"I'll say. She's amazing."

"The pro will sing that part tonight, but Daphne is just as good, in my opinion."

"Does everyone agree with you?"

"Many do, and some don't. For instance, there's Corinne Kelsey, one of our quite good altos." He gestured toward a stocky, gray-haired singer two rows down. "She's one of the 'don'ts.' See how she looks like she just ate a lemon?"

"I gather Corinne doesn't like Daphne much."

Riley grimaced. "*Hate* is not too strong a word for it, Piper."

The line for the women's room began at the dressing rooms, snaked along the hallway, and continued down the staircase. Piper held her breath as the women ahead of her descended the stairs in their long black skirts and high heels. One careless move and a stiletto heel could catch on a broken step, ending in a pileup as women toppled over one another. The minutes before curtain time ticked away, and tempers grew short.

"They said no perfume tonight," said a voice that carried up the stairs. "Smells like Corinne bathed in it."

"I did not!" Corinne yelled. "Liar."

"Watch it, Corinne, you'll lose your voice!" someone else shouted.

"Mind your own business, Rhoda. They said no hairspray, but your hair is so stiff a tornado wouldn't bend it."

The woman in front of Piper turned around—Daphne Paige. She was great-looking up close, with deep-set blue eyes and dark strands escaping her bun like bedroom hair. "This is what it's like on concert nights, Piper. You must be getting a bad impression of us."

Piper shook her head. "Don't worry, everyone's nervous before a performance."

Daphne put out her hand and introduced herself. "It's good to meet you. I enjoy your writing in *NYN*."

"Thanks, you sang wonderfully at rehearsal." Piper returned the strong handshake.

"Inspired by the occasion, I guess. When you write about our chorus, please remember that we love music more than we dislike each other." Daphne gave her a confident smile. "When we start singing, all the knots will smooth out."

Someday, after the article was published and she and Daphne became friends, Piper would explain that disregarding conflicts was not her job—the truth was her job. She hoped Daphne would understand and forgive whatever rough stuff her article might contain.

Daphne was studying her. "Piper, I just love your fabulous half-buzz cut and those cool two-tone bangs. I swear I feel like trying something like that. I'm so sick of wearing my hair long and straight or in this uptight bun. Where do you get yours done?"

Piper was about to answer when a hand touched her arm. "Hello, I know you're Piper Morgan, and I presume you know I'm Nicole Jennings-Barlow." It was the maestro's wife on her way up the stairs. "Don't forget the Jennings part of my name if you write about me. So now we're introduced, and we need to talk."

"Sure, about what?" This woman was too affected to be real.

"An urgent matter of great importance to the chorus as well as to my husband's career." Mrs. Maestro spoke sotto voce as Daphne turned away. "It must be attended to at once. I see you're dressed for the concert, so I assume you've dined and are ready to sing?"

"Yeah, if you call 'dining' a quick salad at a coffee shop," Piper said. "I'll be ready as soon as I finish here."

"Meet me outside the women's dressing room in ten minutes. No one must overhear us. We must have total privacy, and I will require your promise of secrecy."

Was she always this bossy? Piper would meet with Nicole Jennings-Barlow—don't forget the Jennings—and find out.

4

"Excuse the cloak-and-dagger," Nicole whispered. "It's not my style, but we can't be overheard."

They were huddled in a corner outside the women's dressing room, where nervous chatter escaped the open door.

"Where's my lipstick?"

"Don't hog the mirror!"

"Who moved my music?"

"You'd think it was their Met Opera debut," Nicole said. "Todd says shaky nerves lead to a smooth show."

"It's less pressure singing in a group, isn't it? No, that's wrong. No one wants to spoil it for the others."

"That's right, no one does." Nicole's eyes were unwavering on Piper's face. She felt herself being evaluated for some sort of risky espionage, and she remembered Riley's description of a whip-smart bully type. She sized up Mrs. Maestro in return, noting her cold blue eyes like glacier ice and hot red lipstick that did not melt the ice.

"Are you ready to listen and keep a secret?" Nicole said.

"Maybe, but why me? We journalists don't like to keep secrets."

"A fair point. There are three answers. First, you don't know us and will therefore be impartial. Second, only one other person is aware of this matter besides myself—not my husband, by the way—and I want an uninvolved party to know. Third," she said, her eyes unblinking, "the information must be made public when the time is right, and you, as a noted arts journalist, are the person to do it."

"I see," Piper said, though she didn't yet.

"Are you willing to hear me now?"

"I will listen, but I can't promise to stay silent indefinitely." Piper tried to hide her impatience. "If I decide what you're referring to needs to be made public, I will have to act on it. But I promise not to do it without consulting you."

The sound of musicians tuning up drifted down from the stage.

"All right, I will trust you," Nicole said. "I'll get to the point quickly."

"Good. We don't want to be late for the lineup."

"No, of course not." Nicole gave a wry smile. "My husband would be most unhappy."

She leaned close to Piper. "You might have heard that our chorus will premiere a piece at Carnegie Hall in the spring—a requiem by an unknown woman composer. Her name is Lisha Lovington, straight from late-nineteenth-century England."

"Interesting. That's the first I've heard about it."

"Women composers were usually overlooked back then, of course. So we're expecting a huge interest in the music. It's an outstanding work. However, something very troubling occurred today."

"Like what?" Piper felt a stir of interest.

"I was home alone getting ready for the rehearsal—my husband had left earlier, you see—and an old *Requiem* manuscript turned up identical to Lisha Lovington's in every way but one."

"'Turned up?'" Piper tried to follow.

"Yes, turned up, which I will explain later."

"Go on."

"There was a different composer's name on the title page. A famous composer's name. So now we have two 'original' manuscripts of the same work. It's quite unsettling."

Piper knew she was supposed to ask which famous composer's name had somehow "turned up," but she did not know the names of many classical composers. Just some B's—Bach, Beethoven, Brahms; a smattering of M's—Mozart, Mendelssohn, Mahler; and, of course, Handel, whose music awaited them upstairs.

"We don't have enough time for you to guess," Nicole said. "It's Edward Elgar."

"Aha." Piper drew a blank. "Oh, I know. I marched to him at my high school graduation."

Nicole gave an impatient wave. "Right, he composed the *Pomp and Circumstance Marches*. But he wrote a hundred other things, too, including several masterpieces. But that's not the point, is it?"

Piper cleared her throat. "No. The point is you want to know why there are two identical manuscripts of this *Requiem,* and who the real composer is." She spoke precisely, to show she'd been listening. "But it's probably by the famous guy, don't you think? That would make more sense."

"'Probably' won't cut it, Piper, and you, as a journalist, should not automatically exclude the unfamous woman. A lot is at stake, for our chorus, for music history, and for women."

Piper stared at her. Quite a burden to put on a piece of music. Right now the music she most cared about was *Messiah,* and they had better go upstairs.

"So now you know the situation. I will inform you when you can write about it."

Piper sidestepped the remark. Once a reporter got hold of a story, it became the reporter's obligation to keep track of it. "I will need more information," she said, taking her notepad from her tuxedo-pants pocket. "For instance, where did you find the second manuscript?"

"Oh, no you don't." Nicole wagged her finger at the notepad. "No making notes. The record of this conversation must be in your head. I will tell you the full story after the concert."

"Who is the other person who knows about your discovery?"

Before Nicole could answer, a man's voice boomed from the loudspeaker. "Ladies and gentlemen, please line up for the stage. This is your five-minute call."

Nicole spun around on her high heels. "Hunter Bell knows. You probably haven't met him yet. Coming?"

Piper followed at a distance, writing in her notepad. Just let the imperious Ms. Jennings-Barlow try to stop her.

5

Barlow peeked from the wings at his darling Daphne. She looked so beautiful bathed in a halo of stage light. In fact, all the women were transformed from their ordinary selves into splendid creatures of art, thanks to their makeovers and the music filling their hearts and minds. The men looked sharp in their tuxedos with whatever hair they had neatly combed.

Barlow savored these final moments before a performance. All the strife fell away: the hours spent coaxing rhythms from singers exhausted by their day jobs; the weekly efforts to inspire and elevate them; the incessant need to ask for their money. Whatever you called his choristers—volunteer, avocational, amateur—the fact was he got paid while they shelled out for dues, concert tickets, and more. It was how things worked in the chorus business. Whoever wrote that threatening letter might resent him for his salary, a modest one by today's standards.

But he would not think about the letter. Not tonight, when he felt kindly toward everyone—everyone, that is, but Hunter Bell, whose complimentary seat in the hall, arranged for by Nicole, was galling. Handsome, long, and lanky, with upper-crust good looks and an affected manner, Bell had charmed the chorus with two lectures so far on the plight of women composers in late-19th century England, including his own great-great-grand-aunt Lisha Lovington. After seeing announcements of her upcoming premiere, Bell had phoned to propose they "fly him over the pond" to enlighten the singers about his aunt's life and times.

One email later and Nicole had arranged to sweep Bell across the Atlantic and pay for his consultant fees from her family trust, no doubt falling for the sculpted cheekbones and rakish dark hair of his headshot. And now they were stuck with the guy for the next five months.

ANGELS' BLOOD | 17

Thinking about it made Barlow gloomy. Well, let his wife flirt. He was in no position to complain.

Chuck, the stage manager, poked his head out from the control room. "Ten minutes, Maestro."

Good old Chuck, taking care of him as always. He could count on Chuck to tell him if there was fluff on his shoulders, or if his tailcoat was split down the back.

The stage had a permanently open curtain, and Barlow, peering out a final time from the wings, saw the house was full. His gaze fell on Nicole among the sopranos, her dark hair pulled into a bun. He nearly mistook her for—but there was no comparing the two. Nicole and Daphne were poles apart.

He closed his eyes and pictured *Messiah*'s score in his mind. The opening orchestra movement appeared behind his eyelids, a reassuring language of musical notes. He spoke that language, and it spoke to him. He was home.

"One minute now, Maestro," Chuck said, and Barlow straightened his bow tie. He opened his baton case and lifted Siegfried from its velvet cushion.

"Go," Chuck said, and Barlow followed the soloists onto the stage.

Worcester, Worcestershire

5 September 1898

Dearest Sister,

Performance can be such a joy when friendly ears are listening. There was no stage tonight, no concert hall, just a grand piano and the happy surroundings of our regular music salon. There, I met a well-known person, I dare not say his name, who showed me the most baffling encouragement. My two songs were scarcely ended before he barreled across the room toward me, a mustachioed gentleman with dark burning eyes. "You must not rest at these," he said, as I stood at the piano, "but must swell these delightful rosebuds into full-blown gardens."

"Yes," I said, attempting not to laugh, "I will do so while waiting for the kettle to boil."

In fact, Harriet, it is not the kettle but Leo's pitiful coughing that has made me unable to compose. The poor child gasps for air, scarcely able to catch his breath before another fit begins. I sit by his bed in a stew of worry, making soothing sounds and coaxing him to drink hot ginger tea. Ten-year-olds should not lie in bed while the sun shines, yet he must rest.

And so my *Requiem* sits untouched on my desk in the kitchen alcove amid a pile of dusty music pages. What holds me back is not just the fatigue trailing me throughout the day, but a darker fear. I will whisper it. *This work must not be a requiem for my own darling son.* I would sooner never write another note than compose a Mass for my beloved child.

John puts on his brave doctor's face as he listens to the boy's chest. He must sleep to care properly for his patients and thus leaves the nighttime vigil to me. So it is I who feel blessed when steam and warm compresses bring our child peace.

Influenza is a terrible enemy, sister. Wrap your little ones in blankets and feed them their vegetables, that they may remain strong and inhospitable to such a dreaded illness.

Now I must flee to the garden, where I may weep without waking John.

My love,

Lisha

6

Barlow looks ecstatic, Piper scribbled, hiding her notepad behind the singer in front of her. *Everything is going perfectly, even better than at the dress rehearsal.*

It was unreal to be part of this magnificent concert, as she was a far less accomplished singer than those around her. She forgot she was here as a journalist and competed to make her voice resound. If she became a permanent member of the chorus, she could sing onstage for the rest of her life.

Her place was on the fourth riser amid a blend of male voices. The bass to her right harmonized with her own voice in flights up and down the scale, while the tenor to her left filled her ear with his lovely tones.

Rapt faces gazing up from the audience. An old man asleep with his mouth open, a young woman texting behind her program. The musicologist Bell has the best seat in the house, a press seat where I would be sitting if I weren't singing. And there's Vicki behind him, looking slim and elegant in her black dress. Damn, I miss our phone calls...

Bell fidgeted in his fifth-row aisle seat during "His Yoke Is Easy." *Look at him, crossing and uncrossing his legs, wiping his forehead, loosening his collar. He looks even more uncomfortable than Theo must feel in the upper balcony.* Was Bell bored, sick, or what? She would find out at intermission.

The stage lights were too bright to see Theo, and Piper hoped he had not been called to some orthodontic emergency. Just in case, they were to meet after the concert at their favorite restaurant, Napoli's, at 39th and Lexington. She looked forward to the easy drive back to the city at what should be a low-traffic hour. As a reporter she needed a car, despite the hassle of parking in Manhattan.

But now the maestro was looking at her, and she brought her eyes back to him.

At the end of Part One, a whisper passed through the risers. "Everyone stay onstage during intermission." The house lights came on, and a bearded tenor named Preston Hancock repeated the instruction in an apologetic tone.

"Preston is like our sergeant at arms, pretending to keep law and order," Riley said, leaning forward. "But he's a total softie, no bite to his bark." Some singers hurried from their end seats, but Piper was stuck mid-row. She felt caged as she watched Daphne exit stage right and Nicole follow soon after. Vicki left her seat in the audience, her slim figure disappearing through the double doors. Then Hunter Bell sauntered out, looking tall and refined in his navy blazer and striped tie. Piper figured he was heading for a glass of wine; she could not picture him chugging a beer.

"Why do we have to sit here?" she asked the bass to her right. He was drumming his fingers on his music book and jiggling one knee.

"Too much trouble to line us up again."

"Are you okay?" Piper said. "You seem nervous."

"Yeah, I'm claustrophobic. Don't mind me."

She slid as far to the left as her chair would allow. "I'm Piper Morgan, in case you missed the maestro's grand intro."

"I heard it." He smiled, sweat beading on his upper lip. "I'm Griffin Sharp. I'd shake your hand but mine is—pardon the expression—wet."

"We've done well so far, Griffin. I'd say you can relax. Maybe close your eyes and you won't feel so claustrophobic."

"Yeah, sure." He shrugged. "I'm sticking it out, like an exercise in character-building. By the way, you can go if you've gotta go, but good luck with the Dungeon bathroom. They ought to make the men use that one. You women should complain big-time."

"I know. That bathroom is a disgrace, and so is the staircase." Piper reminded herself to cover the issue soon as a public service.

"Sing much outside the chorus, Griffin? I like having you next to me. You've got a great voice."

He looked pleased. "Thanks, yeah, I lead a small group. Bass Blast. We sing jazz in a classical style. Sending up the genre."

"Which genre?" Bass Blast could make a good feature for *NYN*. Piper was always on the lookout for offbeat stories.

"Both, I guess," he said, laughing.

The intermission dragged on for the unusually long time of 45 minutes. The singers began stamping their feet, and audience members whistled. The magic of *Messiah* had faded away. At last the house lights dimmed, and Barlow came back onstage. He looked dazed, bowing to the audience again and again. That was weird. He faced the chorus and orchestra with his arms up and kept them up. Weirder still. Then Piper noticed his hands. Where was his sparkly baton? Missing. Where was the downbeat to begin Part Two? Locked in his empty right hand.

Whispers swept through the audience. What was wrong with the conductor? There was a rustle as Griffin Sharp slid into his place, breathing hard. He had been away for a while, but Piper could not recall him leaving.

"Phew, lost track of time," he whispered.

At last Barlow gave the downbeat, and the second half of the program began. It was as if a colorful 3D picture had turned flat and gray. The *Messiah* story was growing more intense, but Barlow had gone slack. His eyes wandered, his arms chopped at the air, and he forgot to give the chorus their cues. The orchestra kept the music going, but even veteran singers got lost. Piper skipped the last half of the Amen Chorus, singing the final "amen" like a drowning person lunging for the shore.

She waited for the audience to boo and hoot, but they exploded with applause—from relief, she figured. It seemed you could not ruin *Messiah;* audiences heard the work they wanted to hear. She would not write much about tonight in her chorus feature—just that an old warhorse had thrilled listeners once again.

The house lights came on, and the singers inched offstage. They moved so slowly, Piper worried she would be late for Theo.

"Let's go!" she shouted, her patience giving way.

An earsplitting scream drowned her out.

7

THE FIRST SCREAM sent the audience fleeing toward the exits. Detective Lieutenant Lucas Knowles, attending the concert on his night off, bolted to the stage. More screams followed, loud and hysterical, as his wife, Midge, added to the racket. "Be careful, Lucas!" she shouted.

Knowles yelled at her to go home, then listened for the direction of the trouble—somewhere backstage. He called the station for backup as injuries mounted on the risers, the men falling on the women, the women falling on one another. Singers with twisted ankles struggled to stand up. A few men traded punches. It would all get worse until he restored order.

"Stay calm!" he shouted, raising his badge in the air. "Everyone stay where you are. We can't let you offstage right now. Officers are on the way."

In the wings a woman threw up into a pail, shielded by a stage manager. Knowles flashed his badge. "What happened?" he mouthed, and the stage manager mimicked a slashed throat.

"Keep everyone onstage," Knowles said, as the singers shoved one another in panic. "You've got security? Get them here pronto."

The stage manager shook his head. "Security went home sick. There's just me."

Knowles shook his head. He couldn't do this alone. He corralled some muscled men in the crowd and asked them to help out. "Stay calm!" they shouted as he ran backstage. "Everyone stay where you are. No one is allowed to leave." The place settled a bit, allowing Knowles to look for whatever mess he was going to find.

A stunned singer stood in the wings. A shame; she'd been singing happily just a few minutes ago. "Blood," she said numbly when he asked what she had seen. He ran down the ramp toward the dressing room in the direction she pointed.

"Look on the Dungeon stairs; a woman is dead," she shouted after him. "We called 911."

"What's the Dungeon?" Knowles shouted back.

"The women's rotten bathroom."

Knowles went into work gear. He forgot the music, forgot Midge as he rushed down the ramp toward a steep, dimly lit staircase some 15 feet from the women's dressing room. Who was that man at the top of the staircase? Slim build, medium height, with a two-toned half-buzzed punk haircut.

Wait, that was no man. It was a woman in a tuxedo missing her shoes. Moving closer, he saw blood trailing down from the top of the stairs. An inert figure lay sprawled at the bottom—a female figure in concert clothes with blood pooling around her. Knowles used an authoritative voice to address the tuxedoed lady.

"Move away from the staircase, ma'am."

She did as she was told, staring as he zigzagged around the blood to reach the still figure below. He felt for a pulse in the throat—none. The neck was sharply angled, suggesting a fracture. Congealed blood obscured the profile, but there was an identifying feature—hair in a bun. It was a popular hairstyle among the women tonight, but this one had come uncoiled, with strands of bloodied hair matted to a step.

"Who are you, and who is that?" the woman in the tuxedo called out.

Knowles ignored her. Police sirens wailed in the distance too soon to be his backup, maybe some local squad looking for action. He took photos on the stairs and recorded notes on his phone: black concert skirt gathered around the knees; empty hand outstretched; plastic pearls dripping blood, one lonely drop at a time.

The bleeding pearls made him queasy. He took a few deep breaths, then regretted it. The stench of the Dungeon bathroom nearly overwhelmed him.

"I said, who are you?" The woman called again. "I'm coming down."

Holding his nose, Knowles focused on the puzzle. If this chorus singer—young, it seemed—had died from a fall, why would the blood start at the top of the stairs? And why enough blood to form a damn river? He bent over, looking for the dead woman's purse.

"If you don't answer me, sir, I will report you to the police when they arrive, and they will arrest you. Do you want that?"

Knowles suppressed a smile. A chorus member, he supposed, glancing up at her. Someone in a trouser role, like at the opera. Then he remembered seeing a few women tenors on stage tonight. "Ma'am, I am a detective, Anderson County Police." He blocked the body from her view. "Please go back upstairs, and do not leave the theater until you are told."

Knowles was unfailingly polite in such circumstances, the better to neutralize the scene as a Black and therefore automatically suspect male. You had to nip problem scenes in the bud before they ended in tragedy, since you never knew who you were dealing with. Would this woman question him in the same scared way if he were white? To be honest, yes, he supposed, given the circumstances. A singer dead, no one else around, and himself out of uniform. Someday he would make this a lesson for Marcus, his six-year-old son.

Behind him, the young woman began to gasp and gag, and he realized she could see the body. "Oh, how terrible!" she repeated, clapping her hand over her mouth. He thought she would be sick, but she got herself together. "So you're a detective? Why didn't you say so? Your turtleneck threw me off. Where is your badge?"

"Night off, ma'am. You should be upstairs with the others." He softened his voice. "You're with the chorus, aren't you?"

She said something about being a tenor and therefore wearing a tux. With dangly earrings, he observed. While he studied her, she said the "R" word. "Reporter." She was a reporter with *NYN*.

"I must know who that woman is for my newspaper, Detective. Do you know her name?"

He shook his head. Had he dared the reporter to show prejudice? If so, he was disappointed in himself. "We will inform the press when we can confirm the I.D. How did you get past the stagehand?"

She gave him a rambling answer he did not follow, a real travelogue he didn't have time for with his forensics team barreling down the ramp. "Never mind; my team is here, ma'am. So go on upstairs now, and we can talk more later."

She handed him a business card. "I'm Piper Morgan, and I'll call to follow up. Your name is?"

He told her, and she turned to go. She was a spunky reporter with something appealing about her. Bravura to spare, but he didn't hold that against her. You had to be bold in a profession like hers, or you wouldn't last a day.

8

A COP DIRECTED PIPER to the front rows of the theater, where about 100 people were already seated. Half the chorus, some orchestra players, and audience members who had lingered too long after the first scream.

The chorus women were huddled in the rows behind her, their black concert outfits like mourning clothes. Piper kept thinking about the crumpled figure at the bottom of the staircase. A figure so still, bloody, and dead, it was hard to imagine it was ever a live person.

She could have prevented this tragedy if she had written about the perils of the women's restroom. But bathrooms were not a sexy story, and now it was too late.

She phoned Theo from her seat. "I know I've kept you waiting, but the most terrible thing...."

"What terrible thing? Are you okay?" The line buzzed with chatter and clattering plates.

"Yeah, but someone died backstage tonight, fell down the stairs. I hope it wasn't someone I met today. The police are about to address us."

"That sounds awful, hon. Look, I'll get takeout and meet you at home. Hurry back and it will still be hot."

He sounded sweet, considering he'd been waiting an hour. "I can't, Theo. I've got to file a news story after the police question everyone, including me."

"You're kidding, right? A news story about a fall? Boring! Don't sit around there, hon. Come home as soon as they finish with you."

"Yeah, well, I can't promise anything, Theo. This is what reporters do. We wait around and report, no matter how long it takes. Like orthodontists fix broken braces at all hours?" She hated to be nagged while she did her job. It was one reason she resisted marriage.

"I don't like it, Piper. You'll be driving home in the middle of the night, alone. What if that poor woman didn't fall but was pushed? Murdered by some weirdo. How do you know he isn't still out there, waiting to strike again?"

She bit her lip. "Your cop brother has told you too many tales. The killer was a pair of high heels. I'm sure it's as simple as that. Don't wait up for me. Bye."

Would Theo's only sibling would show up? Brandon Shay, formerly known as Brandy, Bandaid, or Bandit, but more recently as Copper Don. She would call him tomorrow and ask if there was foul play on the Dungeon stairs, and she'd promise a bottle of Dom Pérignon to get him talking. Copper Don was a sucker for the finer things, having risen from a delinquent youth in a law-abiding family to the proud status of police lieutenant.

Since joining the force, Copper Don bragged that his crooked path to success was better than his big brother's more conventional tooth-straightening one. The ego match went on, though Piper knew the brothers' mutual love outweighed their lifelong rivalry.

She would not endanger Copper Don's job; she would just ask a small favor.

A female cop called for silence. Piper's palms began to sweat as she waited for the dead singer's name.

"Listen up, folks. Detective Lucas Knowles here is going to ask each of you some questions. Relax, snooze a bit, and we'll have you out of here as quick as we can. If you cooperate, it will go faster."

Knowles looked smaller than he had on the staircase, as though tonight's events had shrunk him. "You all have a right to know why you're being detained," he said, his forceful voice enlarging him again. "A choral singer named Daphne Paige died in a fall in this hall tonight, and we treat all such incidents as suspicious."

Daphne! Oh, no. Piper's stomach lurched. It felt like a personal loss, though she had known the woman only five minutes. Long enough to be impressed.

Detective Knowles's words sank in. *We treat all such incidents as suspicious,*

ANGELS' BLOOD | 29

What if Daphne's fall on the stairs was not an accident? What if someone deliberately pushed her down that metal menace? Piper shuddered, then felt a shiver of excitement. Had a brutal crime been committed under her nose? Whatever had happened to Daphne, she resolved to wring every detail from this tragic story, no matter how awful she felt about it.

"We're going to find out how and why it happened," Knowles was saying. "And that's why we need to speak with each of you one by one in a tent we've set up in the lobby. Beginning with you, Maestro." He nodded at Todd Barlow, a disheveled mess whose untied bow tie hung crookedly from his neck.

Piper called out, "Excuse me, Detective, what time did the accident occur?"

"The station will release the details to the press." Recognizing her, he spoke in a softer tone. "About nine-forty, Ms. Morgan."

Around her, people were sounding off. "We were onstage the whole time, dammit!" a woman with a scratched violin case said. "We didn't do anything wrong."

"Except play a B instead of a B-flat," someone shouted, and the other musicians laughed.

"How about during intermission, Nancy?" said a man whose cello occupied its own seat. "Were you onstage then?"

Nancy sank lower in her seat. "Not the whole time," she mumbled.

"But we were!" a soprano sang out. "We all had to stay onstage. The whole chorus is innocent!" The last word ended in a shriek.

"Shut up, all of you, so we can go home," another voice said. "No one is accusing anyone of anything."

Piper made notes mechanically, her excitement dulled. Whatever had happened, Daphne was gone. The vibrant person whose voice had soared through the concert hall just hours ago, the new friend she would never have, was dead, her voice stilled, and for what? For the sake of sexy shoes. Piper filed the facts she knew and would call Copper Don tomorrow for more. If he had sensational news, she would be ready.

When it was her turn, she entered the lobby tent and sat down across from Detective Knowles. He smiled from his seat behind a makeshift desk, and she smiled back. They had a history now.

"Here's the spunky reporter."

She saw him check out the toes peeking from the high-heeled sandals she had put back on her feet. "Nice to see you again, Detective."

"Regarding our earlier meeting, Ms. Morgan, I'm obliged to remind you that you were an unauthorized person at an accident scene." His expression became stern. "You disobeyed orders, which gives the press a bad—some would say an even worse—reputation. I hope you don't make it a habit."

Piper felt a wave of indignation. "My work demands that I act quickly, Detective. As I told you, there was too much chaos onstage to get the proper permissions. I ran down to the Dungeon without thinking. I apologize if I got in your way."

He gazed at her, his brown eyes soulful under half-moon lids, and she got why people might spill every troubling detail of their lives to him. She wondered if he would slap her with a fine.

"No need for apologies. We'll let it go this time. How well did you know Ms. Paige?"

"I met her for the first time today."

"Under what circumstances?" He looked ready to take notes, so Piper told him about her conversation with Daphne while they waited in line for the women's room.

"You mean the Dungeon bathroom? You were on the Dungeon stairs?"

"Yes, people call it that." The word sounded strange coming from him. "I meant to write about that awful staircase but—unfortunately, I never got around to it." She winced with guilt.

"I see." He glanced up from his notes. "Did you notice anything special about Ms. Paige at other times today? Onstage, for instance?"

"Well, yes, she sang a terrific solo at the dress rehearsal. Tonight the pro sang it but not half as well, in my opinion. Daphne's voice—I mean it had such sweetness and purity...." Piper choked up, unable to go on.

Detective Knowles nodded. "Several people have commented on the young woman's lovely voice. I wish I'd been at that rehearsal to hear it."

ANGELS' BLOOD | 31

It sounded like genuine regret coming from a hard-nosed detective. "I was lucky," Piper said. "Do you like choral music, Detective?"

"It's in the top five—first comes opera. I was here tonight in my capacity as a ticket-paying music lover."

Piper smiled. He was nice.

"I didn't mention this downstairs, but I noticed you singing onstage. You seemed to be enjoying yourself."

"I was. What I didn't tell you is I sang for an assignment about the chorus."

He leaned toward her. "If you interviewed Ms. Paige in connection with your assignment, we would like to see that material."

"Oh, no, I didn't get the chance to interview her." She spoke quickly, knowing she would never give her notes to the cops, not even to him. "Was it more than an accident, Detective—I mean, was Daphne murdered?" The question leaped out of her mouth.

"We'll look into that, but why do you ask? Do you have reason to suspect otherwise?"

"No." She thought of the sour-faced alto, Corinne, who might have hated Daphne enough to trip her or push her down the stairs. But that was a wild conjecture.

Knowles waited a beat. "All right, back to the events of this evening. Did anything else stand out for you? As a reporter, you'll have a keener eye than most people."

Barlow's odd behavior stood out, but she might have made too much of it.

"It seems you have something in mind, Ms. Morgan."

"Uh—yes, I do." She ran her hand through her bangs and let the hair flutter between her fingers, a comforting childhood habit. "The intermission was very long, you see. Then, when Todd Barlow finally came back onstage, he kept pausing." She crossed her legs in her satiny pants and felt the fabric tickle her calves. She wished she were somewhere else—in bed with Theo, say, or getting to know this interesting detective in a bar.

"Go on." He was writing.

"Well, his conducting was nothing like in the first half. I am not a music critic, but he seemed unfocused." This felt disloyal, but it was true. Anyway, poor conducting was not a crime, though others might disagree.

"Anything else?"

She recalled the missing baton.

"Ms. Morgan?"

"The conductor used a baton in the first half and not in the second."

Knowles cocked his head. "Did he ordinarily use a baton? For example, at rehearsals?"

"I don't know. I only attended the dress rehearsal."

"Did he use it then?"

"Yeah, I noticed because it sparkled in the stage lights. In a way, he seemed at one with it—a silent musician with his instrument."

The detective smiled. "Very poetic. Anything else?"

She shook her head.

"Thank you." He handed her his card. "Please call the station if anything further comes to mind."

"Sure, and I'll call you to follow up about the investigation." She leaned forward to give him another of her cards, in case he had lost the first one.

"Thanks." He pocketed it. "I'll make sure you get a pass to our five p.m. press conference tomorrow. Along with my old pal Hardy Wheeler."

Piper's back straightened at Wheeler's name. *NYN*'s phlegmatic chief crime writer turned in maybe one story a month, usually about tempests in teapots. He had the curiosity of a stone and the passion of a brick, but he'd be plenty riled up to see her in his territory.

Well, too bad. She, Piper, was the one on the scene, and this was her story, not his. It was not a crime story, anyway, at least not yet. But she had a feeling—no, more of a secret wish—that it soon would be.

Worcester, Worcestershire
15 September 1898

DEAREST SISTER,

Last night I dreamed that my music flowed like a river. If only I could find the means to make that vision true! I tire of the constant pull of the household, the expectations set upon women like myself. Your encouragement is of the highest value, Harriet. Without it I should no doubt go mad. I only hope Tom knows what a treasure he has in you.

The good news is Leo has had a spell of good health, and his young doctor assures me that he can and will get well. I will compose again! It's no use pretending that a child does not turn a mother's heart inside out. A father's, too, though differently.

I shall now dust off the *Requiem* and produce music fit for an angel. I will prove, as though proving were necessary, that a woman can indeed produce a grand work. Curses upon George Upton and his rotten theories.

Harriet, do you recall the gentleman I mentioned who has shown an interest in my songs? Perhaps you have heard of Mr. Edward Elgar, the Englishman who composed *Caractacus* and *King Olaf*, which has a longer title but never mind! Elgar lives here in Worcester, and when I showed him one of my piano sonatas at a salon, he insisted I send it and other works to the Academy, posthaste. "New blood, my dear! An essential ingredient," he said in his genial way. He has boosted my confidence up a notch, Harriet. Hope with me that this time is the charm!

ALL MY LOVE,

Lisha

9

KNOWLES was immune to shock, or so he thought. But alone in the tent, after the last interview was done, he was shaken by the fatal fall of the singer whose lovely voice had risen above the choral mix. Everyone he interviewed mentioned the special voice of Daphne Paige.

Tragic that her last words on Earth were sung to Handel, music to live by, not die by. And not fair that it happened while he was out with Midge. Made him feel responsible somehow, like he'd been sleeping on the job.

Knowles had worked hard for the force, rising to third-grade detective with ease. But he was stalled, for reasons he suspected but did not want to believe. Being promoted to second grade, and then first, would mean a rising salary and a heftier pension. Word was that racism and cronyism were behind the creeping careers of numerous Black detectives, including himself. *NYN* had run an article that Midge laid out for him on his dinner plate one night. Full of facts that made her raise hell. "Don't let them do this to you, Lucas. Think about me and Marcus. Your son needs to see you fight!" She kept it up until he exploded that he would rise on his merits and let Marcus learn about integrity.

The chief called saying it was good Knowles was on the scene, and wasn't he lucky to have the white angel all to himself. Knowles told the bastard it didn't matter to him whether Daphne Paige was white, gray, or green. What mattered was she was dead with a face no one would want to look at.

He geared up to close the hell out of the case. It was the kind that grabbed the public by the throat, making them demand justice for the dead woman. He'd had his share of cases about the horrendous deaths of Black women, but they did not carry the same weight with the public. It was unfair, it was racist, it was infuriating, but he was not going to riot about it. He was going to do his job with the fairness he was raised to value.

His young son's voice was never far from his mind: "Daddy, why do you like dead people so much?"

To which he would reply, "It's my job to care how they died, son."

"Do you love them more than us?"

"No, buddy, of course not."

"Then why do you spend more time with them than us?"

A six-year-old would not understand why his work kept him away from home. But someday he would tell Marcus why he had to find justice for murdered people. How it had started with justice for little Black boys and big ones, too—boys like him who weren't always treated right even by Black cops like Daddy—something they would have a talk about soon, and then how his caring had spread out to the whole human conglomeration.

He would explain how his own momma and daddy wanted him to be a doctor, or even a lawyer, though most of those guys were crooks, Momma always said, and that was why they had sacrificed so much to send him to Harvard, so with his brains he could rise to the top. And how, after all that fine education, thanks to scholarships, he disappointed them by becoming a cop. "A cop?" Momma said. "You could've done that for a whole lot less money and in half the time."

"Not really, Momma," he would say to ears that would not hear. His psychology major was sure not wasted. Neither was his Law and Society course. Nor Legal Justice for the African-American Male. When he was promoted to detective, Momma and Daddy began to take pride in him. It was a longer word than *cop,* and its three syllables suggested a higher salary.

He left the Anderson Center and parked at the station for round two with the maestro. He had his reasons for singling out the guy, namely evidence found at the scene. He hoped it could be explained another way, as Knowles held a childish belief that a musician could not commit such a heinous crime. His mind wandered to the dead woman's family, but he would not think about that right now. If you thought about families when people died young, you could not do this job.

He stepped out of the car, ran his fingers through his graying hair, and bent to touch his toes. Too much sitting was giving his 52-year-old back an ache. He used to work all night without so much as a yawn, but now he trudged through the door like an old man. A quick cup of bitter black and he'd be good to go.

Knowles observed the conductor through the clear side of the two-way mirror. Catatonic by the looks of him, sitting motionless and staring at the floor of the interrogation room. Might have to call the doc for a go-ahead to interview the guy. Wouldn't want the department getting sued.

What did conductors really do, anyway? Did they wave a stick to make the musicians play or just keep time once the music started? It was like the way Marcus explained wind. "The trees shake their leaves and wind happens, Daddy."

Knowles entered the room and reintroduced himself to Barlow. Then he started the recorder and stated the essentials—place, date, time, and parties present at the interrogation: the conductor and himself. Barlow mumbled something unintelligible that Knowles took to be "What am I doing here and when can I go home?" which was what they all said. But Knowles did not tolerate mumbling, even by an exhausted maestro.

"Mr. Barlow, I need to ask you some more questions," he said in a tone meant as non-threatening. "Therefore, you need to sit up and pay attention."

A groan passed the conductor's lips.

"Or"—Knowles exaggerated the syllable—"we can do this tomorrow morning at your home, where I imagine your wife will be present, and I will park smack-dab in the middle of your driveway so the neighbors know us guys are present. You know how neighbors like to talk, so which do you prefer, Maestro?"

Barlow lifted his head, his eyelids fluttering.

"Where is your wife? We need to talk to her, too, but she was seen leaving in a hurry before we took control of the exits. It will be convenient for me to speak to her tomorrow morning, along with you." He paused. "If, that is, you prefer a formal home visit."

"No, talk to me here." Barlow was waking up.

"All right, then, speak up and state your name and address."

Barlow cleared his throat and gave an address in one of those leafy villages a short commute from the city.

"Occupation?"

"Conductor."

Knowles nodded. "Who do you work for?"

"I am the music director and conductor of the New York Luminoso Chorus."

Knowles resisted the urge to ask what the hell conductors do.

"How did you know the deceased, Daphne Paige?"

"I already told you at the theater. She is—was—a soprano in the chorus."

"When did you last see her?"

"Earlier tonight."

"Approximately what time?"

Barlow stared into space, his left eye twitching.

Knowles repeated the question, and Barlow knit his brows. "Time is all mixed up right now, Detective. I'm not sure, but I'd say around nine, right before intermission."

"The intermission of what? Say it for the record."

"Handel's *Messiah*." Barlow pronounced it "Hondle" and slurred the S's.

"Nice piece," Knowles said, to establish a rapport. "I've always enjoyed it."

The conductor eyed him as though not buying it. He went on to claim that during intermission he had gone straight to his dressing room to lie down, though he knew of no one who could confirm his presence there. The singers were told to stay onstage, he explained, and the orchestra members could not see his door from their dressing room.

Knowles was familiar with the center's backstage arrangements but wanted to test Barlow's memory.

"Explain the setup of the dressing rooms for me, please. I need to understand the crazy maze down there, so be specific about both levels beneath the stage."

"Well, one level down there are separate dressing rooms for men, women, and the orchestra—the musicians have a divided room of their own. Next level down there's a women's bathroom and some utility rooms they use for storage." His eye twitched again on the word *utility*.

"You just said the singers had to stay put during intermission, yet according to numerous people we questioned, Ms. Paige left the stage," Knowles said. "Why do you suppose that is?"

"I don't know; maybe she had to use the bathroom. We let them do that."

"You mean the bathroom that's two levels under the stage."

"Yeah, there's a decrepit staircase going down."

"Decrepit? In a modern facility like that?" It was a fancy word for a man so recently in shock.

"Yeah, they've neglected it, but there are other bathrooms. It's complicated."

"Enlighten me."

The conductor became more animated. "The soloists have private bathrooms in their dressing rooms. I have one, too, but I lock my dressing room so I can rest during intermissions. The musicians have two bathrooms in their dressing room, but they don't like to share with the chorus. Chorus men have a bathroom in their dressing room, but chorus women don't. So they have to use the one I mentioned."

"The one down the decrepit staircase."

"Yeah, because the elevator is always out of service."

Knowles evaluated the proceedings so far. The conductor had come around, but he seemed in complete denial about his soprano's bloody death. No weeping, panicking, or faltering with words. And less flustered than might be expected during a late-night questioning after a strenuous performance.

Knowles fiddled with his video recorder. "You returned from intermission to continue the concert," he said in an even tone. "Did you begin conducting immediately?"

"Yes."

"You didn't pause to be sure everyone was in their place on the chorus risers?"

Barlow looked startled. "Pause?"

"Mr. Barlow, people have said you waited on the podium a long

ANGELS' BLOOD | 39

time before continuing the program. That you appeared lost and confused and were looking around the stage. Can you explain that?"

"Uh... I don't know. I must have been thinking about the music that came next. I might have blanked out for a minute."

"Once you came to after this 'blanking out' period, did you see Ms. Paige in her place on stage?"

Barlow stared at him. "I told you, the last time I saw her was right before intermission."

Knowles stroked his chin. "I see. By the way, do you usually conduct with a baton?"

Barlow seemed to flinch. "Yes, when I'm conducting an orchestra."

"Did you use a baton during both halves of the concert tonight?"

Pause. "Not in the second half."

"Why not?" Knowles said. "You still had to conduct the orchestra, right?"

"Yes, but I, uh, I forgot my baton in the, uh, in my dressing room. During intermission."

"You forgot it? Really? On the night of a concert? That sounds strange to me." Knowles stroked his chin again. "Can you describe your baton to me, Mr. Barlow?"

The conductor's mouth quivered. "It is quite special, not an ordinary stick. It has what they call a pearlescent shaft and a pear-shaped handle made of rosewood."

"I see. Anything else special about it?" From his seat the baton had looked to Knowles like any other. But he'd had no reason to focus on it.

"It has an inscription from my parents. When I..." uh... graduated... from... the... conservatory." He winced, his chin wobbling.

"What's wrong? You look upset, Mr. Barlow."

"The baton means a lot to me, and—I'm not sure where it is." He collected himself. "See, my parents supported me, and it wasn't easy for them. They would have preferred me to choose a more secure profession, but they always believed I would succeed."

Knowles nodded. He thought about the hopes parents had for

their children, his own hopes for Marcus. He felt sorry for the conductor. Poor fucking guy to get into this mess.

"What was the inscription?" he said in a softer tone.

"'For a life in music.'"

"Very nice."

"I must get it back, Detective. But I wasn't allowed downstairs to look for it... after the concert... after the, uh, death... I...." His voice trailed off.

Was the guy acting? Did he really not know where his baton ended up? "Tell me about Ms. Paige," Knowles said. "What kind of person was she?"

Barlow sat up straighter. "Well, she was a quick learner. I knew a little about her family situation, and I know she worked awfully hard at her job—being a nurse, I'm told." He paused and blinked several times. "A selfless person; that's how I thought of her."

"Selfless? You mean she didn't want things for herself?"

"Well, that's how it seemed to me—at first."

"Then what happened?"

Barlow rubbed his forehead and shrugged.

Knowles rephrased the question. "How did your impression of Daphne Paige change?"

"I—uh, I saw she was more determined than I realized. She wanted me to make her a soloist in our concerts, and she got kind of adamant about it."

"Mr. Barlow, don't make me pull teeth. How was she adamant?"

"Uh, well, she kept asking me."

"And what did you answer?"

"I said it was a long shot because she didn't have a conservatory music background with, you know, credentials and awards. But I didn't rule it out, because she was making a lot of progress." The conductor coughed and pulled at his collar.

"So she might have had a solo role with your chorus in the future?"

"Yes, but nothing major." Barlow coughed again. "A few lines of music, maybe, but not a main role. I didn't lead her on about that."

Knowles leaned forward. "Yet she kept asking?"

"Yes, she did."

This opened a whole new line of inquiry, but Knowles's eyelids were drooping, and Barlow was losing his voice. He could let the guy go home because 99 percent he wouldn't fly the coop.

"That will be all for tonight, Maestro. Be back here tomorrow morning at eleven a.m. sharp. Wash your face, show up sober, and so will I."

10

A TAXI DROPPED BARLOW at his door at 4:00 a.m. As he entered the silent house, exhaustion overwhelmed him. Dropping his coat on the floor, he flopped onto the couch.

"Nice performance," a low voice said.

"Nicole! You're up."

He turned on the light. There she was in the armchair across from him, her legs crossed under her short silk nightgown.

"Of course I'm up, you idiot. Do you think I could sleep after what happened tonight?"

"No, but—it's not as though you two were friends. . . ."

"Oh, cut the crap, Todd."

Her eyes were red and swollen. It wasn't like Nicole to cry. More likely she'd been drinking, but he smelled no liquor.

She glared at him through eyes like slits. "Where have you been?"

"The police were questioning everyone. They took me to the station. I have to go back tomorrow."

"What for?"

"They said they investigate accidental deaths." His voice came from a dead place inside him. "They want to talk to you, too, you know."

"How come? To accuse me of murdering your girlfriend?"

He gasped. "I know I've messed up badly, Nic. I was going to tell you everything after the concert. Really. And apologize."

"You think I needed you to tell me? It's been obvious for months you can't keep your eyes off her. Couldn't. If it weren't so sordid, I'd pity you."

He put his face in his hands. "Nicole, I don't know what to say."

"Were you getting ready to leave me? Just waiting until after the concert to break the news?"

"No. I . . . I've been so confused. I never wanted to hurt you. I didn't know what to do, and that's the truth."

"Well, at least you don't deny your affair." She stared at him with vacant eyes. "Of course, they'll question me next. The wronged wife is the first suspect—after the lover himself."

He could not think. His tears flowed from some distant river. "Did you kill her, Todd?"

"Of course not."

"Did you see it happen?"

"No." He blotted his eyes on his shirtsleeve. "I've got to ask you, Nicole, did you have anything to do with this? I saw you leave the stage at intermission. You had a motive."

"Don't flatter yourself," she hissed. "Either way we've got her blood on our hands."

"Why? Not if it was an accident."

"People will suspect one of us pushed her, whether we did or didn't. We're in this together, hubby."

Being in it together sounded reassuring. "I should never have dragged you into this, Nicole. You don't deserve it. You're a good person." His regret was like bitter fruit. "We haven't had a bad marriage, have we, Nic? Say we haven't."

"For heaven's sake, stop blubbering. I can't talk any more tonight."

She stood up, her nightgown sliding over her body. He wanted to press his face against her, feel her warmth. They were in it together, yes, through thick and thin, in sickness and in unfaithfulness. Why was he so blind? How did he think he could live without his wife?

"Please don't leave me, Nic."

She gave a bitter laugh. "Leave you? Because you've got a wandering dick? You had to be using it somewhere." Her voice became businesslike. "Look, Todd, you have to pull yourself together. We've got a major problem, but it's rotten timing, and I'm not going to tell you until we've both had some sleep. Just know we'll have to fight for Lisha Lovington, plus fight off the police and crime reporters. It's going to be a bitch around here. Whatever happens to you and me, the future of the chorus is at stake."

She was not leaving him. The relief drained him of whatever strength he had left. "All right, we'll talk tomorrow. Let's go up to bed."

"I'm going; you sleep on the couch." She turned off the light and went upstairs.

Barlow lay in his crumpled tuxedo, his arms stiff against his body. He was achingly cold, a sense of loss pressing on his chest. Daphne, his wife's trust, and Siegfried, the symbol of his parents' love. The baton that was with him at every orchestral performance for the past 16 years. New tears flowed onto his damp tuxedo shirt. Daphne's death was unfathomable, but the baton was a loss he could grasp. You could not replace a relic like that, once it was gone.

11

Piper stood by the editor's desk, getting her morning fix of his weathered face.

"Sometimes a cigar is just a cigar," he said. "Remember that, Piper."

"Meaning what in this case, Moss?"

"Meaning the singer fell down the stairs." He rocked in his squeaky leather chair. "Story told, story over."

"I disagree. The police are investigating how she died. And there's more to cover here, Moss. Did I mention the dead woman was the conductor's student?"

Moss raised his eyebrows. "So?"

"So, maybe there was more between them. I'll bet there's sex in this story, Moss. Passion. And music. How can you beat that? A high-culture-musical-passion saga, just the kind of thing you love. And don't pretend you don't."

Piper enjoyed the back-and-forth with Moss. He was a beloved old-timer who valued persistence, objectivity, and the printed page. "The day *NYN* abandons print is the day I retire," he would thunder, though he read the news on his phone like everyone else.

He crossed his arms across his wide chest, a stance Piper knew meant "I surrender."

"Hmm, put that way, I'll give you a chance, Piperino. You can share the story with Hardy Wheeler, equal partners. But if it's a dud, no more crime for you." He grinned. "I don't know why I'm so good to you."

Piper shook her head. "No way. Wheeler can chase something else. I want this story."

Moss looked incredulous. "You're piping up again, Piper."

"As I am born to do. Names have consequences."

"Suit yourself. Take on the murder of poor Daphne Paige; you'll be bored in no time. But don't come back without a Page One sob story on the dead gal. Got that?"

"Page One on the way." She turned to go.

"Wait a minute—remind me about your name."

Like a child, Moss liked to hear the same story again and again. His favorites were origin stories, in her case how her artist mother modeled nonconformity but created such domestic chaos that Piper embraced the solid and immutable, whatever could be nailed down. Noticing her early talent, her mother groomed her to be a painter, but Piper had rebelled. Journalism attracted her for its facts and figures, and for the voice it gave her in the world.

One day Mother let her in on the saga of the name.

Father's surname was Piplebury, which Mother shortened to Piper after they were married. The name had a nice ring as well as a practical subtext; their future children would learn to "pipe up" and make a difference. They named their only daughter Morgan, but at 21 Piper switched it legally with her surname for a snappier byline.

That was more or less the story, which Piper kept embellishing to keep Moss entertained. "My mother is disappointed I'll never be a 'grand artiste' like her, but she says she's glad I turned out fairly rational," she said in today's version. She did not add that sometimes she wished she were a real artist and not just an observer with a journalist's hat.

Moss grinned. "I'd say Momma succeeded about halfway. If you were any more rational I wouldn't be able to stand you. Now go and find me all that sex and passion you talked about. I'll expect a follow-up on the singer's death latest tomorrow at five."

Right." She started for her cubicle.

"Wait, Piper."

She turned and saw Moss's flushed cheeks. Bloody dramas in highbrow settings excited him.

"Yes?"

"We'll need deep background on this Daphne woman. Job, boyfriends, family, weird habits, everything. Squeeze it for sympathy and our readers will love it. 'But for a pointy stiletto she would still be with us.' You know what to do."

"I'm on it, Moss. There's a press conference today at four. I'll go and have that follow-up to you maybe even tonight."

"Good." He held up a finger. "But keep Hardy in the dark awhile, will you? Pretend I've assigned you legwork. That'll keep him off your back. All right?"

"Sure."

"One more idea, and don't bite my head off. I think you should work with your friend Vicki Jewel on this. She's known the chorus longer than you have, and she was in the audience last night.."

Piper frowned. "What? How do you know Vicki?"

"She calls here once in a while to pitch a story. I always tell her to contact you. In this case, she's given me some tasty backstage stuff she claims to know better than you."

Piper clenched her teeth. "I'll consult her for background, Moss, but I want to cover this story on my own. Anyway, Vicki isn't a journalist."

Moss studied her with his head cocked. "Do I sense a rivalry? Sure, kid, that's fine. You've got the bloody story." He glanced at his computer. "Hey, something came in while you've been standing here." Moss rolled his desk chair closer to the computer, and the old chair squealed as if in pain. "It's an email from speaking-of-the-devil Vicki Jewel, and she's offering to do you a favor."

Piper rolled her eyes. "Like what?"

"She says there's a guy claiming to be the relative of Lee-shee Lala, the hundred-and-fifty-year-old formerly alive person who's getting a premiere by your chorus. She thinks you should go interview him—she's an editor all of a sudden. But hey, he sounds like a good story; British, musicologist, real upper-class stuff."

"Moss, his name is Hunter Bell. I saw him in the audience yesterday, but I haven't met him yet."

"Vicki says she'll introduce you. Go do it today and get eight hundred words to me by Monday. A mini-profile of the scholarly Brit. Now get going already; I need to work." He saluted her. "Thanks for jazzing up my day as always, Piperino."

Moss meant no harm by the silly nickname. He was an old guy not up-to-date about a lot of things. Would he call a man a cutesy name?

She knew it was a sign of his affection for her.

She was halfway down the hall when he called out to her from his doorway. "You think this chorus will stay in business? Maybe the death will put a kibosh on it."

"I don't know," Piper called back. "They've got another mystery I want to look into. Could be a fantastic public-relations coup for the chorus, but I'm not sure it's a story yet."

He made a puzzled face. "I do love a good mystery. Now go and get some work done, for heaven's sake."

"I'm trying to go, Moss."

Piper left a message for Copper Don about Daphne's death. While waiting to hear back, she read up on Lisha Lovington. It was a short task, since there was only one paragraph in *NYN*'s database.

The art song composer Lisha Lovington was born as Lisha Brown in Alfriston, East Sussex, England, in 1862. As a teenager she hoped to study music composition, but her father considered it "man's work" and would not allow it. Married to the physician Dr. John Lovington, she became a voice teacher and self-taught composer who wrote and performed many successful songs of the day. Among her friends in the music salons of the late 1890's was the English composer Edward Elgar.

How sad that Lovington's father had stifled her dream. "Man's work," indeed.

Lovington's connection with Elgar might explain his name on the second manuscript. But who was the real composer? Lovington had nothing to gain by copying a famous man and presenting the work as her own. Unless fury and frustration had unhinged her.

One thing was certain: Two composers writing identical scores was as unlikely as a bunch of monkeys randomly typing a Shakespearean sonnet.

Nicole Jennings-Barlow was gruff when Piper phoned. "Who is this and what do you want? Don't you realize it's only nine-thirty a.m.?"

"Nicole, this is Piper Morgan, and I need to know if you've talked to your husband yet about the manuscript with Edward Elgar's name on it. I get you might not have had a chance, what with everything that happened last night."

"Exactly right. I haven't told him. We are both devastated by Daphne's death. Goodbye."

"Wait! I can't stay silent about the identical manuscript much longer. I have to tell my editor. Plus, I'm supposed to interview Hunter Bell for *NYN* today, and I'll have to ask him about it. He's an authority on Elgar and—"

"Stop! Not another word!" Nicole was awake now. "You promised you would be silent, and you must keep your word. I don't care about your journalistic imperative. You have privileged information and will suffer the consequences if you speak about it. I'm hanging up now to get ready for work."

The line went dead.

Next, Piper took a deep breath and called Vicki.

"What do you want?" Vicki's voice was cold.

"Moss liked your offer to introduce me to Hunter Bell and wants to take you up on it."

Vicki made a clicking sound. "I've been thinking it over, Piper, and I've changed my mind. I see no reason why you, a well-known reporter, can't go knock on his door by yourself and say you want to do a story on him. You don't need me to hold your hand."

Piper felt a pang. "Why the cold shoulder, Vicki? My editor asked me to call."

"Here's why. Daphne Paige was dead for five minutes and all you cared about was your byline. You could have contacted me for input; you've got my cell number. You could have quoted me in your article. I've known these people for years, in case you forgot."

Piper thought back. Had she looked for Vicki? Probably not. "I don't recall seeing you after the concert, Vicki, and I had to get *NYN* an exclusive before some other outlet picked up the story. I was just doing my job." She didn't say Vicki could have contacted her if she had so much "input" to put in.

"I'm busy now." Vicki yawned into the phone. "What do you need from me?"

"Hunter Bell's phone number would be useful."

Vicki recited it and hung up. The rebuff stung, but Piper would think no more about the expired friendship. She phoned Bell, who shrugged off her request to interview him.

"Not feeling well, flu probably. Highly flattered, though."

"That's a shame." Most people would jump at a profile in *NYN*, even a last-minute one. "Can we talk on the phone instead?"

A phone interview would deprive her of Bell's facial expressions, body language, choice of clothing, and personal surroundings—the details that made a profile come alive. But it was better than nothing.

"Maybe another time," he said in a weak voice. "As I said, I'm not feeling well."

It was a sparkling day with temps in the 40s. Why not go to Bell's apartment on a gamble he would let her in? Flu or no flu, she would get the interview and preserve her perfect record of never losing a story.

Worcester, Worcestershire
20 September 1898

DEAREST HARRIET,

You asked about the music salons. They are indeed a joy, where I may perform my songs and drink fine wine amid kindred spirits. But salons are velvet cages, sister, allowing us women the mere illusion of full artistic expression. In the light of day I labor at my true passion—longer works that the Academy might approve and present with full respect on public stages.

I have recently sent those esteemed judges my piano sonatas and a violin sonata that can hold its own on any stage. Now it is a waiting game, while the learned jury stroke their beards and ponder these works from an unknown woman. But I have reason to hope, Harriet. While my lack of formal theory training limits my exploration of orchestral color, I can modestly lay claim to a harmonic inventiveness and rhythmic playfulness that I am told produces music not unpleasant to the ear. Would so eminent a composer as Mr. Elgar say so, were it not true?

Forgive my immodesty, but with you I need no veils.

LOVE ALWAYS,

Lisha

12

BARLOW WAS SIPPING COFFEE in a coffin. Across the room, Daphne and Nicole kissed as he watched himself watch them. They were so alike, the two beauties, with their long dark hair and slim builds. Why had he not seen the resemblance before? He called out to them, but they did not answer. He reached out, but a force held him back.

"Todd! Wake up! You're moaning in your sleep." Nicole was shaking his shoulder.

He woke sprawled on the couch on a sunny, surreal morning. Daphne was gone, but the smell of coffee remained. If only this waking moment was the dream, and Daphne was still alive.

"What time is it?"

"Past ten. How about some breakfast?"

"All right, thanks." He had not eaten since before the concert, and his stomach was growling.

"It's in the kitchen, Todd. Get up and get it; I'm not a waitress. And shake yourself awake so I can talk to you. We don't have all day."

Then he remembered. He was due at the police station at 11:00.

He stood on shaky legs and smoothed out his wrinkled concert clothes. His head ached as he stumbled into the kitchen, where Nicole had nicely laid out toast, jelly, and a coffee mug.

"Hurry, Todd," she called from the living room. "We have a crucial problem to solve."

"Which one?" Daphne's death, his missing baton, or their broken marriage?

"Just hurry and we'll talk. Bring your food in here. I have a class to teach at twelve."

He carried his breakfast into the living room, where she sat on the couch. "Can you drive me to the police station? I'll drive my car home afterward." He waited for her to sneer, to tell him to get lost.

"Yes, and Ben will be at the jail, just so you know."

"Ben Nelson?" The guy was a well-known defense lawyer and a friend of Nicole's parents.

She nodded.

"Wow, nice of you, Nic. Thanks. You work fast."

"He'll keep you from doing or saying something stupid. Just keep in mind, Todd, my primary goal is to keep the chorus intact. Whatever I have to do, I'll do." Her voice was so cold it hurt.

"Still, thanks."

She shrugged. "As I said, we have a big problem."

"I know." He gulped his coffee, waiting for his wife to say she wanted a divorce.

"There are two *Requiem* manuscripts."

He stared at her, the cup halfway to his lips. "What?"

"There are two *Requiem* manuscripts with two different composers on the covers."

He shook his head like a dog after a bath. "Two different *Requiem*s?"

"Focus, Todd. I'm talking about two identical *Requiem*s with two different authors. Get it now?"

"No." He sat down with his food.

Nicole spoke slowly. "The second manuscript is signed by Edward Elgar. I found it yesterday after you left for the rehearsal. I read it through, and it's identical to Lovington's manuscript."

Barlow rubbed his forehead. "But how can they both be the same?"

"I don't know. Not only is Elgar's name on the cover, the manuscript is in his handwriting on the kind of music paper he used. Hunter authenticated it."

Hunter, the hated name. "Wait—where did you find this so-called Elgar?"

"In the same box the Lovington manuscript was in. I was looking for my concert skirt, which had fallen on top of the box, and on a whim I looked through the box again. I never finished doing that after we found the Lovington."

"*We* didn't find the Lovington, Nic; *you* found it."

"Okay, *I* found it."

"And now you find an Elgar. Except I don't remember ever hearing about an Elgar *Requiem*." He was too distracted to eat. "This is either a big deal or a hoax."

"Looks that way." Nicole sat back.

Barlow took a sip of coffee. "Okay, so this second manuscript is in Elgar's handwriting, and the Lovington manuscript is in her handwriting, but the two are identical musically. Do I have that right?"

She nodded. "Precisely."

"Wow. Who really wrote it?"

"I don't know, Todd. I hope it was Lovington."

He was fully awake now. "Who knows this besides you and Bell?"

"Piper Morgan."

"The reporter? Oh my God, Nicole, why would you tell her? Now the whole world will know. She'll write about it, and the chorus will be screwed."

"How will it be screwed? I don't see your point."

"If Elgar wrote it, Lovington is a plagiarist and no one will come hear her music." A new wave of unreality washed over him. "Unless . . . we present it as an Elgar."

"Not so fast." Nicole held up her hand. "As you said, there's no record of a requiem in Elgar's oeuvre. And how would Lovington get hold of his manuscript? Did she tiptoe through his window and steal it—this unknown work no one had ever heard of? It's still a Lovington, as far as I'm concerned."

"She must have had some reason to copy him. Like a fast track to fame, except she'd have to be crazy."

Nicole made a disgusted face. "Men love to assume women are unstable. It's easier than believing in their talent."

Barlow sighed. "Please, let's not argue. We need to find the truth and square things with the public, the way you said."

"Good." Nicole gave him a half-smile. "Piper Morgan can write an article—a series of them, until we get to the bottom of this. People will be fascinated, and we'll draw a bigger crowd to the concert."

The concert. Beautiful and terrible words. A concert killed Daphne, and another concert lay ahead, the unsullied part of his life with Nicole. But there was no longer an inspiring story to attract the public—how Luminoso was rescuing a forgotten woman from obscurity. This new story was sordid, involving a death, suspected plagiarism, and the conductor's sure-to-be-revealed infidelity. Nothing suitable for a glossy concert brochure. "Maybe it would be wiser—for the chorus's sake—if this was kept quiet after all, Nic."

She laughed. "And you're so wonderful at hiding the truth? Ha! Half the chorus must know you were having an affair, and the other half must know who with."

He reddened. "Don't."

"Why not?" Her voice was like a cold shower. "If I don't leave you, and I don't kill you, I should at least get to torment you, for humiliating me, cheating on me, withholding sex from me, lying to me, and driving me to drink."

Why didn't she cry and scream? She sat unmoving in a silk robe that covered her legs. It struck him that Nicole had a lot of robes. A lot of clothes. A lot of money, too—her own. Plus a lot of ambition. Enough to talk to him about chorus business the morning after his lover died. A lover, he realized, who looked a lot like her.

"You and Daphne look alike."

"What?"

"I said, you and Daphne look alike. Looked. A dream showed me that."

"I suppose you're right. Dr. Freud would find that interesting."

"That's not the point."

"Then what is?"

"Maybe someone pushed her. Maybe she didn't just fall down the stairs."

She stared at him. "And that would mean...."

"Maybe it was you who were supposed to die."

Nicole's mouth opened, then closed. She studied her pedicure, head bent, until at last she muttered, "Give me a break."

"No, seriously. You should be careful. Someone may be out to get you."

Nicole fiddled with her robe, smoothing it over her knees. "Our resemblance, as you call it, is a mere coincidence."

Something possessed him to go on. "Dr. Freud says there are no coincidences."

"Fuck it, Todd, you're spooking me now." She sat up straight. "What are you trying to prove?"

"To be honest, Nic, I don't remember anything about the intermission last night. There's a total blackout in my brain. How do I know I didn't push Daphne down the stairs and make it look like an accident? Maybe I did it thinking she was you." *Or wishing it were you,* he thought.

"My God, that's it!" he cried out. "I did it so I wouldn't have to choose."

Nicole jumped up, the robe fluttering around her ankles. "Now you really are spooking me. You are in shock, and it's making you psychotic. I'm calling an ambulance."

She headed for the phone, but he tripped her. Her robe flew up and she fell hard on the floor, more surprised than hurt. He was surprised, too. It felt good to see her fall.

"I'm not psychotic, and I don't need an ambulance. Later we'll talk about Edward Elgar. He might be just what the chorus needs." Barlow stood up. "Now get the hell up off the floor, get dressed, and drive me to the police station."

Worcester, Worcestershire
20 September 1898

OH HARRIET, NO GOOD NEWS.

The Academy has returned my sonatas with a letter thanking me for my "interest," and informing me that "the schedule is full" for next summer's festivals. Since I met their submission deadline, I smell a rat.

Could the rat be my name, Harriet? "Lisha" is not Richard, Thomas, or Hugh. "Lisha" is blond curls and frilly frocks, though my brown hair waves only slightly and my housedresses are plain. John suggested putting his name on my next submission, but he was teasing, of course.

Perhaps I should have become a schoolteacher as Father wished. The dear man would regard Upton's words as spun gold—having believed composing to be unsuitable for his daughter. Did you know he threatened to withdraw financial support if I continued? I may not have told you this, darling, wishing to shield you from Father's less than noble traits.

But then John came along. Tall, honest Dr. John Lovington. If I failed at music, he had the funds to protect me from ridicule and poverty. So, Father changed the subject to marriage, which he calculated would keep me too busy to compose.

Mr. Elgar does not hold such narrow views of women. From the first, he encouraged me to find a stage where "your talents can breathe." With those words a window opened in my mind that can never be shut again.

LOVINGLY YOURS,

LL

13

Forensics had photographed 16 bloody shoe prints leading halfway down the staircase, reversing direction, and advancing toward the stage. Footprints, the forensic podiatrist said, made by one pair of feet in low-heeled size 11 shoes with a faint herringbone pattern on the rubber outsole.

Knowles studied the photos, figuring a man or woman between five-ten and six-two had worn the shoes. That narrowed the suspects to a couple hundred. "Call when you've got a pool of five," the forensic podiatrist said, and Knowles was working on it.

Though he slept little last night, he was revved by the energy of a new case. Meandering down the hall to the interrogation room, he stood watching Maestro Todd Barlow through the two-way mirror. The guy looked a wreck in the same formal jacket as last night and the same sorry mess of a dress shirt. Ragged in form and spirit, Knowles thought, recalling an old poem. And last night he had looked so fine in those swanky duds.

Knowles's brightest sergeant, Matt Daniels, was coming to help put the maestro through a third round of questioning. Also on hand was the high-priced defense attorney Ben Nelson, who scrolled through a cell phone beside Barlow. Nelson was known for tricks that kept detectives and prosecutors alert.

"Do you think he killed her, sir?" Daniels had arrived, smelling of shaving cream. A trim 25 with blond hair and a razor-sharp intellect, he'd been headed for law school when he made a U-turn and enrolled in the police academy.

"I hope not, Matt, but don't tell anyone I said that." He liked being addressed as "sir" rather than "boss," a more common title in the station. "Sir" was Daniels's own idea, which had endeared him to Knowles at once.

Daniels handed over a lab report that made Knowles scratch his head. One piece of evidence damning to the conductor and another vindicating him. Mixed results that kept a detective's life interesting.

"I only had time to read part of it, sir."

"Read it later; let's do this now," Knowles said as the two entered the room. "Good morning, Mr. Barlow, and good morning, Mr. Nelson. I am Detective Lucas Knowles, and this is Detective Sergeant Daniels."

"Morning," Barlow mumbled, and the lawyer nodded. Nelson was a pasty-faced, 40ish white man with acne scars and a dark comb-over, but his eyes were large and lively. His eyes made you forget the scars.

Knowles went through the preliminaries, starting the videotape and announcing the date, time, and those present. Then he cleared his throat and summoned the resonant tone he had cultivated for such moments. "Mr. Barlow, we have evidence that Daphne Paige's death on the concert-hall stairs was no accident. It points to homicide."

Barlow groaned and covered his eyes. Nelson touched his arm and made a shushing gesture.

"Therefore, Maestro, I must ask you more questions about your relationship with Ms. Paige. It's in your interest to answer fully. Do you understand?"

Barlow nodded. "I want to answer." He glanced at the lawyer.

"To continue where we left off last night, let me remind you that you called Ms. Paige your student. Was she more to you than that, Mr. Barlow? Did your relationship with her ever become personal?"

Barlow ran his hands through the flop of hair on his forehead. "I was her teacher. You could say that's personal."

"In what way? Please elaborate."

Nelson gave a slight headshake and Barlow paused, as if weighing his options. Knowles was familiar with that look before a suspect gave in to an urge to talk.

"Well, I had to think about her emotional state."

"What sorts of emotions?" Knowles prided himself on being a verbal architect, building his case word by word.

"Um, you know, was she happy, stressed, or in some other state that would affect her voice." Barlow shifted in his seat as Nelson, sensing what Knowles was up to, eyed him cautiously.

"What kind of 'other state'?" Knowles sought Barlow's bloodshot eyes. "Look here, please."

"Uh, I don't know, just the usual." The conductor met Knowles's gaze.

"Mr. Barlow, I sense you're holding something back." It was a standard line, since people always held something back from him or themselves.

Barlow mumbled something like "wife."

"Aha," Knowles said. "You don't want it to get out that you and the deceased woman had a personal relationship, is that right?"

Barlow glanced at Nelson. "Tell him," the lawyer said, shrugging. "He'll find out anyway."

"Yes, we had a personal relationship," Barlow said.

Knowles checked to confirm the video system was working. "Was it an intimate relationship?"

"Yes."

"Sexually intimate?"

"Yes, yes." Barlow sounded almost joyful.

"How often were you intimate, Maestro? Once? Twice? Thirty times...?"

"More than I can count!" Barlow burst out. "I loved her, okay?" He began to weep, a dam bursting.

Knowles waited for him to calm down. "All right, I understand. Any idea about who might have killed her, the woman you loved?"

"No." Barlow wiped his tears with his sleeve.

"Someone who might have wanted her dead?"

"Some of the singers were jealous of her. I mean the women."

"I can imagine," Knowles said. "A beautiful woman with an angelic voice, and the conductor's favorite. We'll want some names, Mr. Barlow."

The conductor shrugged. "Okay."

"Was your wife aware of this relationship you had with Ms. Paige?"

Barlow slumped in his chair. "Yeah." He met Knowles's eyes. "She knew something was going on—but I don't know when she found out, because I didn't tell her. I mean, I didn't really admit it to her until last night." He sat up again. "Can we keep Nicole out of this, please?"

Knowles shook his head. "We'll need to speak to her, so I suggest you tell her everything when you get home. Now, when did the sexual nature of your relationship with Ms. Paige begin?"

"Six or seven months ago. After our May concert."

"Who started it?"

Knowles was working the drama, toughening and softening his voice, adding the occasional quiver, and using his eyes to their most electric effect. Nelson tuned in like it was a TV movie.

"She started it," Barlow said. "It was during her voice lesson. She came over to the piano and kissed me."

"You joined in the kiss, I presume."

"Yes." Barlow reddened. "I wish now I hadn't. Maybe she would still be alive."

Knowles raised an eyebrow but let the comment go—for now. "Where were you giving this lesson?"

"In a room in the music building."

"You had sex in that room?"

"No, of course not. We went to a motel."

"You stopped the lesson to go?"

"Yes," Barlow whispered.

Knowles pictured it. A man and woman alone by the piano in a setting ripe for passion. "It's a big leap from a kiss to a motel, isn't it, Maestro?"

Barlow twisted in his seat, as Knowles prepared to push him. Minutiae like who made the first move, and how much the other did or did not resist, provided the flavor of a budding relationship—or a crime. Without such details, Knowles's intuition held as much power as a wet noodle. "I need you to describe that scene to me step-by-step," he said.

"You don't have to do it," Nelson said.

Barlow shrugged. "It's simple, detective. She knew what she wanted, and I went along with it."

"You went along." Knowles kept his eyes steady. "A beautiful young woman comes on to you, a married man, and you just go along with it? Taking no responsibility, Maestro?"

"All right, I was weak." Barlow hunched over the table. "I admit it, I was weak where Daphne was concerned. It was all my fault, everything that happened was my fault, and you're right, I should have said no." He looked contrite. "I'm married."

Knowles glanced at Daniels, listening quietly a few seats away. Normally Knowles excused himself at this point to confer with Daniels in the hallway. But this decision needed no discussion.

"Mr. Barlow, I'm going to let you go home now, but you are obliged to promise you won't leave this county. If you do, I swear we will round you up and throw you in jail. We have possible evidence against you, but our investigation is still proceeding. Do you understand?"

"What evidence?" Barlow sat up straighter. Nelson stood with a scowl.

Knowles took a few deep breaths, keeping his eyes on Barlow as he took an envelope of photos from a folder.

"We have your bloody shoe prints, Maestro. Look at these photographs with your lawyer. We believe the imprints are a match with your shoe size."

Barlow looked horrified as he and Nelson bent over the photos. In fact, the shoe prints were half a size larger than Barlow's shoes. The other evidence they had was far more damning, but he would let the lawyer break that news.

"Matt, it doesn't add up," Knowles said after Barlow and Nelson had left. "The shoe prints don't match, but the baton is Barlow's, no question about that. Covered in Paige's blood and wedged under the staircase."

"How did it get there, sir?"

"Remember the photo of Paige's outstretched hand? Like she was reaching for something? Forensics found the baton directly below her hand."

"You mean like she dropped it?"

ANGELS' BLOOD | 63

"Could be," Knowles said. "Or someone else dropped it and tried to hide it."

"Hmm, good point." Daniels's earnest expression reminded Knowles that Matt was someone's son. He hoped Marcus would have a kindly boss someday, someone who saw he was loved and capable of great things.

"Think of scenarios, Matt. Barlow could have forgotten his baton, like he said, and someone else might have found it and killed her."

"I guess that's possible." Daniels did not sound convinced. "Anyone could have picked up the baton after Barlow left it behind."

"True, and Barlow's fingerprints on it don't mean much, since he used it to conduct that night." Daniels struggled to agree with his boss's logic.

"Whoever killed Paige could have worn gloves and run off through the blood." Knowles looked into space, visualizing the scene.

"But sir, how would the killer know the baton would be there if it wasn't Barlow himself?" Daniels took pains to be polite. "Unless there was some kind of conspiracy to kill her, some kind of group thing."

Knowles enjoyed these give-and-take sessions with his assistant. "So, Matt, you're thinking Barlow left the baton behind for the second perp to kill her with?" He smiled. "That hypothesis leaves out one big question. Can you guess what it is?"

Daniels grinned. "That's easy, sir. I just didn't want to insult your intelligence. Who the hell would plan a murder with a conductor's baton? The thing would break in two."

"Bingo. Our problem is that someone did use the baton to kill her." Knowles handed the forensic report back to Daniels. "Read this all the way through—now that you have more time—and you'll see she was stabbed with it."

Daniels whistled in disbelief. "No shit! Oops, didn't mean to curse, sir. But stabbed with it where?"

"Hold on to your breakfast, Matt. In the eye."

14

NICOLE'S TEXT POPPED UP as Piper set out to visit Bell. *Meeting at 12:45 at our place re the two Requiems. Hunter is Ubering from the city, says you can interview him at our place. By the way, you now have my permission to write about this predicament.*

Her permission, how quaint. With Bell's place cut from the plan, she would drive to Scarsdale, where the Barlows lived. She loved driving, though she regretted the carbon footprint. A car was solitude on wheels, where many a new idea had blossomed as she drove. She headed for the parking garage where *NYN* had a discount.

She would phone Copper Don again on the way. When Theo first introduced her to his brother, Don's restless energy—much like her own—had given them something in common. He had greeted her with "Hi, beautiful" until their bitter argument last year, when *NYN* misreported a case of his and he blamed her by association. Now, when he was not complaining about some reporter's "fucking lousy incompetence," she and Don got along pretty well. She hoped he was over his vow never to speak to a reporter again, including her.

Copper Don would know the latest on the Paige case, and if he said the death was deliberate, she would have a scoop. He would become her anonymous source as she worked a new beat. She could see the headline on her sure-to-be-prizewinning article:

**MURDER IN THE CHORUS—
MESSIAH STRIKES AGAIN**

But she needed details. How, exactly, did Daphne fall? What had she clutched in that outstretched hand? And if she died from a fall to the bottom of the staircase, why did the trail of blood start at the top?

She put on her headphones at a stoplight, merged onto the FDR Drive North, and reached Copper Don on the third try.

"Chorus death?" he said. "You into blood now, Piper? I thought you wrote about paintings."

"I sang in the concert with the woman who died, so I want to know what happened, Copper Don. Was it a homicide? I won't say who told me."

He was silent.

"You know I'm a responsible reporter. I don't name sources."

"I've heard that one before." His tone was bitter.

"But not from me, right? I'm new on this beat, and I'd appreciate your help."

"You promise not to name me in your crappy newspaper?"

"I promise, and it's not crappy."

"Debatable."

She steered back to the point. "I want to announce the news before anyone else gets it. Will you help me? Yes or no. Accident or homicide. One word and I hang up."

"I hear Lucas Knowles is on that case."

"Yep, I met him last night."

"He's a good guy, Piper, I don't want to make any trouble for him. Or for myself."

She assured him there would be no trouble.

"All right. We're presuming homicide. Happy?"

She winced. "Thanks for the info, but no, I'm not happy. Why should I be?"

"Because you get to be a star. Break the news. Break a leg."

"I'm just doing my job, as you are. Can I count on you for news going forward?"

"No, sorry," he said. "I'm not going to lose this job because of you."

"I will never connect you to any information, Copper Don. A reporter's sources are sacred."

"They'd better be, Piper, because someday I'll be your kids' uncle. Anyway, I've gotta go now, tell Big Theo I say hi."

"I'm not telling him I spoke to you. And thanks again."

She hung up and let out a few whoops. Excited, sad, and horrified whoops. She could not file a news alert with an unnamed source, but she would have a head start when the news became official. She called Theo at work to tell him about the scoop, leaving his brother out of it.

Theo was reserved, as though a patient were listening. "I know you're curious, but it sounds dangerous." He spoke in his solemn orthodontist voice. "Can't you get Moss to assign you something else?"

"Moss didn't assign it to me. I'm going for it on my own, and I'm excited to start sleuthing."

Maybe she enjoyed unsettling him, the way her mother unsettled her.

"Well, be careful, okay? I love you."

"I love you, too."

"What are you doing today?" he said.

"I have to cover an arts story. A guy is in town to lecture about his great-great-great long-ago aunt who was a composer. There's a chance she'll get famous at the dead age of one hundred and fifty or something, but it's complicated because she might not have written this certain piece...."

Theo interrupted. "That sounds great, Piper. Please stick to safe stories like this one."

15

"I've got something to tell you," Nelson said.

They were in the front seat of Barlow's car, parked where he had left it last night in the County Police lot. "Something good, I hope." Barlow braced himself for something bad.

"How about we get some heat in here first?" Nelson rubbed his hands together.

"Sure, Ben." Barlow started the engine and turned up the heat, then faced the man who held his life in his hands. "What do you have to tell me?"

"They've got your baton, Todd."

"They do?" Barlow slapped the steering wheel. "That's so great! Thank God! I thought I'd lost it forever."

Nelson's expression stopped him cold. "What's wrong?"

"It's got your lover's blood all over it."

"What? Then it's true! I did it!" Barlow flung the car door open and leaped out, leaned over the curb, and vomited. "I did it. I killed Daphne!" He vomited again, hanging on to the door as it creaked on its hinges.

"Get back in here, for Chrissake." Nelson tossed him a wad of tissues from his coat pocket. "Wipe yourself off and get in. We need to talk."

Barlow got back in the car, shoving the used tissues under his seat.

"Now, stop saying you killed her and never say it again, or I won't defend you. I can't help you if you're intent on convicting yourself. And get that stinking garbage out of here unless you want me to barf, too."

Barlow drove to a trash can and tossed the tissues in.

"All right, now let's get a bite somewhere. Drive, Todd, and tell me everything you remember about the baton that night."

Barlow drove slowly down the street, describing Siegfried's

heft in his right hand, the muscle memory that proved he used his stick to conduct the first half of *Messiah*. "After that I don't know. I left it somewhere."

"Park there." Nelson pointed to a spot near a dark alley, like out of a noir movie.

They entered a dilapidated coffee shop and slid into a rundown booth with cracked plastic seats. The virtue of the place was its absence of customers who might overhear them.

"I'm going to help you remember." Nelson signaled the waitress and asked for two orders of scrambled eggs and coffee. "Close your eyes, and don't open them until I say so. Let your thoughts drift."

"All right." Barlow closed his eyes. He felt hollow, his energy and willpower gone.

"What do you see?"

Barlow found his mind as alive as ever. "I see Daphne. She's glowing."

"Where is she?"

"Onstage. Before the concert. She's so beautiful."

"Does she leave the stage?"

"Yes, at the end of Part One."

"Where does she go?"

"Offstage, and I follow her."

"Go on." Nelson's voice was low.

"She's in a hurry. Way ahead of me. Acting strange. Not like Daphne."

"And then?" Nelson kept the same low tone.

"She wants to tell me something. She's pulling me toward a Dungeon utility room. She's going to put an out-of-order sign on the door."

A waitress brought their order and walked off. Nelson slid the mugs and their aroma away from Barlow. Barlow made a face at the congealed eggs and slid the plate to Nelson.

"What time did that happen?" Nelson pushed both plates to the side.

"About nine-thirty. Intermission is ending. I have to go onstage."

"What does Daphne tell you?"

"I don't want to listen. She says I'd better listen or she'll tell Nicole everything."

"What do you do?"

"I run upstairs."

"With your baton?"

"No."

"Todd, open your eyes."

Barlow obeyed.

"What did Daphne say that upset you?"

"I don't remember. But I feel closer to remembering, Ben."

The lawyer picked up the tab. "Okay, drop me at my car, go home, and when you see your wife, tell her you love her. She cares about you, Todd. She hired me without asking my fee."

"She's been nice." Barlow gulped lukewarm coffee from the nearest mug. "I mean, she's acting cold and angry, and I don't blame her, but she's doing nice things." This was the closest to normal he'd felt all day.

"Follow Knowles's advice and confess everything." Nelson left a tip and stood. "Ask your wife to forgive you and swear to her you didn't kill this woman, even if you think you did." He buttoned his cashmere coat as Barlow grabbed his parka. "Cleanse your mind and spirit and get ready to fight for your innocence."

"My innocence," Barlow repeated as they got back in his car.

"Yes. We are presuming you are innocent and someone else used the baton to kill Daphne. If it turns out otherwise, we'll adjust our strategy. And one more thing," Nelson said. "If you don't remember what Daphne said soon, I'll kick your memory into high gear."

16

THE BARLOWS' STREET was lined with stately houses and immaculate front yards that needed a few rusty tricycles to humanize them. Piper arrived on time at an imposing Tudor and made her way down the slate path.

The doorbell rang with a classical tune, and an unsmiling Nicole opened the door. "We're depressed but not defeated," she said, ushering Piper into a spacious, unfurnished hallway. Dust balls scampered as the front door closed.

"We're meeting upstairs in the study; follow me." She led Piper through the living room and up a sweeping staircase. "Hunter says he has the flu, but don't worry, he's not coughing or sneezing. He's probably just in shock like the rest of us. Wait here a moment," she said at the top.

The house was fancier on the outside than on the inside. If you liked Tudor, which Piper didn't much, then the architecture was impressive, with a wraparound second-floor hallway where she stood waiting. The living room below lacked a distinctive style, though the oak floors gleamed, and a Persian rug, where a piano sat, looked like the real thing.

A musician and an intellectual might not be interested in home decorating, but with their money—judging by the size of the house—they could make the place a showcase. On the other hand, compared to the one-bedroom apartment she shared with Theo, the Barlows lived in a palace.

Nicole emerged from the study and invited her in. Piper felt instantly at home in the room, with its high, bright windows, wood-paneled walls, and twin desks placed side by side on a colorful area rug. Books were piled on one of the desks, while two large bound manuscripts occupied the other. This was the real living room, Piper thought, meaning the life of the mind. The natural world was at hand when the mind wanted to drift; outside, bare trees cast wintry patterns against the sky.

Bell sat leafing through a book at one end of the room, while at the other end an unshaven Barlow lay prostrate on a couch. "For the record, I disagreed with my wife about inviting you here today." He rose as though his bones hurt. "I trust you will report accurately on our meeting."

"Of course, Maestro. I always aim for the truth."

"The truth is slippery, Ms. Morgan." It was Bell, coming to greet them. "You must know that as a seasoned reporter."

Close up, he showed no signs of the flu. Bell was a handsome, aristocratic type in a navy wool blazer and perfectly fitted jeans. Only colorful sneakers hinted at a more casual side. His dark brown eyes were set above knife-sharp cheekbones, and he was taller than Theo. Or maybe he just seemed taller with his perfect posture.

Piper smiled. "I take your meaning, Mr. Bell. By the way, we have not officially met." She extended her hand. "Please call me Piper. I hope you're feeling better than when I phoned this morning."

"Not really, though I'm enchanted to make your acquaintance." Bell gave her a limp handshake, flashing a smile that showed an upper left canine jutting sideways. Piper had noted such dental flaws since meeting Theo.

"So you're here to write a splendid article publicizing the chorus," Bell said. When his smile faded, he looked less well.

"Not quite." Piper bristled at the cynical belief that arts journalists were publicists. "I'm here to cover the manuscript mystery. You know, 'Who really wrote the *Requiem* the chorus will premiere, Edward Elgar or your relative the woman composer?'"

Bell frowned. "Female composer, Ms. Morgan. We don't say 'man composer,' do we?"

Piper shrugged. Bell was a pedant, and pedants lacked sex appeal. "I stand corrected. Whatever the outcome, I'm interested in your aunt Lisha. Like most female composers of the time, she faced appalling barriers, or so I've heard."

"Velvet barriers," he said in a velvety tone.

Nicole stepped between them. "Piper is here in the interest of fairness to your aunt, Hunter."

"And I'm here in the interest of history," he said.

"Also, in the interest of your honorarium." Nicole winked at Piper.

Bell did not respond, but Piper detected a smirk. Nicole was good at cutting through crap. Now she took charge of the meeting. "We've brought Hunter here to analyze the twin *Requiem* manuscripts. He is a foremost authority on English music of the time period, and Todd insisted on getting his expertise."

Piper took out her notepad. "Will any other experts take a look?"

"We're moving ahead one step at a time. By the way, I know you want to interview Hunter for *NYN*. As I texted, you may use our living room when the meeting is over."

Piper thanked her, though Bell seemed to think he was doing her a favor. *A profile will benefit him more than us,* she scribbled in the notepad, drawing an annoyed face in the margin.

It was an unhappy day, considering Daphne had been killed only hours before. Yet no one mentioned her. Were all these people hiding something? Was the murder somehow connected with this meeting? It was striking that the two mysteries had occurred on the same day in the same chorus.

Journalists needed three events to declare a trend. Piper hoped nothing else was in store for New York Luminoso.

Nicole, her face pale without its bright lipstick, was passing a box of white cotton gloves. "No one touches the manuscripts without wearing these, please."

When all were gloved, she faced them. "I propose that only two names are important today, Lovington and Elgar. Do I hear agreement?"

"And Daphne," Piper spoke half to herself, then bit her lip. Reporters should be like flies on a wall and keep out of the proceedings.

Barlow shot her an appreciative glance. "And Daphne."

Nicole raised her arms in preacher fashion. "A moment of silence for our dear departed Daphne—okay, that's it. No more talk of our late soprano. Todd, open the manuscripts, please. Hunter, go stand next to him."

How cold she was, as though she despised Daphne. Piper

jockeyed for a view of the manuscripts, which she estimated to be the length of her own forearm and a foot wide.

"The one with the creamy cover is Lovington's," Barlow said. "The one with the blue cover is Elgar's." He glanced at Piper. "Someone should take notes."

"I'll do it," Nicole said. "She's a reporter, not a secretary."

Piper gave her a grateful smile. Nicole's moods were mercurial, but she was bright and interesting, even possible friend material if you didn't take her jabs personally. And if she wasn't a killer. Piper had made only one friend so far while covering the arts—Pam, a flamenco dancer. Then Pam moved to L.A. and stopped responding to her texts. Too busy clicking her castanets. If you want to make friends, don't go into this business, Moss always said.

Nicole elbowed herself between her husband and Bell, paper and pen in hand. "Take a careful look, Hunter. Do you see any obvious differences between these two manuscripts—musically speaking?" She sounded used to giving orders. "Take your time and be as specific and objective as possible, considering we're talking about a relative you admire."

Bell flipped slowly through each manuscript as Piper looked over his shoulder. She had never seen a full orchestral score before, with a separate line for each family of instruments: woodwinds, brass, percussion, and strings. Symbols were scattered in the margins—squiggles and lines a musician would understand.

The two manuscripts looked musically identical, but the handwriting told a different story. Elgar's was neat and graceful, while Lovington's had a hurried look. Piper imagined her rushing to finish her work so she could cook dinner or tend to a child.

Both manuscripts were in pristine condition, the paper still creamy-white after a century in a box. It was awesome to think how long they had been hidden away.

"Well, Hunter?" Nicole said.

Bell closed both covers and asked for a glass of water. Maybe he did have the flu, Piper thought, seeing his distressed expression.

"You should sit." She held out a chair and he collapsed into it, draining the glass of water Nicole brought him. They all waited for him to speak.

"As you all must have noticed, the two manuscripts are the same down to the margin notes," he said. "I have a strong suspicion about this strange coincidence."

"Yes, go on." Nicole's face was alive with curiosity.

"I believe Elgar was displeased with his efforts at a requiem, and he offered Aunt Lisha the manuscript as a learning device. Instead of trashing it, you see. It was his way of being a friend."

Nicole threw her head back and laughed. "Come now, Hunter. The piece is obviously glorious. Todd and I both think so; don't we, Todd?" She glanced at her husband. "Speaking for myself, anyway, I don't like your trash theory at all."

"Now hold on; let's be analytical," Barlow cut in. "From a musical point of view, this *Requiem* is tranquil—none of the usual fire and brimstone you might expect from it. But more importantly, it lacks the richly orchestrated style Elgar is known for."

"Exactly," Nicole said. "Because Lovington wrote it."

Barlow frowned. "Without coming to an instant conclusion, Nic, I suggest Elgar may have scrapped the piece not because it was inferior but to keep his oeuvre consistent. Which departs from Hunter's view but dovetails with it. But let's let him finish."

"Thank you, Maestro. As I was saying, I suspect Elgar allowed my aunt Lisha to copy the manuscript much the way art students copy paintings of the masters. She had never written a large work and would gain valuable experience in format, orchestration, and the like."

Bell's idea sounds reasonable, Piper noted.

"Don't forget, Aunt Lisha did not have the advantage of composition lessons—did I mention that women were thought unsuited for such schooling? But neither did Elgar, which is remarkable, given the power and complexity of his music."

Bell was too sure of himself, but he knew a lot. All eyes were on him.

"I surmise that once Aunt Lisha finished studying Elgar's work, she stashed both copies away in the same box," he said with a tone of finality. "And that explains the mystery."

Piper waited for someone to mention plagiarism. It was an obvious explanation for the double manuscripts, but it would make no sense. Why would an unknown composer try to pass off a famous composer's work as her own? She would look ridiculous, at best, and risk jail at worst. Unless Lovington and Elgar had some kind of pact.

Bell seemed to read her mind. "Aunt Lisha was not a plagiarist, my friends, just a devoted student of music."

Nicole sighed. "Come now, Hunter, why are you selling your aunt short? And so quickly?" She glanced at her husband for support. "Why couldn't Lisha have composed this beautiful work? I agree she can't be a plagiarist, because she would have nothing to gain."

"Did you have a chance to sight-read the piece, Hunter?" Piper said, cutting in. "If not, what are you basing your opinion on?"

"Its lack of brilliance is obvious," he said, then faced Nicole. "You spoke like a true feminist, and I appreciate your defense of my aunt. However, no requiem has ever shown up in her archive. End of story."

"The end until Nicole found Lovington's hidden manuscript," Piper said. "The story goes on. That's why I'm here."

"Right." Barlow smiled at her.

"And the hidden work has turned out to be a masterpiece," Nicole said. "A real *Sleeping Beauty*."

"Its beauty is a fact," Barlow said. "The rest is conjecture."

"Performing it as a Lovington would be the conjecture," Bell said, scowling.

Why was he taking this tack? He should be upset, Piper thought, considering he crossed the Atlantic to hear his aunt's premiere. And he'd been so proud of her up to now.

"We need to research further," Nicole said. "We owe Lovington that much."

Piper spoke up again, a noisy fly on the wall. "You mentioned a coincidence, Hunter. What did you mean?"

"The coincidence is Nicole finding the manuscripts together." Bell turned to Barlow. "Maestro, while your wife does her research—he made quote marks in the air—"I recommend you find something to substitute for the *Requiem* on your spring program."

"Are you saying the work has no musical value at all?" Piper was unable to stay quiet. "You're implying Todd Barlow doesn't know his music."

Bell rolled his eyes. "Leaving the esteemed conductor out of it, Ms. Morgan, it pains me to say—and you can quote me—that this *Requiem* is a glib work whose beauty is skin-deep."

"I can speak for myself, thank you." Barlow shot Piper a withering look. "I'd like to hear more of the distinguished scholar's view."

Piper bit her lip. "Of course, go on, Hunter, if I may call you that."

Bell nodded at her, then folded his arms on his chest. "To summarize, the work provides a sugar rush, but in a historical context it's a trifle." He leaned back, exhaling. "Those runs of sixteenth notes, the repeated tonic chords— it's like eating cotton candy, sweet but unsubstantial."

"And you've felt this way for how long?" Nicole sounded incredulous.

"Since the beginning, when you first showed me my aunt's manuscript. I didn't mention it then, because I didn't want to spoil your fun."

"You kept your true opinion from the chorus?" Nicole's cheeks were flushed. "I find that dishonest. It's unworthy of your commitment to us. It shows you don't respect us."

"Not at all. I saw no harm in your chorus presenting the work. It's probably no worse than many other things you've sung." Bell smiled. "I was glad Aunt Lisha was getting a premiere, even if the music was subpar."

Nicole fumed in her chair. "Unbelievable."

Piper made fast notes. *Wow, the argument has gone from "who wrote it" to "how good is it" to "does it have any value at all?"*

Nicole put a finger to her chin. "How well do you read music, Hunter? I don't believe you've ever actually heard the *Requiem*. Perhaps when we run through it at Monday's chorus practice, you'll change your mind."

Zinger! Nicole had punctured Mr. Elegant's oversized ego.

Bell looked weary. "I didn't say it was complete garbage."

Barlow erupted in a fury. "If it's so bad, and Elgar wrote it, why didn't he just throw the damn thing away? Tell me that, Bell."

"He did throw it away, old chap. He gave it to my aunt, so she could see that even the greats wrote mediocre music."

Barlow thrust his hand in the air. "Enough! As the conductor and music director of New York Luminoso, I have decided to premiere the piece as the Elgar *Requiem*, discovered posthumously in a closet. The fact is, Elgar will do more for the chorus than Lovington can. We have to look out for ourselves."

"Todd, how could you?" Nicole balled up her fists.

"It's a pragmatic decision, Nic. I hope Piper will inform the public—after I explain it to the chorus, of course. We'll blitz the media from now to May and keep everyone's eyes on us. We can start a contest—'Who Composed This Heavenly *Requiem*? Prove It's Not by Edward Elgar and Win an Award.'" He looked elated, while his wife scowled.

Piper could not believe her good luck. This was great stuff, three intellectuals fighting over a century-old piece of classical music. Moss would be thrilled.

"I need to go home now," Bell said. "This meeting has exhausted me, and I request a car service. I am in no condition to take the train."

Barlow cast a stern glance at his wife, as though warning her not to offer him a ride. Piper thought of the editor, eagerly awaiting Bell's profile. She thought of the five o'clock police press conference, calculating how to chauffeur Bell to the city, do the interview, and get back to Anderson on time. There was a thin line between Superwoman and failure, but she would chance it.

"I'll drive you, Hunter. My car is parked outside."

Worcester, Worcestershire
15 October 1898

DEAREST SISTER,

Answer this—if a novelist like George Eliot can assume a man's name, what stops a composer like myself from doing so?

Honesty, you will say. Yet the world is not an honest place, Harriet.

The dreadful Mr. Upton says women cannot write great music. Thus, a woman's name blinds judges to the quality of her work. If a man composes with beauty, conveys tender feelings, brings an audience to tears, he is praised. He is celebrated as a deep soul with many facets, among them—a desirable feminine side.

However, if a woman composes with beauty, conveys tender feelings, and brings an audience to tears, she is a sentimentalist. She is writing what is expected of a woman: flowery, superficial, "feminine" music. Her work is cast aside. Yet dare she write strong, muscular music, with enough brass to shake the rafters, she is undesirably mannish. Where is the honesty in that?

Harriet, we women composers cannot win, and so we are overlooked and willfully ignored, fated to inhabit drawing rooms rather than concert halls. Happily, Ethel Smyth has broken through with large works, but she is one out of hundreds. Clara Schumann suffered in her marriage while her husband composed for the ages. For all her talents, Robert wanted her at the stove.

I view our plight with a cold eye. Yet I am married to a kind and loving man who, though male, would wish to exhibit no such prejudices against women as I have described. My John depends on me to know and fulfill his needs without a word, so that he may remain pleased with his wife the musician, or should I say magician, who reliably runs the household and in her free time produces sweet musical concoctions. John will never ask me to put away my writing, but he will ask pitifully, and with a hangdog face, what time we shall eat. He will forage through his drawers for underwear yet will never scold if the drawer is empty. I am lucky in my marriage.

Sister, tell this to your darling Pattie: A woman should not marry if she does not intend to be a wife. Yet I think a female artist is equally as worthy of loving companionship as a male artist. Why must she suffer loneliness for her art, whilst he is served by his loving household?

But I hear John returning home and shall now exchange my thinking cap for an apron. I do this not with resentment but with love. I would not betray my beloved husband for all the musical success in the world. Honesty lives in this household, at least.

Off to stir the pots.

MY LOVE,

Lisha

17

"What's all the racket?" Moss shouted into Piper's phone. "Todd and Nicole Barlow—excuse me, Nicole Jennings-Barlow—are fighting about a requiem. I can hear you, by the way."

She described the situation: two manuscripts, Lovington's possible plagiarism, and Todd's defection to Elgar.

"So? Why call me?"

"Because you might not want the Bell profile anymore, if his relative is a plagiarist. I need to know your decision now, Moss, because I plan to interview him while I drive back to the city. He's in my car at the moment." She peered out the leaded windows to check on him.

"Ah. And why wouldn't I want to run his profile?" Moss must be doing three things at once and not listening.

"Because, as I said, his ancient aunt might not have written the *Requiem* the chorus is scheduled to premiere in May." Piper summoned patience. "To repeat, there are two identical manuscripts and the men here think the explanation is Lovington copied a famous guy."

"Sounds like a beautiful mess," Moss said. "Get the nephew's take on the charge. Get the dead aunt's photos, song scores, the works. We'll make her famous in ways she never imagined."

"Infamous, you mean." Moss loved arts stories tinged with scandal. "But remember, we don't know the facts yet. Lovington might be the real composer. I won't let her down without a fight."

Now she was the one shouting.

"That's my girl," Moss said, chuckling.

Piper loved Moss like a father, but 28 was not a girl. "You know who Elgar is, right, boss?" Her tone was teasing.

"What? The gall," he said with mock outrage. "Of course I've heard of him—somewhere. I'm no rube."

"Then tell me what he's written."

"*The Naked and the Dead?*" he quipped.

"Nope. Wrong art form."

Moss could take a ribbing, but Bell was hanging out the car window and pointing at his watch. Piper shouted goodbye to the Barlows and headed out, with Moss talking in her ear.

"You've got a winner on your hands, Piperino. See why I need you in Arts and Culture? I can't wait to read this one! Bring it back alive."

"Bring it back alive" was one of his favorite sayings.

"Don't worry. I'll make it roar."

Bell slept during the drive, then woke and directed her to the prewar building on the Upper East Side where he was apartment-sitting. It sat at an angle to Central Park and across from a mansion-style museum and garden. The neighborhood had class but not one café where she could do the interview. Boutiques were the only shops for blocks.

"I'm feeling somewhat better," Bell said. "We can talk upstairs."

Piper pulled into an adjacent parking garage, and they entered a cozy lobby with carved leather walls where a doorman winked slyly at Bell. Piper hoisted her journalist bag higher to set both of them straight. She was ready to punch and run if Bell tried anything with her.

The tiny, polished elevator had a little round stool where an operator once sat going up and down all day. "Apartment five-oh-eight; follow me," Bell said, exiting first. He led Piper into a duplex with creamy walls and an Art Deco theme, as she made a mental note to avoid the carpeted staircase that must lead to the bedroom.

Bell seemed oddly distracted as he hung up her parka with the sleeves bunched inside out. He proudly showed off his temporary surroundings as though he owned the place: the oversized windows in the airy living room, the posh furnishings, the view of Central Park. She wondered if he was all pretense, unaccustomed to such luxury despite his well-cut clothing and upper-class manner.

"Very nice. What's your place back home like, Hunter?" She imagined him in one of those quaint little cottages the English loved but were damp and uncomfortable.

"A small flat not far from London Bridge. Just the basics—I'm not home much."

"And you live there alone?"

"Usually. Just my Persian cat Nannerl and me, and my girlfriend when she's speaking to me."

"Nannerl, like Mozart's sister." Piper steered away from his love life.

"Indeed. Nannerl was said to be as talented as Wolfgang but overlooked due to her sex." He indicated the walls. "Take a look at the incredible art. What do you think?"

Piper crossed the room to study a life-size plaster bust of a nude woman on a pedestal. It was tucked into an alcove and illuminated by recessed lights, like in a gallery.

Bell studied her with his arms folded across his chest. "What can you tell me about that one?"

"It's exquisite."

"Nice to be surrounded by beauty, don't you think?"

"Yes, especially a George Segal sculpture."

"What?" He gave it a closer look. "I'm surprised Segal had time with all the acting he did."

"It's by George Segal the sculptor, not the actor. I recognize the model—he used her often for his castings. This is quite a valuable piece of art."

"Really? Well, good for you. You know your stuff."

"You know yours, too. Recognizing an inferior piece by Edward Elgar—the way you did this morning—must take a lot of knowledge."

Bell looked confused, then smiled. "That's why they pay me the big bucks."

He gestured for her to sit and collapsed his long body into a recliner. She was relieved he showed no sexual interest in her, unlike past encounters with interview subjects in their apartments. She recalled a hot summer day when she was alone with a famous jazz trumpeter who sat across from her on a slippery leather couch wearing very short shorts. Then there was the jail warden who—but never mind. Bell was a toothless tiger, though his doorman imagined him a lothario.

"A moment, please, to catch my breath." He leaned back on the recliner. "Then I shall cooperate with your mission to interview me."

It was more her editor's mission, but she didn't say so. He opened his eyes. "You said I must know a lot to recognize a bad Elgar. Tell me, Ms. Morgan, what do you consider to be a good Elgar?"

Her mind went blank. "Let me think a minute."

"You're an arts reporter, right? You must know your music."

She cleared her throat. "Well, of course there's *Pomp and Circumstance*." The title popped into her head.

He laughed. "Of course, the *Pomp and Circumstance Marches*, with number one played on many important occasions. We in England call its theme 'Land of Hope and Glory.' "

He hummed a few bars in an off-key bass. "I expected you to say *Enigma Variations*, or the *Cello Concerto*."

"I prefer to be unconventional." She tried for a graceful pivot. "But tell me, how did you decide on musicology as a profession?"

He adjusted the recliner to upright. "Can you guess? It's quite obvious."

"I'd rather you tell me."

"Composer in the family." He shrugged. "End of story."

"You mean everyone spoke to you of your great-great-grand-aunt, and you were determined to follow in her footsteps?"

"Not at all. Aunt Lisha Lovington was my model and muse, but I couldn't compose music if my life depended on it. Or play the piano—an instrument I detest—or play the flute or the violin. I'm simply not a musician in that sense."

"So," she prompted.

"I am someone who knows about music, and can talk about it, and get other people interested in it. Knowledgeable listeners are worth their weight in gold, don't you think? They provide the gold the musicians need to keep going." He paused. "You're following this, I hope. I'm not going too fast for you? Veering too far off the path?"

"No, that's fine." She was writing quickly, using symbols for conjunctions and prepositions. Leaving out a "but" or a "without" could make for ambiguous notes and result in misquotes.

"You have a quick hand," he said, watching her, "but why don't you use a recorder like other reporters?"

"It takes a long time to transcribe, and I'd rather spend my time writing." In fact, she had left the recorder in the car, figuring the interview would be short. Never assume, as Theo always said.

Bell's eyebrows shot up. "How will you quote me accurately without a recording?"

Piper smiled. "Don't worry. I've written dozens of profiles, and no one has complained yet."

He was staring at her.

"What's wrong?" Maybe her stomach growled. She had not eaten for hours.

"Everyone is so business as usual today," he said, shaking his head. "It amazes me. You all are going on as if nothing has happened. Is it always like this in America the day after one of your fellow chorus singers dies? Is violence so common in this country that no one gives a damn?"

His outburst startled her. "We don't know that it was violence, Hunter. Daphne's death was probably a horrible accident." She had to be evasive until the police announcement later today. "Did you know her?"

"Of course. Ms. Paige was fascinated by my lectures. So young, a real tragedy."

"Yes, it's very sad. We won't be so matter-of-fact tomorrow, at her funeral."

Seeing Bell's stormy expression, she changed the subject. "Are any relatives alive who would remember your aunt Lisha?" Her tone was light. "Someone who would be in their nineties today?

"No one living. She had a son, quite sickly, never married. No direct descendants, just some family-tree nieces, nephews, and cousins, including yours truly, four branches away. But Aunt Lisha is a living presence, a living influence."

"How exactly did she influence you? I'd like some details."

Bell sighed. "I'm truly surprised you're continuing to pursue the topic."

"Of course. Life goes on."

Bell let out a guffaw. "Americans! So blunt. A little bit like cartoon figures, don't you think? No, I'm not talking about the tragedy." His mouth curled with annoyance. "I question why you're asking about my aunt instead of about me, since she didn't write the *Requiem* and it won't be her work performed in May."

Piper frowned. "But why you are so sure Aunt Lisha didn't write the *Requiem*? You must have been excited about her to travel all the way to New York."

He narrowed his eyes. "It's my job to know these things. And not to be sentimental when facts put a damper on my expectations."

Moss's voice in her head said to keep an open mind. Maybe Lisha Lovington did not succeed because her music was not very good, and Bell was doing the hard job of handling his disappointment. But if he no longer believed his aunt composed the *Requiem*, why should readers care about her, or him either? His profile should be scrapped, and Moss would agree.

"Thank you for your time." She rose from the couch. "May I have my parka, please?"

"So soon? But you've barely started." Bell braced himself on the arms of the recliner and stood. "Don't assume my aunt's whole oeuvre was worthless. One slip does not define failure. Aunt Lisha wrote many charming short works and plowed on despite rejection after rejection. She is an example for us all."

"I'm glad you still admire her." Piper put away her notepad. "But I doubt my editor will want to continue with your profile now." She waited for her parka, but Bell had his hands in prayer position.

"Sit down again, please. Editors aside, I'd like to tell you more about Aunt Lisha." He bowed and gestured toward the couch.

"All right, for five minutes." She went back to her seat and took out her notepad. "I'm listening."

He had returned to his recliner. "Aunt Lisha wrote small gems, exquisite bouquets of sound, but frankly I doubted she had it in her to compose a whole requiem. I came to New York ready to have my mind blown, as you Americans like to say, but as it turns out, my earlier doubts were confirmed."

"What kind of doubts?"

"I'll be straight with you—you don't mind my calling you Piper?"

She shook her head.

"You may accuse me of sexism, Piper, but Aunt Lisha was a busy doctor's wife and the mother to a sickly boy. She would be too tired at the end of the day for serious composing."

Piper recalled reading about a doctor husband but not a sickly son. "I agree it would be a challenge," she said, scribbling *conflicted view of his aunt.*

"But be clear on one point, if you take nothing else away from our chat." Bell pointed a finger at her. "Edward Elgar was an accomplished composer who had no need to plagiarize a relative nobody. If anyone was a plagiarist, it was my aunt."

Piper suppressed a gasp. So now Aunt Lisha was a "nobody," yet she was the subject of a lecture series that was paying Bell prettily, and she was the reason he had left home to spend several months in America. How thoroughly he had degraded his relative.

"Don't get me wrong. Aunt Lisha had talent. She was skilled at playing piano, according to the yellowing reviews in our family scrapbook, and she composed the score for a musical comedy successful throughout Europe."

Bell raised his chair to a sitting position. "Unfortunately, she stopped appearing onstage when she was still young. Back then it was thought unladylike for women to perform. It held a whiff of vulgarity." He became animated. "Once she was married, Aunt Lisha did not waste energy fighting such views. She channeled her talents into motherhood."

"And into playing piano at salons, from what I've read," Piper said. "With all due respect, Hunter, I'm confused about your opinion of your aunt. On the one hand you praise her music, and on the other you belittle it." His eyes widened as she went on. "You came to this country to hear the *Requiem*'s premiere, yet you don't seem at all fazed by the sudden collapse of it all."

Bell threw out his arms and laughed. "These things happen, as you are old enough to know despite—" he glanced at her playful hairdo—"not looking it. You are naïve if you think life proceeds down a rosy path. But tell me—just between us—who do you think killed that poor Paige woman?" He leaned forward for good gossip. "Assuming she was killed, that is?"

Piper willed herself to remain civil. "Who do *you* think did it—if anyone did? The police said she fell."

"I vote for murder. America is so violent and unpredictable. I find it all very entertaining."

"Right. *And I'm done here.* She stood again to leave. "See you at the next rehearsal. Thanks for your time."

"You mean you're leaving without asking me about Elgar and Aunt Lisha?" He looked amazed. "Your editor won't like your lack of imagination, Piper. They were more than teacher and student, you know. I own a letter from Elgar to my aunt making that quite clear."

Piper let her bag drop. "Is that so? Can you show it to me?"

"That's the most emotion you've shown all day," Bell muttered.

"A personal link between your aunt and Elgar would add weight to the story, Hunter. It would make your profile more attractive to my editor. Does the letter mention the two manuscripts?"

He shook his head, then grabbed at his stomach. "I'm feeling quite terrible. We'll have to continue another time."

"Oh. I'll bring you a glass of water. I presume the kitchen is nearby?" She found it—a narrow space behind the dining room, with a swinging door.

"No, don't," he called out. "It's best if you go."

She came back without the water. "All right. Just tell me where that letter is, and I'll make a quick copy without disturbing you. A printer must be here somewhere."

"You're disturbing me now." He rubbed his stomach. "There is no printer. Thank you for the ride home. Now go."

She had to persist. "But a letter from Elgar could mean the difference between a profile of you and no profile, Hunter."

Bell put his hands over his eyes. "I don't give a horse's ass."

"All right, I'll come back tomorrow. Then I'll help you look for the letter."

Bell flung his hands out. "Goddamn it, woman, the letter is in England! Now get out of here and leave me alone."

Piper took her parka from the closet, adjusted the inverted sleeves, and closed the closet door. "No problem. Just have someone in England overnight a copy to me at *NYN*. We'll need your signature agreeing we can publish it."

He groaned. "I wish I'd never mentioned the damn letter."

"I'll send you an email with all the specifics we need." She headed for the door. "Feel better."

Whatever was ailing him, she hoped she hadn't caught it.

Worcester, Worcestershire

8 November 1898

DEAREST HARRIET,

When I last wrote to Mr. Elgar, I was so bold as to convey my unhappiness with the Academy. That was unwise, as you will see. He has now presented me with the most tempting proposal that is both interesting and rash. And now I will thrust you into this dilemma—my wise and steady sister.

I need your opinion, as I cannot discuss the topic with John. He already suspects Mr. Elgar has decidedly unmusical designs on me. To be frank, John has heard that my new friend likes beautiful women too much for a married man. Not that I include myself in that category, Harriet, no matter what John says!

Moreover, it pains me to think that Mrs. Elgar, who presumably exists, languishes at home while her husband seeks me out at the salons. If his offer is not sincere, I will reject it outright and take no part in depriving his wife of even one moment's peace of mind.

Finally, I would be depressed to learn that an artist like him values me more for my womanly attributes than for my music. That is why, dear sister, I am asking you to read with dispassion the enclosed letter from Mr. Elgar. If you prefer not to be drawn into my predicament, I will understand and love you just as much.

Please accept or decline this request as soon as you are able.

EVER YOURS, YOUR DEVOTED SISTER,

LL

18

Piper stopped by Moss's office before heading for the press conference. "No. I did not see the actual old letter," she told him. "But even the envelope with Elgar's handwriting would liven up the page, right?"

"Hmm." Moss's usual frustrating response when he was busy. He kept his eyes on his computer.

"Okay, I see you're swamped, and I'm leaving. I'll have Bell's profile to you tomorrow. Then I'll beg, borrow, or steal to get the letter for the art department. I'm really excited about this, Moss. Bye."

"Wait." Moss looked up. "I'm killing the nephew's profile. Sorry, I shouldn't have encouraged you to do the interview."

"Killing it? But why?" Her shoulders slumped.

"Because you said the mixed-up music will be played as an Elgar. When that happens, Lovington disappears from the picture. Poof, so who cares about the nephew? Or some letter? I apologize for wasting your time."

Piper nearly cried. "Please don't kill it, Moss. It's a developing story."

"Whatever." He turned back to his work. "We have other stories to run, you know. Your manuscript crime, if there was one, took place more than a hundred years ago. It will take another hundred years to get all the facts."

"But maybe the murder and the mystery manuscripts are linked, Moss. They're both connected to the same chorus."

He looked up again. "Good point, Piperino. Keep an eye on it."

It struck her Moss looked tired. He was past 65 and maybe should retire.

"Moss, I—"

Her voice cracked at the thought of him growing old. Attuned to her as always, he softened his tone. "Come on, Piper, forget it. Why are you so invested in this so-called story, anyway?"

ANGELS' BLOOD | 91

"Because I feel this ancient lady calling out to me. Maybe Lisha Lovington was wronged, and now she'll be wronged twice."

"She's protesting from beyond the grave? I doubt it. As I said, the profile is dead."

Piper made hard fists so her short nails cut into her palms. She would not cry in front of her boss. It surprised her that she even felt like crying, or that she would break down over a story. But she had to fight for Lisha. She turned abruptly and hurried to her car.

As she drove back to Westchester for the press conference, it hit her. Connecting Bell's letter to the manuscript mystery would keep a spotlight on Lovington. Moss loved mysteries—historical, cultural, sexual, the gamut—and he believed readers did, too. With a rush of elation, she phoned Bell.

"What—you again?" he groaned.

"Hunter, sorry to disturb you while you're sick, but it's urgent that someone faxes me the letter you mentioned today, the one from Elgar to Lisha. If you have a pen handy, I'll give you the fax number. We need it ASAP. In an hour or two, preferably."

"Impossible." His voice was muffled as if by multiple blankets.

"Why?" She steered onto the busy Hutch Parkway. "It's the only chance for your profile to run."

"My assistant is on vacation."

"Then get someone else to do it." Piper cursed under her breath.

"There is no one else."

"Then summarize the letter. No, forget it." Quoting Bell would not do. Only the actual letter would do, reproduced in its century-old glory. "When does your assistant get back?"

"Tomorrow."

"That's okay. Please have him do it first thing. Or her."

"Him."

"And we need photos and anything else showing a connection between your aunt and Elgar, or the editor will kill your profile for good. I don't think you want that."

"All right."

She let out a sigh. "That's great, Hunter. Feel better, and I'll see you at chorus rehearsal Monday night. They'll be working on the *Requiem*."

"What? Even though that poor woman died, and the *Requiem* has been disgraced?" He sounded horrified. "Audiences will stay away in droves."

"No, they won't," she said, arriving at the County Police with time to spare. "People will flock to a mystery."

The pressroom hummed as techies set up their equipment, photographers vied for positions on the floor, and reporters chatted shoulder to shoulder on narrow chairs.

True to his word, Detective Knowles had left a pass for Piper at the information desk. Grateful, she grabbed one of the last seats in the room, her mind whirling from the events of the past 24 hours. She was squeezed between a broad-chested man with sharp elbows and a woman fishing chips from a greasy bag. Across the room, Hardy Wheeler slouched in his seat, looking bored. He shot her a quizzical glance, and she nodded. A moment later Detective Knowles, in a suit and tie, entered with another suit and two uniformed officers.

The second suit took the mic and identified himself as the deputy police chief. "As most of you know, a young woman was found dead backstage at the Anderson Performing Arts Center last night," he said as reporters held up their phones or scribbled notes. "We have ruled the death a homicide."

Piper felt sick again when he announced Daphne's name. Did crime reporters ever grow callous? How many of these people had looked into a victim's eyes before tragedy struck, as she had?

The deputy added graphic new details. Daphne died from "a fractured skull and exsanguination" between about 9:00 and 10:00 p.m.

His clipped tone turned sympathetic. "It is always sad when a young person dies, especially by violence. We extend our condolences to her family. Detective Lucas Knowles will now answer your questions."

As Knowles approached the mic, a reporter called out, "So she fell down the stairs?"

"Yes."

"Then why a homicide, Knowles? The fall could be the cause of death, right? The deputy said she bled out."

ANGELS' BLOOD | 93

"There was an incident that made her lose her balance."

"What kind of incident?" someone else shouted.

"That is all we can report at this time."

Piper raised her hand. "Do you have evidence connecting someone to the crime, Detective?" Her heart beat faster—it was her first question on the crime beat.

"As I said, we are not prepared to comment at this time." Knowles nodded slightly at her.

"What about the security camera?" someone in the back yelled. "Did it capture the crime?"

"The security camera wasn't working."

"Witnesses? Suspects?" It was Hardy Wheeler, too lazy even for complete sentences.

"There is one person of interest. No suspects. No witnesses."

"Who's the P.O.I., Detective?" Wheeler said.

"We're not identifying the person of interest at this time. You folks know the drill. We hope to have more for you in a day or two."

Piper noted that Wheeler had asked two questions, two more than she expected. Maybe he knew what he was doing, after all.

19

AFTER A SCANTY PRESS CONFERENCE that left reporters hungry, Knowles liked to ruminate with Sergeant Daniels about the evidence or lack of it. In this case no DNA other than that of Paige, as she had not helped by pulling out her killer's hair, gouging his or her skin with her fingernails, or causing the culprit to bleed onto her clothes. No eyewitnesses or anyone claiming to hear her scream, though more than 1,000 people were in the hall at the time.

"Maybe there was no time to scream," Daniels said.

"You're right, Matt. The coroner's report says she suffered a fatal brain injury from an eye stab that severed an artery, followed by a cracked skull from bouncing down a flight of metal steps. When she landed, she could no longer scream or do anything else, for that matter."

Daniels whistled softly. "It's worse when you put it that way, sir. Let's talk about the evidence we do have." Daniels liked to focus on the positive.

"You mean the contradictory evidence," Knowles said, pulling him down a peg, but gently.

"Well, we do have the murder weapon, sir. No disputing that."

He had shown Daniels the forensic team's find: a 16-inch conductor's baton caked in the victim's blood, though how you killed with one of those things was a puzzle. You had to be rock steady and precise to aim such a skinny object at a small moving target like an eye, especially if the victim was struggling or falling.

"The perp must be the conductor," Daniels said, but Knowles was not so sure. Barlow's fingerprints were on his baton, along with Paige's, but that did not prove he killed her.

"If Barlow told the truth about losing the stick, then someone wearing gloves could have picked it up and done the deed, Matt. I'm sure you also thought of that."

"Of course," Daniels said, and Knowles smiled at his earnest tone.

Knowles still could not see Barlow doing such a vicious thing, "Whoever did it, it's horrible to think about—that poor woman pulling the baton from her eye as she falls to her death."

The level-headed Daniels looked thoughtful. "Can you really die from something in your eye, sir? I mean, I got stuck by a branch once, and it healed."

"Having researched that question, I say yes. Paraphrasing now, if the object penetrates deep into your eye socket, and travels through the cranial cavity to your brain, it can cause a severe bleed that kills you. I read about some teenage kid who died when a fishing reel hooked his eye instead of a fish."

"Ouch, like a horror movie. That conductor must have a lot of rage inside him."

"But our other evidence clears him, Matt. You saw the forensic podiatrist's report about those bloody size eleven shoe prints. The maestro's shoes don't fit. They're ten and a half."

"Maybe he likes to wear roomy shoes for concerts. Maybe he wore someone else's shoes that night. Nothing is for certain, right?"

"Right, but no worries, Matt. The perp's out there, and we're gonna get the son of a bitch."

Worcester, Worcestershire

12 November 1898

DEAREST HARRIET,

I enclose Mr. Elgar's letter and send you loving thanks for agreeing to advise me. If you, a learned schoolteacher, can find nothing wrong with his proposal, I shall assume that the distinguished gentleman means well and wishes to help me. In that case, I would consider accepting.

Conversely, if you are outraged, I will fling the proposal to the wind.

Rest assured that Mr. Elgar—Edward, as he begs me to call him—is one of the warmest and most agreeable persons I have ever met. Otherwise, I would surely have torn up his letter at once and not bothered you with it.

Whatever you answer, Harriet, I promise to listen. Otherwise, my nerves may set me upon a path I shall live to regret.

AWAITING YOUR REPLY, I AM,
YOUR DEVOTED SISTER,

Lisha

20

Piper was leaving the press conference when Nicole Jennings-Barlow phoned. "I must meet with you tonight. We need a strategy to change Todd's mind about presenting the *Requiem* as an Elgar."

Piper's shoulders sagged with fatigue. "Can it wait a few days? We just met this morning. The Lovington concert is still five months away."

"It will be the Elgar concert if Todd gets his way. I hope you feel as I do, Piper— pushing Lovington aside is wrong. She needs her day in court, so to speak. And we're the only court she has."

That was true—only the two of them seemed to care about a musician treated unjustly a century and more ago. "All right, I'll meet with you, but just for an hour. Where?"

"Anderson café at eight p.m., top floor of the library. I'll grab a table."

Nicole waved from the back of the café. "So good to see you, Piper," she said. "It's been a hell of a day."

"Yeah, for me too." Piper dropped her backpack on a chair. "You and Todd must be devastated about Daphne."

"We aren't, but he is." Nicole rolled her eyes.

So Daphne had come between them, and Nicole wanted her to know. Maybe Todd was cheating on her with Daphne, which would explain Nicole's cold attitude this morning. "Do you want to talk about it? The bad day, I mean. Anything personal will be off the record."

"No, thanks, I just want to talk about Lovington." Nicole gave a tired shrug. "Can I count on you to take her side in this *Requiem* mess, Piper?"

"I can't take sides, not publicly, anyway. Journalists can't be advocates." The smart Ms. Jennings-Barlow should know that.

"But you're a woman and a writer, Piper, and you know how women are discounted by the patriarchy." Nicole gave her an icy stare. "Don't be such a good little reporter. Don't you want to make a difference? People read your stuff, and you can influence them. Speak out on behalf of Lisha. Protest the restrictions against women!"

Nicole's words stung. Objectivity was baked into Piper's reportage, or as close to it as she could get. *NYN*'s reporters kept their opinions to themselves unless invited to express them. Yet here was Nicole, openly demanding she take sides.

"I'm not an opinion writer, Nicole—not yet, anyway. But I do care about Lovington, and I'll report on the story as it unfolds."

Nicole looked disappointed. "It's so important that Lovington gets a chance."

"I agree."

"Let me lay it out a different way, Piper. Journalists seek 'the truth'"—she made quote marks in the air—"but sometimes there are higher values than truth. This is a moment when a woman's whole creative life is at stake. And she represents centuries of women. You get that, right?"

"Sure, I get it. I know women have to fight for their creative lives. But you're focusing on someone from so long ago. Why not focus on someone alive?"

"I'm with you, and that's the point!" Nicole cried out. "Lovington is long gone, but her work is alive. That's because music never dies. Yet now, at a crucial moment, a man threatens to destroy her one last opportunity at recognition." She sat back. "See?"

"The *Requiem* might not be her work, Nicole."

Nicole blinked. "Do you even know which man I mean? The one threatening to destroy her last opportunity?"

"Let me guess. Edward Elgar."

"No."

"Hunter Bell?"

"No."

"I would say my editor Moss McCarthy, but you don't know him. That leaves your husband, Todd."

"Yes. Did you hear how fast he put his money on Elgar this

morning?" Nicole looked disgusted. "He's planning a big media campaign to build an audience for our so-called Elgar concert. Hunter has no decision-making power over New York Luminoso, but did you see how he threw his aunt to the wolves today? It made me sick."

"Yeah, me too."

"We must stick up for Lisha. And prevail!"

Students at other tables turned around. Were any of them Nicole's students? What kind of reputation did she have here at Anderson? Piper guessed she was admired and feared.

"It's closing time, Nicole. We should go."

"I'll repeat my question. Can I count on you to take Lovington's side? Think what a powerful ally you can be with your byline. Why not submit an opinion piece, or must you just blindly report?"

Piper noted how Nicole threw words around. "I don't *blindly* report, Nicole. And there are things about the *Requiem* dispute that trouble me." Library lights flashed as she went on. "You're assuming Lisha Lovington was persecuted for being a woman in a man's field, and that's why her music was rejected back then."

"Damn straight."

"But weren't a lot of male composers rejected, too? Hasn't it always been that way? Not everyone can become a big name in the music world, right?"

Nicole might be smug, but she was a good listener. She did not interrupt as Piper went on. "The symphony orchestras back then must have turned away plenty of male composers, just like today. There are standards, and a work has to meet them."

"Men set the standards, Piper." Nicole enunciated carefully. "Even more so back then. At least women today have a chance to be heard, and a chance to fail. That's more than Lisha Lovington had."

"I guess we agree life isn't fair," Piper said. "But do you really have no doubts that Lovington wrote the *Requiem*?"

"Yes, of course I have doubts, but we must swallow our doubts and support her." Nicole leaned forward. "It's a matter of loyalty, Piper. We said we're premiering her work, and we're going to premiere it. If someone else wrote the *Requiem*, that's not our problem. We vote for Lovington."

"Your husband will call it an Elgar."

"We must work to prevent that."

"I'll do what I can," Piper said.

Worcester, Worcestershire
14 November 1898

DEAR SISTER,

Did you dispatch your letter on an eagle's wing? I sense you are angry at me for even considering Edward's proposal.

But I have not lost my powers of judgment, Harriet. I simply judged it best to seek your opinion before refusing Edward. Now I will answer your questions, to reassure you of my sanity.

Yes, I remember what our dear parents taught us. We must not lie, cheat, steal, or cause harm to others. We must value honesty, sincerity, and loyalty; be respectful, and always obey the law. We children went forth grounded in a strong morality, not knowing what lay ahead but possessing a fine and proper set of values with which to meet the world.

But then life stepped in, Harriet. Life with its twists and turns that a noble morality never envisioned. When veils are lifted, and the "good" become treacherous, we must seize the weapons at hand and strike out on our own behalf.

Mr. Elgar and I are both adults, aware of the risks in any endeavor. I know that you do not want me hurt nor my reputation ruined, which are the same thing. I love and thank you for your clear counsel to refuse this offer, and I will refuse it. You are sensible, and I am headstrong. Your strength will help me resist.

MY LOVE,

Lisha

21

BARLOW WEPT as he drove to the funeral home. The news reports said Daphne was murdered, making him fear anew he'd killed her. Oh, Daphne! Wiping his eyes, he nearly collided with another car. Impossible that he would never see her again, breathe in the scent of her hair. Had it been only two days? His sense of time was distorted, along with his judgment. He should not be driving.

He grew calmer thinking about the funeral agenda. There would be speeches, but music would speak for him; he would lead a select New York Luminoso ensemble in *Messiah*'s Amen Chorus. What if he started blubbering during the music? Like broadcasting to the world that he loved Daphne.

And he did—had—would love her always.

If he had brought that threatening letter to the police, would she still be alive?

The sun sent a shaft of light through the clouds, reminding him of how his wife and lover gazed at him from the soprano section—as if he were the sun. He should have ended the pretense, but which one to choose? Daphne made him happy, but Nicole kept him edgy. Because of Nicole he pushed the chorus to perform music by new composers, and it was she who had brought the forceful and thrilling Lovington *Requiem* to his attention. But surprise, surprise, Lovington had not composed it after all.

He would never say this to his wife, but it was obvious why the *Requiem* was forceful. Edward Elgar had written it.

Daphne's closed casket rested in pine needles and rosebuds at the front of the chapel. The place was packed, with the grieving mother in a wheelchair at the end of the first pew.

After the hymns, prayers, and eulogies, the singers stood and sang "Worthy Is the Lamb That Was Slain." Barlow conducted, his gut heaving with cramps.

Afterward, Barlow tried to flee to the restroom, but mourners kept reaching out to him. "Thank you, so moving," "a beautiful ending," and "a perfect send-off," over and over, as if he were the Messiah himself. He finally got away and made it just in time.

"Coming to Dodi's?" A heavily rouged older woman approached him as he exited the restroom. She introduced herself as "Daphne's Aunt Dora."

"I don't think so—who is Dodi?"

Aunt Dora pointed to the woman in the wheelchair.

"She's my sister, Daphne's mother. She'd be honored if you would come. You must, you know; it's only right."

Barlow gulped in panic. "So sorry, I can't make it today, Ms. Dora. Please give your sister my deepest condolences."

Aunt Dora stared at him, her rouged cheeks a lurid red, her face expanding to fill the room. This woman knew about him, and Daphne's mother knew, and who knew how many other people in this stifling chapel knew. Daphne must have told her mother about their affair, and her mother told her sister, and from there the word spread. Everyone politely kept mum except this clownish woman, who had the nerve to judge him. If he murdered Daphne, and persistent rumblings in his intestines told him he had, he must go home and figure out what to do.

Take the torn-up letter to the police, for starters.

22

Piper lingered in the church to make notes. *Nice touch, members of the chorus singing at Daphne's funeral. Todd Barlow looked heartbroken. No doubt about it—he and Daphne were having an affair.* It all came together. The tense vibe at the manuscript meeting, the cold way Nicole shot down Daphne's name, the furious argument afterward. The Barlows' marriage was in trouble, and Daphne Paige was the reason.

Could Nicole have killed Daphne out of jealousy? Piper's heart beat faster as she wrote notes in the quiet church. *If Todd was in love with her, Nicole would have a strong motive to get rid of her. I saw her follow Daphne off the stage at intermission. On the other hand, Todd came back so late after intermission—maybe he killed her? He also had a strong motive, if he felt his personal life closing in on him.*

She noticed a woman in a wheelchair and went to greet her. "Hello, are you Mrs. Paige?"

The woman nodded. "And you are?"

Piper introduced herself. "I sang *Messiah* with the chorus and heard Daphne sing at the dress rehearsal. I am sorry for your loss, Mrs. Paige. Your daughter seemed like a wonderful person."

"Morgan...you're the one who wrote that first news article, aren't you?" said an older woman who appeared behind the mother, her rouged cheeks matching her eyes. "I mean the article about what happened to Daphne? And the one saying it was a homicide? You write very well."

Thank goodness they didn't turn their backs or make disgusted faces. "Thank you, yes; I am covering this sad story."

"Excellent," the rouged woman said. "Such a dreadful crime should not go overlooked. Please keep reporting on this tragedy, Ms. Morgan. I'm glad they assigned someone like you to cover it."

"Me too," Mrs. Paige said.

Piper's hopes rose—if the mother and the other woman liked

her, they might talk to her about Daphne. "May I ask your name?" she asked the second woman.

"I am Daphne's aunt, Dora Stringer. I flew in from Seattle last night to be with my sister. But I'll be returning home tomorrow morning."

Mrs. Paige began to cry.

"Come now, Dodi, there will be many other people around." Her sister patted her back. "You'll hardly miss me." Her eyes met Piper's over the mother's head. "I would stay, but my husband needs me at home. By the way, will you be coming to the house, Ms. Morgan? It's just down the road in Pelham. You're welcome to join the crowd."

"Thank you, I'll stop by. And if you need help after Dora leaves, Mrs. Paige, I can spare some time tomorrow. I helped my mother when she was sick. How about if I come late morning?"

It was presumptuous of her. Theo hated it when she worked on the weekend. And tomorrow was Saturday, when there were errands to do at home. But it was a win-win plan. Piper would help the mother, and the mother would help her by talking about Daphne. Pelham was only 30 minutes from the city, a fast round trip.

"That's very sweet of you, dear," Mrs. Paige was saying.

"Yes, it is," Dora agreed.

"How is your mother doing these days?" Mrs. Paige said.

"She's much better, thanks." The cancer had retreated, and her mom was painting every day.

"Very glad to hear that," the two women said in unison.

Piper called Copper Don before leaving the church.

"I can't talk to you about police cases anymore, Piper, if that's why you're calling."

"Please, just one more question." She spoke fast. "What made Daphne fall? Detective Knowles said 'an incident' made her lose her balance."

"I just don't get why you're so interested, Piper. You don't write about this kind of dirt."

"The crime happened on my beat; that's why. I knew Daphne slightly, and I need to know what happened to her."

Copper Don was silent a moment. Piper pictured him chewing on his lower lip, a habit Theo shared.

"You know you're asking me to risk my job."

"Just tell me this one thing, and I won't ask anymore. What was the incident?"

He groaned. "You didn't get this from me. And it's the last time I'm answering you. I mean it, Piper."

"I understand."

"She was stabbed. Now I gotta go."

"Wait! Stabbed where? Just finish the sentence."

"That's my answer."

A deep breath. "Come on, Copper Don, please. Where was she stabbed?"

"In the eye, dammit."

Piper was too shocked to thank him.

23

Piper raced to her car and phoned Moss. "Hot tip, Moss—a scoop." She sat hunched over the steering wheel, too stirred up to drive. "Daphne Paige was stabbed in the eye. I'm going to write it up after I make a condolence call to the mother."

"Slow down, missy. Who's your source?"

"I can't tell you."

"Can't use it, then." She heard his chair squeak and imagined him swiveling at his desk "We don't use unconfirmed anonymous tips."

"Moss, this is real!" She tapped her toe in impatience. "Let's say I got the confirmation from the detective, but he asked me not to report it—would we go with it anyway, even if it helped the killer? Would that be ethical?"

More swiveling and squeaking. "Look, hon, I've got a shitload of work to do today. Please, pretty please, take a course in crime reporting? On your own time, when you've finished your present assignment?"

"Okay, sure, Moss." Her cheeks burned.

"Look, I don't mean to be harsh, and you're a damned good reporter," he said, his voice softening. "But if you want to work the crime beat, you gotta learn a lot on your own. Your question is complicated. Do some reading. Talk to Hardy—he's been around. I just don't have the time to be your editor and your professor at the same time."

"I get it, Moss, really." She blinked back tears. It was like talking to her father all over again—the only man who could make her cry. As an adolescent she would mouth off at Dad, then cry at his hurt expression. But she would never mouth off at Moss.

"You were supposed to announce the news of a mystery manuscript yesterday, and for some reason you didn't. I believe you're still our Arts and Culture reporter, yes?"

"I'll do it today, Moss." Which meant she'd be working late into the night. "But this eye-stab thing is major, and I'm the only reporter who knows about it." He would relent; he always did. But not this time. "You know the drill, kiddo. No creditable source, no story."

Piper sighed into the phone. "All right, I'll give the manuscript mystery my best."

"You always give it your best, and you are appreciated. Now I've gotta get some work done."

"Okay, but here's a heads-up—Hunter Bell called his aunt Lisha a 'relative nobody' who obviously plagiarized Elgar. Too bad she's not here to defend herself."

"Deadly sad. Jazz up the mystery and the misery, and we'll post it tomorrow. Page One of Arts and Culture in Sunday's print edition. Now go write the hell out of it, as only you can do."

"I will, Moss, thanks."

"And here's a last bit of wisdom. Beware getting sucked into the sensationalism of the Paige murder case. In the long run you'll remember the composer-wannabe and her posthumous fling at stardom, not some dead woman's bloody eye."

We'll see about that, Piper thought as they ended the call. Driving toward Pelham, she read a new email from Nicole while stopped at a long red light. It was headed "Park Bench Conundrum."

> *"What I desire is liberty to go walking alone, to come and go, to sit on the benches in the Tuileries Gardens. Without that liberty you cannot become a true artist. You believe you can profit by what you see when you are accompanied by someone, when you must wait for your companion, your family! Thought is shackled as a result of that stupid and continual restraint.... That is enough to make your wings droop. It is one of the main reasons why there are no women artists."*
>
> Simone de Beauvoir used that quote in The Second Sex, Piper. It's from the journals of Marie Bashkirtseff, a young Ukrainian-French painter writing in Paris in 1884.

The quote rang true—only a free mind could be fully creative. But didn't men feel the same constraint waiting for women? Piper parked in front of the Paige house, pulled out her phone, and replied to Nicole.

What about the nineteenth-century female writers who succeeded? Like Jane Austen, George Eliot, Charlotte Brontë. They must have had men in their lives. And look at artists like Mary Cassatt, Rosa Bonheur, and Cecilia Beaux. But I do sympathize with Marie on her Tuileries bench. I've felt that way waiting for Theo.

Nicole's response was swift. *Piper Morgan, do your homework.*

Doing a quick search, Piper learned that Austen never married, Eliot was not officially married until the last year of her life, and Brontë died nine months into her only marriage.

As for the nineteenth-century painters, neither Cassatt nor Cecilia Beaux ever married, and Rosa Bonheur had domestic partnerships with women. Only Berthe Morisot was married to a man for any length of time.

The verdict was in: Marriage—especially to men—stifled creative women. But was Nicole's email a cry for help or a warning? Was it an implication about Lovington or Nicole's own feminist position?

Droopy wings to be discussed, Piper replied.

Worcester, Worcestershire
24 November 1898

MY DEAR EDWARD,

You may think I have retreated in horror from your recent proposal. To the contrary, I believe your "game" was born of a genuine desire to clear an easier path for women composers like myself, who must bear repeated rejection without a sensible explanation. Not horror, then, but careful contemplation has led to my decision.

Before answering, I must say I admire your playful and productive imagination with its freedom from convention. Imagination is my path, as well, though there are constraints upon it. One cough from my fragile son distracts me so that my budding "Sanctus" movement dies on its stem. A mother's love must eclipse her ambition. Her mind cannot be wholly open while her child is ill, as the borders of her heart are too porous to keep fear at bay.

Might the disagreeable Upton have a point in judging our sex? I say no. Women can and do compose great works, but our art requires a receptive intellect and an environment suitable for creativity. For a devoted mother of a sick child, such conditions may be acquired only through selfishness or the services of a full-time nurse. Most women have neither the perversity for the former nor the resources for the latter. Therein lies the dilemma, as a woman who would allow her children to wilt whilst her art flourishes is an unnatural woman indeed.

Moreover, the man of most households can freely achieve because the woman does the worrying, soothing, and administering. My husband loves our sick boy yet leaves home each morning confident that I will carry on, and I do.

These points may help explain why I have decided to respectfully decline your offer.

I will continue to compose when life allows, though I would prefer a more concrete sphere like the law, where precedent outshines invention and conformity rules the day. Perhaps I care too much for conformity to risk my reputation in the manner you have suggested.

WITH MY SINCERE GOOD WISHES,
I REMAIN YOURS IN FRIENDSHIP,

Lisha Lovington

24

Visitors streamed through Mrs. Paige's open door carrying dishes that aroused Knowles's appetite. He came empty-handed, but his contribution would trump the food. He would catch the killer.

As he advanced through the somber gathering, he spotted the reporter with the colorful hair near the bereaved mother. But how did Piper Morgan get to Dorothy Paige before he did? There she was, holding the woman's hand. Morgan had a talent for showing up and writing things up. He had read her articles, and they were good.

"How do you do? I'm Detective Lucas Knowles." He showed the mother his badge. "When you're done with Ms. Morgan here, I'd like to ask you some questions. I'll be over there." He pointed to the refreshments table.

"No, wait." Piper Morgan stood. "It's your turn with Mrs. Paige, Detective. I'll make sure they save some cookies for you."

The mother mustered a smile for her. "You are such a kind person, dear." She gripped the reporter's hand. "Please help yourself to the food—you girls are so thin these days."

Piper Morgan gently extracted her hand and turned her sharp eyes on Knowles. "I've been wanting to talk to you in person again, Detective, and now fate has made that easier." Her smile had a teasing edge.

"You mean Hardy isn't covering this?"

"I've got the assignment, so you're stuck with me."

She had a spark, but the press was still a pain. "Hardy has whatever we've released so far, Ms. Morgan. I'm not at liberty to discuss anything off the record."

"I understand, but now that I've got you in the flesh—so to speak—I'd just like a minute or two of your time. I'd really appreciate it."

Knowles was not used to polite reporters. "Okay, if you can find me. I'll be heading out fast."

"I'll find you. See you in a while, Mrs. Paige."

Knowles felt a pang of pity for the mother. He could not imagine the pain of losing a child. If something happened to Marcus—well, he always stopped that thought right there. You bring a tiny being into the world, and before you know it they're human creatures who feel and think and know. Even at four months Marcus had been a person, aware of his surroundings, letting you know what he liked and damn well didn't like. You looked into your child's eyes and saw the human race, a mystical experience he did not describe to Midge, because the right words would not come. "Who are you, and where did you come from?" were the unspoken questions on his lips around Marcus.

His work demanded that he ask grieving parents about their children, poking and probing for any shred of a clue. Who would want to hurt their child, and why? Hard questions that piled on the pain, but someone had to do it. He straightened his tie, cleared his throat, and summoned his strength. Then he bent over the woman in the wheelchair. "If you don't mind?" He indicated the empty chair the reporter had left.

"Of course, Detective. Have a seat. It's a little noisy, but we can shout if we need to."

Maybe he should not have expected revealing talk about the daughter she had lost so recently. A grown daughter with a life this mother might know little about. He got the basics—age, schooling, job, work schedule—but most of the mother's answers were slow and brief. He did not have a full picture, but he did not come away empty-handed.

Mrs. Paige's eyes narrowed when he asked about her daughter's recent behavior. "I'm sure Daphne had reasons for everything she did." She firmly shut her mouth, and he made a mental note to follow up.

As he approached the curb where he had parked his Dodge Charger, the reporter called to him from the driveway. "Hey there, Detective."

"Hello, Ms. Morgan."

"Please call me Piper." She approached him, a slim woman in a maroon parka whose hair shone in the sunlight. He had to admit he liked the silvery streak, but he would not address her informally. "I wanted to ask if you could confirm something I heard this morning. Is it true Daphne Paige was stabbed in the eye?"

"Who told you that?" Knowles regretted the sharp tone. The cold wind was making him short-tempered.

"Just an anonymous tip." She pulled up the hood of her jacket.

Knowles cursed to himself and exhaled a puff of steamy breath.

"Is it true, Detective Knowles?"

"It's freezing out here, Ms. Morgan. Come sit in my car a minute."

She looked surprised but got in the passenger side when he opened the door. "You're asking where the victim was stabbed," he said, settling behind the wheel.

"Yes." She had a notepad in her hand and a pen poised to write. "Can you confirm that it was in the eye?"

"You're new on this beat, aren't you, Ms. Morgan?"

"I'm Piper, remember. Well, yes, it's a new beat for me, but—"

"You might not be aware that the police don't release information like that. I don't know where you heard the rumor you're inquiring about, but I have nothing to say. This little chat is not my usual style—far from it—but meeting you under these circumstances, well—you might say it's softened me a bit. Not enough, though, to harm our case."

Her pen hovered in the air. "But the public has a right to know, Detective. Where she was stabbed matters."

He should not have invited her into the car. There was a comfort to her presence that bothered him, made him want to put their heads together to get her view, but also to find out what she knew. It was a professional urge after all, he thought, relieved.

"I think what matters most to the public is a murderer behind bars," he said. "Don't you agree?"

She was scribbling in her notepad, unaware of his brief inner turmoil. "Then your answer is no comment."

"Correct."

She was silent a moment before opening the passenger door.

"Thanks for your time, Detective."

"Have a nice day, Ms. Morgan. Stay in touch."

An envelope from Maestro Todd Barlow was waiting when he returned to the station. Inside were a note and some paper flakes. *I received a threatening letter stinking of perfume. I tore it up, and here are the pieces.* Knowles sprinkled the pieces on a clean sheet of paper and sent them off to forensics for analysis.

25

KNOWLES MULLED what he knew about Mrs. Jennings-Barlow. Professor. Childless. Wife of choral conductor. Her university headshot showed a tense, strong-featured face with dark hair pulled behind her ears. No hint of a smile. Man-hater? Maybe. Murderer? You never could tell.

He had the desk send her to the interrogation room.

"Am I a suspect?" Jennings-Barlow asked when Knowles walked in. She indicated the guy seated next to her. "This is Mr. Damon Fielding, my lawyer."

The two shook hands, then Knowles did a double take. The conductor's wife was smaller and older, but there was a definite resemblance to a photo in his file.

"You had me for a moment, ma'am. I'm sure people have mentioned your strong resemblance to Daphne Paige."

"Yes."

"Not to alarm you, but you might want to be extra careful for the time being. Until we catch the killer."

"You mean the murderer made a mistake and is coming back for me?" Spoken with sarcasm and a look of amusement.

"Just a precaution, ma'am. Some people would hire a bodyguard."

A flicker of a smile crossed her face. "Thanks for your concern, Detective. Please get on with the reason you brought me here."

Knowles liked this part of his job—matching wits with sharp people like this woman, by all accounts a powerhouse. He readied the recorder for the usual procedure. "We need some information from you. Please state your full name, address, and phone number."

"First answer my question, Detective. Am I a suspect?"

Knowles sized her up. Bold, not easily intimidated. Aware that as the wife of a man whose girlfriend was murdered, she would be an obvious suspect. But he could start out nice and slow. If she had a solid alibi, he would not have to ruin her day.

"No, not yet. I just want to ask you a few questions. So please state...."

"I know what you need." She gave her name and address in a low, husky voice. Surprisingly low, since if he remembered correctly, she sang as a soprano in the chorus.

"Ms. Jennings-Barlow, how well did you know Ms. Paige?"

"Not well."

"But you sang together in New York Luminoso—a terrific chorus, by the way—isn't that true?"

"Yes. It's true that it's a terrific chorus."

"And you sang together with Ms. Paige in the soprano section," he repeated. "Right?"

"Yes."

"The chorus conducted by your husband, Todd Barlow."

"Correct." She colored slightly at the name.

"Why do you think you're here, Ms. Jennings-Barlow?"

She glanced at her lawyer. "I am here as Todd Barlow's wife."

"Do you love your husband?" It was a sudden question, meant to shake her up.

The lawyer leaned toward her. "Don't answer that."

"No comment." The voice precise, the face a mask.

"Were you onstage the night Ms. Paige was killed?" Knowles aimed for the whipping sensation of a non sequitur.

"Yes. I sang with the chorus."

"Did you leave at intermission?"

"Yes, briefly."

"What time did you return?"

"It was nine-ten. I remember telling one of the other sopranos we had twenty minutes to kill."

He studied her face. Was she toying with him? No, her expression was somber.

"Excuse the pun, Detective, I obviously didn't mean it literally." Her hyper-alert attitude softened.

"Which soprano did you say that to?"

"I don't know her name."

"Isn't that unusual—in your position, not to know everyone in the section?"

"Not really. I don't socialize at chorus. I avoid the politics that way."

Knowles let the remark settle. "Tell me about the politics."

"It's a tedious subject."

"I'll judge that."

She gave an annoyed sigh. "Very well. My husband gives a few chorus members singing lessons. It's a helpful way for him to contribute to our income. Some of his students believe he will groom them to be soloists, but they are deluded."

"How so?" Knowles said.

"Soloists don't rise from the ranks of an amateur—excuse me, volunteer—chorus. They are groomed at conservatories and universities. They rise through the fire of recitals, music panels, and competitions."

"You mean someone with a beautiful voice cannot decide later in life to become a solo singer?"

"They can decide whatever they want. What they can achieve is a different matter."

He wondered how her acidic comments went over in the chorus. And in the classroom. "Are you saying your husband, a noted choral expert, is paid to help 'deluded' singers achieve their impossible goals?" He watched her face. "A singer like Daphne Paige, for example?"

She held her head high. "That's a trick question which I prefer not to answer."

Knowles leaned in closer. "I've heard that with your husband's lessons, Ms. Paige was close to becoming a soloist with the chorus."

"Frankly, I doubt it. But if it's true, whoopee for her." She examined a fingernail.

Fielding spoke up. "All this is irrelevant, Mr. Knowles. Get to the point."

Knowles glanced at the lawyer and turned back to the lady. "Regarding this soprano you spoke to during intermission, it would be helpful for you to find out her name. Someone will need to testify to your being onstage from nine-ten until the music resumed."

"Fine."

"Where did you go for those ten minutes offstage?"

"To the bathroom in the Dungeon. As you well know, it's located two floors below the stage. Down a staircase in disrepair that should have been replaced years ago."

"Perhaps someone saw you in the bathroom."

"Yes, Diva Daley. We walked back to the stage together."

"And you stayed onstage after that?"

"Yes."

Knowles made notes. "Ms. Barlow, I will not ask about your view of your husband's private life at this time. However, in my conversation with him something came up that has led to this interview."

"I see."

Still cool. Impressive self-control. "Due to his offstage behavior, did you wish to harm Ms. Paige?"

"No. I didn't wish anything about her."

"It would be natural if you did. And you do sound angry."

"Fuck you, Detective. I answered the question."

Fielding put a hand on her arm, while Knowles kept his face impassive. So far, she had cursed a lot less than the usual customers. With a personality like razor blades, she didn't need to curse.

"Why weren't you in the concert hall after the concert?" Knowles spoke with studied cool.

Her face stayed neutral, but she was breathing hard. "It was a long day. My husband wasn't himself and I felt depressed. The harpsichordist left quickly and I asked her for a ride."

That made sense. The harpsichordist would not have to pack up an instrument.

"When did you learn of Ms. Paige's death?"

"There was a commotion before I left. Then, while I was waiting for the harpsichordist to get her car, I heard people shouting about someone dying backstage. No one knew who at first. Later I heard it was the Paige woman."

"I'm surprised you didn't go back into the hall to find out what happened."

"Frankly, I wanted nothing to do with the chaos. I told you I was depressed, and I had a splitting headache, too."

If Diva Daley and the unknown soprano could vouch for Nicole Jennings-Barlow's presence onstage at the time of the murder, and the harpsichordist could confirm leaving the hall with her directly after the concert, the maestro's wife would be off the hook. Knowles would let her go, pending further inquiry into those questions. Maybe one day he would hear her take on her husband's affair. Something to look forward to.

He stroked his chin, reflecting on the absurdity of a chorus singer killing at intermission, then returning to the stage to finish the concert. Stranger things had happened, which was why Knowles loved his job.

Midge had planned a family trip to Birmingham over Christmas "to give Marcus quality time with his grandparents." Her unspoken meaning: At least her parents would spend time with the boy. Knowles loved Marcus intensely, but a man had to do his job. As for Birmingham, the timing was bad. He would not leave with a murder to investigate and a killer on the loose. He still lacked a complete portrait of young Daphne, though she appeared to be a sterling woman with not one bad word said about her. The hospital where she tended pediatric AIDS patients called her a gem. The neighbors described her as sweet and devoted to her disabled mother. Chorus members recalled her as lively and attractive, though distracted at times. "She always had a lot on her mind," said the talkative one, Diva Daley, who would not or could not specify.

Knowles might never know the burdens Daphne Paige carried, and that was hard to accept. It was what he disliked most about investigating homicide cases—the loss of fertile clues as a victim's lifeblood ebbed away.

There was one slightly open window. Piper Morgan, with her empathy skills, could get something from the mother. But it was unlikely she would share it with him. He would have to read about it in *NYN*.

26

Piper reached past the pillow for her buzzing phone. "Yeah?" She was half asleep.

"Get-together at Diva's at eleven today. Everyone's bringing food."

"Who is this calling so early on a Saturday?"

The woman identified herself as a soprano. "Diva thought we should talk about Daphne. Celebrate her life, vent about her death. Spouses and sig others welcome."

Piper calculated the day's obligations—drop in on Mrs. Paige, and then this weird party. "Okay, I'll be a little late." She repeated the time and address for Theo's sake.

"You go," he said from under the blanket. "I'm off to the gym today."

"Enjoy." She dragged herself out of bed. "Looks like a workday for me."

Mrs. Paige answered the door without her wheelchair. "It's good of you to come, but the place is a mess."

"That's okay. I'll help you clean up, and we can talk some more about Daphne, if you're up to it."

"You are too nice for a reporter. Come on in."

Mrs. Paige moved into the living room by pressing her hands against the narrow walls of the hallway.

"Why do you say I'm too nice?"

"The other one came too early today, and I wouldn't let him in." Mrs. Paige settled herself on the couch, pushing her wheelchair aside.

"What other one? Do you remember the name?"

Mrs. Paige squeezed her eyebrows together. "Something about a wagon. A wheeler."

"Mr. Wheeler also works for *NYN*. I apologize if he was

inconsiderate." He had been inappropriate, too. Why was Hardy nosing around her story?

"But you're not inconsiderate." Mrs. Paige's face lit up. "You're a doll."

Piper took in the sofa cushions in disarray, the half-eaten food on plastic plates, and the crumpled napkins on the floor. "Let me help with this clutter. I'll get a garbage bag."

"No, no, visitors shouldn't work." Mrs. Paige motioned for her to sit. "Let's talk. It's easier when I'm busy chatting, you know? Then I don't have to think too much."

Piper moved a magazine aside and sat on the sofa, much as she had done when visiting her mom. "Are you doing all right, Mrs. Paige? I mean, it can't be easy." She fumbled for words.

"You mean without my daughter? I'm still finding it all hard to believe, you know, that Daphne isn't just out somewhere about to return. Death is so final, but it's only a word at first."

"Shouldn't someone be with you? I mean, to substitute for Daphne?" She bit her lip, realizing her mistake.

"No one can substitute for Daphne."

"No, of course not, I shouldn't have said that. I just thought...."

"Many moments of 'never again' lie ahead of me. I don't know how I'll get through them. But right now—it's like I told you. Like she's out for the night. Or away at her...." Mrs. Paige became quiet.

"Yes? Away where?" Piper reached in her bag for her notepad.

"That man, Lucas Knowles, he found out Daphne was divorced. I never talk about that. It's amazing what those detectives can find out."

"How long was she divorced?"

"Why are you asking, dear?" The woman frowned.

"Mrs. Paige, you know I want to report on the progress being made in solving Daphne's case." Piper spoke carefully. "It's a very shocking one, and I want to do sensitive writing about it. Her friends—where she went, who she went with—those things could be crucial in finding out who killed her."

Mrs. Paige eyed her. "I'll think about telling you."

"Good." Piper waited quietly.

Mrs. Paige ducked her head. "Actually, I think I'd prefer to keep that information private. Daphne was a private person."

"I understand," Piper said, scribbling *Ask again later*. "But tell me, did Daphne live with you after the divorce?"

"Most of the time. But what can I get you to drink, Miss Morgan? Some mint tea, perhaps? Daphne always made me a cup before lunch."

"Please call me Piper. Actually, I'm more of a coffee fiend, but may I make a cup of tea for you?"

Mrs. Paige smiled. "I'll say it again—you are very sweet for a reporter. The teabags are in the cupboard over the toaster. The kettle is on the stove. And you can call me Dodi."

"Great, I will," Piper called out from the kitchen. No microwave here; she'd have to heat the water in the kettle. This slowed the rhythm of her interview, but she picked up the beat as she brought the steaming teacup into the living room.

"Dodi, did Daphne have any enemies that you know of?" Piper carefully placed the cup and saucer on a side table, where Mrs. Paige could easily pick them up.

"Enemies? Why, no, dear." Mrs. Paige looked offended as she sipped the tea. "People loved my daughter."

"I'm sure they did," Piper said, sitting down on the couch. "I was impressed with her myself. What kind of hobbies did she have?"

"Well, the usual—cooking, movies...."

"Anything you'd consider unusual?"

Mrs. Paige put down her teacup. "My goodness, Piper, why are you asking me so many questions?"

"I need to get to know Daphne in order to write about her, Dodi. Remember, someone might read my articles and have a clue for the police." *Or for me,* Piper thought.

Mrs. Paige began to fidget. "Well, I wouldn't call it a hobby exactly, but I can tell you that Daphne liked having men around." She looked nervously at Piper. "She really loved men. I always wondered if it was because she lost her father so young. Right on the brink of womanhood, you know?"

"I see. Did she have boyfriends at a young age?"

"Not exactly." Mrs. Paige looked unsure. "Well, maybe I should tell you. Especially if it will help find the murderer." She stumbled over the word, pronouncing it "mudder."

"I'm listening."

Mrs. Paige twisted her hands in her lap. "I'm going to say it fast, before I change my mind. I told you Daphne loved men. The truth is she liked to have more than one man around at a time. The more the merrier, I'd say."

"You mean a couple of different boyfriends?" Piper tried to get the picture.

"No, I mean three or four men at once. In the same room, know what I mean?"

"Oh, I see." Sounded like Daphne was into group sex. But how did her mother know?

"She liked women, too." Mrs. Paige averted her eyes. "It really didn't matter what sex they were. She would bring them here, and sometimes"—her voice dropped to a whisper—"sometimes they looked quite young. It didn't seem right."

Piper blinked a few times. "Did you speak to Daphne about that? You would have a right to object to something illegal happening in your home."

Mrs. Paige sat up straighter. "Naturally I did! She swore everyone was of legal age. I tried to live with it. Daphne was an ideal daughter in every other way."

"She took good care of you, from what I've heard."

"Yes, she did." Mrs. Paige nodded emphatically, her teacup swaying. "And what I described to you didn't happen every night. Mostly on weekends." She dabbed at the spilled drops on her lap. "At first."

"And then more often?"

"Oh, yes. And it was so blatant!" Mrs. Paige was red-faced and bristling. "Daphne didn't care what I saw. She'd walk right past me and up to her room with those people at her heels. Didn't introduce me, even though I was sitting right here in my chair. Like I was invisible."

This was not the sweet young woman Piper had met. "I don't want to upset you further, but I've got to ask. Dodi, did Daphne— did she make money that way?"

"Heavens, no! She wasn't a prostitute. I wouldn't be surprised if she paid them! Every size, age, and color. I don't know where she got them."

"Then you didn't know any of these people?"

"Now, I didn't say that, did I? And the noises!" Mrs. Paige went on, the words pouring out. "My God, it was like a barnyard here some nights. The groans and moans. My daughter's voice, the way she cried out, like she was hurt, like she was dying...." She put her face in her hands. "You can't imagine. And then she would send them home and come down to make me tea. Just like that. And not say a word about it. Like she was throwing it all right in my face. I should have thrown her out." She set the teacup down hard on the side table.

Piper's wrist hurt from writing so fast. She wrote without looking at the notepad, keeping eye contact with Dodi. She had brought her recorder but hadn't activated it in time.

Daphne—a caring person with a fierce need for independence. Made concessions to no one, especially her mother, defying convention with her lifestyle. Or something like that. Trying to stay positive here.

"One night she brought home a large group, like a club," Mrs. Paige said, and Piper stopped writing to listen. "A lot of men and one woman headed upstairs to Daphne's room. Well, I put my foot down. 'You will not have an orgy in this house!'"

"And did they leave?"

"Daphne led them out." Mrs. Paige pinched the skin between her eyebrows. "All she said was 'I'm an adult and can do what I want. If you don't like it, I'll live elsewhere.' And she didn't come home for three days."

"That must have been awful for you." Piper felt a pang for the woman. "Could you talk with anyone about it?"

"Well, I see a psychologist about"—she indicated her body—"my condition, and I told him what Daphne was doing. He said, 'Your daughter has a 'sex-u-al ad-dic-tion.'" Mrs. Paige pronounced the term syllable by syllable, her face screwed up. "He said it was a sickness and I should get her help. Which I did."

Poor Dodi. She had to deal not only with her daughter's death but with these awful memories, too. And poor Daphne, to be so obsessed. "Dodi, will you allow me to write a short news article saying you described this problem of Daphne's? I promise to be respectful."

Mrs. Paige looked hesitant.

"Remember, people may come forward with information about the killer."

"All right." The woman sighed. "I'm so relieved you aren't judging my daughter harshly, the way that other reporter did."

Piper tensed. "You mean Wheeler?"

"He's the one. He was here late last night, too."

"Really?" Why had Wheeler butted in after Moss assigned her to cover the story?

Mrs. Paige noticed her surprised expression. "Yes, he came after you and that detective and everyone else left."

"What did you tell him?"

"Just that Daphne had a sexual problem. I didn't go into detail. He asked to see her bedroom, but I didn't trust him. I said no. He wasn't interested after that. He left pretty fast."

Piper would have to leave fast, too, to file a story before Wheeler did. "Well, Dodi, I have to be going now." She stood.

"Wait a second, please, dear?" Mrs. Paige looked away, her cheeks pink. "It's not easy to tell you these things. For a while I felt like murdering Daphne myself, though I'm ashamed as a mother to say that, knowing she was sick. But to have such a daughter—well, they call it other things now, but in my day she was a slut."

Piper winced at the word. Life must have been hell for both women in this house.

"But I was young once, too." Mrs. Paige hoisted herself up so they were face-to-face." I liked men just fine before I got sick, and I still do. When I understood Daphne needed help, everything changed."

"In what way?" Piper hoped mother and daughter had reconciled before Daphne died.

"At first, she told me to mind my own business. But my

psychologist arranged things, and she went to her first appointment about a week ago. It seemed like a weight came off her shoulders." Mrs. Paige sounded wistful as she led Piper to the front door, using her hands-on-walls technique. "She apologized to me for her behavior, and of course I forgave her."

"That's good." Piper paused at the door. "By the way, did Daphne bring home anyone from the chorus?" She was wondering about Todd Barlow.

Dodi thought a minute. "The chorus? Oh, she loved that group. Maybe there were some folks here and there; it's hard to be sure," She rolled her eyes. "They weren't here to sing, you know."

"True." Piper stifled a smile. "Now, think hard, Dodi. Did anyone Daphne knew ever get really mad at her? Mad enough to kill her?"

Mrs. Paige frowned. "There was a Clayton. I don't think he came to the house, but he called once looking for Daphne. He sounded like a gangster, if you ask me. I remember him because his name was unusual. Also some woman with a husky voice—Cora, or Corina. She said Daphne had better call her back, or else. Daphne just laughed it off when I gave her the message. She was never afraid of anyone."

Corina sounded like Corinne Kelsey of New York Luminoso. But Clayton—Piper did not know anyone by that name. "Dodi, you've been standing for too long. I'll be going now, but call me with anything else you remember. My number is on the card I gave you yesterday."

Mrs. Paige smiled. "I will. It's comforting to speak to you, dear. I'm sure you'll write a fine article."

Piper posted a news brief about Daphne's addiction from her car. It gave the story a sordid twist, but delicacy had no place where murder was concerned—or where selling newspapers was concerned, Moss might say. She fought with her conscience, but in the end it was Dodi who led her to reveal the news.

Sadly, Daphne had no say in the matter.

27

PIPER WALKED up Diva's front path with a bag of warm bagels and a backpack full of reporting tools— notepad, pens, cell phone, digital camera, digital tablet, charging cable, and a backup digital recorder with extra batteries. All to capture the vibe and "bring it back alive" to Moss.

She was deep into the murder story now, feeling her way in a mystery where someone, or several someones, had a lot to hide. A clue to the killer's identity might slip out at the party. The killer himself or herself might be there, a familiar face no one suspected until she, Piper, discovered the truth. That would make some story.

It struck her the day was ripe for the Third Event, a third chorus crime to increase the mystery's cachet. For instance, a killing at the party, or multiple killings if the guilty person hated the chorus enough. The thought was alarming, but a reporter went forward no matter what. She clutched the bagel bag tighter.

Diva lived in a yellow Cape Cod house trimmed in green paint. It was like something out of *The Wizard of Oz*, where Munchkins might jump out of the bushes and greet you with a song. But no one was singing today; the scene was set for mourning, with tissue boxes placed inside and outside the door.

Piper was late, but it did not seem to matter. An alto took the bagels and ushered her into the crowded but solemn living room. Diva, in black leggings and a long white ski sweater, came to hug her, then flitted around filling bowls with nuts and chips. Her shining eyes and pink cheeks made her look pretty. "Isn't it wonderful to have everyone together?" she kept saying.

Clusters of singers stood quietly picking at the refreshments. Preston Hancock, his beard shaved off, walked aimlessly from room to room. Off to the side, Corinne Kelsey stood alone, scowling and looking over her shoulder. Piper sensed a current of fear in the group. Her eyes teared as she thought of Daphne's violent end.

"Smoke in your eyes?"

It was a deep, husky voice, and Piper turned to see Griffin Sharp in a sky-blue shirt that showed off his hunky physique. His handsome face was drawn, as if Daphne's death had hit him hard.

"Hi, Griffin." She was glad to see him, remembering how they had sung *Messiah* together.

"Hey, Piper. Can we talk?"

"Sure, where?"

"Grab some food and meet me in that corner." He pointed to an alcove where potted plants soaked up the sunlight. Piper made her way to a refreshment table nearly the length of the small dining room. Todd and Nicole Barlow stood at opposite sides of the table with their backs to each other, and Piper sensed she had it right. Todd and Daphne had been lovers, and this "party" was agonizing for Nicole.

Her face was pale, but Todd's devastation showed in his hunched shoulders, disheveled hair, and shadowed eyes. Had he been swept up in Daphne's addiction? If so, both he and Nicole would have a motive to kill her—Todd out of fear and Nicole out of anger and a desire for revenge. Piper hoped they each had an airtight alibi for their whereabouts during that endless *Messiah* intermission.

Nicole sidled over. "Writing about Lisha Lovington soon, Piper? Maybe today? Maybe yesterday?"

"It's on my list for this week," Piper said with a smile. "Catch you later."

Normally, she would be annoyed if anyone but Moss hounded her about a story, but this was not a normal day. She put salad on a plate and headed toward Griffin's corner. People stared at her backpack as she passed, as though it might explode any minute. Should she stash it in a closet? But then her tools would be out of reach. Besides, everyone here knew she was a reporter.

She reminded herself of her own "first rule" of journalism: A reporter was by definition an outsider, and if you couldn't take it, you should quit the field. Otherwise, keep your head up and your eye on the goal—getting great material for your story.

Griffin was sitting alone, watching the crowd. "Someone here either did it or saw whoever did it." He seemed to be speaking to himself as Piper approached.

"Who do *you* think did it?" She pulled up a chair and waited.

"Someone wanted her gone, and now she is." His tone was caustic. "But you'd never guess it from the eulogies coming up. They'll be dripping with hypocrisy."

"Can I quote you?" Piper grabbed her notebook from her bag, noticing that Griffin had used pronouns instead of Daphne's name.

"I insist you do."

It calmed her to take notes while a killer might be in the room. She narrowed her eyes and scanned the crowd for a murderer type. But there were only the chorus people, looking like their usual selves. "It's a big turnout, Griffin. We should all stay alert."

He gave her a long look. "You don't strike me as someone who scares easily, Piper."

"I don't. My imagination scares me more than anything."

His lips curled into a half smile. "A lot of folks are absent, by the way, whatever that means."

Piper noted two of the missing: Hunter Bell and Zandy Stewart. Other singers were also absent, but Piper knew them only by their faces.

"I won't name names," Griffin said. "But if I were investigating this crime, I'd look at the women who wanted to be soloists. I'd look at the men who wanted to make it with Daphne and the ones who did make it with Daphne, and then I'd look at the men and women who loved all of the above."

"Phew. Quite a list."

"Add ambition, lust, pride, and jealousy, and you've got a seething stew of possibilities."

Piper jotted it down. *A seething stew of possibilities.* Griffin was poetic and hot, but he was not flirting with her. He was using her for something, but what? Neither of them had mentioned the Barlows, the twin elephants in the room. She figured he had a theory about them and the deceased interloper who had likely ruined their marriage.

That same interloper—Daphne—might have ruined something for Griffin, too. Did he kill her out of jealousy? Her mind raced. Griffin had returned late after intermission, out of breath. Earlier, he acted nervous and jumpy, blaming it on claustrophobia. Piper felt a shiver. Could he have killed Daphne after Part One and then sung Part Two? That would make him a cold-blooded murderer. If his motive was jealousy, Todd Barlow had better look out.

"I'm guessing you were one of the men who 'made it' with Daphne; am I right?"

"That's blunt. Why do you ask?"

"Just a feeling."

He gave her a quizzical look. "You do know I'm gay, don't you, Piper? My husband, Clayton, couldn't make it today."

Clayton! Dodi Paige said someone angry named Clayton had phoned Daphne.

"I didn't know. Now I know not to trust all my vibes." She tapped her forehead in a "stupid me" gesture.

Griffin smiled, a real smile that reached his eyes. "The truth is I was bi before my marriage—I still am, but I'm into monogamy now. Anyway, I knew Daphne before she married Preston. I knew her well during their short so-called marriage and after their not-so-surprising divorce. We became close friends after the sex stopped."

Piper let it all register, including the "sex" kicker. Daphne and Griffin made sense, but Daphne and Preston Hancock were an odd couple. Did Daphne's sex addiction start during their marriage, and if so, how did the gentle Preston handle it? It would be a nightmare for a new husband, but would he kill for it years later?

"You're wondering if Preston killed her. The chances are one in a hundred thousand."

"Why are you so sure, Griff, if I may call you that? He might have been deeply hurt."

"No, they were the wrong match, and he was grateful to get out when he did. I happen to know because he confided in me. He wasn't even upset enough to quit the chorus after their breakup."

"He looks ten years younger with his beard shaved off." Piper turned to Griff. "Maybe he's deeply grieving. In some cultures, people cut off their hair to mourn."

"And in others they let their beards grow. Whatever, Preston is not the killer, so don't waste your time thinking about him."

Piper wrote the name *Preston*, then put an *X* and a question mark through it—the question being Griff's reliability. "I guess you've known Daphne better than almost anyone, being lovers for so long."

"Lovers, such a quaint term." Griff studied his hands. "Lovers as in two wild animals going at it."

Piper bent over her notepad to hide her reaction. Griff was sly and seductive, and he knew the power of words.

"It's been over for a long time." He glanced sideways at her, as if aware she was aroused.

"I'd like to meet your husband sometime," she said when her heartbeat slowed. "Where is he today?"

"Clayton keeps away from groups; he's a loner."

"But he's got you."

"He says I make him feel alone, so it works." Griff laughed. "Clayton didn't know Daphne, and he didn't kill her. He was upstate at a family event that night, so don't waste your time on him, either."

His smile faded, and Piper wondered if he was deliberately implicating himself by eliminating others. She put an X through Clayton's name, too, but a name could be rewritten.

"I'll bet Detective Knowles will get around to questioning you further, Griff. I'm sure he'll find your insights valuable about the sexual dynamics of the chorus."

Griff looked unsure if she was teasing. "The topic interests me. Sex underlies everything."

"I'll keep that in mind." She stood up. "I'm off to mingle and do some eavesdropping."

"Hold on." He grabbed her hand and pulled her close. "You're a clever reporter, so I'll tell you something in confidence," he whispered. "Daphne was a certified sex addict. You won't hear that in the speeches today."

"Really?" Piper pretended surprise. "Thanks for the tip."

It seemed Griff wanted her to suspect him and was disappointed with their discussion. Distracted by the idea, she nearly collided with Corinne Kelsey, coming toward her from the dining room. "Corinne, can we speak a minute?" Piper wanted her take on Daphne's singing voice. But Corinne walked on. "Maybe later, maybe never," she said over her shoulder. What an odd person she was.

Vicki arrived with a casserole dish as if she were a bona fide chorus member. Griff, near the door, greeted her with a kiss on the mouth. The casserole tilted, and Piper, passing by, reached out to level it. That brought a dirty look from Vicki, who marched into the kitchen without saying hello.

Piper set out after her. "Vicki, wait up; let's talk things through."

"No thanks." Vicki kept her back to Piper as she unwrapped the casserole—some kind of lasagna.

"Look, I know you like Griffin." Piper had guessed the man in Vicki's heart even before the kiss. "I was interviewing him, nothing more." She wished Vicki would get over her crush and the married Griffin would stop encouraging it.

Vicki whirled around. "Haven't you figured out by now that I represent Griffin's vocal group as well as the chorus? It's a professional relationship. You think all I care about is a man. How dense you are."

Piper took a step back. "Then you must still be angry about that news story I wrote."

Vicki shrugged. "Forget it. The world keeps spinning. Let's party."

She walked off as Nicole entered the kitchen. "Having fun, Piper? Ah, there's the coffee—want a cup?"

"No to the first question, yes to the second. Is it supposed to be fun?"

"Only if your idea of fun is the macabre." Nicole poured two mugs and handed one to Piper as they returned to the crowded living room.

"Why macabre?" Piper paid close attention.

"Someone killed the charming Ms. Paige, but no one is mentioning how grisly and shocking it all is. Everyone is acting suspicious of everyone else but pretending to be friendly."

Was Nicole pretending? She was as cool as ever, with no sign of a guilty conscience. On the other hand, she resembled

Daphne more than ever today, even with her long hair hanging straight.

It was best to be candid. "Nicole, are you being careful? I'm sure you're aware of your resemblance to Daphne."

Nicole frowned. "Why does everyone keep saying that? I'm always careful."

"I'm asking because the killer might be here today." Piper stifled the next logical remark—the killer might be looking for her.

"What a bore, of course the killer's here," Nicole hissed. "What am I supposed to do about it?"

Piper opened her notepad to a clean page. "Who do you think it is?" She lowered her voice.

Nicole glared at the notepad. "Damn it, Piper Morgan, can't you have a normal conversation without taking notes? Come off it."

Piper lowered the notepad. "Sorry."

"Look, I...I like you." Nicole stumbled on the words. "I thought you could be someone to talk to. I don't make many friends—not being the girlie type. Neither are you, but you're all work twenty-four seven. It's a shame."

Piper hid her surprise. "I'd love to be your friend, Nicole. Can you wait until after I finish writing about the chorus—and the crime?"

"That's cool, if I'm still around. You probably consider me a suspect, but I didn't do it."

"That's good."

Nicole's face relaxed. "So how does it feel to cover a murder?"

"I'm new at it, but in my reporter mode I feel detached and protected from harm. Of course, that's just an illusion." Piper gave a light laugh. It felt good to clear the air.

A couple rose from the couch, and she and Nicole sat down. Piper noticed beads of sweat gathering in the V-neck of Nicole's black designer sweater. Her hands trembled, too. Nicole was afraid, though she pretended otherwise.

"I hope I haven't made you more nervous, Nicole."

"No, I feel better around you. In fact, Piper Morgan, I'm putting you in charge of my fate. If I get murdered, don't throw a party for me. Hold a reading. Make it a murder mystery. Then offer a reward to find my killer. Are you with me?"

Piper nodded, not sure if she was serious.

"Nobody brings food; they contribute to the reward," Nicole went on. "Do you accept the assignment?"

Piper played along. "Absolutely, I'll take care of everything." She lowered her voice.

"Nicole, this is off the record, but at the café you implied Todd and Daphne were having an affair. At least that's what I picked up." Piper drew in a breath, emboldened by her own audacity. "If it's true, I can't imagine what it must be like for you to be in this house today. I'm amazed you had the strength to come."

Nicole's eyes watered. "Thanks, Piper, I really appreciate your saying that. I'll be heading out soon, before the phony eulogies start."

"Looks like Todd is going with you."

Across the room, Todd was in his parka, trying to break through Diva's wall of chatter. "I wish that cute not-to-mention-single Hunter Bell had come today," Diva said loud enough for all to hear. "He was nice enough to call and say he couldn't make it, but I wish he were here all the same." She threw up her hands. "I guess we'll just have to wait till Monday for some words from him."

"He lives in the city, Diva, so it's hard for him to get here," Todd said.

"Trains are running, right? And buses, taxis—I would have thought...." Diva's voice trailed off.

"Patience; you'll see him Monday. Thanks for the party. I wish I could stay, but I've got some kind of stomach bug."

Diva jumped backward. "Yikes, go home and rest, Maestro. I don't want people getting sick here. Go, go, go!" She made pushing motions with her hands.

"Clever excuse," Nicole whispered to Piper. "I'm going; let's talk soon."

Nicole's warmth made up for Vicki's coldness. Piper said goodbye and looked around for Vicki. She would patch things up without restarting the friendship, because her mother always said not to burn bridges.

She found her old friend in the dining room. "Look, I'm sorry for hurting your feelings. I should have tried harder to consult you on the story about Daphne's death. Please forgive me."

"Sure, whatever." Vicki shrugged.

"We can still meet at Captions for coffee, if you want."

"Yeah, why not?" She gave Piper a cold smile, excused herself, and walked off.

Diva called out, "Time to gather around the fireplace, everyone. Come and let's honor Daphne with our memories." She trilled this message several times, her voice bordering on hysteria. Piper took out her notepad and headed toward the wood fire, hoping for a bonanza of quotes. Corinne stopped her on the way, enveloping her in a sickly floral scent.

"To be clear, Ms. Morgan, I don't talk to reporters. It's a long-standing allergy, so please don't ask again. Adieu."

Diva scurried over and piled on the rebukes. "Would you mind terribly standing at the back, Piper? So we won't feel self-conscious when you write down our words? Thanks ever so." And she scurried off again.

It was puzzling. These people seemed to fear her. Were they protecting themselves or the chorus? Couldn't they see that the chorus was already damaged and her reporting could help repair it? On the other hand, if Daphne's murder had been some kind of conspiracy, she, the dogged reporter, threatened the cover-up.

In which case she was in danger, too. But her audacity might protect her.

"Folks! Listen up," she shouted, moving to the center of the living room. "I'm new to New York Luminoso, but I feel we're all in this together." Her voice grew stronger as she went on. "You're such a talented and dedicated group of singers. It would be a shame if we let Daphne's murder ruin the chorus's reputation."

People were listening, so she continued. "I believe my reporting can help by telling people the truth, so New York Luminoso will live on and keep making wonderful music."

Zandy Stewart, who had arrived late, put a comforting hand on Piper's arm. Griffin Sharp mimed silent applause, and Riley Webb shot her a grin. There were grumbles about the media, and some people turned their backs, but Piper felt better.

Now she hugged the wall as choristers grabbed chairs or sat down cross-legged on the floor. Speeches followed about what a kind person Daphne was, how sweet, helpful, pretty, and talented. Clichés and platitudes, nothing insightful. How many of these people knew about her addiction? Which singers were her sexual partners—besides Griffin and presumably Todd? One, two, or many? They would learn the truth about Daphne this weekend, when Moss ran the addiction story. Piper figured the story would make her even more unwelcome in the chorus.

There was a scream and a thud as someone fell to the floor.

"Diva saw Daphne's ghost and fainted," a young alto cried out.

"Whoever killed Daphne, confess!" Griffin boomed in horror-movie style, coming forward to help Diva get up.

She stood shakily, leaning on him. "Too much excitement, I guess." She gave Griffin a coy smile. "I'm fine; let's go on."

Nicole turned up at Piper's side, laughing. "From the macabre to the ridiculous. Ghosts; what's next?"

"How nice that you stayed for the fun." Piper laughed, too. "And to be the ghost yourself. Diva might have seen you and freaked out."

"Yeah, it's a new role for me. We keep trying to leave this place but can't. Like that old Buñuel movie."

"Come, I'll lead the way." Piper reached for her hand.

"Thanks, but I'm waiting here for Todd. He really does have stomach troubles."

Todd scuttled toward them, holding his midsection. If he threw up on Diva's floor, it would be a fitting end to a mess of a party. But he made it outside and was gulping fresh air when Piper and Nicole joined him.

"Going to the car," he blurted, rushing off.

"Be right there," Nicole called after him, "I've got something to say to Piper."

Piper waited.

"I changed my mind—no mystery reading," she said straight-faced. "If something happens to me, make it a Shakespeare reading, and then everyone sings 'Ode to Joy.' I'm the epitome of joy in an imperceptible way."

"Yes, I'm beginning to see it," Piper said.

Worcester, Worcestershire

13 December 1898

MY DEAREST HARRIET,

A burden has been lifted since I refused Edward's proposal. Your advice was sound and reasonable, and I do thank you for it. Yet there was a wily justice in Edward's plan to address the wrongs inflicted on women like myself, who are engaged in serious music composition.

Why do you suppose a man like him has taken such an interest in my pursuits? When I posed the question, he said he had long awaited success, which he is now finding since turning forty, and sees a kindred spirit in me. The Academy are fools, he says, as they worship conformity more than invention. He confided an earful to me at a salon last week.

"You must persevere, Mrs. Lovington," he said, and so I shall.

With Leo improving, the *Requiem* is flourishing, Harriet. The manuscript lies before me, music sheets fanned out in happy disarray. I dream that someday the work will be performed in a grand hall by a full chorus and orchestra, though I may no longer be alive to hear it. Then let an army of music lovers chase the witless Mr. Upton out of town and stamp out his kind.

Your gentle sister has cranked up her fighting spirit! Be glad!

MY LOVE,

Lisha

28

Moss never called on a Sunday, but here he was, furious. "You're in big trouble, missy,"

"What happened?" Her heart pounded.

"Pissed-off emails happened, texts happened, you name it. Accusing you of bias in your 'mystery manuscripts' story. The real mystery is how you could have filed such a slanted piece."

"Moss, I...."

She had sprinkled the article with several quotes from Nicole and one from Todd, where he declared Elgar to be the *Requiem*'s author. Piper hoped astute readers would grasp her not-so-hidden message to side with Lovington, but she had succeeded too well.

"Here are some choice excerpts. 'Why would your writer side with a plagiarist? Is it just because she's a woman?' And another: 'Why quote that feminist bitch Nicole Jennings-Barlow so much?' And my favorite. 'You're a radical feminist newspaper and I'm canceling my subscription.' Want to hear more? There's plenty."

"No, that's okay. Did you get any emails liking the article?"

"Of course, an equal number if not more. But that's not the point, is it? We should not know your position on the issue. Do you have a bias in the case?"

"Um—I don't think so, Moss. The conductor's wife has some strong opinions, but I'm still figuring out what my opinion is."

"I'd prefer you not to have an opinion, Piper. At least not in print. Write the news fairly. Be a journalist and save your opinions for cocktail parties. Later, after you've piled up a few more kudos, we'll consider your personal viewpoints."

"But Moss, I did try to be...."

"Try harder. Read and revise. Be aware of your tone. Make sure your quotes are balanced." He sighed. "I should not have to tell you these things. I rely on you to do the job right."

Piper's face grew hot. Had Moss read the piece before running it? He trusted her, he always said, but shouldn't an editor prevent a writer's gaffe—if this was one? She had to defend herself.

"Moss, I see now that female artists have always been second-hand citizens in the art world. Men want them to look pretty and make the coffee and feed them dinner so they—the precious men—can work without being disturbed. But then the women...."

He cut her off. "Nice speech; here's what's wrong with it. First, you're generalizing about us male jerks. Second, things are tough all over. Take a look at the story on page one today about disease and crime in the homeless population. As if being homeless isn't bad enough."

He paused, and Piper wondered where he was calling from. It occurred to her she knew little about his personal life.

"What you're writing about is the past," Moss said. "Edward Elgar—he's already won the game. He's Sir Edward Elgar now, you know."

Piper lifted an eyebrow. "Someone has done his Google homework."

"You got me interested, so take a bow. Look, history remembers Elgar, but no one has heard of your Lovington lady."

"But don't you see, Moss? No one has heard of her because she—"

"Stop! You don't know the reason. Maybe her music was lousy. But let's move on. I'm thinking of putting that nephew's profile back on the list."

"What?" Just like Moss to present a bouquet after bombing you.

"Yeah, the readers are interested in this Bell and his deader-than-dead aunt, so let's keep them happy. But focus on him, please, not her."

"Okay, Moss, I've interviewed the guy." Piper could hardly believe her ears. "I can whip up something pretty fast."

"Fast isn't working for you, kiddo. I'd prefer good journalism."

She gulped. "Well, sure, Moss."

"So have it to me by Wednesday. And keep your opinions to yourself."

"Will do. I'm starting the minute we hang up."

Moss paused. "Good update on the sex addiction, by the way. I prefer three sources, but I'll settle for two. It'll post tonight, even though I don't approve of smearing dead people."

"What if it leads to a killer?"

"We'll see."

Piper started Bell's profile with a positive twist. Here was a scholar who came to the U.S. on what might seem like a fool's errand. He would not bask in his great-great-grand-aunt's belated glory, but he was a popular lecturer on music history. Choruses like New York Luminoso looked forward to his talks each week. He was a success in America, so maybe it was not a fool's errand, after all.

That was the gist. She would give it an hour of work and be done with it.

Todd Barlow had a different take when she called him for confirmation. "I feel embarrassed for the guy," he said. "It's humiliating to learn the relative you admire was unbalanced enough to copy a famous composer. Looks like Bell traveled all this way for nothing."

Piper fished for a more upbeat answer. "But I've noticed people really enjoy his lectures. What do you think of them, Maestro?"

Barlow paused. "He's knowledgeable about the period."

Weak, but she would work with it. Now she must throw the "fool's errand" question to Bell, to be fair. He would surely give her a strong positive end quote. A great kicker.

His answer was blah. "Life evolves. We must take what comes."

Then he called back. "Permit me to give you a different response to your question regarding my aunt. I'll speak to you tomorrow night at chorus; is that fine?"

"All right. But I will decide which quote we use."

Worcester, Worcestershire
18 December 1898

DEAREST HARRIET,

Though I made clear to Mr. Elgar that he is not to proceed with his plan, he continues to write to me. Yet he hardly speaks about music at all. He describes the simple pleasures of flying kites as he watches storm clouds gather, putting me in mind of Beethoven's thunderstorm. I sense a roiling spirit beneath Mr. Elgar's buttoned-up shirt, and a child's temperament concealed in his dignified manner. The full mustache beneath his aquiline nose hides whatever expression his lips might show, and I have grown curious to see how they look.

No, I am not falling in love, Harriet. I am happy with John, who shows me a tender concern in all aspects of our daily life. Yet here is an artist like myself who has opened his heart to me. He says I am beautiful, a shock, as I draw quite the opposite conclusion when I look in the mirror. He must be nearsighted, though I confess I am not displeased. He says I look aristocratic and judges this by my nose. Where this is going, I do not know. I wish to divert our contact back in a musical direction, as I need a knowing friend to face the horrid and exclusive music Establishment.

Have I told you that Edward—Mr. Elgar—loathes the Establishment? I suspect a sense of inferiority stemming from his own humble origins as the son of a shopkeeper. He says he has never had a composition lesson, though I don't believe it, as I have listened quite recently to one of his wind quintets of 1878.

"In this we share a handicap, my dear Lisha," he told me, knowing I, as a woman, have not been allowed into theory and composition classes. But how else might I learn to master musical complexity? Edward pooh-poohs my resentment over this affront, saying I have quite enough ability to overcome the challenge. What strength he gives me, sister! My spirits rise whenever a small white envelope appears, addressed to me in his familiar handwriting.

"We shall triumph, Mrs. Lovington," he wrote last week, as though we were partners in some surpassing struggle. And perhaps we are.

Trusting you, Tom, and the children are well.

All my love,
Lisha

P.S. You might wonder whether John is suspicious on account of this attention from a married gentleman. I must ask your discretion and indulgence in this matter, Harriet. There is no point in presenting John with any worries, as I do not feel myself slipping in any way. Rest assured I shall converse with him about Mr. Elgar when I must. In any case, John is quite taken up with responsibilities to his patients and pays scant attention to what falls through the mail slot.

29

Knowles judged Griffin Sharp to be a man of clear focus whose paranoid nature showed in his darting eyes and swiveling neck. Such men were tough as hell to engage in normal conversation, not that Knowles's interviews approached anything like normal conversation.

He settled Sharp in the interrogation room and buzzed Daniels to join them. During the usual preliminaries, Sharp's demeanor was cool and his answers candid. Possibly too candid, as though he had practiced them.

"Did you leave the stage during the *Messiah* intermission?" Knowles asked.

"Absolutely, yes, I did. Without question. I went down to the Dungeon staircase."

"To use the men's room?"

"No, sir, the men's room isn't down there. I was looking for the security guy I got to sub for me that night. To make sure he was at his post."

"Sub for you? Please explain."

Sharp was a smooth talker with no nervous tics. "I was singing, so I couldn't work. But the bum called in sick and didn't cover his ass."

A few more questions and Knowles knew the secret Sharp kept from the chorus. He worked eight-hour shifts as a security officer at Anderson Performing Arts Center. Though he'd had the night off to sing, he'd felt compelled to check the environs of the so-called Dungeon.

"And it was good I did," Sharp said, making large-knuckled fists. "Because I'll know never to call on that rotten stinker to sub again."

He was either a good liar or truly angry about a murder on his turf. Which, if he had been on duty, he insisted, "never would have happened." He cursed when Daniels told him the lower-level security camera was out for repair.

"Puts me in jeopardy on duty," Sharp said, a scowl twisting his Hollywood features. "Makes me vulnerable to crime and random accusations."

"What was your relationship to Daphne Paige?" Knowles used the abrupt manner he favored.

"She was a friend." Sharp's eyes swiveled away.

"Just a friend? Nothing more?"

"There was more a long time ago. It stopped."

"Who stopped it?"

"I did."

"Why was that?"

"Too hot to handle. Together we were fire, dangerous."

Knowles raised his eyebrows. "Dangerous for her?"

"No, for me."

So Paige was his Achilles' heel. "And after it stopped?"

"I watched out for her. She was going to crash."

"Was she open to your watching out for her?"

"No. She pushed me away. I watched from a distance."

"Man to man, tell me," Knowles used a gentler tone, "were you in love with Ms. Paige?"

Sharp looked down. "It doesn't matter. I couldn't help her."

"Did you kill her?"

Sharp snapped to attention. "Are you nuts? What the fuck?"

"You might have resented her. Wanted her to be with you or dead."

"No, I didn't kill her." Sharp looked straight at Knowles. "But I know who did."

Knowles rubbed his chin. He maintained steady eye contact with the tense man seated across from him.

"Aren't you going to ask me who?" Sharp narrowed his eyes.

Knowles did not tolerate such baited questions. "Mr. Sharp, this is not a game. If you had evidence about this murder, you were obliged to come forward immediately. Why have you waited until now?"

Sharp was unfazed. "It's complicated. Not my business to run my mouth off."

"You may provide your opinion and we may disregard it. In any case, it will not be made public."

Sharp studied his well-manicured nails. "I'd look into the conductor if I were you. That's all I'll say, and you can throw me behind bars for all I care."

Knowles was not throwing him anywhere. "Speaking of bars, Mr. Sharp, did you ever sing in a jazz bar?"

Sharp's eyes widened. "Yeah, I've got a group, Bass Blast. You've heard us?"

"Damn, yes. Ten rumbling voices—Bass Blast, good name. Unusual. I enjoy your gigs."

"Thanks. Can you keep my Anderson job confidential, please?"

Knowles shrugged. "There's not much confidential about a murder, Mr. Sharp. But we'll try."

30

BARLOW WISHED he could call in sick tonight, the first chorus practice without Daphne.

But he had to go; the singers would expect his *Messiah* "postmortem," as the wrap-up after a concert was called. Tonight the metaphor cut too close to the bone.

He would not be overly critical of them at this painful time. He would walk the thin rope of tact and praise their singing, which in fact had been quite good. You had to go gentle with folks who sang for enjoyment and not dwell on their flaws. Those twangy diphthongs and flattened vowels would improve in good time—even if he had to reach into their throats to make it happen.

Besides, who was he to criticize? His own performance had been messy in the second half—he knew it, and they knew it. He had fumbled *Messiah* badly and would humbly accept their complaints. But now they would move on to the *Requiem,* music to lift their hearts. No rowdy voting on who wrote the damn thing, either. His would be the final word, and it was an Elgar. Period. As the music director, he was the decider.

A Lovington would bring the chorus honor, but a newly discovered Elgar would bring them fame. Not to mention a paying crowd. Nicole had to trust him on this.

"Let's sing!" Barlow said after the feedback discussion. Then Diva Daley raised her hand, and Piper Morgan, seated closer to the front than usual, started taking notes. Double trouble, but he'd plow through it.

"Yes, Diva? And by the way, let's hear it for Diva and her tribute to Daphne the other day."

Someone called out, 'How ya feeling, Diva? Wooooo...." and everyone laughed.

Diva shot up from her seat, looking well recovered. "I'm just fine, and I don't believe in ghosts. Someone thought they'd play a practical joke, that's all, only it wasn't funny." She turned to Barlow. "But aren't you going to say something about Daphne, Todd? Everyone's waiting to hear you speak, since you were too sick to do it at my house."

Barlow cleared his throat. "Well, of course I—"

"We should all say a few words." Zandy Stewart broke in, ever sensible. "And by the way, I read the news this morning"—she turned to glare at Piper, seated behind her—"and all I can say is Daphne isn't here to defend herself against the slanderous charge of being a sex addict. I don't think anyone should mention it."

"But you just did," Riley Webb said.

"Forget it!" It was the bass Nixon Fox, one of the few times Barlow had heard him speak. He was a librarian with a fringe of white hair who sang well and minded his own business. "Her private life was private, and if she had a problem, that's a shame. We shouldn't go on as if nothing happened, but let's do it respectfully."

"Right!" others joined in, Preston Hancock among them.

Barlow had to nip this in the bud. "Folks, we shared a lot about Daphne on Saturday. Let's focus on our music now, as Daphne would have wanted."

"How do you know what she wanted?" a low alto voice called out. It was Corinne Kelsey, the bulldog.

"I can only imagine, Corinne. Daphne cared about this chorus, and she would want us to act like one—by singing."

"Hold on, Maestro." Nixon Fox again. "Why not give the people who couldn't make Diva's party a chance to express their thoughts? Five minutes less singing won't hurt us, and then we'll have closure."

"Fine. Anyone who has something to say, please do so." *Without mentioning sex,* he pleaded silently.

"How about a moment of silence first?" Diva said. "It's the least we can do."

Barlow's chest constricted as they gazed up at him. He bowed his head, and the chorus followed. It felt good to stare at the floor, to let the moment linger. He lifted his head and cleared his throat. "Now for a few comments; then we sing."

ANGELS' BLOOD | 149

"You start, Maestro," Riley said.

Barlow flushed. "Okay, here goes. It will be sad to carry on without such a wonderful person singing among us. Especially since we lost her through an act of senseless violence." He surveyed the room, wondering if the letter writer was here.

"She was a damn good singer, right, Todd?" Corinne prompted with an edge to her voice. "In fact, she did a lot of things well, didn't she?"

Her winking tone brought a gasp from Zandy and a stab to Barlow's gut. Behind Corinne, Piper Morgan kept scribbling, no doubt to expose more chorus secrets to the world. But not much about Daphne was secret anymore, including his love for her and hers for him.

"Todd?" Corinne was waiting.

"Yes, indeed, she was a very fine singer," Barlow said, ignoring the innuendo. He added without thinking, "What you all might not know is that I occasionally gave Daphne voice lessons, and she was this much away from becoming a soloist." He pinched his right thumb and third finger together, leaving a small space. "Her musical potential was unfulfilled, but she made an impact on the world."

"And an impact on a bed," Nicole whispered to him as she breezed in late, looking chic in a new black outfit instead of her usual rehearsal sweats. She headed to reporter Morgan's row and sat down.

Nixon rose to his feet. "I missed the so-called party, folks, out of choice, since a party seemed wrongheaded given the circumstances. But I liked Daphne, and I want to say she was a beauty, with that great posture and pretty hair. Yet she wasn't full of herself; she was modest, unlike a lot of young ladies today." He sat down, red-faced.

Buckley Walters, a rotund bass who needed two chairs, called out from his seat. "She always said hello to me."

Barlow adjusted the score on the podium. "This has been heartwarming. Now, if I may...."

"Excuse me." Zandy again, sounding troubled.

"What is it?" Barlow heard his own impatience.

"I don't think many know Daphne worked as a nurse and took care of her mother at the same time. We all saw the mom in a wheelchair at the funeral."

Nicole began to cough.

"Her mother has MS," Diva called out. "That poor girl was going for a master's in social work. Just about a perfect person—well, almost perfect. The good ones always get killed."

Cough, cough. Barlow wondered if anyone else heard it.

Griffin Sharp stood. "That's plain irrational, Diva. Good people don't always get killed. No need to make things worse than they are. But people who get killed are often good. That's a better way to say it."

"Well, thanks so much, Mr. Not-a-Professor," Diva shot back.

"Enough! Let's sing." Barlow glared at Diva. "Open your *Requiem* music books, please."

"The Lovington?" someone called out. "Or the Elgar?"

There was laughter. Bell gave Griffin a thumbs-up sign, and Griffin, an inscrutable loner, saluted him. Their chummy rapport gave Barlow a kick in the gut, and he felt the loneliness of a leader. But now he had to set a serious tone.

"We will assume Elgar wrote this special piece, folks. Eyes here, and let's get some work done tonight. Sopranos, watch my beat. Basses, unglue your eyes from your music books. Sing to me!"

During the break, an argument started at the refreshment table. "Professionals sing solos! Not everyone can do it. Not even if they studied with Maestro Barlow." It was Corinne Kelsey, thrusting out her chin at Berry Dunn, a fellow alto.

"Where do you think professionals come from?" Berry shouted back. "They study. They master the repertoire. Sometimes they rise from the ranks—like ballerinas!"

"Dream on, Berry. You'll never be a soloist without a degree from Juilliard. Or from the University of Mediocrity. Why don't you admit it?"

"You're so over-the-hill you can't even imagine ambition anymore."

"Yeah?" Corinne's face was purple. "Well, my ambition is to get as far away from you as possible. So I can hear the music

ANGELS' BLOOD | 151

instead of your atrocious singing. Your off-key growling is more like it."

"Friends, please!" Griffin Sharp stepped in to separate them, and the women retreated, like prizefighters, to opposite ends of the room. Griffin was a mysterious fellow, but he knew how to keep him, the maestro, above the fray.

"Sir, may I have a word?" It was Bell, even more unctuous than usual.

"What is it?" Barlow said as Piper Morgan's head snapped to attention. Could Bell be making it with the reporter? He would not put it past him.

"I am not totally certain about the Elgar authorship, you know?" Bell stood below the podium with his back to the chorus. "I'd hate for New York Luminoso to look uninformed, foolish, intellectually lazy—you get the drift."

"Get to the point so we can sing." Barlow could barely contain his dislike of the man.

"The point is it is imperative for me to have the manuscript checked out with another Elgar authority," Bell went on sotto voce. "The most expert one in the world is in London."

"I thought you were an Elgar expert yourself."

"I am a late-nineteenth-century-British-music expert." Bell spoke through his nose, lowering his eyes and lifting his chin. "I must take the second manuscript to London to be sure. A copy will not do."

"You're asking my permission?"

"That's right, old boy. I'll need you to give me the manuscript. Is that fine?"

The manuscript of a newly discovered Elgar could be worth millions. Bell had only to find a second expert to authenticate the score and flee to an auction house, where he would collect his ill-gotten fortune. No way would he, Barlow, hand it over.

"Not fine, old chap." Barlow watched Bell's face fall.

He had, of course, made copies of the piece months ago, using the Lovington manuscript for study purposes. He had delayed putting the Lovington original in a bank vault, spending much of the past five days in a haze, but would do it tomorrow.

Lucinda, the accompanist, sounded a chord. The break was

over, and Morgan rushed to the spot where Bell held up the wall. "Remember I'm still waiting," she whispered, loud enough for Barlow to hear.

"I don't have it yet."

"Then I'll use the first one. Unless you call me tomorrow morning."

Barlow broke into a sweat. What were they talking about? It was time to get rid of that gossipy Piper Morgan, a teenager wannabe with her wacky hair. She was useless anyway. Where was that feature she promised? The chorus needed good publicity with a murder hanging over them.

But now, ah, listen to that music. The chords cut through his anger, touching his heart. Calming, yet its chromaticism gave it an edge. Barlow recognized Wagner's influence in those aching tone shifts. His eyes teared up. The *Requiem* sounded gorgeous the way Lucinda was playing it, with a fluidity far surpassing his own choppy piano style.

Lucinda lifted her fingers from the keys, and applause filled the room. Piper Morgan clapped hard, her face glowing. Bell's hands remained at his side.

"That was just the first movement, my friends," Barlow said. "Let's hear the next."

Lucinda arched her hands slowly over the keys, and a hush fell over the chorus. Barlow closed his eyes and yielded to an almost erotic pleasure. This second movement reminded him of—he searched for the comparison; yes, that was it—Gabriel Fauré's *Requiem*, a sublime late-nineteenth-century work that shimmered with peace and hope.

Lucinda played for 45 rapturous minutes, continuing through each movement without interruption. No one coughed or talked. At the end, the entire chorus stood and applauded.

"Amazing," people said in unison. Some wiped away tears, Barlow along them.

He motioned for everyone to sit, then addressed them. "To find a new work like this in any era is a gift. To know it was hidden in a box for a century is sad. But we will have the honor of presenting it to the world. We are lucky indeed."

The singers began another round of nods and comments. Barlow had rarely seen them this enthusiastic. After they quieted, he went on. "How can we describe this work, whose effect I see on all your faces? Let me try, if I may. Overall, it has none of the fire and fury of the usual requiems—think of Verdi's thrilling version, originally written as opera." The singers' eyes were fastened on him. "This one lacks the heartbreak of Mozart's 'Lacrimosa' movement, but shares its lullaby quality with Brahms's *German Requiem*. I would place it in the tradition of Fauré, whose *Requiem* is uplifting and ethereal, without Verdi's heart-pounding fear."

"I can't wait to sing it." Diva Daley called out.

"Thank you, Diva, and I hope everyone feels that way." He had more to say, but Bell was waiting to lecture.

"Hunter is going to speak about the prejudices faced by women composers in late-nineteenth-century England. But first, let me say, as your music director, what a fine achievement this *Requiem* is, though it does not follow Elgar's usual style." He loved the way they were listening to him, with real respect on their faces. "As some of you might know, Elgar was a master of bright orchestral color, of sudden mood shifts, of muscular as well as tender melodies."

He drank in their enthralled faces. "Only a master could sustain such control as in this great piece or achieve such conceptual unity. We are privileged to premiere this gentle, soulful *Requiem* from the pen of a great composer who was later knighted by the queen. How satisfying that Elgar was not afraid to show his tender side."

Nixon Fox raised his hand again. "I've done some research," he said in his slow, scholarly way. "Elgar not only completed this *Requiem* in 1899, according to you, Maestro, but he also composed *Enigma Variations* the same year and finished another big work, *The Dream of Gerontius*, in 1900. Quite a remarkable output, wouldn't you say?"

Barlow thought about the energy of genius, how inspiration swept time aside in the act of creation. "Yes, thank you, Nixon. It's astonishing that Elgar completed these three great works in such a short time. What a gift to the world and to our chorus, as well."

Piper was scribbling in the back row, writing about the *Requiem*'s triumph, he hoped. If her articles brought an audience in May, she could sing in the chorus for as long as she liked.

Worcester, Worcestershire

22 December 1898

Dear Harriet,

Since refusing Edward, I have become more restless every day. I must try to make sense of this longing in order to snuff it out. There is gossip: Mr. Elgar strays from his devoted wife and helpmate Alice. He fancies the wavy hair and sparkling eyes of younger women, indeed much younger than I.

I would abhor to be in their camp, reduced to my physical appearance. Yet the attention he pays me, by mail, in person, is like the warmest, most fragrant June day. Who could run from such joy?

Edward speaks of my music, not my hair, my soul, or my smile. Moreover, we are near to the same age, he being less than a year older, almost a twin brother. My femaleness is like a chain keeping me from the freedom my male twin enjoys, which perhaps is what attracts me to him. He is myself reflected in him. He is the fully blossomed "myself" that I wish to be.

Oh, Harriet—why do we crave another being as urgently as an itch craves a scratch? How are we to distinguish between true love for another person and wishful self-love? I cannot search for these answers with John, though he is my dearest and nearest friend. I am on fire, unable to eat or compose. Edward knows nothing of these feelings, unless he is clairvoyant, which would not surprise me. I promise you, sister, I shall do nothing indiscreet. I am no Madame Bovary. I shall not jump in front of a train. My family needs me. Yet I need him.

Please, rip this up after you read it. Better yet, before you read it!

As ever, L

31

BELL LOOKED SCHOLARLY in a button-down shirt, his glasses balanced on his forehead. He faced the chorus with an earnest expression, then spoke in a subdued tone.

"For the past few weeks, I have talked about the social issues holding back female composers of the late-nineteenth and early-twentieth centuries in England," he said. "One was my own great-great-grand-aunt Lisha Lovington. Recent reevaluations have determined that the Requiem we heard tonight was not her work. But she was a fine composer of her time."

Nicole pressed a sharp elbow into Piper's arm. "Say nothing," she whispered. "We'll get the truth out when we're ready."

Piper flinched at the presumptuous "we." It was her job alone to decide what "truth" to release about the Requiem, and when to release it. But Nicole meant well.

"Right," she whispered back.

"We've also discussed women's restricted musical opportunities." Bell leaned toward the chorus, and the chorus leaned toward him. "I have spoken about women being denied the vital composition and theory classes that were standard for men, and the stigma attached to respectable women displaying themselves onstage as they performed or conducted their own works." He studied the faces of his listeners. "The morés of the time also prevented a woman from traveling alone—or going out alone at night—for fear of being thought a prostitute."

"Why did the women put up with it?" Piper called out.

Bell held up his hand. "Excuse me; questions later, please. Think about it—is it any wonder that a composer who was also a suffragette leader, my aunt's contemporary Ethel Smyth, took to dressing like a man?"

Bell got the chorus's attention without begging for it the way Barlow did. No one seemed to notice his quick dismissal of Piper's question, which she'd hoped would lead him deeper into his topic. *I can see people's attraction to Bell but don't feel it myself,* she jotted in her notebook.

"Before I close, here's a question. How many of you have heard of the nineteenth-century American music critic George P. Upton?" No hands went up. "Upton thought women had no business composing music. What you're about to hear is his opinion, not mine." Bell opened a book and read aloud: "*Woman lives in emotion and acts from emotion, but cannot sufficiently separate herself from emotion to create great musical art.*" Protests rang out across the room. "Hold on, there's more." Bell flipped through the book as the chatter quieted. "Here it is. *To bind and measure emotions, and limit them within the rigid laws of harmony and counterpoint . . . is a cold-blooded operation, possible only for the sterner and more obdurate nature of man.*"

He looked up as if awaiting an outburst. When it came, he waited for quiet. "I will now end with a paraphrase of Upton's views: If the women are busy composing, who will take care of the men? Women's proper role is to inspire musical men."

The room filled with gasps and laughter, and Nicole leaned toward Piper. "Upton is so atrocious he's irresistible. I'm surprised nobody shot him."

"Agreed," Piper said. "He's the perfect villain."

Critics like Upton had crushed the spirits of artists like Lisha Lovington. How sad she had died without ever hearing her *Requiem* performed—if it was her *Requiem.*

Unable to sleep, Piper left the bedroom at 2:00 a.m. and took her phone into the kitchen. A text from Vicki was on the screen. *Urgent we talk.*

Piper texted back. *Call now if you're up. I can't sleep.*

The phone chimed a minute later. "I can't sleep either," Vicki said. "Great talk tonight in chorus. Hunter Bell is really good."

"Sorry I missed it."

"What's on your mind?" Talking to Vicki in the dead of night was like old times.

"I read your article about Daphne being a sex addict, and now I'm absolutely sure about something. I need to tell either you or that detective about it, and it might as well be you. Then you can tell him."

It might as well be you. How cold. "Tell him what?"

"Griffin is the killer."

"What? Why do you say that?"

"Because he was obsessed with Daphne. I'll bet he was in a jealous rage about all those people she slept with. Swear you won't tell anyone I told you this."

"I won't. Go on."

Vicki lowered her voice. "I saw him near the Dungeon stairs at the end of intermission on *Messiah* night. No one else was around. He was just standing there, like he was waiting for someone."

"What were you doing there? I'm surprised they let an audience member backstage."

Vicki sniffled. "No one 'let' me. I followed Griffin to see what he was doing." Her voice cracked. "Don't judge me, Piper. I'm not over him."

"Wait—did you sleep with Griff? You told me it was a professional relationship."

"First it was a crush, a long time ago. And now he's got a husband and I've got a case of depression."

Poor Vicki. Guys like Griffin were hard to resist. "You've got to pull yourself away, Vicki. Please, find someone to talk to, okay? I'm worried about you."

"Yeah, yeah, all right. Will you tell the police about Griffin being the killer? Then I can stop thinking about it."

"What do you think happened? Was he waiting to kill her when she came up the stairs?"

Vicki blew her nose. "Yes, I think so. Your news story convinced me. I finally connected the dots."

"Did you speak to him when you saw him?"

"No. I went back to my seat. I don't think he saw me, but maybe he did."

Piper felt scared for her—Vicki was her friend again, whether she knew it or not. "I've always meant to ask you about Griff, but

ANGELS' BLOOD | 159

you're so private. I thought you'd be annoyed. Do you think you're in danger?"

"I don't know," Vicki whispered. "I just hope he'll be locked up so I don't have to find out."

"Wow. You love him but you want him locked up."

"I never said I loved him. I said I wasn't over him. Even so, I'd join the chorus if I could sing worth a damn. Connecting through music is so emotional and passionate. There's one more thing, Piper."

"Tell me."

"Griffin was exciting yet calm. You wouldn't think he had a temper at all. But I've seen him—go berserk. It only happened once, but I saw what he was capable of."

"Violence?"

"Almost. He was defending his horror of a husband before they were married. Someone shouted an anti-gay curse at Clayton, and Griffin grabbed the guy by the throat. He told him to apologize, said he'd strangle him if he didn't."

Piper pictured Griff grabbing Daphne like that. And stabbing her and pushing her down the stairs to her death. A hideous image.

"There's a rage inside that man," Vicki said.

Piper took a calming breath. "There could be a very good explanation for why Griff was near the stairs around the time of Daphne's murder. On the other hand, he does sound like a tightly wrapped firecracker. I want you to call Detective Knowles at the police station first thing in the morning and tell him exactly what you just told me. Insist that your information remains anonymous, for your own safety."

"Okay, I will."

"And be careful. Keep away from Griff."

"I'll try," Vicki said.

After the call, Piper sat thinking in the dark kitchen. If Griff was near the Dungeon staircase at the exact moment Daphne walked upstairs, he must have had a premeditated plan to kill her. But Vicki had described him as hotheaded and impetuous, more likely to strike on impulse.

Vicki was too distraught to be logical. All the same, Griff could be guilty.

32

Alone in the dark living room, Barlow reflected on the rehearsal. It had gone well after an awkward start, when the singers demanded more eulogies for Daphne. But he'd held things together, not weeping or embarrassing himself.

Then Nicole embarrassed him with her whispers and coughs. And now she was out, though it was past midnight. "I forgot some papers at my office," she told him after they got home. He hoped she was safe.

A sound at the front door made him jump. "Nicole, is that you?"

No answer. He got up to see.

A figure stood silhouetted against the streetlight. "It's me, Todd," a familiar voice said.

Barlow switched on the light. "Corinne Kelsey! What are you doing here?"

"I need to speak to you." Cold air rushed through the open door.

"Not now, Corinne, it's late. How did you know where I live?"

"I followed you." She shut the door behind her. "I'll just be a minute."

Revulsion gripped him. "No, please go. I need my rest after chorus rehearsal. Phone me tomorrow."

She did not move. "I came to apologize for the brawl at rehearsal tonight. I haven't fought with a woman since junior high."

Thank goodness she sounded rational. "It's all right; no one was harmed. Now you must leave." He made motions toward the door. "Please go."

But she stepped farther into the house, bringing her repulsive scent with her. It smelled like rotting flowers and old dog poop, and then he knew.

"Oh my God, Corinne, it was you! You sent that letter."

"So glad you liked it." She smiled with gleaming teeth and headed for the living room.

"No way." He grabbed her arm. "You are trespassing. We'll talk about the letter, but now I want you out of here."

She wrestled his hand away. "Listen to me, you phony. I am as good a singer as Daphne Paige." Her spittle sprayed his face. "There's no reason you can't give me a solo in our next concert. I've been studying the Lovington music, and there are lines I could sing."

He would have reasoned with her if she hadn't sent a crazy letter. "Get a hold of yourself, Corinne. Leave now and I will not press charges. You need help."

"It doesn't have to be a big solo, just something to show your belief in me. I've seen you smile at me when I sing, Todd." She bared her teeth. "You've turned your light on me, and now I must shine. You must not deny me a chance." She thrust her forefinger at him. "Audition me, and if you find me lacking, teach me the way you taught Daphne Paige. I will pay you the fee you deserve."

Her odor was drifting through the house, upstairs to his study, his bedroom, his music books. It would pollute his life, his hopes for a new start with the wife he had betrayed.

"You know soloists rarely come from the chorus, Corinne." He clenched his fists to keep from shoving her out the door. "Soloists have conservatory training; they have established careers. Very few break through from nowhere." He must be nuts to try reasoning now.

"Hogwash!" More spittle. "You said Daphne was close to being a soloist. I heard you. We all heard you. Why Daphne and not one of us? Why not me, dammit?" Corinne thumped her chest.

She was flushed and trembling, hideous and menacing. Never had he been this afraid of a woman—except Nicole, but in a different way. Corinne was a coiled spring. And the rotten scent of her perfume masked her fear. She was ill, he realized now. She was obsessed with Daphne, with fame, with him. Maybe she was off her medication.

"Come now, Corinne. Go home, get some sleep, call me tomorrow. We can work this out."

"No. Agree to make me a soloist, or I will campaign to have you fired—for favoritism, loose morals, and exploiting a minor. That filthy whore and you worked together to lure my son. She stole his virginity!"

So that was it. He winced at the accusation but felt a moment of sympathy for Corinne. Her face was purple. Would she have a stroke in his living room? But she had called Daphne a whore. And a pedophile. She had to be stopped.

He put a firm hand on her back and moved her toward the front door. To his surprise, she did not resist. When they reached the door, she swiveled and kissed him on the mouth. He tried to pull away, but her mouth locked onto his, a large mouth with prominent teeth. He imagined a giant insect releasing its poison. What if Nicole came home and saw him like this? She would laugh.

Their mouths made a sucking sound as he pulled away. Corinne staggered out the door, down the front steps, and onto the slate path. As she caught her balance, he saw Nicole coming up the walk.

"For God's sake, Nic, where have you been?" he called out. "I was worried!"

"I told you I was going to my office. What's going on? Why is she here?" Nicole looked Corinne up and down. "Is this something I should know about?" She smiled at her joke. "A bit too much perfume, Corinne, dear."

"She wants singing lessons." Barlow shrugged.

"After hours?"

Corinne glared at them. "Think it over, Mr. Maestro. I'm finished here."

"What a shame," Nicole said. "We'll miss you when you go."

"It's freezing out here." Barlow pulled Nicole into the house and bolted the door. "How cool you are. I couldn't get rid of that woman!" Thank goodness she hadn't seen Corinne kiss him.

He reached out to hug his wife, to celebrate her being safe and sound.

"Nothing doing." Nicole dodged him. "Not in the mood. Was dear Corinne going to shoot you?"

"I don't think so. She is crazed, don't you think? She's the one who sent me that letter I told you about." Only he hadn't told her about it, he remembered now.

"What letter?"

ANGELS' BLOOD | 163

"Never mind. Corinne threatened me; I didn't want to worry you. She says I should make her a soloist or else."

"Or else what?"

"I don't know."

"I'm going to call the police." Nicole took out her phone.

He did not stop her. "They have a letter she sent me; it had a disgusting smell."

"I wonder if she killed Daphne." Nicole looked thoughtful. "She had a fit of jealous rage about your precious Miss Paige, and she snapped. On the other hand, I don't think so. She's too desperate to be loved."

"But she could have done it." Barlow favored any scenario that excluded him. And here was his wife, coolly discussing his dead lover as if they were a pair of married movie sleuths.

"I'll follow up with Knowles first thing in the morning. It's always so good to talk to you, Nic. I was happy to see you on the front walk." He gave her a warm smile.

"Yeah, because she was about to kill you."

"No, it was for yourself I was happy. For the sight of you. I've missed you."

He reached out again, but she held him off. "None of that. I'm off to bed now—by myself." She started up the stairs. "Make yourself comfortable on the couch. Sleep as well as a guilty man can sleep."

"Wait! You don't really think I killed Daphne, do you?" The name of his lover was an off-key note in their living room.

She shrugged. "Who knows? You're guilty of cheating, and you've hardly apologized for it. You're wallowing in that woman's memory and still worrying you killed her. It's pathetic. You're pathetic, Todd."

She was right. He was pathetic.

33

Knowles sat at the breakfast table reading Piper Morgan's article, his eyes growing wider. He had not figured the singing angel for a sex addict, but if Morgan was correct, and he had no doubt she was, he had some catching up to do.

Men and women, the article said. Paraded through the house in front of the disabled mother. Despite his effort not to judge, the image appalled him.

Knowles stood, stretched his limbs, bent to touch his toes. He felt a twinge in his hip and straightened carefully. What he needed was a good mountain hike to think things through, followed by a long, strong massage.

He finished his buttered bagel and bitter black, then called Daniels with the morning schedule. First, question the woman who intruded into the Barlow home at 1:00 a.m. Then get going on the sex-addiction angle.

The intruder case would be fast. "We don't want her charged, just questioned," Ms. Jennings-Barlow's voice message said. "We hope you'll scare the hell out of her, Detective. Any more harassment and we'll make a formal complaint. By the way, she admitted sending Todd a threatening letter."

The message gave the intruder's phone number. Organized people like Jennings-Barlow ruled the world, his father often said.

"Pay close attention to this woman, Matt." They were outside the interrogation room, watching Corinne Kelsey inside it. "Harassment can be a symptom of worse impulses. This could be our murderer."

"Got it, sir," Daniels said, and Knowles smiled. Of course he got it. Smart people like Matt did not need to hear things twice, which was why they were invaluable underlings. The trouble was they did not stay underlings for long.

Entering the interrogation room, they faced a large middle-aged woman with salt-and-pepper hair and defiant gray eyes. Knowles introduced himself and Daniels and started the recording, stating the date, time, and names of those present.

"Do you know why you're here, Ms. Kelsey?" he said as both he and Daniels sat down.

"That bitch reported me." She met his eyes without a blink.

"A couple whose house you entered late last night without an invitation said you harassed them. They also accused you of mailing a threatening letter to their home." He stopped to keep her off-balance. "However, they are not pressing charges on either matter at this time."

"Then why am I here?" Her eyes flashed beneath graying brows.

"I want you to explain the letter you wrote to Maestro Barlow, the one in which you threatened him."

"It was a joke." Her face turned red. "It meant nothing."

She huffed and puffed about the unjust behavior of some conductors when charmed by a stunner like Daphne Paige. "To be born beautiful is no achievement," she informed Knowles, raging on as he held back the retort that neither was it an achievement to be born white, or wealthy, or two-legged. He'd figured out long ago that no one fully appreciated their own inborn advantages.

"If the letter meant nothing, why did you send it?"

She fidgeted with her handbag. "To warn him about the monster who ruined my son's life. He was sixteen when she got hold of him. It's a damn good thing she's gone." She leaned back, arms crossed against her chest.

"Why didn't you press charges? If what you say is true, it was a crime."

"I should have. I was going to. I didn't get around to it."

"Did you kill her?" Knowles said.

"No! I'm angry, not crazy."

Well, maybe not, but she was handicapped, as we all were in one way or another. Her particular handicap was believing she'd been dealt an unfair hand as a plain woman in a beauty-obsessed society. Such perceptions led to retaliation for real or imagined slights. Kelsey should count her blessings, he wanted to tell her, because nothing trumped the disadvantage of wearing dark skin in the United States of America, whether you were male or female, beauty or beast. He would have liked to chat with Kelsey about these things, but this was not a cocktail party.

"What size shoe do you wear, ma'am?"

She snorted. "My feet are enormous, Detective, just the way I like them. Would you like to know my bra size, too? It's 40F."

Nope, he had not intimidated her. Maybe he should have stared at her longer. "We're doing a routine shoe check of everyone onstage the night of Ms. Paige's murder. You can expect someone from our department to follow up. You might want to make a list of people who can confirm your whereabouts during the intermission of *Messiah*, the concert you participated in with the New York Luminoso Chorus."

She knew where she had sung; the last words were for the recording.

"Yeah, sure." Said with venom.

She was either innocent or cunning, with two strong motives to kill Paige: envy and revenge for her deflowered son. If Kelsey's shoe size matched the killer's, Knowles would not be surprised.

"We'll be in touch, Ms. Kelsey. Now please remove your shoes and give them to my assistant here. You'll get them back shortly."

"Like at an airport." Kelsey scowled. She removed her black Nikes and dropped them into the evidence bag Daniels held open.

Daniels closed the bag and whispered to Knowles, "We got a new message on the tip line, sir—just came in." Knowles left the room and heard a shaky female voice on a speaker-phone. "I wish to report this to Detective Knowles as an anonymous witness. On the night of Daphne Paige's murder, I saw a man at the top of the Dungeon stairs at the end of intermission. His name is Griffin Sharp, and here is his contact number."

Knowles pondered the message. It was one thing for Sharp to check on the sub he had arranged for the evening, and another for him to be seen at the exact spot of the crime. "Damn," Knowles whispered to no one.

34

Moss boomed his impatience through the phone. "How's that profile of the Brit coming along?"

"It's only Tuesday morning," Piper reminded him. "I've got till tomorrow." She was walking to *NYN* through a wintry Bryant Park, its skating rink and holiday craft shops not yet open for the day. "I need a final comment from Bell and some photos from his assistant. Those visuals will really bring his aunt alive."

"Alive as in what?" Moss's old desk chair squeaked in the background. "As in someone who didn't compose the music people thought she did? We could fill the universe with the things people didn't do."

Moss was great at juggling stories, writers, and deadlines, but sometimes he dropped his imagination. "The Lisha Lovington saga isn't over yet." Piper joined the mob crossing 42nd Street. "Watch and see."

"I await her next resurrection, but I won't hold my breath. Anyway, remember your assignment isn't the dead lady, it's the great-whatever-nephew. Send the profile, but don't be crushed if we still kill it. The ancient dame isn't relevant in the least if Elgar wrote the damn music, so neither is her charming Brit relative, unfortunately."

Piper was close to tears as she entered *NYN*. If Moss killed Bell's profile for the second time, and Todd Barlow performed the *Requiem* as an Elgar, Lisha Lovington would fade back into history, unknown, a zombie who had tasted new life and lost it—twice. She thought about the work that had moved everyone at last night's rehearsal, and the waves of maternal love washing over the chorus. Lisha must have composed it, unless—Piper argued with herself as she reached her cubicle—this was a tender work by Elgar. Didn't people make a game of trying—and failing—to identify which gender wrote a piece of music?

If only she didn't have a reporter's brain, examining all the angles. Philosophers like Nicole were less concerned with "facts" and more interested in the essence of things. The essence of the *Requiem* was its effect on the listener, on her, Piper. She would stand by her opinion that the *Requiem* was composed by a woman. At her desk, she texted Nicole:

> *Do you think romantic feelings in music can be distinguished from other feelings of love? Like, if Elgar wrote the Requiem, he could have been expressing paternal love for his daughter, Carice, or a love of nature, or passionate love for some new crush. I've read he fell in love with younger women several times during his long marriage to Alice, his adviser and editor.*

Nicole replied: *Excellent questions but irrelevant to our cause.*

The Lovington materials arrived—two published songs and four sepia-toned photos in the style of the day. One: An attractive fortyish woman with dark curls framing an oval face. High forehead, wide-set pale eyes, straight, narrow nose. Lisha, presumably. No identification on the back of the photo, just a pair of empty brackets.

Two: A studio shot of the same woman in a flowing white dress, cradling a baby. A classic Madonna and Child pose. No hint of the sitter's personality, though excellent print quality. No ID, just a pair of empty brackets on the back.

Three: Arty-looking people at a music salon. The same woman as in the other photos seated at the piano in a high-necked dress with a shoulder ruffle. Piper had read about those elite gatherings in private homes, where like-minded people shared the latest in literature and the arts. Musical women of the nineteenth century thrived in such protective settings, where they could perform their art away from the public eye.

A caption on the back read, "The lovely Lisha Lovington plays to the delight of onlookers." At last, an ID confirming Lisha as the woman in three photos so far. Here she looked happy and at home, fingers curved gracefully over the keys, head tipped back at a flirtatious angle. Was Elgar looking on? Piper scanned the photo for his luxurious mustache but did not see it.

A search for a doctor type was futile, too. Who would wear a stethoscope to a salon? She wondered if John Lovington knew about Elgar's attention to his wife, and if so, whether he tolerated the flirtation to help her career.

Piper longed to time travel and get those answers.

Four: The same Lisha, gray-haired now, posing on a street corner with a younger woman who resembled her. A sunny day with deep shadows, the women squinting and smiling in their wide-collared coats. They held identical books with flowery covers and empty brackets in each corner. A caption on the back of the photo read, "Lisha and Harriet in Fitzrovia-London—1900."

Researching Fitzrovia, Piper learned it was a London neighborhood where many artists congregated in the late 19th century. George Bernard Shaw lived there, as did Virginia Woolf in the early 1900's. Lisha and Harriet could have been coming from a concert of Lisha's songs, carrying the books that held the scores.

The phone interrupted her thoughts.

"Hunter Bell here. I read your sex-addict article today. Anyone can see Paige was self-destructive. She probably hurled herself down those stairs."

"I seriously doubt it." Piper adopted his brusque tone. "By the way, I received the photos and song sheets from your assistant today. The Elgar letter was missing, and we need it."

"Right, I'll fix that."

"And what about this Fitzrovia photo your assistant sent? Who is Harriet? I haven't read about a daughter, but this woman resembles Lisha."

Bell drew in a sharp breath. "Harriet is my great-great-grandmother on my father's side—Aunt Lisha's younger sister. She's just a name on my family tree, but according to family lore, she was a reserved person with a sharp, inquisitive mind. She wanted to be a scientist, but marriage killed that dream. Instead, she lived vicariously through Lisha and was devoted to her."

"So that's the line you're descended from."

"Yes, I'm a product of the son of the son of Harriet's son. She was Harriet Bell."

"Were she and Lisha close?"

"Seems so. Great-Great-Grandmother Bell kept all her sister's letters and mementos, a treasure trove that unfortunately was passed down to Harriet's daughter's descendants, not her son's. They're a narrow-minded, peevish bunch who want nothing to do with me. Real dullards."

"Who is the caretaker of this 'treasure trove'?"

"Never mind that. You don't need anything from my aunt's archive for my profile."

"Except the letter you mentioned. The one I keep asking for."

"I said you'd get it. But look here, I want to give you my new closing comment. Are you ready to take notes?'

"Always ready."

"Then here goes. 'New York Luminoso is a joy to work with. I wish I could stay forever.' How is that?"

"Very diplomatic." And drab. "Tell you what, Hunter. You give me the archivist's name and contact info, and I'll use this quote for the profile. Otherwise, I can't guarantee it won't end on a sour note, given your latest appraisal of your aunt's music."

Bell gave a dry laugh. "A respected journalist making a deal? Well, I never."

"Take it or leave it. And I'll have to connect with the archivist before my deadline today, say by four-thirty."

"Fine. The person you want is a cousin of mine in California. Name of Amelia Martin, age about thirty-five. Not a nice person, though she lives in a beautiful place, South Pasadena, all hills and valleys and fruit trees. Her grandfather was Harriet Bell's grandson, descended from her daughter. My cousin fancies herself an archivist though she has some kind of drudge job." He snorted. "Delusions of grandeur, I'd say."

"Thank you. Now I'll need your cousin's email and phone number."

Bell relayed the information, then chuckled. "I visited Amelia this morning and found her most uncooperative. So good luck with the archive."

"This morning?" He'd been at the chorus rehearsal last night.

"Are you in California now?"

"Indeed, took an early plane for some family business. Sleep is overrated, you know. Life is too short to worry about it."

Piper's neck tingled. Bell was a strange man, but if Lisha was a plagiarist, neither he nor his quirks would matter. "For both our sakes, I hope Amelia and I connect before my deadline."

"What's your stake in this game, Ms. Morgan?"

"The truth about Lisha Lovington, Hunter. And you should want it, too."

Worcester, Worcestershire

26 December 1898

DEAREST SISTER,

Today my mind is circling around the same three-note phrase. Perhaps I am overly tired from our happy Christmas, but there is another reason the composing is stuck. I will tell you, but please do not scold.

Harriet, I cannot stop thinking about Mr. Elgar. I am wondering—what is he like in all his facets? When he sips his coffee, when he sets his mind to a line of music, when he glimpses a woman's knee. I have never before felt such a yearning to know another person.

He says I am a romantic, like him, and that it is wonderful to be a romantic. I adore his "Salut d'Amour," have you heard it?

Rest assured that I am not in love with Mr. Elgar. Not yet. Not ever, and we shall not consummate our relationship with anything more than a firm handshake.

But he is curious too, Harriet! And how he looks at me, as though his eyes were twin mouths that would drink me in.

YOUR SISTER

LL

35

BARLOW'S HEAD ACHED as he read Piper Morgan's article. It sent him reeling to the medicine cabinet for aspirin, which he tossed in his mouth like peanuts.

Daphne—his Daphne. But she hadn't been his at all.

And now he remembered something new. After Daphne said the terrible words that hurt him, he had felt humiliated, enraged. He remembered running up the stairs as Daphne called to him from below, "Todd, wait." But he did not wait. She had reached out to him with something in her hand. "Wait," she said again, and this time he turned around. Was that when he struck her? It was not far-fetched to think so. He almost struck Corinne last night but wasn't angry enough to do it.

But he had been furious at Daphne, causing her to fall and die. He was sure of this now. He had killed her.

He rushed from the house without saying goodbye to Nicole. Earlier, he'd told her he was going to a regional conference at Anderson University, one of those soul-searching bores about attracting young audiences to choral music. Hunter Bell would be there, he figured, a good reason to stay away.

He drove, picturing the staircase. When the Performing Arts Center came into view, he grew nauseous. The terrible place that had taken Daphne's life. He sped past the Anderson exit.

36

Piper left a message for Amelia Martin requesting a call by four o'clock Eastern time. Then she waited—sifting through press releases, answering emails, and checking social media. At 3:30 she went for coffee. At 3:50 she printed out the two Lovington song sheets.

"Puddles" was for children. "Love Amid the Roses" was sensuous and adult, its pages stained and torn as though much used and cried over. Maybe the stains were Lisha's tears.

It struck Piper that if the harmonic patterns in the love song matched those in the *Requiem*, it might prove Lisha the true composer. Something to discuss with Nicole.

Amelia Martin called at 4:20, speaking with a hybrid British-California accent and ending sentences with a question mark. "Call me Amelia, not Amy? Americans love nicknames?"

Piper said she would. "Are you in music, too, Amelia?"

"Nope, film. I'm an editor?"

Piper figured that was a statement, not a question. She grabbed her notebook. "Your cousin Hunter said you oversee the Lisha Lovington treasure trove. Will you share some of your great-great-grand-aunt's letters for an article I'm doing? They could shed light on a controversy about her."

"Which controversy?"

Was there more than one? Piper explained the plagiarism issue without mentioning Elgar.

"I seriously doubt Auntie L would copy anyone based on what I know about her? She was an upstanding, talented woman? Only dire circumstances would make her stoop so low?"

"I get it, Amelia, but we have these two identical manuscripts with two different signatures. Maybe not getting her work performed was a dire circumstance for her. Maybe she wanted to have her name known in any way possible. Some people—uh, it was suggested she became unhinged."

"That's absurd. Who signed the other *Requiem*, by the way?"

"Edward Elgar."

Amelia let out a guffaw. "Whoa, that's rich. According to family legend, Auntie Lisha and Elgar had a passionate extramarital affair. Supposedly it ended badly for her."

Piper gripped the phone. "Really?"

"Yeah, that's the controversy I thought you were calling about."

Piper whistled softly. "Amelia, I want to get to the bottom of this. Your aunt's reputation—and the Lovington family name—could depend on it."

Amelia laughed again. "You sound so serious? But there are no direct Lovington descendants, so no worries there. There's just us Bells, and we're a large, unruly lot with a variety of surnames? We feast on family scandals."

Piper winced on Lovington's behalf. "Amelia, would you please look in the archive for letters that mention Elgar? They may hold the answer to the manuscript mystery."

Amelia sounded amused. "I don't mean to take this lightly, Piper, but Hunter has been exaggerating, as usual? He always needs to sound so important? What he calls the 'archive' is a dusty carved wooden box of letters and a few songs and piano scores passed down through the generations. There is no grand archive, and our aunt Lisha is beloved only by us."

"But you'll send what you find?" Piper had picked up Amelia's singsong. "I'd like copies?"

"Sure, after I dust off the box." Amelia's tone changed. "How well do you know my cousin Hunter?"

"Not well. I heard him give an excellent talk, and I've interviewed him. He called me this morning after visiting you. He sure works fast—he was at our chorus rehearsal in New York last night, charming us all."

"Yes, his face was at my door at eleven this morning," Amelia said. "I got rid of him fast."

"Doesn't sound like you like him much."

"He's a damn snake, pardon my French? Always after money,

jumped from career to career until he pounced on our great-great-grand-aunt's connection to Elgar. Now he's made himself an expert on Edwardian-era music. Frankly, I don't think Hunter cares that much about music?"

"Music history, then?" Piper said.

"He cares about himself and his schemes, whatever they are? He's tried for years to get hold of Auntie L's original letters. He tried again today? Of course, he can never have them."

"Why is that?"

"Because I can't trust him. We're missing an important letter from the collection, and there's a strong chance he took it? That happened years ago. As I said? He's a snake."

"What was the letter about?"

"Frankly, it was in the category you're asking about. Elgar wrote it to Auntie L, lots of interesting chitchat."

Could that be the letter Bell owned? Piper made notes but stayed clear of the family argument. After they hung up, her image of Lovington shifted from musical dynamo to amateur. Probably neither was accurate. Piper had imagined a perfect woman, but if Lisha had an adulterous affair, she was no angel. And she might be a plagiarist, too.

She called Nicole to fill her in.

"Piper Morgan, I'm impressed," Nicole said.

"You are? Why?"

"Your article this morning was a shocker—but not to me. I got a kick out of it. 'Let's correct the angelic image of the murdered gal and tell the world she was a sex addict.' Nice going."

"I just wrote the facts." Piper gulped. Maybe publishing the article was a mistake.

"And I'm glad you did. As I said, I'm impressed. Any Lovington news?"

Piper relayed Amelia's phone call and the rumored affair. "Amelia said she would send any of Lisha's letters that mention Elgar. Meanwhile, how about you and I get together and look at two of Lisha's songs? We can compare them style-wise with the *Requiem*. Are you free tonight?" She held her breath, half-expecting Nicole to laugh or dismiss her.

"Yes, excellent idea," Nicole said. "Come around seven. Todd's at a conference."

Piper filed Bell's profile to Moss, then ate takeout in her car. She did not feel her usual relief after filing an article. The Elgar letter never showed up. She now believed the letter existed, but Bell had bluffed about owning it.

It was a wild, moonless night, the wind whipping through the bare trees. Piper parked at the Barlows' curb and tripped over a fallen branch; nothing serious, a slight knee abrasion. She brushed herself off and was halfway to the front door when she saw the police car in the driveway.

Hurrying through the unlocked front door, she heard a man's voice, then Nicole's, coming from the upstairs hall.

"The only thing I can think of is an article saying the manuscript was in my closet," Nicole was telling a cop as she motioned to Piper. "My husband may know more about it—he could have taken it himself, but I haven't been able to reach him. He turns off his phone when he's at conferences."

"How did it get in your closet?" The cop, a skinny, red-faced guy no more than 21, was making notes.

"I put it there. It was in a box of old music a friend gave me as a gift—she found it while cleaning out her grandmother's attic."

"Ma'am, you put the box in the closet before you knew something valuable was inside?" The cop was practicing the polite tone he had been taught.

"Right, I looked through most of it but obviously missed something. The manuscript in question was near the bottom."

"Can you estimate its value?" The cop frowned above his pencil.

"In the seven figures if the composer whose name is on it really wrote it. It's a mystery, you see."

The officer whistled. "Millions of dollars for a few pages of music? Wow."

"Crazy, right?" Nicole shrugged at Piper, who had come upstairs.

"When did you first notice it missing, ma'am?"

"Today. But it could have been taken days ago. I looked for it today because this friend and I are meeting tonight to discuss that mystery I mentioned." She gestured at Piper.

The officer looked reluctant to get into the matter. "But you say your husband may have taken it?"

"Possibly, but it would be highly unusual for him not to tell me."

Nicole slapped her forehead. "Oh! I just realized he might have taken it to get an expert opinion at the conference. I apologize for taking up your time, officer. My husband will be home later, and we'll know for sure if we're talking about a theft."

"Since there was no breaking and entering, ma'am, I doubt if theft was involved, but you never know. Call again if you need us."

"Right. I mean, the closet does look a mess, but Todd might have been in a hurry." Nicole spoke half to herself. "I guess we have to keep the back door locked."

And the front door, too, Piper thought; she had walked right in.

"Yep, good idea." The officer tipped his hat and left.

"The Elgar manuscript—is it missing?" Piper said when they were alone.

"Afraid so." Nicole looked pale and worried. "It's possible I moved it, but I don't remember doing that. Or maybe Todd took it, as I told the cop, or maybe someone's hiding in the house right now, waiting for a chance to escape with it."

Piper looked behind her. It was creepy to think a thief might be hiding in the house, so desperate to get out he—or she—might kill whoever was in the way. What if the manuscript thief was Daphne's killer? She and Nicole should get out of here.

Nicole stayed calm. "I'd be screaming if I were sure Elgar's manuscript is valuable, but it has little monetary value if Lisha wrote the *Requiem*, which is what I'm hoping for." She cocked her head. "Paradoxically, the manuscript is more valuable to me as a Lovington, because it shows what women can accomplish even when the odds of success are low."

Nicole pinched the top of her nose. "All this vagueness and uncertainty has given me a headache. The back-and-forth nonsense about the piece is awful. On the Elgar side, it's all about money. I hate disruption because of money. It's soul-sucking."

She gestured to Piper to sit on the couch. "I'm pouring myself a glass of wine. Want one?"

"Yes, thanks, if you're sure you don't want to run from the thief." Piper settled herself on the worn but comfortable couch. She didn't want Nicole to know she was a bit of a fraidy-cat. Or, as she liked to describe herself, a brave person with a scared person's imagination.

Nicole poured a generous amount of velvety Merlot into a delicate wineglass. On the one hand, it was lovely to be here with this highbrow woman in her dusty but interesting house. On the other hand, it was a dark night with a howling wind, and they were two women alone. Piper could not shake the thief-in-the-house-needing-to-get-out scenario Nicole had described.

"I'm glad you're here but also surprised." Nicole curled up near Piper on the couch. "Have you taken my side and become a crusader for Lovington?"

"No, not a crusader—but I can't get that woman out of my mind. What if she didn't plagiarize Elgar? Looks like we're the only two people on the planet who care."

A cracking sound sent them to the window. Trees thrashed in the wind, and a monster branch had bounced off the house. Nicole stuck her head out the front door. "Eek, it's a mess out there. Get thee to the piano quick, Piper, before the roof caves in."

Piper obliged—it was all quite exciting, the stormy night, the scary house, and now music from beyond the grave. Was Lovington sending them a message? Piper groaned at her own silliness.

"What's wrong, Piper?"

"Nothing. It's the perfect night to hear Lisha's music."

They sat down together at the piano, resting their wineglasses on an old music notebook. Nicole scribbled on the back of a loose page and slid the paper to Piper.

BEST NOT TO DISCUSS LOVINGTON IN CASE SOMEONE IS LISTENING.

YOU THINK A THIEF IS IN HERE? Piper wrote, sliding the paper back to Nicole.

IT'S POSSIBLE!

A manuscript thief would need the world to believe Elgar wrote the *Requiem* so he or she could cash in on it. Anyone knowledgeable who disagreed would have to be silenced, including a journalist casting doubt on Elgar's authorship. That's me, Piper thought with a shiver.

MAYBE WE SHOULD LEAVE THE HOUSE, NICOLE.

NO LET'S SING THE SONGS.

Piper shrugged and took out the song sheets. "These were written by a young cousin of mine," she said with a wink. "They're not very good, but we can have some fun until your husband gets home." She wiggled her eyebrows to emphasize she was acting. They both drained their wineglasses.

"Oh. Well, fine. I'll plunk them out on the piano." Nicole poured two more glasses. "I'll be right back."

She took two bronze pokers from their stands at the fireplace. "Weapons," she mouthed to Piper, setting the pokers by the piano.

Piper decided to stay until Todd got home, so Nicole would not be alone.

Nicole began playing "Love Amid the Roses" and sang in her strong soprano. Piper harmonized down a third. The lilting rhythm, minor key, and melancholy lyrics made the song memorable.

"Let's sing it again," Piper said, winking, "to be sure it's as terrible as it seems."

This time their voices were more confident and expressive. They fell silent when they finished.

"You're right, the song is terrible." Nicole scrawled GORGEOUS!

"Such silly lyrics," Piper said. SO ROMANTIC, I LOVE IT! MAYBE IT'S ABOUT LISHA AND ELGAR.

As the room became chilly, Nicole threw a faux-fur throw across both their laps. "Now let's do the children's song—it's probably even worse than the other one."

"Right, let's have a good laugh." Piper felt cozy and happy sharing the throw and Lovington's music with Nicole. The children's song was about an upside-down puddle world. Rippling couplets evoked children at play.

"What a silly song!" Piper wrote, CHARMING.

"True, it's nonsense." SHE'S GOT REAL TALENT.

They looked at each other. "What time do you expect Todd?" Piper said.

"In a few minutes." Nicole turned the song sheet over and wrote, I HAVE NO IDEA.

"That must be hard for you." Piper would not put up with Theo roaming around without contacting her.

"I'm used to it. Maybe he's crying over that woman's grave. Maybe he's out looking for someone new. I haven't given him much of my—shall we say wifely—self for quite a while, and vice versa." Nicole shrugged. "It takes two to kill a marriage, Piper. Obviously, this isn't for publication." Nicole played loud chords to drown out their conversation.

"Of course not. Are things beyond repair?"

"Maybe not. Todd's been contrite. He's a suspect in the murder, you know. Both of us were questioned, but I think they're waiting to arrest him. They don't have anyone else." She laughed dryly. "I'd make a perfect suspect, but the cops decided my alibi is solid—thank goodness."

"Yes, thank goodness." Piper's tiny cloud of suspicion vanished. "Do they have something on Todd?"

"I'm pretty sure. Like, no one has returned his baton to him. I can't believe it wasn't found in the building."

"You think they're holding it?"

Nicole stopped playing, her hands frozen over the keys. "I don't know. I'm going to go see Knowles and tell him Todd didn't do it. He didn't, you know. He's not capable of murder."

"No, of course not." But he was capable of cheating, lying, and hurting his wife. Piper felt protective of Nicole, who could be brusque and unlikable but was surprisingly tender when you got to know her.

Nicole touched her hand. "You feel cold. Are you scared?"

"I was, a little. But not anymore."

"I've been play-acting for your sake," Nicole said.

"And I've been acting brave for yours."

"That's funny."

"It is."

They burst out laughing. When Nicole held up the music sheet with their writing on it, they laughed until tears rolled down their cheeks.

"You should go home." Nicole dried her eyes. "Your boyfriend will think I kidnapped you."

"I'm waiting to be sure you're safe."

"Thank you."

Night had settled around them. The room was dark except for one triangle of light on the piano keys. At the sound of a slammed door, both women froze. "I'll go see what that is," Nicole said, taking a poker along.

"Be careful!" Piper decided to follow her, but which way had she gone? She stepped into a hallway and called Nicole's name. No answer. Then a figure moved toward her, the face a blur. "Who...?"

A cold hand touched her arm.

Piper screamed and punched at the air. "No! No! Stop!"

"What the hell is wrong with you? I was just trying to steady you. You were about to faint." Todd Barlow hovered over her in a hooded parka.

"Todd? I couldn't see your face. Oh my God, I thought you were a thief." Piper covered her mouth and waited for her heartbeat to slow. "That was you slamming the door, right?"

"No, the wind pushed it closed. What do you mean a thief? Where's Nicole?"

"She's checking on the noise. She'll explain."

"What will I explain?" Nicole said, coming into the hallway. "I heard a scream. Oh, hi, Todd. So, you were the noise we heard. Why did Piper scream?"

"She thought I was a rapist-murderer-strangler-thief." Barlow dropped his coat on a chair. He looked haggard in the dim light.

"You okay, Piper?" Nicole said.

"Yup, false alarm."

"Why did you come in the back door, Todd? You never do that."

"The wind knocked a fat branch against the front. Why was the back unlocked?"

"My fault," Nicole said. "I keep forgetting we've ditched the open-door policy." She glanced at Piper, who sensed a spat on its way.

"You don't want Corinne Kelsey slitting our throats, do you?" Barlow said, as the three went into the living room. "Remember? You told me she snapped and killed Daphne."

ANGELS' BLOOD | 183

"That's true, I did say that. I wouldn't put it past her."

Barlow turned on the lights. "Why don't you two sit down?" He collapsed on the couch. How about pouring us some drinks, Nic?"

"Sure. But looks like you need sleep more than a drink."

Piper could hardly bear the suspense. When was Nicole going to ask about the missing manuscript? If Todd had it in his briefcase, the night would be salvaged. Otherwise—she braced herself for an emotional scene.

Nicole poured Todd some Merlot. "You brought the Elgar manuscript with you to the conference today, right?" she said, handing him the wineglass. How cool she was, not to mention her civility toward her cheating husband. "Please say yes."

"What? No, why?"

"Come this way and bring your wine." She motioned him toward the kitchen. "We need to talk, and it's warmer there. You too, Piper."

Piper felt trapped in a domestic drama. "First I need to call Theo—to tell him I'll be home late."

She was leaving Theo a voicemail when she heard a loud clatter. "Fuck it, no!" Todd yelled.

Piper hung up and ran into the kitchen. Todd sat slumped at the table as rivers of wine ran down a wall and pooled on the floor amid shards of broken glass. Candles flickered on the table, and Piper hoped Todd would not throw those at the wall, too, burning down the house with the three of them in it. Nicole stood beside him, as though he might need emergency aid.

"Who did it?" He covered his face with his hands. "Who knew where to find that manuscript?"

"I told you, it could have been anyone who read Piper's article. The one saying the manuscript was in a closet in our house."

Piper caught her breath. There was nowhere to hide.

"Don't the damn editors delete things that violate people's privacy?" Todd glared at her. "Don't writers know what to keep from the public?"

"I feel awful, guys." Piper's lips were trembling. "I shouldn't have given out that information." She felt a hot rush of guilt. There was no escaping the truth that the theft was her fault.

"No use crying over that now." Nicole sat down beside her husband. "The point is the Elgar manuscript is gone. You were planning for us to get rich with that manuscript, weren't you, Todd." She leaned toward him. "You know, do the premiere, get the world's attention, make a fortune auctioning off the score, in that order."

"Ah, auction it off." Piper felt stupid. "I guess it is valuable, even if Bell thinks it's worthless."

Nicole gave her a withering look. "Bell is full of shit, Piper. He said it was worthless so we'd think so, too."

"Of course it's not worthless," Todd growled. "At least we can agree on that." He was calmer now, and Piper began to breathe normally.

"Piper can testify that the house was in perfect shape when the cop was here," Nicole said. "Right, Piper? I mean, it didn't look ransacked."

"No, you're right."

"What does that tell you?" Nicole said.

"That the thief didn't have to make a mess searching for it. It was someone who read my article."

"I wouldn't put it past that loony Corinne to steal it," Nicole said. "She'd do anything to lord it over us. Don't you agree, Todd?"

"Corinne wouldn't know what closet to look in. She was never in our bedroom."

"Well, that's a relief," Nicole rolled her eyes at Piper, who smothered a giggle.

"Didn't you tell me you showed the manuscript to Hunter Bell the day you found it in your closet?" Todd said. "The day of the *Messiah* concert and the day. . . . " He winced.

"The day of the night Daphne was killed." Nicole finished his sentence.

"Wait." Piper turned to Todd. "I spoke to Hunter on the phone today. He said he asked you to lend him the Elgar manuscript and you said no. He sounded angry about it."

"No surprise there," Nicole said. "He wanted to auction it off before we did. A newly discovered manuscript by a master. He saw millions of dollars in his future. Or pounds, in his case."

"Getting a second opinion was a ruse," Piper said.

Nicole's downcast eyes showed she felt guilty, too—for opening her bedroom closet and maybe more to Bell. And Todd had not thought to put the manuscript in a vault. They all shared in the blame, as Todd, with his agonized expression, seemed to realize.

"The chorus can still do the premiere, though, can't they?" Piper tried for the bright side. "You still have the Lovington manuscript. And all the copies."

Nicole shook her head. "Piper, you're not getting it. Whoever has the second *Requiem* manuscript—Hunter, most likely—can do anything they want with it. Like make up some false claim of ownership or invent some untrue story to stop us from singing it. Whoever took it might dump it in a trash can. There are multiple bad scenarios; forget the loss of money from an auction."

Piper imagined a dark pit of greed. "But isn't it finders-keepers with a manuscript that old? You found it—or at least your friend did and gave it to you. It belongs to you."

"Maybe not," Nicole said. "If Elgar wrote it, one of his descendants might have the rights to his manuscript."

"He has no living descendants." Todd cut in. "I've looked him up. The only child of his marriage, a daughter named Carice Irene Elgar, did not have children. But he could have some illegitimate descendants out in the world, along with some fourth- or fifth-generation nieces and nephews."

"But would those people really have more right to his manuscript than Nicole does?" Piper said.

"Good question," Todd said. "We'd need a lawyer's advice on who owns it, assuming the thief stakes a claim. That would cost us time and money."

"What a mess." Piper wished the floor would swallow her up.

Nicole's eyes watered. "Now I can't prove Lisha Lovington didn't plagiarize Elgar. We need both manuscripts for my plan, and it would have worked."

Todd pounded on the table. "Stop it, both of you! Nicole, get on the phone with Detective Knowles right away. Confirm that a valuable manuscript has been stolen. I'll talk to a lawyer about performing the score."

He turned to Piper. "I see no problem with your writing an article about the theft. It is news, after all. Nicole and I will be glad to give you interviews, won't we, Nic?"

"Yes."

Piper felt her life was a fast-moving train, with assignments and mishaps following one after the other. By now she was too tired to keep up. It was time to go home.

Worcester, Worcestershire
6 January 1899

DEAR SISTER,

I hope you are sitting down, for I have dizzying news.

Though I have written to you profusely of my feelings, I did not confide how intrigued I remain by Edward's proposal—the one I refused. Your sensible guidance reached my mind, but not my heart.

Not wishing to upset you, I took a daring step on my own and recently made him a reverse proposal of more benefit to me. Today I am writing to tell you he has accepted it. My head is spinning with excitement.

Harriet, we have a plan that will change my life forever.

I will tell you more at a later time. Meanwhile, promise not to repeat what I've told you to another living soul. I swore to Edward that you would not. Tear this letter to shreds after reading it, and mail me the shreds. I trust this will not take too much of your time or attention.

YOUR DEMANDING BUT LOVING SISTER,

Lisha

P.S. Be happy for me! I feel the most thrilling sense of freedom.

Worcester, Worcestershire

6 January 1899

Dear Edward,

My hands trembled this morning when I received your letter. I can hardly believe that we will embark upon this new escapade together. As you know, it is a departure from my usual ways. I pray no unforeseen consequences will bring harm to either one of us.

I will be discreet with my husband, son, and closest friends. However, I have let slip a word to my trusted sister, who has never in any way betrayed my confidence. If this worries you and you wish to reconsider, I will think no less of you. You will remain in my mind—and in my heart—as a dear and generous friend.

Yours with gratitude,

Lisha L.

37

THE THEFT of an antique music manuscript would not send chills through most detectives. But after reading Piper Morgan's article, Knowles hurried to get Ms. Jennings-Barlow on the phone.

She spoke before he could say a word. "I talked to one of your men last night, Detective, so I assume you know the details by now."

"Yes, and—"

"Imagine you're running a marathon, and someone puts a wall in your path. My husband has been studying the Lovington for months, but now our performance may be canceled forever."

"However, I—"

"It's been traumatic for Todd, piling on to the unresolved murder."

"I see." Knowles at last completed a sentence.

"It's also a serious situation for New York Luminoso, our audiences, and culture in the region. With the score in dispute and a manuscript stolen, we've got no premiere, no forthcoming revenues." Her voice cracked. "In short, we're toast."

"Ms. Jennings-Barlow, I called to assure you we're going to find the manuscript. We've got the FBI and Interpol on the lookout, so it can't get far."

"That's good."

"We will be in touch when—"

"One moment, please, Detective." Her tone softened. "If Elgar is the true author, his manuscript could be auctioned for upwards of six figures. Maybe seven." She paused as if to let the news sink in. "But if Lovington is the author, Bell is in for a nasty surprise. The manuscript might draw a couple hundred at most. But I would be no less grateful for its safe return."

Knowles whistled. The manuscript was either a treasure or trash, according to the lady. But she was hinting at a reward, whatever the outcome.

"One more thing," she said. "On Monday night Bell begged my husband to give him the Elgar manuscript for further evaluation. Todd said no; interesting, yes? We're counting on you, sir. Goodbye."

Knowles searched his database for recent police interaction with Hunter Bell. Nothing there but a routine interview Daniels conducted the day after the Paige murder, containing nothing of note besides the flu Bell suffered on concert night and the following day. Daniels, not wanting to catch the bug, interviewed him on the phone.

Knowles asked Daniels to search London police records for Bell's name, then contacted the FBI to stop Bell from leaving the country with a "culturally significant" manuscript. He hoped Bell and the manuscript were not already airborne—en route to London.

Did this kind of thing happen often in choruses? Surely, such groups offered escape from the ugly world of crime. Knowles was no singer, but he imagined choruses as havens where individuals surrendered their egos to become one beating heart. If the vibe was as confrontational as life on the street, he did not want Midge joining one. She'd had her eye on New York Luminoso since *Messiah* night, despite the tragedy that followed.

It was his lunchtime, time for food and music. Knowles closed his office door, punched up Pergolesi's *Stabat Mater* on YouTube—the sublime Claudio Abbado version—and bit into his meat loaf sandwich. Something smelled foul, and it wasn't the meat loaf. Two mysteries in one chorus were one mystery too many.

Nicole Jennings-Barlow turned up at his door as he was leaving for a meeting. "I must add something to our phone conversation," she said. "It's about my husband's baton."

Knowles ushered her in, surprised by the coincidence. His meeting had been called to discuss the baton.

"What about the baton, ma'am? I'm afraid I just have a moment and can't ask you to sit."

"I don't need to sit, I need to talk."

She looked as well put together as always, but her usually precise lipstick was smudged, a possibly significant detail.

"Please, what do you want to tell me?"

She fixed her startling blue eyes on him. "You might have heard that my husband always uses his baton with an orchestra. He says he feels naked without it."

"Okay."

"It's not just for beating time, Detective. With the baton, he can trust that the musicians are watching him. Even if they aren't, which is often the case. That goes double for the chorus."

"The singers don't always watch the conductor?" Knowles played with her a little.

She threw back her head and laughed. Seeing the row of straight white teeth, he laughed, too. "I gather that's an inside joke."

"Detective Knowles, most choral singers are not trained musicians. They don't memorize the words, and many don't read the notes so well, either." He waited for her point. "If they look up to watch the conductor, they may lose their place in the music. But if they don't look up at him, he is displeased. It's a catch-22, see?"

"I see. And now, regrettably, I must go, but thanks for stopping in." She had not said much, to his disappointment.

"Wait, please." She blocked his way. "I came to say my husband did not kill Daphne Paige. But I have a very strong theory about what happened."

Knowles sighed with impatience. "We need evidence, ma'am, not theories."

"This is psychological evidence, Detective. I knew my husband was having an affair from a hundred little details. But besides the Paige viper, he may have had another lover as well."

Knowles looked at his watch, and she held up a finger. "I don't discount the possibility that something is up between him and Griffin Sharp, another member of our chorus."

That was a new angle. "Interesting, but now I must. . . ."

"The Paige viper more powerfully gripped my husband's psyche—along with his other parts—as Todd is not gay or bi. But as you know, sexuality is fluid in most people. I can imagine my sniveling husband being swept away by the handsome Griffin, with his rock of a—shall we say, personality."

"And so?" Knowles prompted.

"So, I suggest something went very wrong between Todd, Griffin, and Paige during the past few weeks, and it led to her death. Adieu."

Knowles thought about the lady's last comment as he hurried toward the meeting room. Distracted, he nearly knocked into Daniels, who was rushing toward him.

"Chief just spoke to me, sir," Daniels said, panting. "Says he wants an arrest in the Paige case right away, or better, yesterday."

"Izzat so? What else did he say?"

"Said it's been a week and you need to get it done." Daniels fixed his gaze on his superior.

"He has someone in mind?"

"Yup, the conductor. Chief said, 'Ninety-nine percent it's him, so what are you guys waiting for?' Those are his exact words, sir."

Knowles had a sinking feeling. He trusted his gut, which throbbed with elation when things were going right. Now his gut told him things were going wrong, and the chief's hassling was just a part of it.

38

BELL'S COUSIN AMELIA MARTIN called the next day. "Piper, guess what. There are tons of Elgar references in Auntie L's letters?"
Piper clutched the phone. "Really? Like what?"
"Like how she and Elgar met at London music salons and hit it off? I can see why Lisha liked him. He treated her like an equal—at least before he got world-famous? I'll bet their affair was real."
"Amelia, please scan some of those letters and email them to me right away."
"I've already done something better? Look for an email in two minutes."
"Thank you!"
Two minutes later an email popped up on Piper's office computer:

> Hi— So many letters, wow! I used my judgment as a filmmaker to create a collage that gives the flavor of their relationship. I hope you like it! It paints a picture of a woman falling in love.
> I did have to cut some lines to shape the storyline, but that is my art. And don't worry about thanking me with any recompense. Perpetuating Auntie L's sacred memory is payment enough.

Piper was wary of the words *cut* and *shape*, and with good reason. Amelia had taken excerpts from Lisha's letters and fashioned them into a story—history according to Amelia. Elgar's name appeared often, but without context. The "collage" was worthless.
Piper called Nicole to vent. But would she answer after last night's sloppy ordeal?
"Hi." Nicole's tone was cool. "What's up?"
Piper explained about the collage. "It's a cut-and-paste job.

"How can we get at the truth when Amelia Martin decided on her own what the truth was?"

"What do the fragments say?"

"I've only skimmed them, but it's some kind of love story."

"Hmm. Doesn't sound enlightening."

"No." Piper was fuming. "I'd like to discuss this travesty with you. Can we meet?"

"Let's see; I have a free hour at two. I'll admit I'm curious. Come on over, partner."

Piper exhaled in relief. "Will do—partner."

In her first visit to Nicole's university office, Piper would normally have commented on the decor—thriving plants in ceramic pots, Navajo rugs, and a genuine floral-labial Georgia O'Keeffe painting on the wall. But today she was too tense to notice.

"Look, she even titled the damn thing." She handed Nicole a printout. "'Letter Fragments as Edited by Amelia Martin.' What an egotist. Okay, let's start."

"We'll read through the fragments and discuss them afterward," Nicole said. "Silently, okay?"

"Agreed," Piper became engrossed in Lisha's words, though the true sequence of the fragments was unknown. "Whoa, this is erotic, Nicole. Did you see the part about 'twin mouths'?"

Nicole looked up. "Yup. Do you want to discuss it now?"

"No, not yet."

Next time, Nicole broke the silence. "She was in love with Elgar, for sure. She just didn't want to admit it."

"And he made her a proposal that she refused—but what was it?"

"Let's talk," they both said at once.

"I'm guessing he asked her to be his mistress," Nicole said. "One fragment said she rejected him, and another said she was relieved. It's a logical conclusion, but I could be dead wrong. What do you think?"

"She fantasized about him. I'll bet they had that affair. She mentions an escapade."

"There's a strength in her," Nicole said. "But we have so little to go on. There's nothing here to help us with the *Requiem*."

"The whole 'collage' is about Lisha's love life—as imagined by Amelia. But that's my fault, Nicole. I asked her to find Elgar's name in the letters, and that's what she did. She was just trying to be helpful."

"We need to know more about Lisha's work ethic. We know she had conflicts, because she talks about struggling."

"I want the whole picture," Piper said. "Her work, her family, her love life. Then maybe we'll get at the truth."

A melancholy violin piece played on the car radio as she drove back to *NYN*. It was romantic and heartbreaking, bringing tears to Piper's eyes.

"That was 'Salut d'Amour,' by Edward Elgar," the announcer said.

Piper broke into a smile. It seemed Elgar was right here in the car with her, a flesh-and-blood human being. If only she could question him. "Did you break Lisha's heart, or did she break yours? And who really wrote the *Requiem*?"

Back at her desk, she called Amelia. "Hi, about the collage—"

"I knew you'd love it!" Amelia burst out. "Hey, I forgot to tell you that when Hunter came yesterday, he demanded Auntie L's letters. The originals, of course? Copies weren't good enough for him?"

"Did he say why he wanted them?"

"Something about research. Well, of course I didn't give them to him. Please don't show him the collage, Piper? It will just cause trouble?"

"About that collage—"

"You have my permission to publish it. Then Hunter will see it along with everyone else. I don't know what he's planning, and it worries me? Fortunately, the collage only shows snippets of letters, so they can't do him much good."

"About those snippets, Amelia. We'd prefer complete letters—without ellipses."

"Oh." Amelia's tone turned cold. "I thought you were calling to thank me for my efforts? It took quite a while to assemble that romantic narrative."

Piper bit her lip. "Thank you, of course! My colleague and I so appreciate the time you took. But would it be a lot of trouble to email me the letters just as they are? It would be so much help in figuring out the double-manuscript puzzle."

Amelia was silent.

Piper explained that she was working with a colleague on Lisha's behalf, even though she was not supposed to admit it publicly as a journalist. "I'm afraid this colleague and I are the only ones fighting to recognize your aunt's achievement—if she did write the *Requiem*—and to show she wasn't a plagiarist. The complete letters are our only hope of finding the truth."

"I care, too," Amelia said.

"Oh, that's wonderful. Will you help us again? With the complete letters?" She repeated it so the words would sink in.

"Sure. And remember, Hunter's got something up his sleeve, so watch him like a hawk, Piper. Goodbye."

"Wait!" Piper yelled into the phone.

"Yes?"

"The snippets mention a proposal Elgar made to Lisha. Please be sure to send any letters you find about that. It's very important, Amelia. And we do have to hurry."

"I get it. The time to act is now."

"Exactly. Or your ancestor will be out of the picture for good," Piper added for drama.

"That would be a shame."

"I'm glad you agree. Now there are three of us fighting for Lisha."

39

AMELIA CALLED BACK sounding contrite. "Piper, I have not been totally up front with you? I did not share with you a letter my mother gave me when I was ten? She said it showed women's strength and I should read it often."

"Sounds like something I should see. May I?"

"Yes, and here's the thing—it's about a proposal Lisha made to Elgar, just what you wanted." Amelia squealed with excitement.

"Please fax me a copy right away." Piper would walk barefoot across hot coals to get hold of such a letter. She would sit in her office chair until the sun went down to wait for it.

"I've never wanted to share my letter before, but if Auntie L can have a happier afterlife, who am I to block the flow?"

"Amelia, do you know about a letter from Elgar to Lisha that Hunter owns? He teased me with it but he won't let me see it."

"Yeah. That's the one he probably stole, though I have no proof."

"Or he invented it," Piper said.

Amelia's fax arrived quickly. "Here's my special letter, but there's a surprise, too. You'll see Elgar's response, which I taped to Auntie L's original years ago."

Amelia signed the fax: *"Enjoy, I am A.M."*

Piper wished Nicole was with her as she read Lisha's words:

Worcester, Worcestershire
29 December 1898

My dear Edward,

My mind keeps drifting to your recent proposal, such that I cannot sleep, work, or tend with full attention to my family. Though I did decline your bold suggestion, it has burrowed deep into my brain, buzzing day and night like a demented bird. In order to find rest both as an artist and a mother, I will now make you a proposal of my own.

My Requiem is near completion. I work on it steadily, thanks in no small part to your encouragement. Tonight an idea has come to me as I sit in my kitchen and my husband and child sleep in their beds. Such dark, quiet hours can be dangerous times, when the most bizarre notions may masquerade as sensible. If you find my proposal outrageous and impossible, you must tell me and I will understand. In any case, the demented bird will stop its buzzing.

But if you agree to it—our adventure will begin.

Here is the proposal: I will send you my completed Requiem, and, if you think it worthy of your attention and time—if you think it worthy in the larger sense—you will rewrite it in your own hand and put your name on it. You will then submit it to the Academy as your work. Should the Academy reject it, I shall know that my Requiem is not up to the required standards, though you judged it to be deserving.

However, if the Requiem is accepted for performance, you will identify me, Lisha Lovington, as its true composer. The benefits to you, dear Edward, are threefold: making the Academy blush, as you have said you wished to do; helping a friend to succeed; and using your influence to make music a more just endeavor.

No subterfuge is without its risks, however. I should deeply regret any poor light that might reflect on you as an unplanned consequence of this "game." Please consider well before replying, for no success of mine must come at a high cost to you, whom I so greatly respect and admire.

Edward, none of us knows how long we may have to live on this Earth, nor how long our spiritual strength will endure to steel us against society's disapproval. But I immodestly wish to reassure you that I have copious *visions of peace and beauty to give to the world, and the Requiem is just a beginning. You see now what your kindness and attention have instilled in me. Am I monstrous?*

*With my best regards,
Lisha Lovington*

P.S. If the Academy accepts my work under your name, I shall always wonder whether they would have accepted it under my own. I am willing to bear the cost of not knowing, however, for my true goal will have been achieved—to have an orchestra breathe sound into the notes I have written, which would otherwise lie forever mute upon the page.

Piper reread the letter to fully grasp its boldness. An upstanding woman was asking a respected composer to join her in a game of deceit. It did not add up, unless Elgar had proposed something of equal dishonesty.

She phoned Nicole. "Major development. We must meet."

"I'll come to you," Nicole said.

"Nice window, nice view, better feng shui if you'd move the desk sideways, but what's the major development?" Nicole said when she arrived. "I hope it's not too complicated, because I'm hungry and Todd is bringing in Italian."

She sat down in a side chair as Piper handed her the letter.

A few minutes later, Nicole looked up with an awed expression. "Extraordinary, what a woman."

"I know. She's not only creative and sensitive but shrewd."

"She took charge of her own life," Nicole said. "She broke free of convention, transgressed the rules, defied her own upbringing, and took steps toward artistic freedom. And she did it as a lady, pardon the expression. She never would have taken such a step earlier in her life."

"Whatever Elgar proposed, he set her in motion," Piper said. "Even though she refused it."

"Maybe it's in a letter Amelia left out."

"I'll bet it's in the letter Hunter claims to own. Amelia thinks he stole it. In any case, it's missing."

"Hunter is so different from my first impression of him." Nicole shrugged. "He was so gallant and elegant—which he still is, in a way, but—you know."

"Yeah, I know what you mean. But back to Lisha. Do you think Elgar carried out her proposal? Oh, wait a minute—another fax is coming in. It could be Elgar's response."

"Oh, goody." Nicole clapped her hands. "The linguine can wait."

Piper picked up the fax. "Here it is! In Elgar's handwriting."

Nicole smiled. "And to think you hardly knew who he was a few weeks ago."

"Yeah, well." Piper felt herself blush. "How about reading it aloud?"

Nicole began reading.

3 January 1899

My dear lady,

Your letter has moved me nearly to tears. I can only say of course send me your Requiem and we shall see. Do not rush the ending or avoid the reworking on my account, for I shall gladly receive your manuscript whenever it arrives.

I daresay if you are a monster, then I am an ogre and a devil for stirring your hopes.

I look forward to testing the integrity of the esteemed Academy. Have no fear—it is more likely that a "poor light" will be shined on them than on me, and anyhow any personal pain would be worth bearing.

I should alert you, however: If those fools reject 'my' manuscript, i.e. your manuscript, it will not mean your work is inferior, dear Lisha. More likely it will be to spite me, or because someone has eaten too much greasy bacon for breakfast, or stayed up too late playing whist. In any case, he will have lost his sense of judgment.

What a bold heart you have, my dear friend. It is an honor to know you.

*With appreciation—and in expectation,
Edward E.*

P.S. The Academy may find something amiss when they see "my" music. Of course, it will be nothing like my music, for it will be your music. To head off suspicion, I shall send them a well-phrased note about trying out a new musical style. Holding my nose, I shall say I wish to know their opinion, which I do not, as they are overly concerned with past forms and often blind—or deaf—to genius. I must hastily add, however, that I am gratified to be accepted by their distinguished selves. EE

"He has a sardonic personality," Nicole said. "But he seems to genuinely like Lisha."

"I noticed that. And he respects her, too."

"Yes, and we know he carried out part of the plan. We have Lovington's *Requiem* in Elgar's handwriting on his music paper in his ink and with his name on it. We just don't know what happened after that."

"Like, why is there no record of a requiem in either of their names?" Piper wrinkled her brow. "And how did the two manuscripts wind up in your box?"

"Those are the big questions, I agree."

"It's certain now she didn't plagiarize him," Piper said. "He did the copying, but at her request. I never would have thought of that."

"Something went wrong."

"But what?" Piper's voice rose. "And how will we ever find out?"

Nicole looked down at the two faxed letters in her lap. "We may never know the whole story, Piper. This may be the closest we may ever get to clearing up the mystery."

"It's not close enough." Piper ran her hands through her hair. "I've got to find more evidence."

"Good luck with that. Meanwhile, I'll put a stop to the media ads Todd is preparing. The ones saying, 'Come hear New York Luminoso perform a brand-new Elgar.' I think everyone can agree that Lovington is more likely the author."

"Good! And I'll try to get Moss to run an update. Like 'Stay tuned, folks, Lisha Lovington ain't twice-dead yet.'"

Nicole was smiling again.

"What, you liked my joke?"

"I'm remembering a time when you wouldn't take sides. What happened?"

Piper thought about it. "I heard the *Requiem* at chorus rehearsal. A talented composer created a strong and powerful work that was never performed, and why? Because she was a woman. We have a chance to make things right."

"But how do you know for sure she wrote it?" Nicole teased.

"I don't. But I'll stake my career on it."

40

Knowles headed to the bedroom early. He needed to think, and his best thinking spot was in the dark, alone under the covers on his side of the bed.

"Feeling all right, babe?" Midge knew him as a night owl.

"Yeah, just got a lot to mull over."

She didn't argue, one of the many reasons he loved her.

He was halfway up the stairs when she called out in a girly tone she rarely used, "Want to do some mulling with me?"

Knowles cocked his head at her. She was the best listener he knew, but he kept his home life strictly separate from nasty crimes. "You know I can't. But I'll tell you this much. The chief wants me to arrest someone I have doubts about. I get why, but I don't want to do it. This person strikes me as a gentle soul, and my instincts are pretty good."

"Then don't do it, Lucas." Midge gave her head a firm shake, hoop earrings swaying.

"It's not so simple. There's evidence this person did it. There's a motive, too. It would wrap things up nice and tidy for the department, and everybody could get back to normal. No more worrying about a killer on the loose."

"Except maybe he's not the killer." Midge narrowed her eyes in that way she had.

"Who said 'he'?" Knowles said. "Maybe it's a she."

"I know who you're talking about, Lucas. That conductor we saw at *Messiah*. I got a feeling. Am I right?"

"Can't tell you that, babe." Knowles continued up the stairs. "'G'night."

He pulled the comforter over his bare flesh and settled himself in bed, sighing at the smooth feel of the sheets. For the millionth time he wondered how Midge did it, kept things so clean and fresh with a job and a young child at home.

He should pitch in more, but tonight he had to work on his day job.

The quiet, the darkness let him focus on the pros and cons of arresting the maestro. He remembered Barlow during the interrogation, his head bent on his arms. Hypersensitive guys like him shouldn't stray. Knowles shuddered to think what Midge would do if he pulled anything like an affair.

He thought about the shoes—how the maestro's were a tad too small, Corinne Kelsey's tread didn't match, and Griffin Sharp's might not matter because of his believable alibi. Some of Paige's dozen or so sex partners had not been fully investigated, and a few chorus members still needed further questioning, including Hunter Bell—not an official chorus member but close to the Barlows.

Knowles let out a frustrated sigh. So many loose ends, so much speculating to close a case. The conductor was the perfect suspect, passionate, private, and probably devastated to know he had shared his lover with half the county. Did finding out about her sex addiction make him snap? The article outing her ran after her death, but she might have admitted her illness to him on *Messiah* night. Such a confession could provoke a murderous impulse in even a mild-tempered man.

Barlow had a motive and an opportunity. The victim's blood was on the baton. No more dragging his heels on this. Tomorrow, he would arrest Barlow for murder.

41

Barlow's teeth chattered in the cold. He wore a thin prisoner's jumpsuit, his toes freezing in cloth slippers. Everything hurt, from his throbbing forehead to his inner cheeks, made sore by nervous biting. Confined within the walls of his solitary cell, he tried to make sense of things.

They had arrested him at his home at 6:00 a.m., escorting him down his front path and into a police car. Nicole watched from the door, pain in her eyes. They had been happy once, with their house, the chorus, and music. Civilized and comfortable. Trees! Little animals! He loved them all and missed them already.

They said he had the right to remain silent, but he couldn't stop saying he was innocent.

In the cell he let it go, Nicole, the chorus, the concert stage. Music, the heart and soul of his life—they would take it away from him. They would not let him conduct an orchestra or a chorus; he was no longer the maestro. Who would buy tickets to a concert led by a suspected killer? He would not.

He moaned in his cold cell, unable to stop.

Detective Knowles was meaner than Barlow remembered, the questioning room gloomier.

"Did your girlfriend try out your baton the night of the concert?" the detective said.

"No one holds my baton but me. It's a special baton, and I don't pass it around for fun."

"There was blood on your special baton. Black, thick, and congealed." The detective held a folder under Barlow's nose. "These photos prove my point. What do you have to say?"

Barlow clamped his hand over his mouth, sickened at Siegfried's condition.

"My client has nothing to say," said Nelson, at his side. "He has professed his innocence, and as such he cannot account for the blood on his baton. Keep in mind that after my client misplaced it, anyone could have picked it up, including Ms. Paige herself. Maybe she fell on it when she tumbled down the stairs. Maybe she stuck herself with it while she was pretending to conduct. Who knows? While the baton was out of Mr. Barlow's hands, anyone could have used it to commit the crime."

A useless fan clicked in the dead air. Click, ta ta click, ta ta, like a broken metronome.

Detective Knowles raised his voice. "I maintain your client killed the victim with the baton and then tried to hide it under the stairs, where my team found it. Do you still claim you lost it, Mr. Barlow?"

Nelson answered for him. "My client stands by his story that he lost the baton at the end of intermission. He has been traumatized by his student's murder and remembers little about the evening."

The dark music of their voices washed over him. Nelson was fighting for him, but Detective Knowles thought he was guilty. Then the detective left the room, and the dark music stopped. When he returned, he looked like a kid with a new toy.

"A guy just walked into the station and said he needed to unburden himself."

"Who?" Barlow and Nelson spoke in unison.

"His name is Griffin Sharp. He described a club of which he is a former member. Are you a member of any clubs, Mr. Barlow?"

Barlow shook his head. "I belong to the musicians' union, and they have a clubroom where we can shoot the breeze. Sometimes I drove my wife to her book club, but I didn't read the books, so I wasn't invited to stay." Barlow wondered what the guy was getting at. "I'm not a clubby kind of guy, Detective. Music takes up most of my time."

"Mr. Sharp was describing a sex club."

"You mean orgies? Orchestral sex?" Barlow snorted. "I prefer duets."

The detective lowered his voice. "Do you deny knowing Griffin Sharp?"

ANGELS' BLOOD | 207

"Of course not. He's a bass in my chorus."

"He says you two shared a sex partner, Daphne Paige." You might have been jealous of him, a handsome guy like that involved with the woman you loved. You might have been angry at Daphne for sharing herself with him. Then, in your anger, you killed her."

Barlow gasped.

"What's wrong?" Nelson nudged him. "You look pale."

"I just remembered something," Barlow whispered.

Nelson called for time alone with his client. Detective Knowles gave them ten minutes and left the room.

"Are you all right?" Nelson leaned toward Barlow. "Didn't you know Daphne had been with this bass, Sharp?"

Barlow grimaced. "Nothing is clear. I remembered something about Griffin."

"Try to remember. Give it a go."

Barlow shook his head. "It's gone—like a dream."

Nelson gazed at him steadily, a reassuring stare. "I've studied hypnosis, Todd. It was during my psychology phase in college, and I got the knack. I can uncover your memories of intermission."

"But what if it turns out I did it—killed her? Will you still be my lawyer?"

"We're going to prove you didn't," Nelson said.

Worcester, Worcestershire

2 Feb. 1899

OH HARRIET,

How hard it is to wait for what we desire! I continue to anticipate a letter confirming Edward's receipt of my *Requiem*, which I mailed to him on 4th Jan. Will he fulfill his agreement to go forward with the plan? I do not know. I have hurled my music into a chasm where it may reside for all time, unheard but for the angels. Though I flatter myself that the angels would take notice.

If only my imagination could retreat to its former borders and escape this boundless uncertainty. I am in a vast wood with silence all around.

Lisha

42

Moss was pressing for the chorus feature. "A jailed conductor—fantastic. Have it to me in two days max."

Piper faced the editor across his desk. "It's terrible timing, Moss. It'll make the chorus look bad."

"Are you kidding? It's great timing!" McCarthy threw out his arms. "You wanted to cover the bumps and warts of a chorus, right? This one couldn't be bumpier and wartier. Murder and mayhem; who could ask for anything more?"

"The headline would be what? 'Conductorless Chorus Contemplates Calamity'?"

"Excellent alliteration!" Moss exploded with joy. "Come on, Piperino, you know how to do it. Make it juicy—jails, singers, cloaks, and daggers. Have fun with it. This one's gonna write itself."

"Oh, sure." She rolled her eyes.

"It's all set up." Moss stood, exhilarated. "We've run your backstories on the dead singer's sex addiction, the lady composer's plagiarism charge, and the valuable missing manuscript." He kept count on his fingers. "Now take a step back and give us a wide-angle view of the chorus. How are they handling a murder in their midst? Have they taken sides on the *Requiem*? And what's the British dude's role in all this? Get some great quotes and make it throb."

"I'm guessing the British dude took the manuscript," Piper said, hands on her hips. "He knew exactly where it was, thanks to my article."

"So did thousands of other people who read it." Moss shrugged.

"Wish I'd deleted that info."

"Anyway, today I'm researching the story of 'Who Really Wrote It.' I'd rather spend my time on that."

Moss sat again, his old chair squeaking in complaint. "Piper, do you have any idea how popular your articles are? People will eat up the chorus feature, now more than ever with the conductor jailed." He leaned back, putting his feet up on his desk. "My God, we'll sell papers like the old days," he said, grinning. "Get it done, get it over with, and bring it back alive."

"Oh, all right." She sighed.

"Just keep your rear in the chair till it's finished. Make a pretty cake from the rotten ingredients. And meet the deadline. I've got other pieces to edit, you know." He smiled to show he was teasing.

"I'm incredibly proud of you, Piper."

"Thank you, Moss, that's nice to hear." And she meant it, but now she should pipe up about a raise, an assignment to the crime beat, even an occasional opinion column—something to reward her for her hard work. Moss had floated the idea of selling her articles to a newspaper syndicate, but she'd heard nothing further about it.

Back at her desk, she tried out a lede. *Music is like a mother who gathers her weeping children in her arms.* No, Moss would gag. Everyone would gag. She deleted the weeping children.

She was staring at the blank screen when her phone chimed. "Todd's innocent, you know," Nicole burst out.

Piper had meant to call. "Oh, Nicole, it's so awful about Todd's arrest—would you like company? I have a deadline but I'd be glad to come over."

"Not necessary, thanks. Listen, they're rallying for Todd outside the jail. I thought you should know."

"Who is?"

"The chorus. I'm going there now, if I can find the energy."

Piper grabbed her things. "I'm on my way."

An hour later, as she was pulling up to the county jail, Hardy Wheeler phoned—an event as rare as the Tooth Fairy checking in.

"Hey, Piperino." He was too lazy to invent his own nickname.

"It's not a good time, Hardy."

"You busy?"

"Yup, practicing my parallel parking."

"Let me guess. You're at the jail?"

"Yeah."

"You heard about the bloody baton?"

Piper nearly drove over the curb. "What? No."

"Then let me be the first to tell you."

"Yes, please tell me fast, Hardy." He didn't seem to know this was her story.

"Ooh, how hungry we are! But I'll tell you, 'cause I like your guts. They've had it for a week, a music baton caked in Paige's blood, found at the scene."

"Wow, that's big." Copper Don had let her down, but Hardy had come through.

"There's a press conference at eleven. I can't make it, but I left a present on your desk, a police press pass on a pretty chain. You've made my work more fun, and I can't wait to beat you to the murderous finale. Bye."

"Wait!" she yelled. "Where did you get this info?"

"Can't tell you. You rookie crimemongers need your own sources. Just get to the PPC on time."

"PPC?"

"Police press conference, and get with the lingo."

"Okay, anything else?" He was gone.

She jumped out of the car, her mind spinning. Was Todd guilty, then? She shuddered but tingled, too, as she hurried toward the demonstrators. Hardy was right, she was hungry.

Fifty-odd chorus members paced outside the jail in the bitter cold, singing *Messiah* choruses and waving signs that read "Free Our Music Man." People stopped to listen as guards on duty rocked their heads to the music.

Piper approached a talkative alto. "Yes, we argue with Todd a lot, and sometimes he disrespects us in a polite way. But I've learned so much from him." It was a common theme in Piper's interviews as she moved through the crowd—the mutual love-hate relationship between the singers and their conductor. And now, when he needed them, they were here, shivering but firm in their loyalty to him.

Would they still support him when they heard about the bloody baton? And how would Nicole cope with being married to an accused murderer? Piper didn't see her in the crowd.

Moss was wrong; the chorus story was still developing, and she would persuade him to hold off running it. She posted a news brief from her car.

None of these New York Luminoso members seem concerned that Maestro Todd Barlow, arrested this morning for the murder of Daphne Paige, might be guilty as charged. Just an irrelevant detail in this impromptu festival of the arts, a midwinter pageant to mark a cold, bloody, and unforgiving December.

43

Detective Knowles entered the pressroom and announced an arrest in the Paige murder case. The suspect, Maestro Todd Barlow, was cooperating with the police. An alleged murder weapon had been recovered from the scene. Further details would be made public at a later date.

Hands waved in the air. What was the murder weapon, where was it found, how did it relate to the suspect?

"I'm not at liberty to say," Knowles answered each time. "This is a sensitive investigation, and we request your cooperation."

"Is there a chance at bail?" Piper called out.

"We'll let you know, and thank you all for coming."

As Knowles left the podium, Piper rushed to ask him about the bloody baton. But no luck; her way was blocked by a horde of reporters shouting questions. How many of them knew about the baton besides her?

Then he was gone, beyond reach behind a door.

Driving back to the city, she phoned Nicole. "You doing okay?"

"Yeah, mostly. I didn't make it to the jail—I was packing to crash with my folks upstate for a while. But then I thought, No way, I'm not leaving. It may sound nuts, but I want to stay and help Todd."

"Oh, I'm glad. I'm here for you, Nicole, whatever you need. Any time night or day, I'll be there."

"Very good to know; thanks, my friend." Nicole choked up and so did Piper, her tears blurring the road.

She was at her desk, writing, when Bell's call came. "I've got the Elgar manuscript and wanted you folks to know. Hope you haven't been too busy looking for it."

"Hunter?" Piper clutched the phone. "Don't you know you're wanted by the police? You stole a valuable manuscript."

"I stole nothing. I happened to drop by the Barlows' before I left for California—being in the neighborhood—and the door was unlocked. No one was home, but I thought I'd do you all a favor by getting a final appraisal of the Elgar. I took it with me to show a guy I know at UCLA."

"Just a minute, please." She reached for a notepad, spilled a cup of coffee, then rummaged through the drippings for a pen. "Okay, you say you 'took' it?"

Bell coughed and cleared his throat. "Yes, to see if he would confirm my opinion, a plan nearly thwarted by our possessive maestro, who wants the manuscript for himself. I was going to leave a note, but my taxi was waiting. A very long, dull story, I'm afraid."

"Yes, a very long story about a very quick theft. You didn't call or email the Barlows to let them know. You traveled to California with the stolen manuscript, and now you've got it with you. But soon the cops will have it."

"How you exaggerate, my dear. If they find me, I'll know who to blame."

"Are you threatening me, Hunter? I'm recording this conversation, so be careful," she bluffed.

"Record all you want, because I've done nothing illegal. A lawyer friend confirmed I own the manuscript by virtue of the letter I mentioned to you, the one Elgar wrote to Aunt Lisha." He paused. "Therefore, I will keep the manuscript, and if I decide to sell it, I alone will manage the proceeds. It's rightly mine."

"What did the expert at UCLA say?" Piper played along.

"The same thing the fools at the auction houses said. They all have their heads up their you-know-where."

"Auction houses?" She wrote fast notes. "And what was their opinion?"

"Just some nonsense about the music not being in Elgar's style. The idiots! It's not in his style because he didn't intend it to be. Still, he wrote it, all right. It's his handwriting, his music paper. Authenticated by others besides me. I will give you their names and phone numbers."

"Save it, Hunter. I'm doing some writing now, talk soon."

She hung up and called Detective Knowles, holding on until his office connected him

"We know the manuscript is in Hunter Bell's possession," she said, describing the phone call.

"Where was he calling from?"

Piper smacked her forehead. "I didn't ask. He sounded so close I assumed he was home."

"You can sound close and be in China."

"That's true." She felt stupid.

"We've got people on his trail. If he calls again, contact me at this number." It was a different number from the one she had called.

Her cell chimed again ten minutes later. "You hung up before you heard my point," Bell said.

She might miss her deadline for the first time ever, but no matter. She hurried to an empty cubicle, grabbed the desk phone, and called the number Knowles had given her. Meanwhile, Bell was talking into her cell, using words like "proof of ownership" and "vast market of private collectors." She tuned him out, waiting for Knowles to pick up.

"What do you say to that?" Bell said, and Piper panicked, having no idea what he had just told her.

"I say you've got a lot of nerve," She figured that covered a lot of bases. Where was Knowles? They had spoken three minutes ago.

"You're going to have a scoop, and I'm going to get rich," Bell said. "But the money won't be mine to squander. I will spend it on a cause you and the Barlows will approve."

"Hello?" Knowles's voice sounded in her other ear.

Piper lifted her cell away from her mouth. "He's on my cell phone now."

"Don't you want to know what the cause is?" Bell said.

"Yes, I do."

"We'll need your permission to ping your phone and locate him," Knowles said over the desk phone.

"Of course. Yes, you have it."

"What do I have?" Bell said.

"A worthy cause, I assume," Piper thought fast.

"We're trying to track him now," Knowles said. "Keep him talking. Put him on speaker."

She pressed the speaker button on the cell and hovered over the desk phone. "What is this cause, Hunter?"

"The Lisha Lovington Fund for Neglected Female Composers. Aunt Lisha was swimming upstream against the tide of male chauvinism, and she finally cracked. She disgraced our family, but I will restore her name."

"How will this 'fund' work?"

"Each year a deserving female candidate will receive twenty thousand dollars to support her work. Talented women will not have to stoop to the tactics Aunt Lisha used to succeed. The awardees will have a cushion in hard times and an endorsement from the music world. Women matter, which I don't have to remind you."

"Where will the money come from?"

"That's where you come in," Bell said. "You're going to publicize the fund in your newspaper, so it will grow from the millions in seed money my manuscript will bring."

"Is that so?" Keep him talking.

"Your articles are syndicated, you know. People are reading about Aunt Lisha's plight in California."

"Whoa, what?" Moss had neglected to tell her this news.

"Are you all right?" Knowles cut in. "Bell is a person of interest in the murder case, so be careful."

"He is?" She gulped. "Yes, fine."

"I'm glad you agree with the plan," Bell said. "Who are you talking to?"

"Just one of the other writers. Look, Hunter. . . . "

"The phone sounds funny. Am I on speaker?"

"No," she quickly said. "My phone is old and sounds weird sometimes. I was saying I need to know what you want us to publish. I must see that letter."

"I will find you and show it to you."

"Bring it to me at *NYN*," she said.

Worcester, Worcestershire

30 April 1899

Dearest Harriet,

Having missed the announcement of Edward's upcoming premiere, I am obliged to you for informing me.

Now I see why I have not heard from him since sending him the *Requiem* on 17 January. He must set his mind on his coming concert and not bother with tricks for my sake. Truly, I am a near stranger to him.

John and I will be in London at the time of the premiere and shall endeavor to attend. I wish Edward well with his new work and will write at once to tell him so. So ends my excitement about our "game." It is no fun when only one is playing. We all must learn to put disappointments behind us.

But on to other news. Leo has a new doctor, and we are hoping for a more promising treatment. The poor boy asks pitifully how long he will have to endure his condition and refuses to be consoled, locking his door and sobbing on his bed. It is no life for a sociable eleven-year-old, and my heart breaks for him.

It's a shame Pattie broke her leg by falling from a tree. Please kiss my sweet niece and say her Aunt Lisha wishes her a speedy recovery. When I see her, I shall applaud her bravery for attempting such a climb at a mere seven years old. Motherhood must be the most taxing of all occupations.

My love,

LL

Worcester, Worcestershire
5 May 1899

DEAR EDWARD,

I wish you much success with the premiere of your new work next month at Royal Albert Hall. My husband will be in London for a medical conference mid-June and I shall accompany him. As good luck would have it, I was able to secure what were possibly the last two tickets to your concert, and I greatly look forward to hearing the new *Enigma Variations*. Its title suggests a clever mystery.

WITH MY SINCEREST GOOD WISHES,

Lisha Lovington

P.S. I now understand why you have not had time to address my *Requiem*. Do not worry about it in the least. I know you will attend to our agreement when your schedule allows.

44

Barlow cried out for her, the wife he had deceived. He did not blame her for staying away—he had neglected her for Daphne. Oh, Daphne. In his cold and lonely cell, he reflected on the truth. Daphne made you feel loved, but she didn't love you. She loved the idea of you, the idea of men. She tried to tell him that during the intermission, but he was too deeply wounded to hear. He fled to stop her terrible words.

An apology, she called it. A mission to apologize to all the men she had hurt.

All the men. He saw fields of them, stretching from horizon to horizon. Men she had let touch her, possess her, too many men to apologize to in one lifetime. How did she have the time, with a job and a dependent mother, and a dream of a solo career? He'd nurtured that dream, but she had been cruel.

Late afternoon, Nelson appeared. "You're getting bail. Those folks demonstrating had something to do with it."

"What folks?"

The lawyer raised his eyebrows. "You don't know? Anyway, it's a mixed blessing. Unless you have a rich relative, forget about it."

"How much?"

"Eight hundred thou."

He blinked. He could not ask his in-laws. Not after what he had done.

Nicole arrived, her eyelids puffy. "I believe you're innocent," she told him. "You could never kill someone."

"I hope you're right." His hand shot to his forehead with the rubbing habit she hated.

"Stop rubbing, dammit!" As though it was his worst offense. "You need to look presentable. I'll bring acne cream next time. I'll bring anti-itch cream. Just stop it."

"Okay, I stopped, see?" He put two hands in the air.

She sighed. "Better." She moved closer to the partition. "It's time you tell me what happened, Todd. Tell me everything, and don't hold back because you think you'll hurt my feelings. Just talk to me the way we used to talk, and I'll try to help."

He stared at her serious face, her knotted brows. She cared, and that gave him hope. "I was down in the Dungeon with Daphne." He cringed at his confession. "She said something and—I got the hell out of there. I was raging mad, I admit it. Raging like an animal." He wiped his brow on his sleeve. "Maybe I did something to her. That Knowles fellow, he thinks I did, and my baton doesn't help. You know about that?"

"No, what about your baton?"

"It has Daphne's blood on it. I saw pictures."

"Not good." She looked thoughtful. "But it doesn't mean you did it."

"Deep down I don't think I could have done it. You know me, I even catch moths in a jar to take them outside. Same with spiders, and...."

Nicole rolled her eyes. "Yeah, and the ones you don't catch I've got to kill. What did she—Daphne—say that got you so mad?"

"I...I don't remember all of it." He cringed again. "But it showed me I was wrong about her."

Nicole pursed her lips. "You know, every human being has the potential to kill. I thought you did it, Todd, even though I told Knowles you didn't. That's why I was going to leave town. I couldn't stand being home, looking at the furniture you touched. But then I started thinking about it. Something is off, but I can't say exactly what."

Tears came to his eyes. "Thanks for being on my side, Nic. I love you, I always have, but you're one tough...."

"Bitch?" She laughed. "I wear the title proudly. What's new here?"

"I've got to come up with eight hundred thou. For bail."

She rolled her eyes. "Daddy's going to hate this."

"What?" His heart leaped to his throat. "You'll ask him?"

"What do you think, I'm going to let you rot in jail? Daddy will get you out. Mother won't stop him, but she could if she wanted."

He pumped his fists. "That's great, Nicole! We can make music again!"

"Yeah, I've got too much invested in our programs to see them flushed down the toilet."

Their visit would end in five minutes. "I've got something else to tell you," Nicole said. "We know where the so-called Elgar manuscript is."

"Oh, thank heavens. Where?"

"Bell took it and won't give it back. He says he owns it."

"But it's ours! I mean, yours."

"Yes, he stole it and we'll file charges. What will your bail restrictions be?'

"I don't know."

"Talk to Nelson. See if they'll let you conduct chorus rehearsals. Any bastards that won't sing with you can go to hell. We've got work to do." Her face softened. "We've got a woman depending on us, Todd. Yeah, she's an ancient dead woman, but I want to see this through. Will you back me up on that?"

"Oh, I get it now." He raised his voice. "I've got to say the *Requiem* is by Lovington to get your daddy's bail money."

"Don't be an ass," Nicole hissed, as the guard eyed them. "There are no strings to the bail money. I'm not demanding you make my case for the Lovington *Requiem*. It would just be easier if we were both on the same side."

His heart thudded in his chest. Maybe he would have a heart attack and die. He slumped in his seat, expecting the worst. Nicole waited, unmoving.

"Good, you're calming down," she said.

All at once he was exhausted. "Sorry about the tantrum." He rested his head on his arms.

"You've been through a lot, Todd. It's made you half crazy." Her voice reminded him of his mother when he was sick as a kid. Kind and patient. Bringing him buttered toast and letting him sleep it off.

"Are you really that sure about Lovington?" he mumbled into his arm.

"One hundred percent."

"Why?"

"Because the Elgar manuscript is fishy."

He lifted his head and saw her dreamy look. "I can feel Lisha in the music, Todd. I can see her composing at the kitchen table with children tugging at her skirt. It's a struggle, but after months or years she's done it. Her major opus is complete."

"What happened to it afterward?" he said. "Why would the *Requiem* disappear for a century, then turn up in an attic? Did Lovington compose after that? What facts do you have?"

"She composed small pieces, Todd. She took five steps backward and began writing children's songs again. Not that there's anything wrong with children's songs, but she didn't move on to oratorios, though she had the talent."

Barlow's hand flew to his forehead, but he caught it in time. "That's a real shame."

"Damn right it is."

"I will reconsider my opinion. But I need to think it over without you pressuring me."

"All right."

They sat quietly until the five-minute signal. "Before you go, I want to ask for your forgiveness," he said. "For what I've done in the past, and for whatever stupid things I might do in the future. Will you forgive me?"

"I'm trying to forgive you, Todd. You thought I didn't know about that woman. Or care."

"I'm going to make it up to you. There's no one like you, Nicole. I'll be a better man, a better husband, if you'll take me back."

A smile played on her lips. "You won't screw around anymore? You'll keep your dick in your pants?"

He reddened. "The thought of sex makes me sick, Nicole."

Her laugh rang through the sterile visiting room. "How exciting! All work and no sex. Let's get cracking."

45

"Don't judge by appearances, Matt. Take a guy like Barlow—a softie, worried he might have killed his girlfriend. Not the murderer type."

"Yeah. I read the transcript, sir." Daniels, stopping by Knowles's office, looked thoughtful. "He didn't try to hide it or deny he did it. You think he's a sociopath?"

Knowles shook his head. "I don't know, Matt. What if it was a bizarre accident?" He leaned back on his old leather office couch. "What if Barlow took his baton to the bathroom for no particular reason. My mother told us about a radio program from her childhood where a guy carried the trash to his office instead of throwing it out. Absent-minded, you know? Could be Barlow took his stick to the john and forgot it there."

"Right. And the killer picked it up. But we've established that's ridiculous, sir."

"Indeed. Premeditated homicide by music baton is absurd."

Daniels continued on his way, leaving Knowles alone to mull things over. He was about to go for coffee when his phone rang.

"Detective Knowles? Piper Morgan here, following up. I tried to speak to you at the press conference but you left quickly."

He smiled, expecting a few pleasant moments. "Ah, Ms. Morgan, sorry about that. On a separate matter, we've looked into our friend Bell. Interpol has no record of art theft on him, and neither does the FBI. We're still investigating him, as we are other individuals."

"I see. He has no criminal record at all?"

"None. Unfortunately, we failed to locate him through his cell phone this morning. Did he say he flew somewhere?"

"He said he'd been in California."

"He may have deliberately turned off GPS." Knowles was talking to a reporter longer than usual.

"Detective, Bell says he couldn't have stolen the Elgar manuscript because it belongs to him. He says a letter he owns proves that. Will you still arrest him for theft?"

"That depends on whether the Barlows file a complaint. We're watching his New York residence and may need you to contact him again."

She offered to do whatever she could to help recover the manuscript. "Regarding the Paige murder, Detective, I have reason to believe you have Todd Barlow's baton with Daphne Paige's blood on it. Can you confirm that on the record, please?"

A bolt of anxiety shot through Knowles. Who the hell was leaking? "Where did you hear that?" His own voice was sharp in his ears.

"Uh, from someone who is usually accurate."

"No, I can't confirm it on or off the record, Ms. Morgan. You'll have to wait on that score like everyone else."

He'd give the ambitious Ms. Morgan a scoop one day. After she'd learned some tact.

46

VICKI CALLED with a bombshell. "Todd was jealous of Daphne's relationship with Griffin and killed her for it."

"What?" Piper said. "Who says?"

"Griffin, and I believe him."

"You told me Griffin was the killer," Piper said impatiently. She was off to an emergency chorus meeting and had no time for Vicki's new theory.

"I was wrong."

"But you were so sure." Piper drummed her irritation on the steering wheel. "You even reported him to Detective Knowles. What new information do you have?"

"I just believe Griffin, that's all." Vicki's voice was cold. "Even though you tried to poison me against him."

Piper saw where this was leading. "I deny that, but let me call you later. It might be tomorrow because I've got a meeting tonight. After that I'll be with Theo."

"Yeah, rub it in. You being a couple and me being single."

"Stop. I'm hanging up."

"Wait!" Vicki yelled. "I was kidding and it came out wrong. Here's what I wanted to say. Griffin says both he and Todd were Daphne's victims. It was a sick bond, but Griffin pulled away and Todd never could. He thought he was the only man in Daphne's life. So, he killed her in a jealous rage when he found out the truth, that he was one of many and Griffin was there first."

The scenario was plausible.

"I'll be at the chorus meeting, too," Vicki said, "for the sake of my work. But we can't talk there." She sounded more like her old self. "So have a good night and lots of great sex, but don't tell me about it, okay, Piper?"

As if she ever would.

* * *

Diva Daley was presiding at the podium. "We've got to take the long view, in case Todd's not acquitted. I'm heading the search for someone superqualified to take over."

The place was half-full, but Corinne Kelsey was there, an odd person with a lot of grievances. "Some of us members are qualified to conduct, but nobody even considers us," she said in a bitter tone. She was dressed in sweats like an athletic coach, and Piper thought she would like Corinne better if she did coach kids. So far, every attempt to interview her had failed.

"Are you referring to yourself?" Diva said.

"Well, I am a trained musician." Corinne thrust out her chin. "I've played the piano since childhood. If anyone can negotiate a score, I can." She crossed her arms over her chest. "I cannot comprehend why some of us are routinely overlooked, just because we are not the shiny object of the week."

"Shiny object?" Diva twirled her jeweled pen. "I thought our shining object was good music and great singing."

Corinne's face turned red. "Don't we want a sub until the situation is resolved? I can do that. It would save us money."

Not a bad idea, but she's a loose cannon, Piper jotted in her notepad. Nicole had told her confidentially about Corinne's threatening letter and midnight invasion; if she harassed the Barlows any further, they would press charges and Piper could write about it.

"My friend Corinne has a point," Zandy Stewart said. "She can lead us for a week or two. Then, if God forbid Todd is convicted, we can hire someone new."

Griffin Sharp stood. "Let's not waste time, people. The board has voted to line up a pro in case Todd doesn't return. Two candidates will try out at the next rehearsal. So, with all due respect, Corinne, let's get on with it."

Corinne, fuming, stormed out.

"I'll make sure she's okay," Zandy said, running after her.

Piper raised her hand. "Diva, will you be asking for views about Elgar vs. Lovington?" She was glad to see Diva looking healthy.

"Yeah, will we get a chance to weigh in?" It was Riley Webb, sitting next to Vicki and Griff.

ANGELS' BLOOD | 227

"A lot of us are trained musically," a soprano said. "A chorus committee can look at the score and offer an opinion. It will give us something constructive to do."

Nixon Fox, who had found his speaking voice since Daphne's death, raised his hand. "Diva, I think the chorus should get involved, and maybe Piper here could write about us singers for a change." He turned to her. "Weren't you supposed to write a feature about New York Luminoso? You got sidetracked, don't you think?"

All eyes turned toward Piper. "It's true, I did get sidetracked," she said. "But I promise an article will run soon."

Griffin hopped up to join Diva on the podium, as Vicki watched him adoringly. Could Vicki have killed Daphne? She had a motive—jealousy. How long was she offstage on *Messiah* night? She said she went downstairs to follow Griffin, but did she stay there when he returned to the stage?

Piper tried to remember. She had not seen Vicki after intermission, nor was Vicki among the audience members the police interviewed. The reason she didn't consult Vicki for the news brief was Vicki wasn't there.

She could have committed the murder and fled.

Piper's stomach was in a knot. Vicki had acted so irrationally lately, first implicating Griff in the murder and now Todd. Was she covering up her own act of rage?

Griff spoke from the podium. "There's something constructive you can do, folks. Study your scores like crazy over the weekend. It doesn't matter who the real composer is. Let's amaze the two candidates Monday night so they'll beg to conduct us."

Piper had another sickening thought. What if Vicki and Griffin murdered Daphne together? Those two could be a present-day Bonnie and Clyde. Vicki had crossed a boundary when she cozied up with the married Griffin. She was beyond reason. There was no telling what she might have persuaded him to do.

Worcester, Worcestershire

20 June 1899

My dear Edward,

*E*nigma Variations continues to play in my mind, reminding me that art can penetrate a heart as easily as lightning cleaves a tree.

It was my pleasure to attend the premiere with my husband, John, whom you may recall from Vanessa's salon in March. John, too, was deeply moved. We were especially taken with the beautiful "Nimrod" movement.

Edward, you have inspired me to aim higher still with my own music, and for that I thank you.

With warmest admiration,
affection, and congratulations,

Lisha Lovington

47

Vicki screamed into Piper's phone at 6:00 a.m. "Griffin, he...." She began to sob.

Piper sat up in bed, her heart pounding. "What about him? Did he hurt you?"

"No! He's dead!" Vicki gasped. "He had a heart attack."

"Oh my God." Piper clutched the phone. How could Griff die? He was so young and vital, and he looked fine last night.

"I can't live without him, Piper. What am I going to do?"

Piper thought of the beautiful way Griff sang *Messiah* with her. "Did he have heart trouble before this?"

"No. He's so strong. I don't understand."

"Was he on drugs?"

"Absolutely not. Griffin hated drugs. He wanted to maintain a pure mind."

That sounded like Griff. "How do you know what happened? Did Clayton call you?"

"No, I... I went to see him earlier this morning," Vicki gave a long shudder. "Don't scold, Piper, I had to see him. But Clayton wouldn't let me past the door. He just yelled Griffin was dead of a heart attack and I caused it." Anger flared in her voice. "He said Griffin was at the morgue and I could see him there."

"How cold! What time was that?" She asked by habit, as though it mattered.

"Half an hour ago."

Piper pictured it—Vicki leaving home in the cold, dark morning to speak to Griff, presumably still in bed with his husband. Not only had she lost her bearings, something else was off. If Clayton had not let her in, how did she know for sure Griff was dead? Unless she killed him.

She fought off an urge to scream. "Where are you now?"

"In my car, driving around. I'm in a daze."

"You shouldn't be driving. Meet me at *NYN*. We can talk over coffee at Captions."

"No. I'm going to be with Griff. Goodbye."

A call to the morgue confirmed Griffin Sharp was deceased, cause of death pending. The death would be termed suspicious, of course. Griff had at least one underlying condition—he was the ex-boyfriend of the murdered Daphne Paige.

That made two unexpected chorus deaths in nine days. Piper had joined the chorus nine days ago. Had she caused these people to die? She felt numb, but her heart kept pounding.

48

BEN NELSON HAD ARRANGED an early-morning meeting for the Barlows, held in a private jail room with the cameras turned off. Todd Barlow savored the touch of freedom and was eager for a bigger taste.

"Who has the Elgar manuscript now?" Nelson was saying.

"That wretch Bell has it," Nicole said. "But we're going to accuse him of theft, and the police will get it back. Piper said Knowles got the FBI and Interpol involved."

She spoke with her usual confidence, sitting in the narrow chair with her perfect posture and precise lipstick. She's as cool as I am jittery, Barlow thought, admiring his wife.

"On the other hand, what if Bell really does own the manuscript?" Nicole tapped her chin. "Could he sue us for performing it, or slap us with a horrendous fee?"

"That's complicated and not my area," Nelson said. "A work that old is not subject to copyright, but there are separate laws about the physical manuscript. You'll have to ask someone more qualified."

Barlow felt a twist in his gut. "But if it's a Lovington we don't have that problem, right, Ben?"

"As I said, it's not my area, so you might want to wait and see."

Barlow groaned at this new roadblock. He turned to his wife. "Nicole, I've been wanting to ask you this. Why did you show the Elgar manuscript to Bell in the first place? I mean, what was he doing in our house that day?"

Nicole glanced at the lawyer, as if the question were too private to answer in his presence. Barlow cringed, convinced his suspicions were warranted. While he sneaked around with Daphne, Nicole and Bell had an affair.

"Hunter came for a ride to the *Messiah* dress rehearsal, Todd. He lived in the city, remember? Took a taxi to our house from the train station? He happened to walk in just after I found the Elgar manuscript. You don't honestly think there was something illicit going on between us. That man is revolting."

Barlow decided to believe her. He felt a surge of elation. "Nicole, I've made a decision. For my bail project I'll compare the *Requiem* with Elgar's other works. If I don't find the evidence to convince me he wrote it, l will consider performing it as a Lovington."

He saw her eye roll. "Okay, in that case I would *definitely* perform it as a Lovington."

Nicole exhaled with relief, and Nelson smiled at them approvingly.

An unspoken question troubled Barlow. What if he were convicted of murder? Then all the music would stop, along with everything else he cared about.

Nicole touched his arm. "Don't look so dejected, Todd. I'll help you with your Elgar project."

He brightened. "You will?"

"Sure. I'll bring you scores to analyze."

He felt a surge of love for her, the wife he did not deserve.

Nelson clapped his hands with joy. "It's great when couples cooperate, Now, Nicole, I need some time alone with your husband. Do you mind?"

"Not at all. I just remembered an appointment."

"At seven a.m.?" Barlow said, but Nelson gestured to let her go.

"Now we'll do an experiment," Nelson said when they were alone. "Do you remember anything more about concert night?"

"Yes." Barlow focused his mind. "Sometimes I hear Daphne calling to me. When I look, she's holding something. That's a new memory."

"Do you see what she's holding?"

"No."

Nelson moved his chair closer. "Todd, as I mentioned, I've studied hypnotism. I knew it would come in handy someday. This is the day."

"It'll never work on me," Barlow said.

"We'll use an extra ingredient—music. I have permission to play it here. Now, please close your eyes and open them when I say so."

"Come on, Ben, why?"

"Just do it," Nelson said, and Barlow shut his eyes.

Nelson placed his cell phone on an end table. "Okay, we're ready to start. Sit comfortably and breathe deeply. Don't speak unless I tell you to, and try to keep your mind clear. Do you understand?"

Barlow nodded, and Nelson spoke softly to him for what felt like a long time.

There was a clicking sound, and choral music filled the room.

"Oh, that's. . . . "

"You were not told to speak. Now, Todd, what is the name of this music?"

"*Messiah*, by George Frideric Handel."

"What part of *Messiah* are we hearing right now?"

"The last chorus before intermission. 'His Yoke Is Easy, and His Burthen Is Light.'"

"We are onstage at the Anderson Performing Arts Center. The first half of the concert is coming to an end. How do you feel when you hear this music, Todd?"

"Light. And happy."

"Happy about what?"

"The concert is going well. And Daphne wants to see me."

"When?"

"During intermission. She put a note in my pocket."

"And when does intermission start?"

"When this chorus is over."

"All right, it's over now." Nelson turned the music off. "Where are you going?"

"To a utility room in the Dungeon."

"Why?"

"Daphne will be there."

"How do you know?"

"It was in the note she gave me. It said, 'Be careful on the stairs.'"

"What will you do in the utility room?"

"We will have a quickie."

"Are you going there right away?"

Barlow shook his head. "No, I must wait. No one can see us together."

"You've waited. Now, are you walking or running?"

"Running. So happy."

"Is Daphne waiting for you there?"

Todd frowned. "Yes. But not smiling. Not happy. Her clothes are buttoned up."

"What does she say, Todd?"

"She says, 'Why did you bring your baton?' She's angry."

"What do you do?"

"I put the baton on the floor. 'I didn't mean to bring it,' I say. I go to hug her."

"What does she do?"

"She pushes me away. 'Stop,' she says. 'I've got something to tell you.'"

Nelson turned the music back on, and Barlow lifted his arms to conduct.

"Give me your attention, Todd. What do you think Daphne is going to say?"

Barlow swayed to the music. "That she's pregnant. 'Are you pregnant?' I say, and she laughs. 'No, but that would make this easier,' she says."

"Go on." Nelson lowered the volume of the music.

"She says, 'I see other men, and women, too. You're not the only one, and I don't love you. I don't love you, Todd. I'm sorry for lying to you. I apologize.'"

"What do you do then?" The lawyer's voice rose above the choral singing.

"I run up the stairs, trip, almost fall backward. I'm so sad."

"Does Daphne call after you?"

"Yes! She's at the bottom of the stairs. She says, 'Don't forget your baton!' She has my baton, and she's walking up the stairs to give it to me."

"Do you meet her halfway and take the baton from her?"

"No, I keep going up, I'm late."

"Are you angry at her, Todd? About what she told you? Angry enough to kill her?"

"No, not angry, sad. Crying."

"Do you turn around and stab her with something sharp?"

"No."

"A knife hidden in your white tie and tails, perhaps? Or your baton?" The lawyer's voice was feathery soft.

"No."

"Do you push her down the stairs, Todd? Do you push her really, really hard?"

"No, of course not," Barlow said in a normal voice. "I have to hurry back to conduct the second half."

"Open your eyes, Todd."

Barlow opened his eyes. "I never touched her once that night." Nelson turned off the music. "Todd Barlow, you did not kill Daphne Paige. Now we have to convince a jury."

Waiting to be released on bail, Barlow pondered his life. Who was he? Not a killer, that veil was lifted, but a maestro without his musicians, a conductor without his music. He missed his singers, and he loved them. He could not wait to see them again, to thank them. What a lucky man he was.

When he got home, he learned of the new tragedy. Griffin Sharp dead of natural causes. The death reminded him of Daphne, and it struck him Corinne Kelsey might have killed her.

Nicole laughed at this theory. "Just like a man to think a woman will kill for you," she said, rolling her eyes. "I've thought it over, and she's not the murderer."

"Then who is?" he said later that night.

"Someone else. Maybe Hunter."

Barlow snorted. "Hunter Bell? Come on, I don't like him—in fact, I detest him—but I don't see him killing anyone. He's too highbrow."

"But not too highbrow to steal."

"He took the manuscript for evaluation."

"He stole it."

Now they were in bed, where a tentative hug turned into a real one. Barlow all but crushed his wife in his arms, and she did not pull away.

49

AT 5:00 P.M., Moss poked his head into Piper's cubicle. "I've got an assignment for you, Piperino, and you've gotta hurry."

He had nixed a news brief on Griff's death, pending more information. It was chilling that the world kept going as though a person had never lived. But people cared—tributes to Griff were posted on social media and the chorus website, texts and emails lamented his death, and the public was invited to his wake tomorrow.

Piper was not ready to mourn. She needed information. Did Griff die from natural causes or foul play? Were the two chorus deaths related or coincidental? If related, who hated Daphne and Griff enough to kill them both?

She could think of a few people.

She sighed. "Where am I going, Moss?" She and Theo were meeting for dinner, where she planned to pick his brain about sudden heart attacks. He had studied medicine before switching to orthodontia—better hours, or so he had thought.

"Some group's throwing a wingding at the Anderson Center." Moss raised his graying eyebrows. "It's up your alley—five current women composers, some kind of special occasion."

"Five female composers, Moss."

"Whatever, it starts at six, so just get over there. Take a break from all the drama and have some fun." He took off down the hall.

"Are you going to send a photog, Moss?" she yelled, catching up with him at the elevator.

"Damn, I forgot," he said, as they rode down. "Grab some pics with your phone cam, would you? And ask for P.R. pics of the gals. Bye, I'm late for the wife!"

Piper considered inviting Theo to come, but he disliked contemporary music. He would fidget and complain. "Can we switch dinner to tomorrow?" she said, calling him from the car. "Moss threw me a last-minute assignment."

"An assignment about the murder?" His voice had an edge.

"No, it's about female composers—living ones." She hesitated.

"Did you hear about Griffin Sharp, the chorus member who died this morning?"

"Nope, been working since seven. Sorry to hear that."

"He was a young guy, supposedly had a heart attack. There's no sign of foul play."

"Then why say 'supposedly'?"

"Because I'm a reporter," Piper said, "and we need to see for ourselves."

"My skeptical sweetheart. Okay, then, enjoy the concert. I'll warm up the bed for you."

The lobby buzzed with attractive people sipping wine. Piper was glad she had dressed for dinner in a blue velvet blazer instead of her usual jeans and scuffed boots. It was an unfamiliar crowd, but there was Detective Knowles, looking suave in a beige turtleneck and black pants. He was sipping champagne with a dazzling woman. Maybe the velvet blazer would divert him from his sexy date, and he would talk to her about Griff.

"Detective, how nice to see you." Piper managed a smile.

"Well, if it isn't reporter Piper Morgan." Knowles returned the smile. "Ms. Morgan, meet my wife, Midge Mitchell Knowles."

"Oh, how nice to meet your wife." Piper extended her hand, which Midge gave a warm shake. The woman was a knockout in her low-cut red sweater, black leather skirt, and strappy black stiletto heels that lifted her to her husband's chin.

"Are you both fans of classical music?" Piper said.

"Lucas is a major music buff. He likes to try new things; don't you, Lucas?" Midge's teasing tone suggested more than music.

"My wife is into choral music. Tell her, Midge."

"That's right. I want to audition for that chorus you sing with. I've got a couple of lady friends who want to try out with me."

"That would be great," Piper said. "The chorus is aiming for more diversity."

Knowles and Midge exchanged glances. "For show or for real?" Midge said.

"I sense they're sincere, Midge, but I get your point. Let me email you the details. What's your address?"

Knowles stepped forward. "I'll take care of it. In fact, Ms. Morgan, we should connect before the music starts. Midge, will you excuse us?"

"Sure thing, Lucas. See you in there."

Piper reached for her notepad, expecting details about Griff.

"I tried to leave my wife home, but she insisted on coming." Knowles spoke quietly. "We've got word Hunter Bell may be here. I don't expect serious trouble, but we'll be looking to take him in."

"Wow." She had forgotten about Bell. "But is Griffin Sharp's death suspicious, Detective?"

"One thing at a time, Ms. Morgan. We consider Bell unstable, so stay alert."

Piper felt a chill. "You really think he's dangerous?"

"That is our assumption, or we wouldn't be here."

A gong sounded, and Piper and Knowles headed separately to the center's smallest theater, the Jewel Box. Scanning the theater for Bell, Piper nearly bumped into Corinne Kelsey in a cocktail dress. Piper greeted her, but Corinne moved on with glazed eyes, as though she had stumbled into the wrong event.

Piper edged toward her press seat, passing the names of female composers taped to each aisle seat. Women from the past: Hildegard of Bingen, Barbara Strozzi, Marianna Martines. And ten women who had won the Pulitzer Prize for music since 1983: Ellen Taaffe Zwilich, Shulamit Ran, Melinda Wagner, Jennifer Higdon, Caroline Shaw, Julia Wolfe, Du Yun, Ellen Reid, Tania León, and Rhiannon Giddens.

In her seat, she tried to relax. Why would Bell come tonight, knowing the police were looking for him? And how could she sit listening to music while Griff lay in the morgue?

She would be professional and focus on the program. The list of works ranged from atonal to melodic, jazzy to ethereal. Each composer could boast an impressive number of performances. Yet, shamefully, their compositions were packaged as a group, as though none could hold up on their own.

A male moderator led a talk-back before the intermission. "If you closed your eyes, could you tell whether a man or woman wrote the music you just heard?"

The largely female audience booed, and the composers, seated in a semicircle onstage, spoke their minds.

"We always hear that."

"No one asks that about music written by men."

"Music isn't male or female—it's just music."

"I dare you to explain the difference."

Piper stood up. "Excuse me, but why ask that question? Each of these fabulous works can be discussed from much more interesting angles, and we would all learn something."

The moderator gave a rote answer, and intermission began.

A hand touched Piper's back, and she turned to see Bell's sweating face. "Come to the lobby," he whispered. His breath was hot on her neck as he leaned forward. He looked unwell, his complexion greenish-white, though he was dressed impeccably in a navy blazer.

"Come now, while there's time." He motioned her toward the exit, where Knowles and Midge were on their way out.

She followed Bell at a distance, curious to know what he wanted. Thank goodness Knowles had his eye on him and would protect her.

But Knowles was not in the lobby, nor was his wife. Maybe a child was sick and they had gone home. Piper felt a sudden loneliness, adrift in unfamiliar waters with only her instincts to guide her. She felt—not exactly fear, but concern that things with Bell would go wrong, and she would be blamed.

He was waiting for her behind a tall, wide-leafed plant. It was a ludicrous attempt at camouflage, and she laughed. "I'm surprised to see you here, Hunter. A wanted man in public like this."

He gave a dismissive wave. "That's ridiculous; I have no reason to hide. I figured you'd be here, so I brought something to show you."

He took a small cream-colored envelope from his blazer pocket. "This is the family heirloom I told you about."

The letter. The envelope looked genuine with its faded blue ink, grayed edges, and old stamps—the kind collectors loved.

"May I see it?" Piper reached out, and Bell slapped her hand, hard.

"Ow! Why did you do that?"

"Because you are rude and impatient." He pressed the envelope to his chest, no longer the suave lecturer with insights about women, but someone who might be dangerous. She rubbed her hand, feeling the first shiver of fear.

"I know you want to see this letter, and I want you to see it." He dangled it in front of her. "But first you must promise to publish every word of it in the *New York News*."

"But—"

He held up a warning finger. "You will publish this so the world will know how Edward Elgar offered my great-great-grand-aunt a stage, but not even his generous influence could bring her a lasting success."

Piper shook her head. "I'm not the publisher, and I can't make such promises."

"Nonsense," he said, his voice hoarse. "You are a star reporter and can do whatever you wish. You must also agree to write the following words, which I will dictate."

He cleared his throat, closed his eyes, and spoke in the velvety tones that had charmed the chorus women. "The *Requiem* was certifiably composed by Edward Elgar, no matter what others might say. Mr. Hunter Bell is accepting bids on this virgin Elgar masterpiece and can be reached via the New York Luminoso Chorus. After the May premiere of this historic piece, the price will rise significantly." He opened his eyes. "You supply the address, Ms. Morgan."

Instinct told Piper to flee. Bell had undergone a personality change, and there was no telling what he might do. She turned to go, but he grabbed her wrist. "Wait, I am not finished speaking." He leaned close, his breath sour.

"Women are often deluded about their talents, as was the case with Aunt Lisha," he said in his lecturer tone. "Upton was not wrong, you see. The women composers we're hearing tonight are deluded, too. Their talent is mediocre to nonexistent. They are riding the waves of good intentions and wishful thinking."

Women composers? Defending the misogynist Upton? Bell was no feminist. It was all an act. Only the letter buried in his pocket was presumably real. Publishing it could be a good thing, without his addendum. She would write about this confrontation instead, and *NYN* would deal with any backlash.

"Don't look so sad, Ms. Morgan," Bell said, misreading her expresssion. "When you publish my letter, I shall be fulfilled and you will be famous." His eyes narrowed. "But you must do it tonight."

The lobby lights flashed. "I told you I can't guarantee it will be published." She kept her voice level. "I'm returning to my seat now because I'm on assignment here. But first let me read your letter, so I can see what you want us to publish." She extended her hand again.

With a quick motion, Bell pressed something hard and cold into her rib cage. "Don't stall. Agree to my demands, or you will feel severe pain."

Piper calculated what to do. People were passing by, returning to their seats. She and Bell might look like lovers as they stood face-to-face. No one would guess he was shoving a gun—or what felt like a gun—against her delicate organs. Where was Knowles? She needed him now. She must do something before the lobby emptied out, leaving her alone with Bell.

"Detective Knowles!" she screamed, gambling that he was nearby. "I'm here with Hunter Bell, the man who stole the second *Requiem* manuscript. He has a gun. Please help me!"

Startled audience members hurried past, some staring as if they'd stumbled onto a bit of performance art.

Bell pressed the gun harder into her ribs. "You're bluffing, you bitch. There's no detective here. Scream all you want."

"Help me, Detective!" Piper waited for a blast and oblivion.

Seconds that felt like hours later, three burly men in plain clothes surrounded Bell. Knowles spoke from behind the men, his distinctive voice resounding through the lobby. "Let her go."

Piper froze as fear gripped her body. "Please, he might shoot me." She hoped none of these men would do anything stupid.

One of them shoved Bell to the floor, while Knowles pinned his hands behind his back and searched for weapons. "Handgun." He passed the gun to the team. "Arrest him."

An arm encircled Piper's waist—it was Midge Knowles, leading her away from the scene. "My husband may look slight, but he's all muscle," she said, a take-charge woman with a soft voice. Piper moved numbly along, then stopped cold.

Bell's letter was on the floor. It must have flown from his hands when he was knocked down. She broke away from Midge and pounced on it.

"What's that, honey? Something of yours he was trying to steal?"

It was an insert from the concert program. "No, it's nothing," she said, her eyes tearing in disappointment. "Your husband must have what I'm looking for."

50

GRIFFIN SHARP'S DEATH required an autopsy, over his husband's objections. Knowles disliked going against the wishes of a grieving spouse, but Sharp had been in excellent health with no issues but an allergy to shellfish. An autopsy was necessary to rule out foul play. Knowles pondered the term. *Foul play* was quaint and bloodless, better suited to a rugby game than a homicide investigation. "Murder most foul," he muttered as he drove Midge home from the concert hall.

"What's that, Lucas? I'd say you prevented that journalist's murder tonight."

"Just thinking, baby." He had not told her about the second chorus death, because she did not need to know.

"You think that well-dressed man would have shot Piper Morgan if you weren't there?"

"I must assume yes." He glanced at her serious profile as he braked for a red light.

"Then thank goodness you were." She squeezed his free right hand, the one she always complained should be on the wheel.

After dropping Midge at home, he drove above the speed limit to the station. The autopsy should be nearly over by now.

"Heard we lost a maestro and gained a musicologist." Daniels met Knowles in the hall. "The guys say the musicologist was babbling about some letter."

Knowles smiled at his assistant's enthusiasm. "We're not rushing to reassure Mr. Bell that his precious letter is safe, Matt."

"Check. Have you read it, sir?"

"Not yet, but I'll fill you in after I do. That reminds me, there's someone else who should know it's safe."

Piper Morgan had nearly lost her life tonight for the sake of an old piece of paper. He would call her tomorrow with the gist of the letter they had confiscated from Bell, then give her an exclusive on whatever the autopsy report said. Two gifts for a brave young woman he had come to admire.

In truth, the letter baffled him. It was not just old; it was a puzzle beyond a detective's expertise. Moreover, he did not see the big deal, as it was signed by a composer unknown to the average person. "Edgar *who?*" Midge would say.

He himself knew Edward Elgar from *The Music Makers*, a choral beauty, and the *Cello Concerto*, which he preferred to *Enigma Variations* by a mile. More soul and less pomp, was how he compared them, except for the "Nimrod" section of *Enigma*, but don't get him started on that dazzler.

Music was Knowles's safe haven. But with two musicians dead and two others arrested in the past ten days, he was obliged to drag it into the fray.

"He's a fancy-looking dude," Daniels said the next morning, as they watched Bell through the glass. "Surprising he'd wind up here."

"Nah, anyone can wind up here, Matt. We let him catch himself to find out what he's after."

"Money," Daniels said with a knowing shrug. "Watch and see. It's always money at the bottom of it."

Knowles smiled at how young and sure of himself Daniels was. Probably never lost more than five minutes' sleep over anything, but time would change that.

Before entering the interrogation room, he ordered a shoeprint analysis, as he did with everyone now. Then he turned to Daniels. "You know, Matt, except for Bell's letter being sent from the same composer whose name is on the mystery manuscript; and the mystery manuscript being the same one Bell saw in Nicole Jennings-Barlow's closet the day of the murder; and Nicole Jennings-Barlow resembling the murder victim; and her husband being the guy who was going to premiere the mystery manuscript music with his chorus; and Daphne Paige, Barlow's lover, being a member of that chorus, I don't see a big connection to her murder."

Daniels let out a guffaw. "Where does Griffin Sharp fit in?"

"I don't know, but we'll find out."

As they entered the Interrogation Room, Bell waved his hand to get on with it, as if Knowles were his servant. Racist son of a bitch? Knowles was not one to make such assumptions. The man was cornered, and cornered people were not unlike wild animals, giving it their best snarl. Animals, as far as he knew, were not racist.

Well, let the pompous fellow snarl away. Daniels completed the check-in routine, and Knowles began. "Mr. Bell, I don't know why you waived your right to have a lawyer present here, but let us proceed."

"I waived it, sir, because I expect you to release me."

"You committed crimes nonetheless. Holding a young woman at gunpoint last night, breaking into the Barlows' home, and stealing a valuable music manuscript. Do you have anything to say?"

"The door was unlocked," Bell said in a smug tone.

"You also made several telephone inquiries at American and European auction houses, hoping to sell something that was not yours. We have ample proof against you, in case you try to deny it."

Knowles felt Bell looking down his nose at him, a familiar sensation from his childhood in a mostly white town. He knew how to contain his rage, but this pompous jerk could make it boil over. Daniels, aware of this, hand-signaled Knowles to stay cool.

Knowles hand-signaled back that he would. Then Bell defused the tension by saying something absurd.

"I couldn't have stolen the manuscript you're referring to, because I own it."

"That so?" Knowles cocked his head. "How do you figure that? To the best of my knowledge, Ms. Nicole Jennings-Barlow owns it."

"History will bear me out, sir. As soon as my letter is returned to me, I will clearly show why the manuscript is rightfully mine." Bell pointed his chin in the air. "I suspect that reporter stole the letter from me. It disappeared last night after your nasty crew manhandled me."

"We have your letter in safekeeping, Mr. Bell. But a man of your erudition should know that threatening someone with a gun has criminal consequences."

"I would never pull the trigger," Bell said with a look of distaste. "I hate the sight of blood."

"That's beside the point. We know what you were after with the manuscript you stole—money. Please tell me in your own words how the letter proves your ownership."

"Bring it here and we will parse it line by line."

"No, we'll do things my way." Knowles was already sick of the man. He looked at his watch. Piper Morgan should be at the station by now to help him figure out the letter. She deserved thanks, and if Griffin Sharp's autopsy results were in, she would get her reward.

"As I have an unexpected meeting that cannot be postponed, we will continue this interview in thirty minutes." He motioned to Daniels a few feet away. "Lieutenant Daniels, please escort Mr. Bell to a comfortable room, where a guard will keep him company until we resume."

Piper Morgan was waiting in his office, looking fresh and recovered from last night's fright. She raised his spirits with her bright, unwavering eyes and lack of self-seriousness. He found her sexy, but not in a seductive way. You could see she didn't hate men, didn't want to kick them in soft places, like so many women he had met.

Plus, she was a trouper, ready to work on a weekend after a rough night. "That was some concert, huh?" she said, shooting him a smile. "You want me to review the part you missed?"

He grinned. "What I heard was mostly delightful, which is high praise from a Baroque fan. How was Part Two?"

"I missed it—for the first time ever, I botched an assignment."

"I'd say you botched nothing, Ms. Morgan. We nabbed a thief thanks to you."

She blushed. "Hey, it was nothing. But I'm guessing that's not why you asked me here."

"Right." Knowles cleared his throat. "I need your literary expertise." He removed Bell's letter from an evidence box. "Mr. Bell claims this letter we confiscated proves he owns the manuscript he stole. Please read it and tell me what you think."

Her face lit up when he handed her the letter.

3 November 1898

My dear Mrs. Lovington,

I was distressed to read in your letter of 14 October that the Academy has rejected your sonatas. Since it was I who recommended that you submit them for next summer's festival, I take their refusal personally.

Moreover, I loathe the prejudicial tradition that dishonors music by women. Dear Lisha, your songs are sublime. Larger works await your pen, and the world awaits the fruits of your labor. I am confident that with your talents you shall succeed.

But in the meantime, may I offer my meager help? I propose a game in which we shall play a little joke on all the stuffed shirts who might exclaim: "But how dare a woman write a symphony? An oratorio? Would not a nursery rhyme be more to the point?"

Here is the game: I shall write a requiem and put your name on it. The pompous devils will reject it ("by a woman indeed!") and then I will come forward, to the dismay of all who have bestowed upon me their highest honors. They will have been tricked into rejecting one of their supposed "favorites." What satisfaction their red faces will bring!

The next step, dear lady, is for you to compose a work for when the farce shall be revealed. Make it your best music, for all eyes will be upon you when we hold a joint concert in the finest hall at our command. At the end there shall be laughter, lessons learned, and a fine bit of amusement for us to share.

Please agree that this is a wondrous plan. At your earliest word I shall commence writing.

Yours ever, Edward

* * *

"What's wrong, Ms. Morgan?" She was scowling.

"How clueless and cruel of Elgar," she burst out. "Only a man could be that condescending."

Knowles was crushed—she was a man-hater after all. "See? I completely missed that. And here I thought Elgar was doing the lady a favor."

"A rotten trick disguised as a favor. He couldn't have cared less about Lovington's rejection by the Academy. Her predicament was amusing to him, even though her future hung on the whims of those narrow-minded men."

This was not the soothing interlude he had expected. "Aha," he said, trying for a cheery tone. "So, Edward Elgar was not an enlightened specimen of manhood, and that disappoints you?"

"You bet it does." She crossed her arms and looked away.

Knowles sighed. "Here's the point, Ms. Morgan. Why do you think Bell values this letter so much? He says it proves he owns the Elgar manuscript, so he can't be charged with theft. But I don't get it."

Piper skimmed the letter again, then clapped her hand to her mouth. "Here it is—the sentence that led Bell to steal the manuscript. I missed it on the first reading."

She pointed to the line *I shall write a requiem and put your name on it.* "When Bell read about the Lovington *Requiem* to be performed in New York, he must have thought it was the one Elgar referred to in his letter. That's why he came to the U.S. in the first place—to get his hands on the manuscript."

"Go on."

"He came expecting to see a work attributed to Lovington but really composed by Elgar. I'll bet he planned to sell that manuscript for millions—as a never-before-heard Elgar work."

"Sounds credible." Knowles watched Piper as she gathered her thoughts, a clearheaded person with infectious enthusiasm.

"Once here, Bell ingratiates himself with the Barlows, who show him a *Requiem* manuscript—but it's in his *Aunt Lisha's* familiar handwriting, signed by her. He instantly realizes this can't be the *Requiem* he's been searching for, which is supposed to be in *Elgar's* handwriting.

"Because that's what it says in this old letter we took from Bell last night."

"Yes."

Knowles perked up. "But then the conductor's wife finds an identical *Requiem* in Elgar's handwriting after all, attributed to himself and not to the woman composer. And Bell, being a musicologist, knows the handwriting is authentic."

"Exactly."

Ms. Morgan seemed to find it perfectly clear. "I have seen another letter that explains the existence of that identical manuscript," she said. "Bell either doesn't know about it or he's being cagey."

"I'm kind of lost, Ms. Morgan." He wished Daniels were here to take notes.

"Okay, Detective, let me give you an analogy. Bell's letter is like a puzzle piece that almost fits but doesn't."

Knowles signaled her to go on.

"Bell has to force the manuscript to fit his letter—the way people force puzzle pieces—so he can cash in on it. But a forced piece is never the right piece." The young woman sat back, looking pleased with herself.

Knowles began to see the light. "Your theory is Bell stole the manuscript in Elgar's handwriting and concocted his own story for the auction houses. Is that right?"

"Yup, you've got it."

"Thank you, Ms. Morgan. You've persuaded me that Elgar is the true author of the *Requiem*, and that he either forgot about putting Lovington's name on the cover or changed his mind at the last minute. Now you can go write your scoop. You've cracked the mystery with your logic."

Her cold expression surprised him.

"Not at all," she said. "I don't agree that the mystery is cracked. You men just won't consider that Lovington could have written this gorgeous work." She shot up from her seat. "But Lisha hasn't had the last word yet, I promise you, Detective. Logic only goes so far."

Morgan's cheeks had turned an attractive shade of pink. Knowles liked her even better for her outburst; never mind that she had insulted him, essentially calling him a sexist. In that she reminded him of Midge, who often talked herself into that tiresome corner.

"I see you are passionate about this issue, Ms. Morgan. But back to my original question. Why do you suppose Bell believes he owns the Elgar manuscript? There's nothing in the letter explaining that."

"I suggest you ask him." She stormed out without saying goodbye.

Worcester, Worcestershire

24 June 1899

HARRIET,

You asked if I bear animosity toward Mr. Elgar. No, I do not. Envy is among the worst sins, for it implies ingratitude for what one has. I have a good life, a loving husband, and the will to succeed at my music. I will keep at it, never fear.

Yes, the music world has awoken and lofted Edward to the sky. I too have read about his success with *Enigma Variations* and of course am pleased for him. Thank you for enclosing the newspaper reviews, which could not contain more superlatives if the writers had memorized the dictionary.

As to your suggestion that I ask Edward to return my manuscript, I find it hasty. I will give his newfound fame a chance to settle, then send a gentle reminder. I have already mailed him a sincere note of congratulations, which was the right thing to do.

When one succeeds, we all succeed, Harriet. Edward struggled for so long that it gives me hope.

AS EVER, YOUR LOVING SISTER,

L.L.

51

Piper argued with herself as she drove too fast to Nicole's. Had she missed the point of Elgar's "wondrous plan"? If he could embarrass the academy and benefit Lisha at the same time, how was that bad?

She would talk it over with her friend.

"So much is happening," she said when Nicole opened the door. "What should we talk about first, Bell's Elgar letter or Griffin Sharp's death? I presume you're going to his wake later?"

"Good morning and come in." Nicole was in a bathrobe, her hair dripping wet. "Here's what I have to say about Mr. Sharp." She blotted her hair with a paper towel. "It's a shame the chorus hottie is dead. He and I never got along, but no worries. He has plenty of mourners in the chorus without me showing up. And you're one of them." She gave Piper a knowing look. "I've seen you looking at him."

"That's ridiculous and irrelevant. He might have been killed, you know. They did an autopsy. Does that interest you?"

Nicole cocked her head. "Hold that thought while I get a towel." She headed for the staircase. "Help yourself to those croissants but please keep your voice down. Todd's asleep upstairs."

Piper paced the kitchen. The room was tidy, with no sign of the broken-wineglass mess from last time. Nicole returned quickly, wearing gray velour sweats and a white towel wrapped around her hair. She looked like an ad for an upscale gym.

"Sit, Piper."

Nicole sat at the table while Piper kept pacing. "You think Griffin didn't have a heart attack, Piper? It's true he was young for that kind of thing."

"It's fishy." Piper perched on a stool. "Maybe the person who murdered Daphne had something against Griff, too." She caught Nicole's expression. "But don't worry, they can't accuse Todd. He was in jail."

Nicole stared at her. "No, not Todd. But now you've got me thinking about it. You're right. This could be major. A double murder in the chorus."

"Yeah, creepy. By the way, Hunter Bell has turned into a nut. He stuck a gun in my ribs last night and talked crazy about owning the Elgar manuscript." Piper filled Nicole in on the scene.

"First a theft, then threatening bodily harm with a gun." Nicole frowned. "Shocking behavior for a musicologist. And to think I once found him attractive—but never mind, were you scared?"

"Not too scared to plant a swift knee in his groin, which I would have done if Detective Knowles hadn't shown up."

"How exciting, like cops and robbers. Coincidence?"

"No. Knowles was expecting trouble."

Nicole dropped the upbeat tone. "You're feeling all right, Piper? No aftereffects?"

"I'm fine." And she was—a good sign for an aspiring crime reporter.

"Griffin was fascinated by Bell," Nicole said. "I watched him during that last lecture, and he was spellbound. Do you think it's possible he cheated on his husband with Bell? And somehow that led to his death? Like—his husband took revenge?"

Piper shrugged. "My friend, you have cheating on your mind. And who could blame you? Anyway, my guess is Bell is straight."

"That's irrelevant," Nicole said. "Anyway, what about the letter? Do you have it after all the turmoil?"

"Knowles kept it as evidence, but I read it. It made me furious."

"Tell me before I die of curiosity."

"It's a beautiful old letter, full of beautiful sentiments, but it adds up to an ugly proposal to make Lisha a pawn in a shaming game." Piper told Nicole everything she remembered.

"Sounds to me like Elgar was truly trying to help Lisha and other women by exposing the Academy's prejudices," Nicole said. "We have to remember the time period and the straitjackets women had to bear back then."

"True, and it was a busy time in Elgar's life. Soon after he proposed the 'game,' *Enigma Variations* made him a huge star." Piper's voice rose to a shout. "But you can't deny he tried to use Lisha!"

Nicole put a finger to her lips. "Keep it down, please. Todd needs his sleep; he's home at last, on bail, but home. Sleeping in jail is no fun, I'm sure."

"It's great he's home." Piper's voice dropped to a whisper. "As I see it, Elgar showered Lisha with flowery language, pretended to care, only to humiliate her—someone who never had half his chance to succeed."

"But he didn't humiliate her, Piper, because she didn't give him the chance. Give her some credit. She rejected the proposal to put forth his work as hers, though I'll bet she was tempted. The proof is in the proposal letter she wrote to him."

Piper took a breath. "True. We read that one so long ago." It had only been a few days but seemed like months. "Wait! That letter is in my office, but I typed the most important sentence on my phone."

She scrolled to find it, as Nicole shook her head with amazement. "A true journalist. How could I ever have criticized you for taking notes?"

"Forget it. Okay, here's what Lisha proposed to Elgar."

> *I will send you my completed* Requiem, *and, if you think it worthy of your attention and time—if you think it worthy in the larger sense—you will rewrite it in your own hand and put your name on it. You will then submit it to the Academy as your work."*

"How smart of her," Nicole said. "Putting the Academy on the spot."

"She turned the tables on Elgar. But he had the last word—which was no word."

"He ghosted her. It's good you're angry, Piper. You're getting more woke, as my students would say. But anger without action is useless."

Piper knew that look—Nicole had a scheme in mind. "Okay, what's up?"

"We're going to settle the authorship issue once and for all."

"Great! You and I?"

"No, Todd and I." Nicole lowered her voice. "He is contrite, Piper. To make amends for cheating on me, he agreed to perform the *Requiem* as a Lovington—but only if his research bears it out. While he's chewing it over, we'll get his musical expertise."

"He'll report his findings to you, you'll report them to me, and I'll report them in *NYN*. Is that what you're thinking?"

"Yes. And I promise to tell you even if the evidence points to Elgar."

"That's fair," Piper said. "What's the plan?"

"Todd is a musical mastermind. I'll provide him with various Elgar scores and ask him to find patterns that also occur in the *Requiem*—calling cards, musical signatures, or whatever term you want to use."

"That's a great idea." Piper beamed at Nicole. "The police have both manuscripts, but Todd can use a Lovington copy to do his research, right? The music is identical."

Nicole shook her head. "No, he can't, and that's the downside of my plan. It's true the Lovington is being held as evidence, and of course we have copies. But we need the actual Elgar manuscript or there's no point."

"Why? I don't get it."

"Todd taught me that all composers leave some kind of unconscious signature on their work—a touch that marks their creative approach. A brand, if you wish. It can be found anywhere, even in their handwriting, which is why we need his manuscript."

"Okay. But wouldn't Elgar have left out his 'signatures' if he was pretending to write as someone else?"

"As I said, these little giveaways can be unconscious. Todd explained that no composer can write a long work without putting a calling card somewhere. That's the nature of art. We are who we are, for better or worse. In Elgar's case, for better, I presume."

"The nature of art," Piper repeated quietly. "Nicole, you've given me an idea. While Todd looks for musical clues in the score, I'm going to do some sleuthing, too."

"Online?"

"No, in Lisha's papers and photos. There's something I noticed but couldn't figure out—until now, when you said 'art.'"

Nicole nodded. "Sounds good. But there's something you must do first. It will demand your many skills but has nothing to do with writing."

"I'm suspicious already. What must I do?"

"Get the Elgar manuscript from Detective Knowles. The police must have confiscated it from Bell—unless, heaven forbid, he sold it already."

Piper remembered the angry way she spoke to the detective that morning, virtually calling him a sexist. She would have to apologize before asking for any favors.

"I owe Knowles a call," she said. "I'll do my best."

Worcester, Worcestershire

15 July 1899

Dearest Harriet,

I agree—it is time to ask Mr. Elgar to return my *Requiem* manuscript. His last letter, a brief response to my note of congratulations, convinced me that his attention has been permanently diverted from our friendship. His tone was quite changed, as if addressing a distant acquaintance and not the soulmate he once declared me to be.

I imagine he is quite taken up with the honors coming his way. No doubt others have entered his world, causing him to lose interest in me. I do not blame him, as society moves in circles that may overlap only briefly. Since Mr. Elgar's success with the *Variations* he has been a stranger to the salons we mutually attended. Yet I am grateful that our circles coincided, if only for a short time.

I am feeling weary, Harriet. Disappointment saps one of energy, but like all things it passes. And perhaps it is just as well that the world did not hear my *Requiem* under the proposed circumstances, without my name as composer. No harm has been done, and that is no small thing.

Onward I go, under my own steam!

Your loving sister,

L

52

Knowles held his nose as he reentered the interrogation room. The place smelled like a gym, minus a gym's energy and good cheer. Bell was already there, shooting Knowles dirty looks. Daniels completed the check-in routine, then stepped out to take a call. Knowles missed his presence, as Daniels would have an alternate view of Bell's testimony—a culturally different view, so to speak. A white view, which Knowles would never say out loud. He hoped Daniels would return soon.

"Repeat for the record, please, Mr. Bell. Who wrote that letter you keep referring to? And who was it addressed to?"

"Whom," Bell corrected, and Knowles clenched his jaw. "Edward Elgar wrote it to my great-great-grand-aunt Lisha Lovington. Not that anyone like you has heard of Sir Edward." He added quickly, "I'm not a racist, just a realist."

Knowles let the comment pass. "Elgar is a noted composer," he said, his eyes on Bell. "Circa 1890s and 1900s. A genuine Romantic behind his British facade, if that's your cup of tea."

"Yes." Bell raised his eyebrows. "You probably looked him up this morning."

"Mr. Bell, how did you come to have that letter?"

"I received it as an heirloom when I was eighteen."

"What special meaning does it have for you?"

Bell smiled. "Do you know what 'Nimrod' means in German?"

"Got me, pal."

"It means 'hunter.' My name, you see? I presume you don't know 'Nimrod' is the title of the most well-known section of *Enigma Variations*, Elgar's famous work. Do you understand now?"

"Tell me."

"Since I am 'Nimrod,' the letter gives me a special connection to Elgar and directs me to my rightful reward."

Knowles raised an eyebrow. "Mr. Bell, we have that letter, and

ANGELS' BLOOD | 259

I fail to see how it directs you to anything but trouble. It appears your greed has overcome your sense of logic. And your reading acuity, I might add."

"I don't know what you're talking about." Bell shifted his long body in the chair, as Daniels reentered the room.

"I'm sure your disappointment is painful," Knowles said, his spirits lifting at the sight of his assistant. He noted Daniels's presence for the record and went on. "You came to America expecting to collect your prize. But events took an unexpected twist."

Bell sat at attention, sweat beading on his upper lip.

"You needed the *Requiem* to be Elgar's work, so you stole the manuscript and pressured other experts to agree with you. You invented a story to persuade them, using the letter you owned. Perhaps you believed in your invented story. But let's face it, you stole that manuscript from the Barlows. Why don't you just admit to the theft, Mr. Bell?"

"Because I own it, as I told you."

"Mrs. Jennings-Barlow does not agree. She received both manuscripts as a gift before you arrived in New York."

Bell shrugged.

"What about the reporter Piper Morgan?" Knowles said. "Where does she fit into the picture?"

"As an annoying person."

"So annoying you had to threaten her with a gun?"

"I wasn't going to use it." Bell looked away.

"It makes no difference. But maybe you would kill a different way?"

"That's absurd."

"Hold that thought," Knowles said. "Let's return to the letter you hold so dear. You knew that if you found the *Requiem* manuscript the letter described, you would be fixed for life. You counted on big bucks from an auction house, believing you alone knew the truth—that Elgar secretly composed the music."

"I waited half my life to find that manuscript." Bell stuck his chin in the air. "What of it?"

Knowles tried for a sympathetic tone. "Mr. Bell, how desperate were you when you first saw your aunt's *Requiem* manuscript in person, courtesy of Nicole Jennings-Barlow? How did you feel when you held it in your hands, evaluated the paper, the ink, the composer's handwriting?" He made his voice resonate for the video. "I'm guessing you felt terrible, since you instantly knew it was Aunt Lisha's handwriting and not Edward Elgar's, as you expected."

He leaned toward the sweating Bell. "All that travel, all that expense, and the certainty a pot of gold waited for you at the end of the rainbow in New York. But your hopes blew up."

Knowles's dramatic skills flourished with a sympathetic listener like Daniels in the room. He went on, his voice full and deep. "After such a bitter disappointment, the appearance of a second manuscript, actually penned by Elgar, was like a miracle. Your dream was not dashed, after all. You could twist that second manuscript to fit your plans."

Bell flicked his wrist. "You don't have a flea's idea what my plans were, because you lack the imagination. You are far off the mark."

"I doubt that. You see, Mr. Bell, after your plans went awry, you needed a great public-relations plan to persuade the music world that a new Elgar manuscript had risen from the earth. That's where Piper Morgan fit in, correct? If she agreed to promote Elgar as the true *Requiem* author, you could reap your millions. But she had a mind of her own."

"I didn't need that hack." Bell snorted. "Any imbecile can see Elgar's name is on the manuscript. But it takes a genius to understand why he changed his plan and put it there instead of Lovington's."

Bell was balancing on the edge of delusion, and Knowles aimed to trip him. "You mean a genius like you."

"You said it, not me."

Knowles leaned toward him. "Please explain why Elgar would put his own name on the manuscript when he had promised to write Lovington's name."

Bell was in his element now. "Listen carefully, as this may be above your head. Obviously, Elgar did it to get credit for his great work, which broke with his usual style and with musical tradition itself." Bell puffed up, showing off his knowledge. "Elgar used his own name despite committing the ungentlemanly act of screwing Aunt Lisha, and I mean that literally and figuratively."

He sat back, looking smug. "Gotcha, Detective, as you Americans like to say. Can I go now?"

"No, Mr. Bell. We have just begun."

53

Piper felt waves of guilt for storming out of Detective Knowles's office. She had behaved like a petulant child and could kiss her longed-for crime beat goodbye. Knowles was supposed to be her ace card, proving she could establish rapport with a vital source. Instead, she'd been rude to him.

Griff's wake added to her despair. It was nightmarish to see his body in its open casket, where he looked like some pseudo-Griff the funeral home had got wrong. She paid her respects and left quickly.

Now she was at Anderson Library, trying to write. An apology to Knowles would help clear the air, and she left a message on his voicemail. Then she requested the Elgar manuscript. It was lousy timing, and she doubted he would call back.

But he did call. "Hello, Ms. Morgan. I only have a minute, but yes, you may borrow the Elgar manuscript. I'm also calling to tell you about Griffin Sharp's autopsy report, which hit my desk an hour ago. You may consider this an exclusive."

"Whoa—hold on half a second, please, Detective." She scrambled to find her notepad. "Okay, shoot."

"We have ruled the death a homicide by poisoning, but we don't know which poison yet. Many toxins can stop the heart."

"I see." She felt a pang. Who would poison Griff?

"I want to thank you again for your courage last night, Ms. Morgan. We couldn't have nabbed Bell without you."

"Glad I could help. Just to be clear, Detective, I don't think of you as a sexist at all. I apologize again. And thanks for giving me the report."

"We're good, then; no more apologies." His voice was warm. "Before I go, I'd like you to think about others in the chorus Sharp might have taken up with after Daphne Paige. Think about the sex club Paige was running, and about Sharp's security job. Call me with any ideas about how these things fit together."

"I will—but what security job?"

"Oh. I assumed you knew. Keep this off the record for now. Mr. Sharp worked as a security guard at the Anderson complex."

Piper shivered. So when Vicki saw Griff by the staircase, he could have been doing his job. The killer might have seen him and thought Griff witnessed the murder. That made Griff a target.

When they hung up, she called Vicki. "So sorry to ask you this, but think back. When was the last time you spoke to Griff?"

"I don't know... maybe two days ago."

"Did he talk about any upcoming plans?"

"Why do you ask? You sound like a detective."

"Griff's death was a homicide, and I'm investigating."

"You mean it wasn't a heart attack? How do you know?"

"Something stopped the heart, and they're trying to find out what." It was not her place to give out details.

Vicki moaned. "I can't talk about this anymore, Piper. It's killing me."

"I understand. But did Griff mention anyone he met with?"

"He stopped listening to me. He was so gaga over that man."

"I know." Piper sighed. "He married Clayton and broke your heart."

"No, that's not who I mean." Vicki gave a bitter laugh. "He broke Clayton's heart, too, by being fickle. If only fickleness was catching, so the other person could forget and move on."

"Wait, who was Griff gaga over?" Piper grabbed her notebook.

"Are you kidding? Every other word was Hunter. Hunter was gorgeous, Hunter was charismatic, Hunter was the sexiest thing ever. I was trying to talk him out of it, which is why I went to see him yesterday morning. But he was dead."

"Talk him out of what?"

"Cheating on his husband. He wouldn't have been able to live with himself."

"Do you think he cheated on Clayton?"

"No, Griffin had *values*." Vicki imitated Griff. "But he would drop anything to be with Hunter. Yesterday he was excited about meeting with him for some reason. Something about Bass Blast. That group was his pride and joy."

Piper's nose itched and her breath was shallow. Her body reacted when her ideas began to cohere. But vital pieces of the puzzle were missing. She must get Clayton to open up, though she had never met him. What a task, but she would try.

Her heart raced as she found Clayton's number and called. "I became friendly with Griffin in the chorus," she said, after introducing herself. "He spoke so fondly of you, Clayton. I thought he was terrific, and what a voice! If you don't mind, I just want to ask you a few questions."

"I don't want to talk to anyone, especially a reporter," he said. "They shouldn't have done that autopsy. Wrong, wrong, wrong; I'm the husband, and I said no. So don't ask me anything. Goodbye."

"Wait, please, Clayton. I have only one question." She steered around the autopsy. "I was told Griffin had a heart attack. Did that happen at home?"

"Here's what I told a detective." Clayton exhaled into the phone. "My husband was supposed to be home by eight-thirty after that chorus meeting. I had a late dinner ready. Instead, he sashayed in at nine-thirty. We ate spicy baked salmon with string beans, and he got violently ill at midnight. At two a.m. he clutched his heart and dropped dead. Any other questions?"

Piper shut her eyes against the image. "Do you know where he went after the meeting?"

"Yeah, there were a bunch of cocktail napkins stuffed in his pockets."

"Where from?"

"Dave's Bar."

Piper knew Dave's, a classy place near Anderson with polished wood tables spaced for privacy. "Do you know if he met with someone there?"

She expected Clayton to erupt in anger. But he was on the hook for serving poisoned salmon to his husband, so he should cooperate.

"I don't know, and I'm hanging up now. I don't know why I'm talking to you at all. I suppose you'll smear my husband all over the newspaper, the way you did to Daphne Paige."

Piper winced. "I've never set out to smear anyone, Clayton. I'm looking for the truth about what happened to Griff. I admired him a lot."

"Yeah, sure." Long pause. "All right, I'll tell you this. Two old music scores were in the shopping bag he brought home from Dave's. Griffin wasn't the scholarly type, so I wonder where they came from?"

"Where do you think he got them?"

Clayton was silent.

"Who were the composers?" Piper said to keep him talking.

"Hold on and I'll tell you." She heard him scurrying, as if eager to give her helpful information. Or to give her the wrong information and throw her off course, in case he was the poisoner.

He returned out of breath. "Here they are—a ballade by Giorgio Capelletti, 1518, and a madrigal by David von Oosterville, 1572. Have you heard those names? I guarantee you my husband never did."

Piper hadn't heard of either composer, but Bell must have had a hand in those scores. She wrote and filed the homicide news, leaving out her hunch Griff had met Bell at Dave's last night—not as a prelude to sex, but to pick up music for Bass Blast. Those rare early-music pieces were the giveaway.

Yet the mystery remained. Both Clayton and Vicki had motives to kill Griff, but what would Bell gain?

Piper drove to Dave's Bar and asked a waitress polishing wineglasses if the police had been there. The waitress shrugged and said she did not speak English. Well, could she speak to Dave? Piper asked. "Dave no here," the woman said, and Piper headed home.

Theo had left a message—he was seeing an emergency patient. The kitchen was dark, thanks to the coming solstice, and she turned on all the lights. She was chilled to her toes though still wrapped in her parka. Why was the world so full of evil? If only Theo were here to cheer her up.

She trudged into the bedroom, threw the parka on a chair, and curled up in bed with the covers over her head. She was drifting off when her phone chimed inside the parka pocket. Forget it, she would not run to answer it. It chimed again and again. She put her fingers in her ears. Whoever was calling could call back later.

When it chimed again, she threw off the covers, fished through the parka, and grabbed the phone. "Yes?"

"You are a vicious bitch, Piper. You made a play for Griffin and never owned up to it. He told me all about it."

"No, Vicki, that's not true." Piper's stomach twisted.

"Come off it, you hypocrite. Griffin told me how you stalked him and fawned over him at Diva's party. How he made you blush by talking about sex. Don't deny it. You were trying to seduce him. But you failed miserably because you don't have a sexy bone in your body. You're cold, cold, cold. And you're nobody's friend."

Piper was too stunned to protest.

"Then, to hide your humiliation, you killed him. And I will get revenge; just wait for it. You won't see me coming." Click. The line went dead.

Piper let her tears fall. Vicki was grief-crazed, but her barbs hurt. And she could be dangerous.

The apartment was on the eighteenth floor, but Piper did not feel secure. Someone could climb up the balcony railings. She moved through each room turning off lights. Now there was only darkness and a distraught ex-friend turned bitter enemy who was harassing her. Who knew what she might do?

Piper brought the phone back to the bedroom and propped herself up against the pillows. When Vicki's number appeared again, she answered quickly. "I hope you're calling to apologize."

"For what, telling the truth?" Vicki spoke with icy calm. "I was stupid to introduce you to New York Luminoso. You ruined my favorite client for me. You ruined chorus for Griffin, too, making him afraid Clayton would get jealous and leave him. You are a sick person, Piper. Very, very sick. Thinking only of yourself. I will tell the chorus all about you. How you promised a helpful profile that never came. How you infiltrated a loving group and now two members have been murdered. Everything was fine with everyone until you came along. You are the kiss of death."

Piper hung up before hearing more.

54

BELL WOULD NOT COOPERATE but went in circles, explaining why he owned the Elgar manuscript and thus could not have stolen it, then blaming his assault of Piper Morgan on temporary insanity due to no one believing him.

Unable to short-circuit the nonsense, Knowles called a break. He told Daniels he needed to think and retreated alone to his office.

The problem was the Sharp case. It was messing with his concentration.

Downing a cup of bitter black, he mulled the evidence so far. Napkins produced by the angry husband, tracing Sharp to a place called Dave's Bar. The owner, Dave, saying two thirtyish men were in the place drinking wine together Thursday night—two bottles of Bordeaux gone in a flash. One of them was possibly Sharp. They paid in cash and left at about 7:00 p.m.

Sharp's husband could not—or would not—say who his husband might have been sitting with at the bar. But a waitress described a table so full of papers that two wineglasses toppled and broke. The mess was still there early yesterday when forensics arrived, enabling them to collect broken glass and a sample of Bordeaux from under the table. Knowles would not rule out poison, but confirming this as Sharp's cause of death, and identifying a poison that matched the autopsy findings, would be a long and involved process.

Knowles was discouraged—or was the early darkness getting to him? He wondered if Piper Morgan knew who Sharp had met at Dave's. On a whim, he called her number. Lively Piper Morgan, a little too lively at times, could banish his blues.

She sounded surprised to hear his voice for the second time today. "Did you happen to learn who Sharp met with last night?" he said. "I read your news brief about his death being a homicide. Well done. You're learning fast."

But she had learned more than he realized.

"Let's agree on an arrangement like last time," she said. "I'll tell you what I know, and you'll give me an exclusive on the case you're working on now."

Knowles stared at the phone as though it had teeth. "That's too broad, Ms. Morgan, considering a lot of reporters are waiting for word on the Paige case."

He heard her intake of breath. "The Paige case suits me fine. I've worked out something important concerning Griffin Sharp. Want to hear my theory?"

Knowles rubbed his chin. "I'm flattered you would share it with me before your readers hear it."

"I tell my readers facts, not theories, Detective. As one creative thinker to another, let's make a deal."

He frowned, cocked his head, then smiled. "All right, Ms. Morgan, you have my agreement."

"Excellent. I'm pretty sure whoever killed Daphne Paige killed Griffin Sharp, too."

"Why is that?"

"A source said Griff was near the staircase at the end of the *Messiah* intermission. The same source suggested Griffin was waiting there to kill Daphne, but then I learned from you he had a security job at Anderson. So he could have been at the stairs checking up on something—not planning a murder, see?"

Knowles raised one eyebrow. "Go on."

"I know Griff returned to the stage before Maestro Barlow did, because I sang next to him. But I'll bet the killer saw him at the staircase and thought Griff witnessed Daphne's murder. Therefore...."

"Therefore, Mr. Sharp had to be eliminated before he could testify to what he saw. Is that what you're driving at, Ms. Morgan?"

"Yes. There is something else, Detective, but it's more speculative."

"More speculative?" Knowles chuckled. "I'd say you're already out on a limb."

"Maybe, but here's a new angle. Three people have spoken to me about Griffin Sharp's attraction to Hunter Bell. I say Griff was

ANGELS' BLOOD | 269

more attracted to what he thought Bell could do for him, namely promote his Bass Blast vocal group. If your team finds poison at Dave's Bar, then I propose Hunter Bell was with Griff that night and gave him some rare early music scores that Griff brought home. His husband told me about them."

Knowles thought about it. "And that means...."

"I'm speculating that Bell killed both of them. Daphne and Griff."

Returning to the interrogation room, Knowles prepared to go into high gear. But just as he began to speak, someone interrupted.

"Sir?"

It was a clerk with a report. "Yes?"

"I believe you've been waiting for this."

Knowles thanked the clerk, and took a look—it was the lab report. As he skimmed it, the room briefly spun.

He cleared his throat and stood. "Mr. Bell, we have been interrogating you about the theft of a valuable music manuscript along with your charge of assault and battery with a weapon. But after reading this paper just now handed to me, I find I must expand the scope of our investigation."

Bell's face fell, and Knowles waited a beat. "Mr. Bell, you are under arrest for the murder of Daphne Paige."

55

A FEW COMPETENT defense attorneys were available on short notice, among them the charismatic Charlemagne Charles. After Bell chose him from a list, Knowles called a recess to await and brief the new attorney.

He invited Daniels into his office to pass the time. "My apologies for keeping you in the dark about the lab report, Matt."

"I've guessed what's in it, sir. Bell's shoes match the bloody shoe prints, right?"

"Yes, it's a perfect match. Bell is at a precipice, Matt. One more push and he'll confess to killing Paige."

"How will you make him do it?"

Closing a case was an art, and Knowles considered himself a Michelangelo of the genre. "It's all in the push, Matt." He demonstrated with his hands. "You've gotta know how hard and in what direction to do it. Kind of like a pottery wheel; ever try one of those things?"

"Can't say I have. But I think I know what you mean. It's about different degrees of pressure."

"You could say that. That's a very good description, Matt."

The bloody shoes proved that Bell had walked through the blood. There was no proof he murdered Paige, except no other suspect's shoes fit the tracks, and no other bloody shoe prints were at the scene. Knowles would have to cajole, intimidate, or trick Bell into a confession, all while dodging the lawyer's best efforts to keep him quiet.

Charles, known in the field as Charming Charlie, was no Perry Mason, but he was a good enough defense lawyer. Daniels briefed him, then went through the check-in routine.

"You don't have to answer any questions," Charlie told Bell.

"I want to answer." Bell looked more worried and less smug.

"You're only here to catch this guy's mistakes."

Knowles got started. "Let's return to that old letter of yours, Mr. Bell, the one written by the great Edward Elgar."

"Sir Edward to you," Bell muttered.

"That letter was crucial to your crooked plan, but your craving for publicity got the better of you. You dangled the letter in front of a reporter, which led directly to your being here today."

Bell turned to Charlie. "Do I have to listen to his incompetent stories?"

Charlie told him to shush, while Knowles fought the impulse to smack Bell. Breathing hard, he continued. "Mr. Bell, isn't it true you tried to get Piper Morgan to write a newspaper article about your so-called Lisha Lovington Fund for Neglected Female Composers? In fact, you tried to persuade her with a gun."

Bell straightened his spine. "Who told you about my fund? Anyway, there's no crime in looking for free publicity. Everyone does it." He studied his fingernails.

"But not at gunpoint. Your so-called fund would be built on the proceeds of theft and fraud. But if Ms. Morgan glorified the fund in the respected *NYN* newspaper, you might avoid charges and wind up a hero to women."

"You don't know what you're talking about."

Knowles smiled; the guilty ones all said that—eventually. "Your efforts to use Ms. Morgan backfired, and here you are. Now we come to the part about Ms. Paige. We know you were at the scene of her death."

Charlie jumped up. "I was not appraised of that information."

"We would have informed you in due time, sir," Daniels said.

"What information?" Bell's eyes opened wide.

"Your bloody shoe prints, of course." Knowles said.

"My...."

"Mr. Bell, you left a bloody signature at the murder scene. My team discovered dried blood on a fancy pair of black, red, and white Burberry sneakers, size eleven, which you were also wearing last night when we arrested you."

Bell looked at his feet, clad in detainee slippers.

"A lab report I received earlier today confirms that the blood type on the shoes matches Ms. Paige's blood type. Further, the tread conforms precisely to the sixteen bloody shoe prints you and only you left at the scene." Knowles raised his voice. "You resorted to murder to satisfy your greed."

"No, wait!" Bell jumped up. "I didn't do it! That woman did it to herself!"

"Hush!" Charlie said. "Sit down."

"Tell us, Mr. Bell," Knowles said. "What happened on that staircase the night of the *Messiah* concert?"

Charlie put a warning hand on Bell's arm, but Bell shook it off. "I saw someone on the stairs. I went down to check on it."

"You went down? Your shoe prints show you going down just far enough to confirm the 'someone' you saw was dead. You did not inform anyone of the incident. I'll ask you again, what happened on that staircase?"

"It was a mistake, I...."

Knowles kept up the momentum. "You went down to a bloody scene, although you hate blood. You wore bloody shoes and kept wearing them after the murder. I suggest you don't hate blood all that much, Mr. Bell. So, I'm wondering why you didn't stay to help Ms. Paige, if you didn't mean to push her. Instead, you let her bleed to death."

Charlie jumped up again. "I demand a copy of that report. The shoe prints may prove my client was on the scene, but they do not prove he caused anyone's death. My client was arrested for threatening a reporter at gunpoint, and that's why we're here. He does not need to address your theories about the tragic death of Ms. Paige." With that, Charlie sat down.

Knowles listened politely with pursed lips, then turned to Bell. "Perhaps you didn't mean to kill the young woman," he said quietly. "Is that possible?"

"Yes! That's it!" Bell looked hopeful. "It was all an accident!"

"You're incriminating yourself," Charlie said.

Knowles went on. "I'm thinking something unexpected occurred that caused a scene on the staircase between you and the victim. It made you flail out and accidentally push her down the stairs. Does that sound right, Mr. Bell?"

Bell was sweating, his face flushed. He shrugged at the question. Knowles envisioned the staircase, a woman in concert clothes, and a desperate man pursuing a dream. He summoned all his hard-won skill, then charged ahead with his conclusion.

"Mr. Bell, you did not mean to push Daphne Paige down the stairs. You meant to push Nicole Jennings-Barlow. You wanted to kill her before she could tell anyone else about the Elgar manuscript she showed you—a manuscript now in our possession. With her out of the way, you could cash in big. Just kill the lady, make off with the manuscript, and live in luxury the rest of your life."

Bell looked stunned as Knowles went on.

"You were confused when you saw Ms. Paige coming up the stairs, looking so much like your intended victim. She bore a strong resemblance to Nicole Jennings-Barlow that night, with her upswept hairdo and black concert clothes. But it was too late for you to pull back. Your arm was in motion. It flung out and struck Ms. Paige, who fell to her death."

"Oh my God," Bell moaned.

"Just a minute." It was Charlie. "My client's fingerprints were not on the so-called murder weapon, the bloody baton. How do you account for that? Moreover, why was there blood at the top of the stairs, if Ms. Paige died at the bottom from the fall?"

Knowles had to be nimble. "Mr. Bell will answer those questions promptly, won't you, Hunter?"

At the sound of his first name, Bell moved his hands off his face. "I didn't kill her," he said in a quiet voice. "I just touched her shoulder."

"Don't talk," Charlie pleaded. "Let me handle it."

"Go on, Hunter, Nimrod, you want to talk," Knowles said tenderly. "It is your destiny as Nimrod to explain what happened on the Dungeon staircase on *Messiah* night. It is your story, the story only you can tell. Tell it, Nimrod."

Bell wept softly. "She killed herself, and that's the truth."

"Go on."

"This woman was coming up the stairs, carrying the baton, like so." Bell was on his feet, demonstrating. "Her head bent like this, her hair up in a bun. I wanted to tap her arm, let her fall naturally without making a mess, but she turned to see me."

Bell's eyes opened wide. "And it was the wrong woman! I couldn't stop it; she fell with that baton in her hand." He shuddered. "She stabbed herself with it on the way down."

"Did you see her do it?" Knowles said.

"Yes, it was horrible. Blood spurting everywhere." He began to retch, and Knowles signaled Daniels to get a sick bag fast.

"If only she broke her neck." Bell put his hands over his mouth. "Something nice and neat. But it was a bloodbath, grotesque." He grabbed at his stomach. "That stick shot into her eye like a harpoon. It was a freak accident, Detective, I tell you. I threw up for two days."

Daniels handed Bell the sick bag, and he vomited into it. When Bell had cleaned himself, Knowles went on. "Did Ms. Paige say anything to you before she fell? This young woman with so much life to live?"

"Yes. 'Out of my way, I'm bringing this to Todd.' Quite a rude person."

"She was bringing him his music baton," Knowles said quietly. "To conduct the rest of the concert." He winced at the waste of it. "Mr. Bell, I say you had a premeditated plan to push Nicole Jennings-Barlow down the stairs to her death—the woman you thought was Nicole Jennings-Barlow. Daphne Paige's death was no accident."

"You have no proof of that." Charlie was putting on an impressive show. "Behind all the theatrics, the fact is she died from a self-inflicted stab wound, exacerbated by a fractured skull. That's what the coroner's report said. She struggled to keep her balance, and in an unlikely and freaky motion she twisted, and the baton she was carrying penetrated her eye, causing her to bleed out."

Charlie put his hand on Bell's shoulder. "In fact, my client never touched the baton, which is incorrectly being termed the murder weapon. It was no weapon at all, just the unfortunate cause of the young woman's death."

Knowles glanced from Charlie to Bell and prepared to deliver the final blow. He spoke in a quiet voice tinged with sadness. "Mr. Bell, you killed a woman you hardly knew, a woman with hopes, dreams, and struggles, a woman with friends, colleagues, and a mother who loved her." His voice caught. "And it was for nothing. How does that make you feel?"

Bell lowered his head.

"My client may be guilty of manslaughter, but not premeditated murder." Charlie said.

"That's for the jury to decide. We will now discuss Griffin Sharp."

Worcester, Worcestershire

3 August 1899

DEAR SISTER,

Upon my request Edward has returned both my manuscript and his own perfect copy. He claims to have taken no further action on the "game" I proposed, being occupied with other matters. I am of course disappointed, as he agreed to my proposal. Furthermore, he wrote no word of explanation nor any pleasantries which might lead me to presume an ongoing friendship.

It was like a dream, Harriet. Brief, exciting, and destined to fade away.

As you predicted, anger has eclipsed my sadness. Mr. Elgar stirred my hopes and then let them drop. But why sit meekly by while this gentleman—of excellent talent, it is true—soars beyond my orbit, as though spun off the sun? Some people rise to glory, while others toil in darkness, and so it has ever been. Each moment spent bemoaning this disparity is a wasted one.

Mr. Elgar's triumph does not deprive me of a triumph. There is no quota here, no limitation on great works. Nor must I step aside to honor him, nor pretend to be an inferior. I owe Mr. Elgar nothing but the respect one artist pays another.

Harriet, the flames of my anger will quickly cool. Mr. Elgar is a man, at home in the world. We women must fight to claim our world, and so I shall. You have my word, and I am ever grateful for your prodding. Leo is waking now, and I must close. Be well and kiss my niece and nephew for me.

YOUR LOVING SISTER,

LL

56

Barlow had not much liked Griffin Sharp, but the guy could sing. His rich voice was full and resonant, with an unforced vibrato. He had come untrained to New York Luminoso, a natural treasure who never missed a rehearsal. Any chorus would be glad to have him, and Barlow never forgot Sharp had his pick. Not to mention his pick of women.

Barlow's thoughts drifted to Daphne and back to the miracle of his being home.

He was still in bed at nearly noon, thanks to Nicole's care in not waking him. He depended on her for everything now, and she did not complain. She even touched him tenderly sometimes. It was strange how new seeds of a marriage could grow from its wreckage.

"Todd?" she called up to him. "I'm off to catch up with some work. There are scrambled eggs in the pan, just heat them up. You know the drill."

"Thank you, I will."

"Hope you find something useful," she said, and the front door closed.

Barlow wolfed down the cold eggs, then settled himself at his desk to work on his assignment—the three Elgar scores Nicole had left for him to analyze. *Dream of Gerontius, Enigma Variations,* and *Pomp and Circumstance March No. 1.*

He would immerse himself in each one, searching for an Elgar "trademark" that might also occur in the *Requiem.* He had missed music keenly during this terrible time and looked forward to the task. He would do an honest job, owing that much and more to Nicole.

He stretched his limbs, leaned forward on his elbows, and opened *Gerontius,* a choral piece. At once he felt the thrill of a conductor's work as he delved into the sonic landscape of Elgar's score. He traveled its terrain, seeing as well as hearing the music, alert for any pattern that might also occur in the *Requiem*.

The exercise brought him closer to the human side of music, so at the end he might say, "Hello, Elgar!" as if recognizing a friend. He did not look for a recurring motif, like Wagner's themes for his operas, but rather for configurations or textures that spoke directly of the composer himself.

It was all so abstract. What was a "texture" in music? You needed metaphor to talk about such subtleties, to make music real to those trying to understand. And that was where he came in; therein lay his talent and skill, the right to be called Maestro.

He closed his eyes, his passion for music welling within him. How fortunate he was in his work, how grateful for it. And more than a little indebted to Nicole for making it all possible. But now he must concentrate and not disappoint her.

Clearing his mind, he dove deeply into the music. The shadows in the room slid north, then disappeared as the sun slipped behind the house. By midafternoon his desk was piled with notes he had underlined and circled in his excitement. To be professional, he double-checked himself by skimming links to Elgar on the Internet. By late afternoon he had found a paper that confirmed his observation, written by a specialist in the music of Elgar's time. He could hardly wait to tell Nicole the good news.

"I found something, Nic," he said when she arrived home at 5:30.

"Great, what?" Her cheeks were red from the cold.

He led her to the piano and pulled her down on the bench beside him. "It's about Elgar's chords. You know how music usually *falls* to a sad feeling with notes going down the scale, and *rises* to a happy feeling with notes going up? Like this." He demonstrated on the piano.

"Sure."

"And you know how the minor key is sad, tense, or suspenseful, while the major key sounds happy, sunny, and uplifting?"

"Of course. So?"

"Well, Elgar goes *lower* to the happy sound. He does it by changing a chord from minor to major as it moves down one note. Like this." He played two chords. "You see? From sad, the music goes down to happy, instead of up. Here's how the the musician put it: 'Elgar descends to sadness, then *falls* into joy.'"

"Wow. Interesting. Are we supposed to be aware of that while we listen?"

"No, the sound makes an impression on us. We don't have to know why."

She looked thoughtful. "And Elgar does that a lot?"

"Yes, I found it in quite a few places."

"But isn't this a common thing composers do?"

"I'd have to research that question to give you a solid answer, Nic. But the musician I found online confirmed what I noticed. He calls it Elgar's 'trademark' in a paper he wrote."

Nicole let the words sink in. "Trademark. Just what we're looking for."

"I know."

Her face lit up, then darkened. "Do chords go down to 'happy' in the *Requiem*?" She seemed to hold her breath.

Barlow smiled. "To be honest, no. The *Requiem* is nothing like this at all."

When he looked up again, Nicole's eyes were shining. "So that proves it. Elgar didn't write it. Lovington did."

He hated to contradict her. "It only suggests he didn't write it. It doesn't prove it."

"Oh, for heaven's sake." Nicole jumped up. "Then what will?"

Barlow shrugged. "Maybe nothing."

She paced the room. "Todd, I told Piper I'm cool with not knowing for sure who the real composer is. But I am not cool with it. We need to know."

Barlow wanted to invent an answer but couldn't think of one. "Can we talk about it over food? I'm hungry."

They ordered in, two entrées for him and a salad for her. "Anyway, Piper is studying the mystery too, from another angle," Nicole said between mouthfuls. "Maybe she can prove Lisha wrote it once and for all."

"Good luck with that. I didn't know she was a musician."

"It's not a musical angle, Todd. Can you please work with her? I know you don't like Piper much, but maybe if you two put your heads together...."

Barlow was suddenly sick of the topic; the day's work had caught up with him. "I don't like reporters in general." It was a cranky outburst. "They snoop, get things wrong, and write dumb things."

Nicole pursed her lips. "What did Piper write that was wrong or dumb?"

"I'm sure there was something."

She laughed. "You're just annoyed because she hasn't written the chorus story yet. And because she didn't interview you. She told me she was saving you for last, and then you went and got arrested."

"That's true, I did." He smiled sheepishly.

"It's good she didn't write about the chorus yet," Nicole said as they carried their dishes to the sink. "It will be a lot more interesting when we can announce Lovington wrote the *Requiem* after all."

He came up behind her. "Pretty sure of yourself, aren't you?" He enclosed her in his arms.

"Someone has to be." She leaned into him.

They stood like that for a while as Barlow savored the moment.

"Oh my God, Todd." She pushed away from him.

"What?"

"We still haven't looked through the rest of the old box in the closet. What's wrong with me?" Nicole hurried upstairs with Barlow close behind her. She dragged the box onto the bedroom floor and pulled out old piano-exercise books, one after another, each gray and ragged with use.

"Did Lovington write any of these?" he said.

"None that I can see. Come look."

Barlow flipped through titles by Czerny, Clementi, and Scarlatti. The names brought back music lessons in his childhood, when he understood the piano was not for him.

"Your friend's grandmother was a pianist, then."

"I suppose. Or a piano teacher. Nothing exciting left in here."

ANGELS' BLOOD | 281

"Shouldn't you throw all this junk out?" Barlow said. "The books are too old and mangled to be of use to anyone."

"I will. But not yet."

Barlow made an appointment to work that evening with Piper Morgan. She had accomplished the near-miraculous feat of securing the Elgar manuscript for a day. Detective Knowles himself gave the okay—saying he was glad to help New York Luminoso clear up its mystery. Barlow planned to announce his final opinion about the *Requiem* at midnight, a fittingly dramatic time for a public statement.

Worcester, Worcestershire

15 August 1899

DEAREST HARRIET,

I wish to clarify my last letter. I have no quarrel with Mr. Elgar. I simply meant that I will not worship him or any man.

The good news is that Leo has greatly recovered, giving me the strength to finish several major works. I am busy composing, though who will hear my works, and where, I do not know. As a wife and mother, I can not join every march on behalf of women's rights, though I have vowed to fight in my own way.

I think often of Clara Schumann—how she stopped composing to run her household and care for poor Robert. Was the world deprived because she gave up her art for marriage? How can we say so, when her husband's music has spread such joy? We cannot know which seedlings will shrivel and which will flourish, or which masterpiece will rot for lack of light. Life is what is and not what might have been. There is another universe for that, and it brings me peace to dream of it.

MY LOVE,

Lisha

57

VICKI LEFT FOUR VOICEMAIL MESSAGES, each angrier than the last. She must be drinking herself into a stupor, Piper thought, her fear fizzling into exasperation.

When her phone chimed again, she ignored it. Then the name Copper Don popped up.

"Hi." She answered quickly. "Do you have something for me?" Her heart beat fast.

"You didn't hear this from me," Copper Don whispered. "Hunter Bell confessed to killing both Paige and Sharp. He said he was afraid Sharp would report him for pushing Paige down the stairs. Knowles got him to admit he did it."

"Bell pushed her? Oh, wow."

Piper was sickened but not surprised by the news, remembering the feel of Bell's gun in her ribs. But why would he kill Daphne in the first place? It made no sense.

"I've got to go," Copper Don said. "There's a press conference at five-thirty. I'll look for you."

Detective Knowles must be happy right now. Would he remember to call her with the exclusive, as promised? Maybe, but she wouldn't count on it. Which meant she must hurry to a Saturday evening press conference 30 miles away with only a moment's notice. But first she called Moss and filled him in. "More to come around six o'clock," she said.

"Nice going, Sherlock, I'll fax you a request for a police press pass with my signature on it. That should get you into the press conference."

"I don't need it, Moss. Hardy already gave me a permanent police press pass—or what he calls a PPP. Hardy is all right, even with his great love of acronyms. I underestimated him."

Moss chuckled. "I suppose you've never wondered why he didn't run with that tip he gave you about the bloody baton."

"Should I have asked about that? I gave up on it when Detective Knowles would not confirm the tip and my anonymous source was silent." Copper Don had bowed out, as he'd said he would—until now.

"Hardy could have gotten a confirmation, but he wanted to give you a break. He can't go on covering crime forever—he's not young, you know—and he sees you as new blood. Anyway, he admires you, Piper, and he bet correctly you would do us proud covering the murders. I look forward to reading your news report tonight."

Piper gulped back tears. She regretted every sarcastic comment she had ever made about Hardy Wheeler. "He's a generous guy, Moss. I had no idea."

She called Todd Barlow from the car to reschedule their meeting. "And I've got a reliable tip to share with you. The police have arrested Daphne's murderer."

"What? Who is it?"

"I can't say more. The killer's name will be online by early tonight. I'll bet your lawyer will call soon to say you're off the hook."

"I'm afraid to believe it."

"For what it's worth, I never saw you as a murderer, Todd."

"Thanks, Piper. You're the nicest reporter I know."

Knowles slapped his forehead as Piper came toward him after the conference. He had meant to call her, he said. Had she gotten everything she needed?

"Yes, I'm good." It was true. How could she resent this man? If it weren't for Detective Knowles and his team, she might be dead right now. Hunter Bell's third victim.

She filed her report from the car.

BRITISH MUSICOLOGIST CHARGED
WITH TWO CHORUS MURDERS

The alleged killer confessed to two crimes, admitting the soprano's death was a case of mistaken identity.

Next, she called Dodi Paige. "The murderer did not intend to kill your daughter, Dodi. He hardly knew her."

"I don't know if that makes it better or worse," Dodi said.

Then she phoned Todd Barlow.

"Now, why would Bell do a thing like that?" His voice was thick.

"Todd, can we still get together tonight? It's not that late, and my boyfriend, Theo, and I can come over to your place for a while. He'd like to meet you and Nicole. And I could use your help with a remaining puzzle."

"About the *Requiem*?"

"Yup."

"Of course. At your service."

"We'll bring wine and cake to celebrate your coming freedom. So please don't fuss."

She would also bring the Elgar manuscript, on two-day loan from Knowles, so Todd could reach his final conclusion.

Piper had a sense of déjà vu when the Barlows opened their door. With Nicole's hair wound loosely into a bun, she resembled Daphne more than ever. She hoped Nicole would not be too spooked when she heard the murder details.

After Theo arrived from the city, and introductions were made, they all gathered in the study. The room looked the same as the fateful day Piper had first met Hunter Bell, except for the now-uncluttered desks and a new coffee table. Unbeknownst to Piper and the others, Bell had murdered Daphne Paige the night before. Remembering, Piper stifled a sob. Tonight was for celebrating, not grieving.

Todd filled four wineglasses and Nicole sliced the cake, distributing plates on the coffee table. Theo was all smiles—Piper had rarely seen him this relaxed. "I've been hearing about 'Todd and Nicole' so much, I've felt a bit left out," he said, glancing at Piper. "I'm really glad to be here."

"We're glad, too," Nicole said. "Piper is like one of the family now."

Piper felt her face grow red. It was no secret—her professional distance from the Barlows had disappeared. But she would rather be friends with them than report on them.

Theo raised his wineglass. "Living with a reporter exposes me to good and bad news before the public is informed. Tonight, Piper told me a great musician will soon be cleared of a murder charge. Let's drink to that."

"Hear, hear," they said in unison, clicking glasses.

Theo's toast was indiscreet, but Piper loved his warmth and easy rapport with the Barlows. She hoped the four of them would become good friends.

She tapped her glass. "Now I propose we drink to another innocent chorus person, Griffin Sharp."

They clicked again, as a silence fell over the room.

"Now," Piper said, "would you all help me figure out the final mystery—the one that caused two needless deaths and made Todd and Nicole's past ten days a living nightmare?"

"You mean, of course, the mystery of the two matching music manuscripts," Nicole said.

"That's the one. I want to know why there are empty brackets on Lovington's song sheets and photos—which I have brought with me. Those brackets are everywhere, floating through space, containing nothing, like some mystical puzzle."

"Piper thinks they're the key to the *Requiem* mystery," Nicole said. "She's got great intuition. Let's see if she's right."

"How can we help?" Todd said.

"By looking for a hidden message. Put on your sleuthing caps and get ready."

After the food was cleared, Piper laid out the Lovington materials on the coffee table.

"These are photo loupes." She held up two small, curved magnifiers. "We'll use them to look for unusual markings. Press your eye to the glass, press the glass against a photo, and slide it around. When you see something unusual, show me."

"What exactly are we looking for?" Nicole said.

"Lines that resemble brackets. We only have two loupes, so you'll have to take turns."

"Let me try one," Theo pressed a loupe against one eye, squinted with the other eye, then slid the loupe along the surface of a photograph. "I see what you mean. Lots of squiggly brackets."

"They're on the backs of the photos, too," Piper said.

"Yup, these squiggles look different magnified." Todd was taking a turn.

"We're looking for a needle in a haystack. But if you see bracket shapes, take a closer look."

Todd handed a loupe to Nicole. "I see one pair of brackets in the lower left corner here." She turned the photo over to see the Madonna pose.

"Try other photos," Piper said. "See anything different?"

"They're sort of random." Nicole zeroed in on a few pairs. "Sometimes in the upper left corner, sometimes in the lower right."

"But usually around the same size, correct?" Piper said.

"Yeah, and there's a dot inside some of them." Todd took another turn.

Piper passed a photo to Theo. "Look at the front of this one and tell me what you see."

"Two women on a street, holding books."

"Now slide the loupe over the books. See anything interesting?"

"Speckles and spots. And a lot of brackets—not so random though. There's one in each corner of the book covers. Surrounded by flowers that look hand-painted."

"Anyone know a book designer?" Nicole said. "Maybe this is some kind of common symbol from the late eighteen-hundreds."

Todd slid a loupe over a song sheet. "It's here, too, folks. Forget book designers; any designer will do. Although this might just be a doodle Lovington used to mark her stuff."

"Personal to her, you mean," Piper said.

"Right," Todd said. "Like a symbol of some kind."

"Let's think about a personal squiggle-doodle unique to the person," Piper said. "Any ideas?"

They all were silent, thinking.

"Everyone doodles, especially when they're bored," Theo said. "You should see my notepaper."

"You're bored straightening teeth?" Nicole had a mock straight face.

"It's a bit like watching grass grow. The changes take place slowly."

"I get that," Nicole said. "Anything worthwhile takes time."

"Exactly." Theo smiled at her.

Piper was not following the conversation. Something so obvious had struck her, it was strange no one had shouted the word. "There's a term for personal symbols. Can anybody guess what I'm thinking?"

"Oh goody, charades," Nicole said. "Sounds like...."

"Initials," Todd said.

"An ego-design," Theo said. "I just invented the term."

Piper grabbed a loupe. "These brackets aren't curved like the usual parentheses, they're straight-edged, with one line jutting out from the other."

"They're mirror images." Todd pressed his eye to the other loupe. "Like a forward L and a backward L, with one turned upside down. A monogram."

"Yes, a monogram!" Piper exclaimed. "Double L for Lisha Lovington. Is that far-fetched?"

"No, it makes sense," Nicole said. "Hurry, let's look at her *Requiem* manuscript. Did you bring it, Todd? Oh, I forgot, Knowles's men took the Lovington from your desk after your arrest."

"I have a copy in my music bag," Todd said, reaching for it.

"Todd's never without his bag." Nicole shot him a smile.

"The original would have clearer markings," Piper said. "Let me try to get hold of Detective Knowles and ask to see it."

"It's Saturday night," Theo said. "Most people don't work all the time the way you do, hon."

"And we're glad she does," Nicole said. "Look at everything she's uncovered. Thanks to Piper, we're almost home—all we have to find is an LL monogram on the Lovington manuscript, and we'll know she composed the *Requiem*."

"We'd have to find it on Elgar's, too," Barlow said, "supposing he copied Lovington to the last detail. But if he wrote it, he would use his own initials."

"True," Piper and Nicole said in unison.

"So, convening again Monday?" Theo said.

"No," Piper said. "Let's clear this up tonight."

Slipping on white cotton gloves, Piper and Theo waited for the Lovington manuscript in a police conference room. They had said fast goodbyes to the Barlows and arrived at Anderson close to ten. A clerk brought the Lovington and placed it before Piper on a glass table. She showed him the magnifying loupe and explained it would not harm the manuscript. He nodded, then surprised her.

"Detective Knowles said to wish you good luck, Ms. Morgan."

She thanked him and began her search, sliding the loupe under the words *Requiem by Lisha Lovington* on the title page. There it was, a tiny double L. The angled lines ended in curlicues, and the dot was more of a squiggle, but there was no mistaking it. Lisha also had placed her monogram on the bottom right corner of every page and on the otherwise blank last page of the manuscript:

$$\mathcal{L} \cdot \mathcal{L}$$

"Here's our proof, Theo." Piper passed the manuscript to him, so he could verify what she had seen. Then they high-fived and sat back with relief. This step had taken less than 15 minutes.

She phoned Todd, though it was late. "Yes, the monogram is all over the Lovington. Can you look for it on the Elgar manuscript and let me know? I'll hold on."

He laughed. Wouldn't she hold a long time while he searched?

"No, you'll see it instantly, if it's there."

Todd returned quickly to the phone. "Yes, it's there. Not EE but LL. Nice going, Piper. I found a musical clue that makes a case for Lisha, but you proved it—it's the Lovington *Requiem*."

58

Four Months Later

CALL ME SOON, lots to tell you.

Piper sighed reading Amelia's email. What could be left to tell? She had wrapped up Lovington's story with the chorus's triumph—the premiere of the critically praised *Requiem*, led by Maestro Todd Barlow. She was reporting now on the devious methods of art racketeers, her first official crack at the crime beat. She phoned Amelia as a courtesy.

"Now, don't get mad?" Amelia said. "When you first contacted me, I gave you only as much of my aunt's archive as I thought sensible? Not every interesting letter? But now that I know how brilliant you are, I've decided to share more with you."

"Like what?"

"Well...." Amelia paused dramatically. "Elgar invited Auntie L and her husband to his knighting ceremony at Buckingham Palace. I've got her embossed invitation with his handwritten note on the back? She thought he had forgotten her, but he hadn't."

"I'm glad to hear that."

"Then there's the pièce de résistance. A special letter."

Piper rolled her eyes. "I don't mean to be rude, Amelia, but I'm working on something new now."

"I know, but just wait until you read this one? It makes the manuscript mystery look like a pebble in a quarry. The letter is my gift to you for the amazing work you've done. I've been busy or I'd have contacted you sooner."

"You can email it to me, Amelia, but I can't promise when I'll read it. I'm taking some time off."

"No problem. You'll have your gift in five minutes."

Piper turned off her phone, tablet, and computer. Later, with Theo lying beside her in bed, she opened her phone and found Amelia's email. Her eyes widened as she read the attached letter. It was as though Lisha was speaking directly to her.

Worcester, Worcestershire
4 July 1900

Dearest Harriet,

When there are fights we cannot win, we must change course. Some day things will be different, as nothing lasts forever and ideas as well as customs change. This morning I confided to John about my experiences with the Academy, and the dear man opened his eyes wide. "What grievous unfairness to women and to my own dear wife!" he said, holding me close. "Apologies on behalf of all men."

If my husband can pause and let in new light, he may one day be multiplied by thousands, or even by hundreds of thousands.

But we live now and not in some future time, Harriet, when women will surely be accepted as the equals of men in both intellect and ability. Today we must take action opposite to what we learned as children. Our parents taught us to tell the truth, but we must lie on behalf of the truth.

I will now reveal my own truth to you.

I have been composing without restraint. A symphony, a cantata, sonatas, even a piano concerto. The bitterness that once weighed on me has yielded to a new strength forged by anger and pain, just as a tree mangled in an ice storm may burst with new leaves in the spring.

I am optimistic that my music will soon find ready audiences, though by devious means. Each new work in which I have invested my whole being will bear not my own name but the name of a man who has never lived.

292 | ROBERTA MANTELL

Harriet, I am inventing men's names for my works as readily as new melodies. I even used the name Upton on a concerto, for giddy fun, but the music was too good for him, and I scratched out the name with the blackest ink.

I am smiling as I write this to you. But that is not all.

Other women have also given up petitioning the Academy under their own names and are resorting to the same trickery. In time there will be many more of us. It is in poor taste, it is wicked, but so is our exclusion due to a baseless prejudice on account of our sex.

The future shall be seeded with women's music disguised by men's names.

You will still find my songs under the name Lisha Lovington. I shall not divulge the pseudonyms on my grander works, but look for my monogram, and you will know they are mine. Each of my manuscripts will be marked by the initials LL—with the second L turned around and upside down as if enclosing a truth—a truth about an outrage.

The others have devised their own methods, which are not for me to divulge. I leave it to the music detectives of the future to uncover our secrets. And uncover them they must, if they wish to learn about the past.

Your loving sister,
Lisha Lovington

Afterword

LISHA LOVINGTON is a fictional character who reflects the history of biases against female composers. For reference, George P. Upton's *Woman in Music*, first published in 1880 by James R. Osgood & Co., defines the parameters of the battlefield where women like Lovington struggled for recognition.

In choosing a male counterpart to her character, I searched for a real composer whose locale, timeline and circumstances lent themselves to a juicy story. No facts of Edward Elgar's life (1857–1934) were changed in this book, though I took liberties with what might have happened between a passionate, married female composer and a not yet superstar male composer—also married and known for his romantic temperament.

The 2010 documentary *Elgar: Elgar: The Man Behind the Mask*, written and directed by John Bridcut, inspired me with its insights about the man and his music. *Letters to Nimrod from Edward Elgar*, edited by Percy M. Young and first published in 1965 by Dobson Books, Ltd., helped to convey Elgar's writing style, though his letters to Lovington in *Angels' Blood* are purely fictitious.

The plot for the book came to me during the intermission of a Handel's *Messiah* concert in which I sang with the tenors. Until that night, it had never occurred to me to write a murder mystery. Music moves us in unexpected ways.

Many thanks to the following:

The author Sarah Lovett, for seeing the potential in this story, and the book's early readers, for their valuable suggestions: Beth Beaullieu, Grace Knight, Suzanne Mantell, Nina Parker, Gilda Schneider, Wendy Sclight, and Marshall M. Wise.

George Smit, for answering legal questions; Christine Miller, DPM, for information about forensic podiatry; and Breanna Contreras, for her music-copyrights expertise.

Members of the Crime Fiction Academy of The Center for Fiction in New York City, for their astute observations; the literary agent Joëlle Delbourgo, for her appreciation of the book and efforts on its behalf; the author Roberta Silman, for her publishing know-how; and Dr. Jay Mott, for his insights and encouragement.

The New York Public Library, for allowing me to examine the original music manuscripts of Edward Elgar, and the late coffeehouse Guy & Gallard, for sustaining me and allowing me to write undisturbed.

The copy editor Joyce Rubin, for her sharp eye; the book designer Rita Skingle, for her fine artistic work; and the website designer Jack Arnold, for both his aesthetic and technical excellence.

Friends and family members who have taken an interest in the book's progress, including—but not limited to—Joseph Berger, Rosemary Foley, Fredda and David Mantell, Phyllis and Howard Rosenthal, Phyllis and Herb Ross, Gilda and Lew Schneider, Wendy Sclight, Amy Small, Ruth Stevens and Leonard Bronfeld, and Batya and Michael Wise.

The author and founder-publisher of Indies United Publishing House, Lisa Orban, for her work on behalf of authors, and IUPH's co-op of authors for supporting one another's publishing goals.
My sister, Suzanne Mantell—writer, editor, and overall book

expert—for her informed and nuanced opinions about writing; my daughter, Nina Parker, for her skills as a perceptive sounding board; my son, Michael Hershenson, who inspires me every day with his love of music; my grandson, Justin Parker, for his creative ideas as we shot hoops in his driveway; and my son-in-law, Chris Parker, for his warmth and generosity.

Thanks to my life partner, Marshall M. Wise, for his support ranging from excellent word-choice advice to urgent fixes for the computer glitches that would have otherwise derailed me. You are always ready to help when it matters the most.

Finally, a shoutout to the public schools that bring music into the lives of children. Simply put, you are indispensable. My education included weekly "singing assemblies" in grammar school and participation in a selective high school chorus as part of my daily curriculum. Those experiences led to decades of singing with the Oratorio Society of New York and the Cecilia Chorus of New York, and, eventually, to this book.

RM

Made in United States
North Haven, CT
24 April 2025

68281494R00166